Cinderella Sister

Dilly Court

Cinderella Sister

arrow books

Published by Arrow Books 2011

2 4 6 8 10 9 7 5 3 1

First published in Great Britain in 2011 by
Arrow Books
Random House, 20 Vauxhall Bridge Road,
London SW1V 2SA

www.randomhouse.co.uk

Addresses for companies within The Random House Group Limited can be found at:
www.randomhouse.co.uk

The Random House Group Limited Reg. No. 954009

A CIP catalogue record for this book
is available from the British Library

ISBN 9780099538844

The Random House Group Limited supports the Forest Stewardship
Council® (FSC®), the leading international forest certification organisation.
All our titles that are printed on Greenpeace approved FSC® certified paper
carry the FSC® logo. Our paper procurement policy can be found at
www.randomhouse.co.uk/environment

Typeset in Palatino by Palimpsest Book Production Limited,
Falkirk, Stirlingshire
Printed in the UK by CPI Mackays, Chatham ME5 8TD

For Hilary Johnson and Margaret James, with thanks.

Chapter One

Shadwell, London, November 1880

Lily had been too busy wrestling with the mangle in the outhouse at the rear of the old dockmaster's house to pay much attention to the weather, but pausing for a moment to brush a lock of damp hair from her forehead she sniffed and wrinkled her nose. She could smell it and taste it even before she stuck her head out of the door and saw the telltale strands of pea-green fog creeping over the brick wall into the back yard. It curled like a sneak-thief's fingers around the men's shirts and underwear as if it were about to pluck them from the washing line.

She sighed and arched her aching back. She hated Mondays. If she ruled the country she would make it illegal for women to spend the whole day slaving over a copper filled with boiling water and strong-smelling lye soap. She would put a stop to the drudgery of mangling, rinsing and then mangling again before the clean garments could be hung out to dry.

She had been slaving away since dawn, and with the sudden change in the weather came the knowledge that the washing would not dry in time to be ironed that evening. Her brothers would have to wear soiled shirts beneath their firemen's uniforms for another day at least, and they would not be happy about that. Then there was Nell, her eldest sister who taught at the Ragged School in George Street; she would grumble bitterly if she did not have a clean white collar and cuffs to keep her grey poplin blouse looking spick and span until Friday. As for Molly, Lily's senior by one year – well, Molly was a trial at the best of times. As Grandpa Larkin said, Molly would try the patience of a saint; she was unpredictable as the weather. She was like the little girl with the curl in the middle of her forehead: when she was good she was very, very good and when she was bad she was horrid. Well, Lily thought, grinning, Molly was not that bad and she certainly wasn't horrid, but she had inherited the Delamare temperament from their artistic mother. Molly worked as an apprentice silk handkerchief dyer for old man Cobham in Sun Tavern Place, and she invariably arrived home with her clothes splattered in rainbow hues, most of which were impossible to remove.

Lily cranked the handle a little faster, feeding the wet garment through the giant rollers with care. She had learned from bitter experience that getting her fingers caught between them was something to be avoided at all costs. Why, she wondered, was life so unfair? Having been born the youngest of six she was expected to stay at home all day and help to keep house while her elder siblings went out to work. Her time was not her own. Of course they had Agnes to do the cooking, but she was more like part of the family than a servant and she was getting on in years. Her fingers were gnarled with rheumatism and her legs were corded with varicose veins, which she was pleased to demonstrate whenever anyone asked her to do anything that she considered to be above and beyond the call of duty. This included washing, ironing, scrubbing floors and beating what was left of their threadbare carpets on the washing line. Changing the sheets and bedmaking also came into this category, although each of the Larkin children had been brought up to do this for themselves. It had been many years since the family could afford a domestic to do the mundane chores, and these had gradually been heaped upon Lily's slender shoulders.

If only Ma had stayed to raise the family she had borne so easily and then carelessly abandoned, but she had run off with an artist, or so Lily had gathered from the whispers that had circulated at the time. That had been ten years ago, and at the age of nine Lily had been considered too young to be told the truth. Some years later Molly had informed her in a fit of temper that she was no better than their mother, who had spent her time painting pictures instead of looking after her children. Ma, she said, had wasted money on art lessons, which culminated in her leaving home to live with her lover, which had created a scandal that had tainted all their lives. According to Agnes, to whom Lily had gone begging to be told the whole story, the man in question had been a louche fellow from an upper class background who should have known better. Lily had no cause to doubt Aggie, who had worked for the Delamare family since she was a girl of fifteen and had been a surrogate mother to the Larkin girls after their mother abandoned them. Lily had spent what was left of her childhood living in a dream world she created in her head. She made up stories about her French antecedents having fled to England in a desperate bid to escape from the guillotine, although Aggie cast scorn on such notions and said they had been Huguenot weavers and not at all high up in the social strata. Lily had not been convinced. She remembered sitting at Ma's knee, listening to tales of wealth and family fortune, sadly lost. Ma had been a bit of a storyteller, but she had been beautiful and she had smelt as fragrant as a rose. Sometimes when Lily was tending to the gnarled rose bush in the tiny front garden, the scent of the red damask roses made her think of Ma, and it always made her cry.

Everything had changed after their mother's sudden flight. Pa had always been a remote figure, spending more time at the fire station than he did at home. Less than a year after Ma left, he had been killed in an inferno that had razed the gutta-percha warehouse to the ground.

The melancholy notes of a foghorn brought Lily back to the present. The yard at the rear of the dockmaster's house was being gobbled up by the fog. The gathering gloom had a yellow sulphurous cast to it and the air reeked of soot. Unless she was very much mistaken a real pea-souper was on its way. Very soon she would not be able to see a hand in front of her face and it would become difficult to breathe. She abandoned the mangling and hurried out into the yard, tugging at the garments on the washing line and dropping them into the laundry basket. Wooden clothes pegs flew in all directions but she did not stop to pick them up. The washing was already speckled with smuts and large flakes of ash had begun to flutter to the ground like black snow. She angled her head, taking small breaths of the foul air, and her worst fears were confirmed. There was a new and more alarming smell polluting the atmosphere – the acrid odour of burning timbers.

Fire – the word sent shivers down her spine. Her three elder brothers had followed the family tradition by joining the London Fire Engine Establishment. Lily had never managed to accustom herself to the gnawing anxiety that filled her heart and soul whenever they were on a shout. She sometimes wished that she was a man so that she could accompany them and not be the one left waiting nervously for their safe return. Hefting the wicker basket into the scullery, she set it down on the deal table by the stone sink. She was about to close the back door when she heard the clanging of a bell and the thundering of horses' hooves as the fire engine was driven pell-mell down Labour in Vain Street. That could only mean one thing. The fire was too close for comfort.

Abandoning the washing, she ran through the maze of passages that had once been the servants' domain in the days when Grandpa was dockmaster and a man of importance. But that was long ago and now he was retired and had to exist on a small pension, a fact that he never allowed anyone to forget. Lily was only too aware that the house had seen better days. The walls were in sad need of a lick of paint and plaster flaked off the ceiling to coat the worn tiles like fallen snow, but she was in too much of a hurry to pay any attention to details like worm-eaten skirting boards and missing banisters on the staircase that curved gracefully upwards from the once elegant entrance hall.

She tried to open the front door but the wood had swelled with the damp and she had to put her foot on the jamb and tug with all her might until it finally gave way with a groan of rusty hinges. She stepped outside and sheltering beneath the tiled portico supported by wrought iron pillars, she peered into the gathering gloom. The dockmaster's house was built on a promontory at the old Shadwell entrance to the London Docks. On a clear day she would have had a good view upriver as far as Sharp's Wharf and downriver to Limehouse Hole, but now she could barely see to the end of the garden path. She could hear the water slapping and sucking at the stone wall and the mournful moan of foghorns from across the water, but as the sound of the fire engine's progress grew fainter she was enveloped by an eerie silence. The London particular had the city and river muffled and bound, imprisoned in a thick noxious blanket of sulphur and smoke.

Lily had not stopped to collect her shawl and she wrapped her arms around her slender body in an attempt to fend off the cold and damp. She stood very still with all her senses alert. She strained her ears for the all too familiar crackling sound of burning timbers and cries of alarm, and through a thick curtain of fog she could just make out a faint red glow in the sky above the river. She held her breath, listening for the reassuring clang of the second fire-engine bell and the accompanying sound of horses' hooves. If it was a large conflagration there was certain to be a second appliance sent from the fire station situated in a converted beer shop in Cock Hill. As soon as the call was raised, her brothers would have donned their brass helmets, fire tunics and boots and climbed aboard the fire engine. Even now they would be hanging onto handles fixed to the body of the horse-drawn vehicle as it sped through the streets towards the scene of the pending disaster. It would only take a few minutes to reach the wharves where the fire might have started in one of the many warehouses or the steam mill, or even on board one of the ships moored alongside.

She did not have to wait long and as the second fire engine rattled past the house she was seized by the sudden need to follow it and see her brothers at work. She picked up her skirts and ran down the path, letting herself out of the gate and racing along Lower Shadwell Street. The pall of smoke and fog was making it increasingly difficult to breathe, and she covered her mouth with her hand. When she reached Bell Wharf the swirling, stinking miasma above the river was as red as a blood orange. She could just make out the burning hull of a large vessel on the foreshore where it lay stranded like a beached whale. At the top of Bell Wharf Stairs she came across a small crowd of onlookers, mostly women from the flour mill a little further upriver. Their clothes, hair and eyebrows were coated thickly in white dust, giving them a ghostly appearance, but their anxious chatter was drowned by the shouts of the watermen, dockers and seamen who had formed a human chain to take water from the river and hurl it into the centre of the inferno.

Lily realised that their efforts were being directed by her eldest brother, Matt, whose stentorian tones drowned even the loudest of the other male voices. Without stopping to think of her own safety, she made her way down the slimy stone steps to the foreshore. Holding up her skirts she stepped over the stinking detritus, weed-encrusted stones and muddy pools where shards of burning timber floated, hissing and spitting out sparks.

'What the hell are you doing here, Lil?'

She turned with a guilty start and found herself staring into the soot-blackened face of her brother Luke.

'I just wanted to make sure you were all right,' she said defiantly.

'Go home, Lily. This is no place for you.'

She hesitated, gazing helplessly at the blazing timbers of the schooner. 'I can hear Matt but can't see Mark.'

'He's working the pump and hose. Now get out of here, there's a good girl. We've got enough to do without worrying about you.' He smiled and his teeth gleamed white in his dirty face.

'Look out there.' Matt's voice carried over the water.

With an ear-splitting crash the main mast of the vessel snapped off and fell into the river, sending up a plume of spray as it hit the seething waters of the Thames. A cloud of steam engulfed the ship and firemen alike, and there was a moment of chaos as men stumbled about blindly in their attempts to dodge baulks of burning timber.

Lily did not know why she had come; something had drawn her to this particular conflagration which was beyond her understanding, but she knew that Luke was right. There was nothing she could do and she would only be in the way of the men who were struggling to prevent the fire from spreading to ships tied up at neighbouring wharves and the warehouses filled with valuable goods. She was about to leave when she saw a smoke-blackened figure struggling towards her. His pea jacket was smouldering and his whole body was racked by a fit of coughing. He was limping badly and seemingly unable to control his gait he barged into her, almost knocking her off her feet.

'I – I'm sorry,' he gasped, as his knees buckled and he sank to the ground, very nearly taking her with him.

'No harm done,' Lily said, making a vain attempt to raise him to his feet. 'Please try to get up and let me help you to the steps. It's too dangerous to stay here.'

He gazed up into her face, but another fit of coughing robbed him of speech. Flaming spars had begun to fall about them like a shower of meteors, but Lily couldn't bring herself to abandon him. She looped his arm around her shoulders. 'You'd best make an effort or you'll end up roasted like a hog on a spit.'

Somehow she managed to get him to his feet and slowly and painfully they made their way to the steps, but he stumbled and fell to the ground. 'Alas, my ankle – I think it is broken.'

He closed his eyes, lapsing into unconsciousness,

and Lily stared down at him in dismay. He was not a big man, perhaps a little over medium height and slightly built, but she would not be able to get him up the steep flight of steps unaided. 'I'll get help. Wait there.' Even as the words left her mouth she realised it was a silly thing to say. In his present condition, the injured man was going nowhere. She raced up the steps, almost bumping into a burly fellow who was on his way down. She peered at him through the choking pall of smoke and fog. 'Is that you, Bill Hawkins?'

'Lily?' He leaned forward, squinting at her through the sulphurous haze. 'What the hell are you doing here? Get on home, girl.'

She had known Bill all her life. He had worked on the docks since he was little more than a boy in the time when Grandpa had been dockmaster. Now he was a big, broad-shouldered foreman in the London Docks, but he still took tea with Grandpa every Friday evening after work, keeping him informed of the goings-on in his old stamping ground. Lily clutched his arm. 'There's an injured man down there, Bill. I think he's broken his ankle and he's soaked to the skin. I can't manage him on my own.'

He glanced at the burning wreck. 'All right,' he said slowly. 'Looks like there's nothing much I can do to help the boys. Where is this chap?'

'I knew you wouldn't let me down.' Standing on tiptoe, Lily kissed his bewhiskered cheek before retracing her steps to where the man lay on the muddy foreshore. She tried to rouse him but Bill laid his hand on her shoulder.

'Leave him be, Lily. It'll be less painful for him if we do it this way.' He bent down and hefted the injured man over his shoulder. 'C'mon, fellah, we'll soon have you put to rights.'

It took them some time to make their way back to the dockmaster's house and visibility was so poor that Lily had to keep stopping to make sure that Bill was following her. It was almost completely dark now and Lily had to fumble to find the doorknob. She glanced over her shoulder. 'Bill.'

His booted feet crunched stones on the path behind her. 'I'm here, girl. Best get this bloke inside as quick as you like.'

She put her shoulder to the door and almost fell into the hallway.

'Who's that?' a querulous voice demanded, and the flickering glow of a single candle sent shadows dancing on the walls and ceiling. Grandpa Larkin emerged from the small parlour that had in past times been his late wife's sewing room. It was his domain now, with a single iron bedstead tucked away in the corner of the room and a wingback chair by the fire, which was kept going night and day, summer or winter. He peered myopically at Bill. 'Is that you, Bill Hawkins?'

'It is I, Mr Larkin, sir. Miss Lily found this poor fellow on the foreshore with a busted ankle and burns.'

Grandpa Larkin nodded and his eyes glittered with excitement. 'I saw the ship on fire through my spyglass. Looked to me like a schooner, heavily laden. Went aground in the fog, did she?'

Lily laid her hand on his shoulder. 'Go and sit down,

Grandpa. Let Bill take the poor man upstairs and then he can come and tell you all about it.'

He drew away from her, scowling. 'I ain't a baby. You don't have to treat me like I was made of spun glass and going to break any minute.'

Bill gave a polite cough. 'Begging your pardon, guvner, but this fellow is no light weight. May I be so bold as to suggest that I follow Miss Lily up the stairs and make him comfortable?'

'You're a good fellow, Bill. I trained you and I'm proud of you.' Grandpa shot a resentful look at Lily. 'And he treats me like a man with all his faculties. I'm not ready for my wooden box just yet.'

'Of course not, Grandpa.' Lily knew better than to take offence at his caustic comments. She flashed him a smile and hurried over to a table at the foot of the stairs where the night candles were kept in readiness to light the family to bed.

Grandpa wagged his finger at her. 'Just remember that we can't afford to pay the doctor. You'll have to get Agnes to fix him up, that is if the old besom can manage the stairs at her time of life.' He retreated into the parlour, slamming the door. The draught it caused almost extinguished the lucifer that Lily had struck on a piece of exposed brickwork where the plaster had crumbled away to leave a jagged crater. She lit the candle, and shielding the flame with her cupped hand she led the way up the wide staircase to the first floor landing, and then up again to the attics beneath the mansard roof. It was here they had had their nursery when they were children, but now the rooms were unused, it being too costly to light fires to heat them. Tiles had been blown off in winter gales and the roof leaked, causing damp patches to spread across the ceiling making patterns that Lily had always likened to illustrations of continents in the school atlas. She opened the door to the smallest of the three rooms and wrinkled her nose at the pervasive smell of damp and dry rot. 'Lie him down on the bed, Bill. I'll go and fetch sheets and blankets.'

Bill crossed the bare boards in two strides and gently set his burden down on the bare mattress. 'You do that, Miss Lily. I'll take his boots off while he's out cold, but he's going to need a doctor and that's a fact.'

Lily screwed up her face as Bill started to ease the boot off the afflicted limb. 'You'd best get his wet clothes off too. I'll see if I can find him a clean nightshirt.'

'This fellow ain't no ordinary seaman. These boots cost more than I could earn in a six-month. He's a gentleman unless I'm very much mistaken and a foreigner too. He must have come off that French schooner that's causing all the trouble.'

'Feel in his pockets. Maybe he's got enough money to pay for the doctor.'

Bill raised the man just enough to take off his singed jacket. He went through the pockets and produced a handful of coins. 'That's all he's got, and it's foreign money, but I reckon it might pay for a visit from the sawbones.'

Lily frowned; one problem at a time was quite enough. 'I'll see to his bedding.'

She hurried downstairs to the linen cupboard on the

ground floor, where she sorted out cotton sheets that had been turned top to bottom many times before being cut and sewn together again, sides to middle. She and her sisters had spent many evenings on such homely tasks, sewing long seams in the flickering light of a work candle until their eyes were red-rimmed and their fingers pricked and bleeding. She found an old pillow with the feathers seeping from a tear that was yet to be mended, but there were no spare blankets. The poor man would freeze to death in the attic room, but then she remembered the monks' seat in the entrance hall where out of sentiment they had stored the horse blanket that used to keep old Trotter warm on bitter winter nights. He had been more than a faithful old horse who pulled the dog cart that took Ma and the girls to church on Sundays. He had been a much-loved family pet and they had all cried when he had passed away at the magnificent age of thirty. At least, the girls had cried, and although her brothers had shrugged their shoulders and walked away, Lily had seen them blink away a tear or two. She sniffed and swallowed hard at the memory. She went to fetch the woollen blanket that was now lacy with moth holes, but it would have to suffice. Holding the coarse material to her cheek the lingering smell of horseflesh, leather and hay brought back memories of childhood days when life had seemed so safe and secure.

An agonised cry from the top floor brought her abruptly back to the present and she negotiated the stairs as fast as she could beneath the burden of sheets, the horse blanket and an old nightshirt that had once belonged to Luke but had been outgrown. She hesitated outside the attic room, bracing herself for what she would find when she entered. She was particularly squeamish when it came to blood and burns. 'Don't be a coward, Lily,' she whispered. 'Stop being a baby and go inside. The poor fellow needs you.'

Bill rose to his feet as she entered the room. 'I'll see to him, Miss Lily. It ain't the sort of thing you ought to rest your young eyes on, but you should send for the doctor to take a look at the poor bloke. He's suffered some burns to his hands and shoulders and his ankle is definitely busted.' He held his hands out to take the bedding.

She tried not to look but her eyes were drawn to the inert figure with nothing to cover him other than his torn and singed shirt. Lily had seen her brothers' bare flesh on bath nights when they were much younger, but the only adult male bodies she had seen were the carved statues in museums and their manhood was always delicately concealed by fig leaves or artistic swathes of cloth. She felt the blood rush to her cheeks and she looked away quickly. 'I'll go at once, if you'll just stay with him until I return.'

Bill nodded and grinned, exposing his one good tooth. 'You get along. I'll keep an eye on the poor bugger until you get back.' It was his turn to flush brick red now and he shuffled his feet. 'Begging your pardon, Miss Lily.'

Lily hurried from the room, but once outside the dingy attic her feeling of relief was tinged with guilt for being such a ninny. Her brothers would tease her mercilessly if they found out that she had run away

from the sight of blood and burnt flesh, an occupa-
tional hazard for a fireman. When she reached the hall
she stopped to put on her shawl, and was wrapping
it around her shoulders when the front door rattled
and burst open to admit Nell. Drops of moisture glistened on the rim of her bonnet, sparkling like diamonds
on the dark hair that had escaped from the confines
of a snood and now curled around her forehead like
the springs from a watch. She untied the ribbons of
her bonnet, eyeing Lily curiously.

'What a sight you look. Your hair is a mass of tangles
and you're covered in smuts. Don't tell me you went
out in this pea-souper.'

'I can't stop,' Lily said breathlessly. 'It's a long story,
but I've got to fetch the doctor.' She made for the door,
but Nell was too quick for her and she moved swiftly
to bar her way.

'Who needs the doctor?' she asked anxiously. 'Is it
Grandpa?'

Lily shook her head. 'No, it's a man who was hurt
when the ship caught fire. Bill's with him now. I've
got to go.'

Nell caught her by the wrist. 'Stop there, young lady.
Who said we could afford the doctor for a complete
stranger, and why is Bill here? It's not Friday.'

Lily could see by the determined set of her sister's
jaw that an explanation was imperative if she was to
be allowed out to fetch the doctor. She launched into
a vivid description of the scene on the foreshore, illus-
trating the story with dramatic gestures. 'So you see I
must fetch Dr Macpherson or the poor man will die.'

Nell made a show of hanging up her bonnet and shawl, moving with the controlled grace that Lily admired so much. Nell was never in a dither; she was always so calm and sensible. Lily wished very much that she could be like her eldest sister.

'I will go and see this person,' Nell said firmly. 'I'll decide whether or not we need to incur the expense of a visit from the doctor. I'm certain he charges by the minute, if not the second, and we just can't afford it, Lily.'

Lily hung her head. 'I know that, but the poor chap had a little money on him.'

'Don't tell me that you went through his pockets.'

'Bill did, not me. He said the man is a gentleman. He could tell by his boots. I didn't think . . .'

'No, Lily, you didn't think. You never do. Just leave everything to me. I'm used to dealing with cuts and bruises and wiping bloody noses at the Ragged School, and that includes dealing with children who wet their drawers and worse.' Nell picked up her skirts and was about to mount the stairs when she paused, looking over her shoulder. 'Where is he? I hope you didn't put him in any of our rooms. He might be running with fleas and lice or have some terrible disease. You are very thoughtless at times, Lily.'

'He's in the smallest attic room. I couldn't find any blankets so I took the one that belonged to old Trotter.'

'Heavens above, what were you thinking of? If he didn't have fleas when he arrived, he most likely will now.' With a toss of her head, Nell continued on her way upstairs.

Lily hesitated, unsure whether or not to follow her, but whichever course she chose was almost certain to be the wrong one. She loved and admired her eldest sister, but Nell was inclined to bring the discipline of the schoolroom home with her. Matt was the only one who could stand up to her when she was being bossy, but he wasn't here. Lily stood in the middle of the hallway, undecided until she heard the sound of shuffling footsteps approaching from the back of the house.

'Lily Larkin, I wants a word with you.' Aggie's voice rolled round the hall like thunder.

It was only then that Lily remembered the basket of damp washing that she had abandoned in the scullery, and the wet clothes waiting to be put through the mangle she had left in the stone sink. 'Oh, bother!' she murmured. 'Now I'm for it.'

Preceded by a wavering beam of candlelight, Agnes bore down on her, moving faster than Lily would have thought possible for a woman who complained so bitterly about her rheumatics.

'What do you mean by leaving the scullery swimming in water and piles of wet clothes clogging my sink?' Agnes came to a halt in front of Lily, standing arms akimbo. 'And what's been going on upstairs? I was having a lovely nap when I was woken by the sound of someone screeching like they was being done in.'

Lily could see that Agnes was genuinely upset. 'I'm so sorry, Aggie. I'll come and clear it up right away. But it wasn't my fault, you see the fog came down and then I smelt smoke and I heard the fire engine go past the house.'

'I heard it but I thought I was dreaming. I still get nightmares about the fire that took your poor father's life.' Agnes peered at Lily, frowning. 'I hope you didn't do anything silly.'

'I know I shouldn't have done it, but I wanted to see the fire.'

'How many times have you been told to stay away from fires?'

'I don't know why I did it, but I just had to go and see it for myself, and I came across an injured man. I couldn't just leave him like that. And then Bill Hawkins came along and he brought him home.'

Agnes glanced upwards into the dark shadows on the staircase. 'So where is this person now?'

'He's in one of the attic rooms and Nell is looking after him.'

'I suppose it's all right then, if Nell says so, but don't expect me to go fetching and carrying for a complete stranger.'

'Of course not, Aggie,' Lily said, giving her an affectionate hug. 'We'll look after him and you won't know he's here.'

'Get on with you, you bad girl. I can see your mother in you sometimes, Lily. She could always wrap people round her little finger if she chose.' The top of Aggie's head only came up to Lily's shoulder, and she was almost as broad as she was tall. Her prune-wrinkled face dissolved into a smile and she gave Lily a gentle shove towards the kitchen. 'Go and finish your chores, and then you can scrub the potatoes for supper to make up for me losing my beauty sleep.' She gave a deep

19

chuckle that made her whole frame shake and Lily knew she had been forgiven.

She was in the middle of mopping the kitchen floor where the water had seeped in from the overflowing sink in the scullery when Nell burst into the room looking unusually flustered. Her cheeks were flushed and there was a sparkle in her eyes that made Lily stare at her in surprise.

'That man is not English,' Nell said breathlessly. 'He is burbling away and I couldn't understand a word he said. Bill said he thinks he came from the French schooner, so that would explain how the poor man came to be in such a state. Anyway, I've sent Bill to fetch Dr Macpherson. I've done all I can for him but you were right for once, Lily; his injuries are quite severe.'

'And how are we going to pay the medical bills?' Agnes demanded. 'We can't even afford meat to put in the stew. The boys won't be happy when all they get is a mouthful of vegetables and a soggy dumpling for their supper.'

'We have meat once a week,' Nell said sternly. 'That's more than most people round here can afford. I have children in my class who have to survive on bread and scrape, and sometimes not even that. They are so thin that their little limbs look like sticks and their faces are pinched and wizened so that they look like little old men and women. If anyone complains about their food just let them come to George Street with me and see how poverty-stricken people live.' She ended with a muffled sob, turning away to wipe her eyes.

Lily dropped the mop and ran to Nell, wrapping her

arms around her. 'There, there, dear Nell. Don't be upset. She didn't mean to criticise, did you, Aggie?'

Agnes shrugged her shoulders. 'No need to get in a twitter. I was just stating a fact.'

Nell sniffed and dabbed her eyes with her handkerchief. 'I'm sorry, Aggie. I'm just tired, I suppose.'

'And you gave your dinner to the poorest children,' Lily said, angling her head. 'I know you did, so don't deny it, Nell.'

'That's by the bye. We have more than enough of everything, just not at much as we were used to.' Nell smiled with her lips, although Lily was quick to note that it didn't quite reach her limpid blue eyes.

'You tell that to young Molly when she complains,' Aggie muttered. 'That girl has ideas above her station if you ask me, just like her mother.'

Lily could see by the expression on Nell's face that this remark, although true, had hit a tender spot. Ma's name was rarely mentioned, and Nell in particular seemed to have suffered most when their mother took flight.

'I think I heard the doorbell,' Lily said by way of a diversion, and almost immediately, as if by some miraculous intervention from above, one of the bells on the board above the kitchen door began to jingle on its spring. 'It must be Bill returning with the doctor,' she added hopefully. 'Shall I go, Nell?'

'No, it's all right, Lily. Since I'll be the one in charge of the sickroom, I'd best take the doctor upstairs.' Nell's hand flew to her head and she patted her hair in place as she left the room.

'Well, I'm blowed,' Agnes said with a meaningful grin. 'She's changed her tune. If I was a betting woman I'd lay odds on the bloke upstairs being young and good-looking, even if he is a Frog.'

Lily stifled a giggle. 'Don't let Nell hear you call him that.'

'I can say what I like in my own kitchen,' Aggie said, rising to her feet and carrying the pan of peeled vegetables over to the range. She reached up to pluck herbs from bunches hung to dry on a beam in the chimney breast, and she sprinkled them into the stew, adding a generous dash of salt. 'He'll cause trouble, mark my words, young Lily.'

'Who? Who will cause trouble?'

Lily turned with a start to see Molly standing in the doorway. The sulphurous stench of the fog clung to her outdoor clothes as if reluctant to release her from its suffocating clutches. She took off her bonnet and tossed it onto the nearest chair followed by her shawl. Her cheeks were flushed with the cold and her green eyes sparkled with curiosity. 'What's going on? I saw Dr Macpherson pulling up in his trap just as Nell let me in, but she wouldn't tell me anything. She just pushed past me and hurried out to meet him. What have I missed?'

'There's a Frog in the attic room,' Agnes said, slamming a lid on the saucepan. 'And he's going to bring strife to this family, I can feel it in me water.'

Chapter Two

'A frog? How did a frog get into the house? A frog couldn't climb all those stairs.' Molly stared at Lily with her eyebrows raised in astonishment. 'Could it?'

Lily dissolved into a fit of giggles. She felt the tension leach out of her as she saw the funny side of the situation. 'N-not a real frog, silly. Aggie means there's a Frenchman in bed upstairs.'

'A Frenchman?' Molly snatched up a carrot that Agnes had missed and bit off the end, crunching it with relish. 'Damn it, I would have been home earlier if I hadn't stopped to chat to Sukey Hollands. What have I missed?'

'You've missed a clip round the ear, young lady,' Agnes said heavily. 'You wouldn't dare swear if your grandpa was in the room, nor any of your brothers.'

'Oh, pooh.' Molly waved the carrot at her. 'They aren't here so I can say what I like. If you don't tell me everything at once, Lily, I'll scream. By the way,' she added, 'did you know that there's a ship on fire alongside Bell Wharf?'

Lily felt a bubble of hysterical laughter rising in her throat, but one look at Aggie's set expression was enough to wipe away her smile. She nodded her head. 'That's where I found the injured man, and it just so happens that he's French. Bill Hawkins helped me get him home and he thinks the chap must be a gentleman because he was wearing expensive boots.'

'He could have stolen them,' Aggie muttered, waddling over to the table and elbowing Molly out of the way. 'Haven't you got anything better to do than stand around chewing a carrot? Shift your lazy body, my girl. Let me get on with my dumplings or . . .'

'Your brothers won't be happy if their supper isn't on the table when they get home,' chorused Lily and Molly in unison.

'Out of my kitchen,' Aggie said, pointing to the door. 'Out now, or there's no supper for either of you.'

'Anyone would think we were still kids,' Molly grumbled as they hurried along the dark passageway towards the room that their mother had liked to call the drawing room, where she accompanied herself at the piano after dinner each evening, and entertained her female friends for afternoon tea. The piano had been sold long ago and the curtains were so faded that all the original vibrant colours were indistinguishable. The floorboards gleamed with wax polish but the carpet squares were threadbare and the chairs sagged, with horsehair erupting from the sofa in springy tufts.

Lily ran to the window which overlooked the side of the house facing downriver. 'I can't see a thing. It's a real pea-souper out there. I do hope the boys are all right.'

Molly threw herself down on the sofa, lying back with her hands behind her head. 'Did you know that the plaster is falling off the ceiling in great big dollops? I wouldn't be surprised if the whole thing collapsed on us one evening when we're sitting round the fire.'

'Thanks for reminding me,' Lily said, turning away from the dismal scene outside. 'With all the excitement, I'd quite forgotten to light the wretched thing and it's blooming freezing in here.'

Molly stretched luxuriously. 'I don't know what you do all day, Lily. There am I slaving over smelly tubs of dye and soggy silk and all you have to do is keep house.' She ducked as Lily tossed a cushion at her. 'Missed! You never could throw straight. Now, tell me about this foreign man in the attic.'

Lily went to kneel on the scrap of carpet in front of the hearth. She had cleaned the grate early that morning and she had laid the fire so that all it needed now was to put a light to it. She struck a lucifer on the fire surround and held it to the twists of newspaper nestling beneath the kindling. 'I don't know anything about him, except that he must have been on the ship before it caught fire. His jacket was singed and his hands were in a terrible state. I couldn't bear to look.'

'Did he speak to you? Was he young and good-looking or was he old and ugly? Come on, Lily, you can do better than that.'

Lily sat back on her haunches, watching the golden flames lick around the glistening black lumps of coal. 'I think he is quite young, but his face was very dirty so it was difficult to see what he looked like. He had black hair, I think, and blue eyes or maybe they were grey. He said a few words in English but he had a strong foreign accent.'

'So how do you know he is French?'

'Bill thinks he came from the French schooner, and Nell said he's definitely a Frenchman. She's the school-teacher so she should know.'

Molly snapped into a sitting position and slid off the sofa. 'I'm going to take a look at this chap. Are you coming with me?'

'I don't know. Nell said . . .'

'Never mind her. She can't tell us what to do. Are you coming or not?' Molly paused as she headed for the door, her delicate dark eyebrows raised and a mischievous smile flirting with her lips. 'I dare you.'

Lily rose to her feet, shaking out her crumpled skirts. 'You ought to wash first. Your hands are green and there are red spots of dye on your cheeks. You'll frighten the poor chap to death.'

'Nonsense. If he's off his head with fever he'll just think I'm a part of his bad dream. I'll race you to the attic.' Molly opened the door but she closed it hurriedly, turning to Lily with her finger raised to her lips. 'Stay where you are. Dr Macpherson is just going upstairs with Nell.'

'I wonder if the boys have got the fire under control,' Lily said anxiously.

Molly made her way back to the sofa. 'You worry too much, Lil. They're big enough to look after them-selves and it's only a rotten old boat that's gone up in flames. Now it would be different if it was a silk warehouse or the dye works. I would worry then.'

'How do you manage to bring everything down to your level?'

'I dunno. Being selfish takes a lot of effort, but I just think of me all the time and I find that works a treat.'

'You know that's not true,' Lily said, giggling. 'You can be quite thoughtful when you try.'

'And you insist on seeing the best in everyone. You're doomed to huge disappointments in life, Lil. You need to be more like me. Expect the worst of people and then it's a bonus if they turn out not so bad after all.' Molly lay back on the sofa and closed her eyes. 'Wake me up when it's supper time.'

'I can't just sit around and do nothing. I'm going upstairs to see if Nell needs anything.'

Molly opened one eye. 'You hate the sight of blood and gore. You'll only faint or throw up all over him.'

'I'll just have to make an effort. I can't spend the rest of my life being squeamish.' Lily made for the door and was about to leave the room when Molly called her back.

'Wait for me. I'm coming too.'

'You're not so selfish after all,' Lily said, smiling. 'You do care what happens to the poor fellow.'

'If you're so interested in this foreigner he must be quite a catch.' Molly jumped to her feet and danced across the floor to push past Lily. 'I'm not leaving him to our resident ministering angel or my pretty little sister. If he's rich and handsome then I care deeply.' She opened the door and crossed the hall, pausing to light a candle before taking the stairs two at a time.

Lily followed at a more sedate pace, thinking that

the world had gone quite mad, and all because of a foreigner who wore expensive boots. She caught up with Molly outside the attic room. The door had been left ajar and Molly cocked her head on one side, straining her ears to hear what was being said inside.

A howl of pain made them both jump and they clung to each other, waiting for the next scream, but there was silence. Molly pushed the door open and they crept into the room. Nell was holding a candle to light the doctor's efforts as he bandaged the injured limb, but the patient appeared to be unconscious. Lily clenched her fists, praying that she would not faint as she fought down a feeling of nausea at the sight of an enamel bowl filled with water and bloodied scraps of cloth.

Molly moved closer to the bed. 'Who is he, Nell?'

'Go away,' Nell hissed. 'And take Lily with you. I don't want her swooning or worse.'

Dr Macpherson looked up from his task and he frowned. 'This isn't a sideshow, young Molly. But if you want to be useful go and fetch some brandy and a glass.'

'Isn't it a bit late for that, doctor? He's dead to the world.'

'It's not for him, you silly girl, it's for me.'

'I'll go,' Lily said, eager to be away from the stench of blood and burnt flesh. 'I know where Aggie hides the medicinal brandy.'

'Bring the bottle,' Dr Macpherson said gruffly. 'I don't want one of Miss Aggie's mean little nips that wouldn't fill a hollow tooth.'

Molly leaned over the inert figure on the bed. 'I wish

he'd open his eyes. I'm sure he's quite handsome under-neath all that soot and grime. Shall I wash his face?'

'Leave him alone,' Nell said sternly. 'You can make yourself useful and get rid of these soiled rags. Fetch me some warm water and fresh cloths.'

'Come along, Molly,' Lily urged. 'I'll fetch the brandy and there's a sheet that's past mending. I'll tear that up if you'll see to the nasty stuff.'

'Oh, all right. But I don't see why I have to do the dirty work.'

Dr Macpherson cast a reproving glance in her direc-tion. 'You look as though you've already been in a bloodbath, lassie. We won't notice the difference. Now get along with you. I have to attend to the poor fellow's burns and it isn't a fit sight for unmarried girls.'

Lily tugged at Molly's sleeve but it seemed that her sister was determined to have the last word. 'Nell isn't married and she's only two years older than me.'

'Miss Nell is a level-headed young woman, most unlikely to have a fit of the vapours. If she wasn't gain-fully employed as a teacher I would be pleased to have her as my nurse. Now leave us, the pair of you. This young man needs my full attention.'

'It's not fair,' Molly said as she and Lily left the room. 'I want to be there when he opens his eyes. If I was the first one he saw when he came to he would be sure to fall in love with me.'

'He might die of fright if he saw you splattered with red and green dye.'

'Well I won't have the chance to find out since it will be Nell he'll see first, and she's the beauty of the family.

29

Everyone says so. You and I are just pretty, although I am prettier than you. I take after Ma and you and Nell are more like Pa.'

Lily acknowledged this with a nod of her head. 'You are very striking, Molly. And you do have lovely copper-coloured hair just like Ma. Mine is just a pale copy.'

'No,' Molly said judicially, angling her head with a thoughtful frown. 'I won't allow that, Lil. Yours is quite pleasing to the eye, in fact it's your best feature. I'd say it was more gold than red, and I'm getting to be an expert in colours and dyes.' She held up her stained fingers, wiggling them and pulling a face which made Lily laugh. 'I'm an artist just like Ma.'

'I can't exactly remember her face,' Lily said wistfully. 'It's all misty and faded in my mind and that scares me. I don't want to forget her.'

Molly gave her a gentle shove in the back. 'Oh, for heaven's sake don't get all mushy and sentimental. She's not dead. She's probably living a life of luxury with that bounder she ran off with. All I meant to say was that I take after her in looks and talent; I'm not like her in other ways.'

Lily did not bother to argue, although privately she thought that Molly was exactly like their mother. She ran lightly down the stairs and was met in the hall by a gust of cold air and the choking odour of the fog and the acrid smell of burning as her brothers entered the house. Matt closed the front door, putting his shoulder against it. 'Damn door – I must remember to shave a bit off it.'

'It's just the damp from the river,' Mark said, shrugging off his sodden jacket. 'The wood will shrink back when the weather improves.'

Luke slapped him on the back. 'Good old Mark, always the practical engineer.'

'Well someone has to have their feet firmly on the ground. Your head is filled with all that poetry stuff you're so fond of, and Matt uses muscle to solve every problem.'

Matt shook his head. 'Shut up the pair of you. I'm cold, tired and filthy. All I want is to get out of these wet clothes and put some hot food in my belly.' He took off his jacket and handed it to Lily, who was hovering by his side. 'Hang it in the scullery for me, there's a good girl.'

'And mine,' Mark said, draping his coat over her outstretched arms.

Luke turned to Molly, peering at her in the candlelight. 'You look like a goblin, Moll.' He thrust his wet garment at her. 'Here, make yourself useful and see to this for me.'

Molly dropped it with a disgusted snort. 'Do it yourself, Luke Larkin. I'm not your slave.'

'Help your sister,' Matt said sternly. 'You can't expect Lily to do everything.'

'More fool her if she waits on three lazy lumps like you,' Molly said, tossing her head. 'Anyway, how do you manage when you're on night watch and have to sleep at the fire station?'

'We look after ourselves, of course,' Mark said, grinning. 'But now we're off duty we've got three lovely sisters to wait on us hand and foot, which is just how it should be.'

Molly narrowed her green eyes, glaring at him like an angry cat. 'I've been working hard all day too and now I'm going for a wash. I don't want our Frenchman to see me looking like a fright.' She poked her tongue out at Luke before heading off towards the kitchen.

'Stop her, Mark,' Matt called out. 'She'll use all the hot water on the stove, and I've had a bellyful of cold water today. I'm not washing in it.'

Mark strode after Molly and Lily heard a muffled shriek as he caught up with her.

'If we had the money we could have a proper bathroom,' Lily said wistfully. 'Well-off people have rooms just for washing and bathing. They just turn on a tap to fill the bath, and they have things called geysers to heat the water.'

'Yes,' Matt said, hooking his arm around her shoulders. 'And we've been called to several house fires where those contraptions have exploded.'

Luke held his hands out to Lily. 'C'mon, Lil. Give me those wet things; you're sagging at the knees.'

She flashed him a grateful smile. 'It's all right, Luke. You go and get dry. I can manage.'

'You shouldn't let Molly get away with it,' he said, frowning. 'She's a proper little minx and she should do her share of the chores.'

'I'll have a word with her after supper.' Matt sat down on a rather rickety hall chair and began unlacing his boots. 'So what was all that about a French chap, Lily? Or was it just Molly's imagination running wild as usual?'

Lily glanced anxiously at Luke. She knew she would be in trouble with Matt if he discovered that she had followed them to the scene of the fire. He was very strict about that sort of thing. 'I – er – Bill Hawkins brought him here,' she said, omitting her part in the man's rescue. 'The Frenchman must have come from the blazing ship.'

'That's right, Matt,' Luke said, with a conspiratorial wink aimed at Lily. 'I saw the fellow staggering about on the foreshore and the ship was a Frenchie, wasn't it?'

Matt kicked off one boot and began unlacing the other. 'It was, but I don't know the details yet. I'll have to get them from the owner so that I can write my report. The crew were a mixed bunch but mostly French, I think, and none of them spoke English. They were all taken to the Seamen's Mission.'

'Except one,' Lily added. 'Bill carried him up to the attic. Nell and the doctor are with him now.'

'Bloody hell, Lily. You shouldn't have sent for Macpherson,' Matt said, rising to his feet. 'We can't afford to pay his fee. The padre at the Mission would have seen to all that.'

'The Frenchman has money,' Lily said hastily. 'All it's cost us is a nip of brandy for the doctor.'

Matt headed for the stairs, his coarse woollen socks leaving wet prints on the floorboards. 'And the old soak will have finished the bottle by now unless I'm very much mistaken. I'm going up to sort him out.'

Luke and Lily exchanged worried glances. 'Oh, dear. Perhaps I shouldn't have told him that,' Lily murmured. 'I always seem to say the wrong thing.'

'Don't mind him, ducks,' Luke said, wresting the damp coats from her arms. 'I could do with a cup of hot, sweet tea and a nip of brandy in it wouldn't go amiss, that's if the doctor has left us any.'

He strolled off in the direction of the kitchen but Lily hesitated at the foot of the stairs, gazing dreamily up into the darkness. Her active imagination had been fired by the mysterious foreigner who it seemed was not just a common seaman. Was he the owner of the ship? Or had he been a passenger; a man of business perhaps, who had come to London to negotiate a lucrative deal? Taking the exotic stranger into the house was the most exciting thing that had happened since Ma ran off with the artist.

Her candle guttered and went out, but she did not dare light another one for fear of being accused of extravagance. Nell kept a strict eye on the housekeeping and she frowned upon waste of any kind. It was almost pitch dark in the hall, but Lily could have found her way blindfold.

A cloud of steam erupted from the kitchen as she opened the door. Pans of water were heating on the top of the range and a fierce argument was going on as Molly and Mark fought over a kettle filled with hot water. Lily was faced with the sight of Aggie brandishing the rolling pin and threatening to knock their silly heads together if they didn't stop behaving like a pair of five-year-olds. Luke had stripped to the waist and was standing in front of the range, drying himself with a scrap of towelling, although it did little to remove the streaks of soot from his torso. His lips were moving silently, which made Lily smile. She knew that he was reciting a piece of poetry as he always did when family squabbles became too much for him and he needed to retire into his own private world. He was no coward, but he would back away from a fight unless it was the last resort. Luke was the peacemaker in the family, Mark the joker and Matt the undisputed leader. Her brothers were so different in their characters that sometimes it seemed hard to believe that they were so closely related.

'You are no gentleman, Mark,' Molly shrieked as he won the tussle for the kettle and carried his trophy into the scullery.

'And you ain't a lady,' Mark called over his shoulder. 'You use language that would make a sailor blush.'

Scarlet-cheeked and patently seething, Molly went to stand by the scullery door, leaning against the jamb with her arms folded across her chest. 'Well, if I do, it's because I learnt it from my brothers.'

'That's enough, the pair of you,' Aggie cried angrily. 'If I hear another word from either of you, you'll go and wash in the back yard. I won't have such behaviour in my kitchen.' She turned on Luke, who had begun to recite his poem out loud. 'And you can stop your drivelling, young man. You fill your head with them heathen words when you could be learning the psalms or reading the Gospels. Your pa named you after the apostles, but he couldn't have foreseen how you would all turn out.'

Lily hurried over to rescue the pan of stew that threatened to boil over. 'Don't you think it's time we

35

had supper, Aggie? The boys have been working hard and they must be starving.'

Aggie shrugged her shoulders, bristling like a small, fat hedgehog. 'I won't stand for childish bickering in my kitchen.'

'Of course not,' Lily said gently. 'And I'm sure Molly and Mark will apologise for their bad behaviour.'

'Blame it on the fog,' Luke said dreamily, picking up his damp shirt and putting it on. 'Everyone goes a little mad in a London particular.'

Aggie cast her eyes up to the ceiling. 'What a lot of nonsense you talk, Luke. Make yourself useful and set the table. And move away from my range, I want to get the bread out of the oven. Lily, go and fetch your grandpa.'

Obediently, Lily went to the door, but she hesitated. 'What about Matt and Nell?'

'They'll come when they're ready. I just hope that greedy gannet of a doctor doesn't think he's going to get fed as well as drinking our brandy. There's not enough to go round for him as well.'

Half an hour later the family were seated around the kitchen table having finished their meal of vegetable stew and bread hot from the oven. Dr Macpherson had reluctantly gone on his way, but it had taken all Lily's tact and diplomacy to persuade him to leave before they sat down to supper. He had sniffed the air like a hungry hound and praised Aggie's cooking, adding wistfully that his housekeeper was sadly lacking in the culinary art. In desperation, Lily had given him what was left of the brandy, assuring him that it would keep out the cold. It was a small price to pay, Matt had admitted reluctantly, as the doctor was notorious not only for having a hearty appetite, but he was inclined to linger after dinner telling tales of his past exploits while he smoked a pipe or two of Grandpa's baccy. Nell said she could understand why he had remained a bachelor all his life as no woman would put up with him, but she tempered her criticism by acknowledging that Dr Macpherson was a good physician. He had tended the young Frenchman's injuries with considerable expertise and given him a dose of laudanum that should make him sleep until morning.

Grandpa Larkin pushed his plate away and leaned back in his chair at the head of the table. 'Well then, tell me all about this Frenchie, Nell. Who are we harbouring under our roof? He might be a felon for all you know.'

'Oh, no, Grandpa,' Molly said hastily. 'He is a gentleman.'

Grandpa eyed her with a cynical twist of his lips. 'If the fellow is unconscious, how do you know what he is?'

'He wears expensive boots, so he must be someone important,' Molly said, giggling.

Nell frowned at her. 'It's no laughing matter. The poor man is in a bad way. He might not be able to tell us anything for days. Dr Macpherson said he's suffering from concussion as well as a fever. His ankle isn't broken, though. It's just a bad sprain.'

'Well, he's harmless enough at the moment,' Matt said calmly. 'With an ankle injury and a whack on the head, he's not going to cause us any trouble for the while. But I suggest we ought to take turns sitting at his bedside until he's conscious and can tell us who he is. He may be able to give me some information about the ship.'

'I'll do it,' Molly volunteered. She glanced round the table. 'Why are you all staring at me like that?'

Mark pushed his chair back from the table, grinning from ear to ear. 'When did you ever offer to do anything to help anyone, Molly?'

'It's not the job for a young girl anyway,' Matt said, rising to his feet. 'We'll take it in shifts. Mark can do midnight until two, Luke can do the next watch and I'll take over at four. If the fellow comes to his senses by morning I'll be in a position to find out exactly who he is.'

'Well, I'm glad you didn't include me in your grand plan,' Grandpa said. 'I don't hold with taking strangers into the house; especially not foreigners. They're all right in their place, but that doesn't mean that I have to trust them, especially in a home filled with young females.' He tapped the side of his nose and winked at Matt. 'If you get my meaning.'

'I do, Grandpa. And I agree with you. Nell can tend to the fellow, but I want Molly and Lily to keep away from him, at least until we know more about his background.' Matt took a pan of hot water from the range. 'I'm going to have a strip-wash, so you girls keep out until I've done.' He glanced over his shoulder at Luke. 'And it wouldn't hurt you to do the same. I can see the tidemark round your neck from here.' He strode into the scullery and closed the door.

38

Grandpa struggled to his feet. 'I'm going to my room, but I'll take a cup of cocoa at nine, if it's not too much trouble for one of you girls.' He looked round the table but Aggie was piling the plates up ready to be taken to the scullery, and when no one volunteered he adopted a martyred expression and sighed heavily. 'You'd think that one of you healthy young girls would take care of their aged grandpa.'

Lily glanced at Nell and Molly and she could see that neither of them was going to offer. 'I'll see to your cocoa, Grandpa.' She was just as tired as the rest of them, but since everyone expected her to act as unpaid skivvy she knew she was outnumbered.

'Good girl, Lily,' Grandpa said with a nod of approval. 'I know I can always count on you.' He shuffled out of the room, holding his hand to his back as if to demonstrate his disability, which seemed to shift to different parts of his anatomy according to his needs.

'He's an old fraud,' Mark said as the door closed on their grandfather. 'I've seen him nip around like a two-year-old when he thought no one was looking.' He slapped Luke on the shoulder. 'C'mon, fellow, let's leave the women to do their work.'

'Eh? What's up?' Luke gave a start, looking like someone awakened from a deep sleep. 'What's the matter?'

'You were day-dreaming, as usual,' Nell said with a reproving frown.

'I expect he was making up one of his boring poems.' Molly made a face at Luke who was blinking like a startled owl.

Lily felt instantly sorry for him. Poor Luke was always the butt of Mark's jokes, and Molly was just as bad. She gave him an encouraging smile.

Aggie was not so sympathetic. 'Both of you boys can get out of my kitchen. I want this place cleaned up so that I can sit by the fire and put my feet up.'

'Get up you jackass.' Mark chuckled as he dragged Luke's chair away from the table, tipping it so that his brother slid from his seat.

'Can't you leave a fellow in peace?' Luke grumbled.

'You heard what Aggie said. You're in the way, little brother.' Mark cuffed him gently round the head. 'The girls have the clearing up to do so you'd best go and soliloquise somewhere else.'

Luke grinned sheepishly. 'Sorry, Aggie. I was miles away. I'll go now.'

'Men. You're all the same,' Molly called after them as they left the kitchen. 'That's right; leave us to do all the work.' She pointed to their chairs, carelessly abandoned without having been tucked back under the table. 'They expect to be waited on hand and foot. You'd think we were their blooming slaves.'

'That's just the way it is,' Nell said calmly. 'And probably the way it will always be. Don't forget they were risking their lives fighting that fire, so perhaps we should be glad to look after them.'

'Nell's right, it's the way of the world.' Aggie lowered herself into her chair by the range. 'Women were put on this earth to look after their men. I don't know what the good Lord was about, but that's how it's always been and that's how it will continue. Anyway, I've done my bit for you all today. It's your job to wash and dry the dishes when Matt has finished in the scullery. I'm going to have forty winks and I don't want to hear you girls squabbling.'

'Bloody hell,' Molly muttered beneath her breath but just loud enough for Lily to hear. 'There must be more to life than this. I'm going to marry the first rich bloke that asks me.'

Nell stood up, brushing crumbs from her skirt. 'I'm going to check on my patient, just to make sure he's all right.'

Molly waited until the door closed behind her sister and she shook her fist. 'She always manages to get out of doing the washing up.'

Aggie opened one eye. 'She does her fair share. Nell took on the housekeeping when your ma ran off and you should be grateful to her. By the way, someone needs to go out into the yard and fetch water from the pump.'

Lily sighed. 'I'll do it or else you'll spend the whole evening grumbling.'

'Right,' Molly said, perking up visibly. 'Good girl.'

It was past eight o'clock by the time they had washed the dishes and put them away. Aggie might pretend to be asleep but she opened her eyes every so often to inspect their work and she insisted that the floor had to be swept and mopped and the table set for breakfast next morning.

After she had finished her chores Lily escaped to the privacy of the bedchamber she shared with Molly and Nell. Everyone else, apart from Aggie who slept in a small room off the kitchen, had gone to huddle round the fire in the living room, but Lily had a secret which she had managed to keep from her family for many years.

Chapter Three

Lily closed the bedroom door, taking care not to make a noise. She knew that Nell was still ministering to the injured man upstairs and the family parlour was directly below. She wanted to be alone, but she knew from past experience that if Molly heard her footsteps pattering about overhead she would come to investigate. Whereas the rest of the family might be content to sit by the fire and relax after a hard day's work, Molly was easily bored and always on the fidget, looking for things to excite her interest. Lily placed the chipped enamel candle holder on the washstand and tiptoed over to her bed beneath the window. She sat down to take off her boots and a shiver ran down her spine. Was it her imagination, or did the shadows seem darker this evening? She told herself not to be so silly. There was nothing to harm her in the room she had shared with her sisters for the past ten years. The oppressive feeling must be due to the blanket of fog pressing against the windowpanes and blotting out the glow from the street light.

By daylight, the room was large and high-ceilinged with ornate plaster cornices, but like the rest of the house it had seen better days. The floral wallpaper was so faded that the pattern of roses and forget-me-nots was barely discernible, and the rugs scattered about on the bare boards were threadbare. It had been their parents' room in happier times, and Lily had vague memories of gleaming rosewood furniture and a brass bedstead with a rose-coloured satin coverlet and matching curtains, now faded to dusky pink. The furniture had been sent to auction several years ago and replaced by a pine armoire with a matching washstand and three narrow iron beds. In one corner, reflecting the flickering light of the single candle, stood a cheval mirror; the one piece that had belonged to her mother that had not been sold, thanks to Nell's eloquent plea for it to be saved. Even at the time, Lily had realised that Nell had been motivated by practicality rather than sentiment. Three girls maturing to womanhood needed a mirror if they were to present themselves to the world properly gowned. Nell was far-seeing and sensible, never one to be led by her emotions.

Lily slid off the bed and knelt on the floor, reaching beneath the iron bed frame to pull out a battered cardboard box in which she kept her most precious possession. Inside it was the only thing she owned that linked her to her mother and she prized it above everything. She took off the lid and lifted out a much smaller wooden box filled with tiny pans of colour. Ma had given it to her for her eighth birthday and she had treasured it ever since, using the paint sparingly to colour-wash the delicate pencil sketches of riverside scenes that she drew surreptitiously when the family were not about. These were executed on the back of pages torn out of old ledgers that she begged from Mr Cobbold, the ship's chandler who lived above his shop in Wapping High Street. His daughter, Flossie, was a voluptuous brunette who had a reputation for being a flirt, but Mark could see no wrong in her and had been stepping out with her for some months now. Lily was often required to carry messages to Flossie, and it was on one of these visits that she had seen Mr Cobbold about to throw an old ledger on the fire. Paper was expensive and Lily had leapt at the chance of receiving a free supply.

She laid out her treasures on the floor: a squirrel-hair brush that had lost some of its bristles, the stub of a pencil that would soon be too small to hold and a penknife with a rather rusty blade that had once belonged to Luke, but he had given it to her when the tip of the blade had snapped off. At the bottom of the box were the torn-out pages from Mr Cobbold's ledger noting transactions conducted ten years ago. Scrambling to her feet, Lily went to the washstand and filled her tooth mug with water from the willow-pattern jug. She went back to sit cross-legged on the floor by the bed, taking the candle with her. Placing it close enough to throw its paltry light on her work, she began to paint.

As she worked, the river scene that she had sketched the previous day began to glow with colour. She recaptured the golden light of the autumn sunshine glistening on the water, and the reflections of the ships tied up alongside the wharves. She lost track of time. She was no longer sitting in a cramped position in a cold, dark, comfortless room, she was living in the picture she created. She could feel the sun warm on her face and hear the swish of the water as it lapped and sucked at

45

the stanchions of the wall beneath the dockmaster's house. In her head she could hear the shouts of the men working the cranes on the wharves, the flapping of sails as vessels left port and the rumble of barrels being rolled over cobblestones.

She was brought abruptly back to earth by the sound of footsteps on the stairs outside the room, and she held her breath, poised and ready to slide her guilty secret back beneath her bed should anyone come in and catch her indulging in her forbidden art. The danger passed and the pitter-patter of feet faded into the distance. Lily breathed a sigh of relief; it must have been Nell coming from the attic room and going down-stairs to join the others in the parlour.

After another half an hour, when her eyes were sore from peering at her work in the dim light, Lily stretched her cramped muscles and began packing her things away. Soon her sisters would be coming to bed. Nell would be horrified if she discovered how her youngest sister spent her free time. She had made it painfully clear that she considered Lily's love of art and painting was to be discouraged, and Matt had agreed with her. He had once caught Lily sitting on the wall outside the house with her paints spread out around her and he had reacted angrily, accusing her of idling away her time. But behind his anger Lily had sensed his deep-seated fear that she would take after their mother. She had tried to explain that drawing and painting were as much a part of her as Luke's poetry was of him, but Matt had simply not understood. She had begged to be allowed to keep her paints, but Nell had taken the box and locked it in a cupboard and Lily, who had been eleven at the time and still pining for her mother, had cried herself to sleep for many nights. She had continued to plead for the return of her paints, but Nell had been adamant. Look where dabbling with art had led their mother, she had stormed. Ma would still be with them if she had not taken up with that dreadful fellow and Lily would go the same way if she wasn't careful. It had taken Lily months to find the key to the cupboard, and when she had rescued her paintbox she had vowed to keep it safe from prying eyes. That was her secret, and so far she had managed to keep it from the family.

A draught of cold air laced with the faint odour of tobacco smoke wafted up from the parlour as Lily made her way downstairs. For a moment she thought she might find her pa seated in his chair by the fire-place, smoking his favourite briar pipe, but when she opened the door it was Matt seated in the saggy old armchair by the fire. With his strong profile and dark hair brushed straight back from a high forehead, he looked so much like their father that it brought a lump to her throat. She slipped into the room unnoticed and went to sit on the window seat. It was draughty here too, but she was used to the cold and she knew that it would get much worse as winter progressed. The old house had been built on a promontory and the cold easterly wind blew from the North Sea, whistling across the Essex marshes and picking up noxious smells from the tanneries, sewage works and manu-factories to the east of the River Lea. It was not the most beautiful place in which to live, but Lily loved her home and the river that flowed past it on its way to the sea, carrying ships to far-off lands and bringing them safely home laden with exotic cargoes. The whole area might be dirty and dangerous, but for Lily the river and its wharves held an endless fascination.

She curled her legs up beneath her, studying the faces of her brothers and sisters with the eye of an artist. Nell, with her dark hair, sleek as a raven's wing, confined in a severe chignon at the back of her neck, was fully occupied turning the collar on one of Luke's shirts. There was something serene and beautiful about Nell and Lily was secretly in awe of her. Then there was Luke who had his head in a book as usual, seemingly oblivious to the rest of the world. His red-gold hair flopped over his forehead and his thick eyelashes formed corn-coloured crescents on his tanned cheeks. His generous lips moved silently as he read, and Lily could relate to his ability to vanish into a world created by words.

Seated on the far side of the fireplace, Matt smoked his pipe, staring into the fire with a faraway expression on his handsome features, and not for the first time Lily wondered why he had not married. He was twenty-eight and she knew several girls who worshipped him from afar, but none of them seemed to catch his eye. He had stepped out with a few of them, but it had come to nothing. She wondered sometimes if he was afraid to give his heart to a woman in case she broke it, as their mother had done to Pa. It was a question that she could not answer, and she looked round for Mark who patently adored girls and had courted quite a few. As if sensing

Lily's unspoken question, Nell looked up from her sewing. 'Where did Mark go, Matt? He really should have stayed at home on a night like this.'

'Where do you think?' Matt said with his lazy smile. 'It would take more than a pea-souper to keep him away from Flossie Cobbold.'

Nell sighed. 'It must be love.'

'He asked me to write a poem for her,' Luke said, brushing the lock of hair back from his eyes for the umpteenth time. 'I couldn't think of anything that rhymed with Flossie.'

Molly was sitting on the rag rug by the hearth, with the tip of her pink tongue held between her teeth as she attempted to renovate a battered straw bonnet with flowers fashioned from scraps of silk. 'What about bossy?' she said, giggling. 'That rhymes.'

'But it's not exactly romantic,' Luke countered. 'And I don't think young Flossie is the type to be wooed by words alone.'

'If it's expensive gifts she's after, she'll be sadly disappointed,' Molly said, stabbing her needle into the plaited straw.

'That's not very fair,' Nell said gently. 'Flossie is a nice girl, even if she is a bit flighty.'

'Flighty! I've heard she'll be very generous to a bloke who treats her to a night out and she'll do anything for a box of chocolates.' Molly glanced round to see what impact her words had, but her grin was wiped off her face and she let out a yelp as she pricked her finger on the needle.

'That serves you right, young lady,' Matt said sternly,

although Lily could see the corners of his mouth twitch as though he was trying not to laugh.

'Yes, that's what you get for being crude,' Nell added, patently unamused.

Lily had to suppress a giggle, but no one noticed her as all eyes were on Molly who had leapt to her feet and gone very red in the face. 'I think you're all horrible. I was just stating the truth.'

Matt burst out laughing. 'Sit down, you silly girl, and get on with turning a hideous bonnet into something even worse.'

Molly retaliated by throwing the offending article at him. 'I hate you, Matt,' she stormed angrily. 'If Pa was still here he wouldn't let you talk to me like that, and I wouldn't have to make do with a bonnet I've had for two years or more. Pa would have bought me a new one long ago.'

'Learn to take a joke,' Matt said easily. 'You'll have to deal with worse than that in life. Just be thankful that you've got a roof over your head and food in your belly. As to Pa having money to throw around, just remember that he was a fireman like the rest of us; it was Grandpa's position as dockmaster that kept you in the style you miss so much.'

Nell glanced at the clock on the mantelshelf. 'Oh, heavens! It's half past nine. Did anyone make Grandpa's cocoa?'

All eyes turned to Lily.

She jumped to her feet. 'I'd quite forgotten, but I'll do it now. Does anyone else fancy a cup? And what about our Frenchman? Do you think he'd like some too?'

50

Nell put her sewing aside. 'He should sleep through the night, but I'd better go and check on him.'

'I'll go,' Molly said firmly. 'I'm going to bed anyway since I've got to be up at the crack of dawn.' She flounced out of the room without waiting for a response.

'I'd better go with her.' Nell half rose to her feet but Matt reached out and laid a hand on her arm, shaking his head.

'Let her do it,' Luke said, closing his book with a snap. 'After all, the fellow is so full of laudanum that he couldn't raise a little finger. Her head is so stuffed with dreams, let her imagine he's a handsome prince who will open his eyes, fall in love with her and carry her off to his castle.'

Lily dropped a kiss on top of his head as she passed his chair. 'You are the only one who understands us, Luke.'

He glanced up at her and smiled. 'I'd like some cocoa, Lily.'

Next morning, everyone was up and about before dawn. Mark and Luke were on the early shift at the fire station and Matt headed off to the Seamen's Mission, where he said he hoped to gain the information about the stricken vessel that he needed for his report. Molly went to work with the utmost reluctance, and Nell left for the Ragged School having given Lily a long list of instructions, mostly concerned with caring for the injured Frenchman. Grandpa stomped off to his room, muttering darkly about some people being favoured above others and getting all the attention, and Aggie put on her bonnet and cloak, saying that she was going to the market to buy meat for supper. Lily couldn't resist the temptation to peep out of the parlour window, knowing from past observations that Aggie's rheumatics would improve the moment she was out of the house. Today was no exception and Aggie went off with a spring in her step which made Lily smile to herself. She had once, when she was much younger, followed Aggie to the market, and had seen her gossiping on a street corner with a group of women. Lily did not know their names, but it was not hard to guess that Aggie's friends were all similarly situated and going to market gave them a chance to get away from their employers and enjoy a good long chat.

Left to her own devices Lily knew that she ought to go up to the attic and check on the injured man, but she was suddenly nervous. Nell had attended to him first thing that morning, and had said that he was conscious but rambling and she feared that he had developed a fever. Lily must look in on him at regular intervals, she had said firmly; he must be given sips of water and reassured that all was well. He must not be allowed to worry.

Lily was undecided. There was a pile of ironing waiting for her in the scullery and the clothes that had not dried yesterday were now hanging on the washing line in the yard and would soon be dry. It was a crisp, cold but dry morning and all traces of yesterday's pea-souper had vanished during the night. The air was now crystal clear and the smoke from the manufactories along the south bank of the river rose in straight plumes into an azure sky. Taking one last look at the sunny scene outside the window, Lily had to suppress a sudden urge to abandon her wearisome household tasks. The sunlight had an intensity about it that only occurred on cold winter days and the light was perfect for sketching. It would be wonderful to be free to do just as she pleased just for one day, but it wasn't to be. She had duties to perform and the first and most pressing was to go upstairs to take a look at the patient.

She turned away from the window, and, stopping to straighten the hearth rug and the cushions on the sofa that leaked stuffing every time anyone sat on them, she made her way slowly from the parlour. The sun slanted palely through the hall windows, catching the dust motes in its beams and turning them into a shower of sparkling gold. The improvement in the weather was more than welcome after the suffocating fog of yesterday, but the sunlight revealed scuffed floorboards in need of a good polish, and as Lily mounted the stairs she noticed that the banisters were thick with dust. There was so much to do, and even if she worked from dawn to dusk the task was well beyond the capability of one person. In the old days they would have had a daily woman to do the scrubbing and heavy work, with the help of a parlourmaid and a scullery maid. She tried not to feel dispirited, and she turned a blind eye to the cobwebs that seemed to have materialised overnight.

Outside the attic room, she stopped to catch her breath and her hand trembled as she opened the door just enough to take a cautious peek at the bed, but all was quiet. She tiptoed into the room and stood gazing down at the face of the man she had helped to save. He was, as she had first thought, very good-looking with classically sculpted features that would not have appeared out of place on the marble bust of a Greek hero. His dark hair was plastered against his head, and his winged eyebrows and eyelashes were the same shade of rich brown. Lily sat down on the chair at his bedside, wishing that she had her pencil and paper at hand. Even in sleep, his was a face that any artist might crave to immortalise on canvas.

He stirred suddenly causing her to rise from the chair with a start. She picked up a glass of water that Nell had left on a stool by the bed and she held it to his dry lips. He swallowed convulsively and most of the water spilled onto the pillow, but he managed to sip a little more. Recalling Nell's instructions, Lily wrung a cloth out in the bowl of water that had been left for the purpose, and she bathed his forehead. He was burning up with fever and she did not know what to do next. She felt alone and helpless and she wished that Nell was there. Even having Molly by her side would have been a small comfort.

The man moaned and Lily leapt back from the bed, biting her lip. She was tempted to run from the room and close the door behind her, but she knew that would be cowardly. She did not want the poor fellow to die of neglect. As a last resort she knelt at his bedside and clasped her hands together. 'Please help me, God,' she said fervently. 'I don't know what to do.'

Almost as if the plea had permeated his fevered brain, the young Frenchman opened his eyes. He stared at her with an unfocused gaze, murmuring something in his own tongue.

Instinctively, she reached out to hold his hand. 'It's all right. Please don't try to talk. You're quite safe here.'

A frown puckered his forehead. 'Where am I?'

He had spoken in English but with a slight accent which intrigued Lily. Growing up so close to the docks she was used to hearing sailors chattering away in their own languages but this was the first time she had come into close contact with a foreigner. She squeezed his fingers gently, speaking slowly and clearly. 'You are in the old dockmaster's house in Wapping. You were brought here yesterday.'

'My ship.' He struggled to sit up, falling back against the pillows with a cry of pain.

Alarmed, Lily reached for the medicine bottle and, following Nell's instructions, measured out a few drops of laudanum into the glass of water. She held it to his lips. 'Please don't worry, sir. You must rest.'

He drank thirstily but his gaze never wavered from her face. 'I begin to remember. The fire – you saved me.'

'No, it wasn't like that. Well, not exactly anyway. I suppose I found you but you were injured quite badly and I had to get help . . .' Her voice tailed off as she realised that he had lapsed into either a deep sleep or unconsciousness; she was not sure which, but at least he was no longer in pain. She knew that she could leave him safely now, but she continued to hold his hand, staring down at his slender, tapering fingers and smooth skin. There were no calluses and his finger-nails were clean and neatly pared. It was the hand of a gentleman. She held it briefly to her cheek, and then, feeling rather foolish, she laid his hand on his chest and pulled the coverlet up to his chin. 'Sleep well,' she whispered. 'I'll come back to see you in a little while.'

Even then she could not tear herself away from the handsome stranger. He seemed so forlorn and lonely up here in the attic beneath the leaky roof. It was cold, and draughts whistled through the holes where the ceiling plaster had crumbled away exposing the gaps in the roof tiles. Lily was certain that her Frenchman was used to far better than this. Perhaps he lived in a beautiful chateau on one of the French rivers. She had read about such places in books that Nell brought home from school when she was preparing the next day's lessons. Ma had loved reading, and although her choice had veered more to gothic novels and novelettes than to anything more literary, she had insisted on teaching her daughters to read at an early age. Lily could remember sitting on her mother's knee and learning her alphabet by studying the text beneath illustrations in the latest fashion journal or the society news page in *The Times*. She knew almost nothing about mathematics, but Nell had taken over after Ma's sudden departure and she had taught Lily how to count and to add pounds shillings and pence, saying that was all a young lady needed to get by.

'Assuming that one day you will marry a man who has a respectable profession and can keep you in a reasonable style,' Nell had told the nine-year-old Lily. 'You will be able to ensure that your cook-general does not cheat you and you will be able to work out your household expenses.'

That had been while they were still reasonably pros-
perous. Grandpa had not yet retired and Pa had still
been alive. Lily felt tears welling up in her eyes and
she blinked them away. It was unlikely that any of
them would marry into the professional classes now.
She could see herself ending up as housekeeper to a
well-off family since that was all she knew. She leaned
over to smooth the counterpane and her fingers strayed
to touch the Frenchman's hair. It was thick and luxuriant and most probably had a slight wave when it was
not slicked with sweat. She had had to force herself to
enter his room, but now she left him with the greatest
reluctance. She would have been happy to sit at his
bedside, waiting for him to open his eyes once again,
but there was work to do downstairs and she would
be in terrible trouble if she neglected her duties.

She spent the rest of the morning in the kitchen heating
flat irons on the range before putting them to use. The
kitchen was filled with steam and the scent of the freshly
laundered linen that had dried outside in the frosty
winter air. She had made potato starch which she used
to ensure a glassy sheen on the sheets, collars and cuffs.
Working feverishly to make up for lost time, Lily had
almost completed her Herculean task when Aggie
returned from market.

'I thought you would have finished this ages ago,'
Aggie said, frowning as she made a space between the
neat piles of clean garments to set the heavy wicker basket
down on the kitchen table. 'You'll have to shift everything out of here so that I can start preparing dinner.'

'I'm going as fast as I can,' Lily protested. 'I've had to keep an eye on the Frenchman as well as do my chores.'

'Foreigners are nothing but trouble, if you ask me.' Aggie took off her bonnet and shawl and hung them on a peg by the door. 'But the Lord tells us to look after the halt and the lame and so I bought an oxtail. It will make a nice stew for the family and the fellow upstairs can sup the broth. In the old days I would have made some calves' foot jelly, but that was then and this is now.'

Lily placed the last few garments on the airer and pulleyed it into place above the range so that the sheets, pillowcases and shirts dangled above them in the rising warm air. 'There,' she said with a sigh of satisfaction. 'That's done for another week. Lord, how I wish we could afford a scullery maid.'

'Don't take the Lord's name in vain, girl,' Aggie said sternly. 'You aren't too old to feel the back of the wooden spoon across your knuckles.'

Lily backed away as Aggie reached for her weapon of choice. Lily knew only too well what it felt like to be at the receiving end of the spoon wielded by an angry Aggie, and she had seen her brothers with tears in their eyes after receiving a smart rap on the head. Only Matt and Grandpa were exempt from such punishment, and of course Nell, who never put a foot wrong and, in Aggie's eyes at least, was well on her way to sainthood.

Lily snatched up the remaining garments, which would be hung over a clothes horse in front of the parlour fire. 'I'll just see to these and then I'll check on Grandpa and the Frenchman.'

'If the doctor comes calling, don't let him anywhere near my kitchen,' Aggie said, tipping the contents of her basket onto the table. 'If that man gets a whiff of stewing oxtail we'll never get rid of him. And there's no brandy left, so he'll have to go elsewhere to get his tipple.'

'Yes, Aggie.' Lily hastened from the room and made her way to the parlour where she lit the fire. Having draped the laundered garments over the clothes horse, she went to check on her grandfather. He was at his usual place by the window, peering at the river traffic through a spyglass. 'Do you need anything, Grandpa?'

He turned to glare at her. 'I've been forgotten as usual. Where was my morning tea? I rang the bell but no one came. I suppose you were mooning over that damned foreigner upstairs.'

'I was doing the ironing, Grandpa. But I'll fetch you a cup of tea now.'

'Too late, the moment has passed. I'm famished and I want my midday meal. I know the old besom has returned from market. I saw her through the window not ten minutes ago, so I know there's food in the house. I have a fancy for bread and cheese and a couple of pickled onions. Oh, and a pint of strong ale would go down nicely.' He thrust his hand into his pocket and drew out a leather pouch from which he produced a silver threepenny bit. 'Take this, but I want the change.'

'Yes, Grandpa. I'll be as quick as I can, but I've got to check on the poor fellow upstairs before I go out.'

His bushy eyebrows drew together in a scowl. 'Never mind him. I want my ale now.' His expression softened and he bared the few teeth he had left in a smile.

'Be a good girl for your poor old grandpa, Lil. I need some sustenance or I'll like as not pass out with hunger and thirst.'

She shook her head, smiling. 'You're an old fraud, Grandpa. You like people to think you're a fierce old thing, but I know different.'

'Get on with you, girl. You're a sight too much like your ma for your own good.'

'Not me, Grandpa. It's Molly who is the spitting image of Ma.'

'No, you're wrong there, Lil. You're the artistic one, and don't try to deny it. I've seen you outside on the wall doing your drawings of the river. It don't matter what Matt or Nell say; it's in your blood and you can't do anything about it.'

'I'll go to the pub and fetch your ale, Grandpa.'

She was halfway down the path when she saw Matt striding towards the house. He had a purposeful look on his face and a set to his jaw that made her suddenly anxious. 'Is anything wrong, Matt?'

He thrust the garden gate open and walked past her, making his way to the front door. 'Not exactly, but we've got to do something about the Frenchman.'

Forgetting all about the ale, she followed him into the house. 'Why? What's happened?'

Matt paused, turning to stare down at her with a worried frown. 'The padre at the mission can speak French and he acted as translator so that I could question the sailors from the wrecked vessel.'

'Don't keep me in suspense,' Lily said breathlessly. 'What did they say?'

'To be honest I couldn't get much sense out of them as to how they managed to ground the ship or how the fire broke out, but I did find out who we've been harbouring in the attic.'

Lily's heart sank. 'Don't tell me he's a criminal on the run.'

'No such thing. His name is Armand Labrosse and his father owns a fleet of merchant ships. They are an old and much respected French family and we have the fellow sleeping in the attic with the bats, rats and a leaking roof.'

'I knew it,' Lily breathed, hardly able to contain her excitement. 'I had a feeling he was someone special.'

'Never mind that. We must make the chap comfortable. Light a fire in Grandpa's old bedroom, and make up the bed. We must move Monsieur Labrosse before he comes to and finds himself in the attic.'

Lily frowned. 'You thought the room was good enough for an ordinary sailor.'

'Well it's not good enough for the son of a rich and powerful man. I could lose my job over this, and if Monsieur Labrosse senior complained to the London Dock Company we would find ourselves out on the street.'

'But why? I don't understand.'

'There are reasons. Just do as I say, Lily, and make up the bed in Grandpa's old room. Our whole future depends on this.'

Chapter Four

'Haven't you finished yet, Lily?' Matt stood in the doorway of the bedroom where their grandfather had slept until his rheumaticky legs made it impossible for him to climb the stairs. 'It doesn't look very welcoming. What in heaven's name have you been doing all this time?'

'I've done my best,' she said defensively. 'I can't help it if everything is old and shabby, but at least it's clean and warm. I've just got to finish making the bed and then you can bring him down.' Matt's impatient tone and critical words were hurtful, especially when she had tried so hard to do as he asked. She had cleaned the grate, which had been filled with soot, seagulls' feathers and crumbling pieces of the chimney stack, and she had managed to get the fire going after several unsuccessful attempts. Not only that, but she had taken the rugs out into the yard and beaten them until her arms ached, and she was now making up the bed with the freshly laundered sheets. Someone would have to go without clean bedlinen for another week at least. To make matters worse, Grandpa's room was directly below and she could hear his bell clanging impatiently as he waited for his midday meal and ale. She shot a resentful glance at her brother. 'You're being very unfair, Matt. I can't work miracles.'

'I didn't mean to criticise you, Lil,' Matt said in a gentler tone. 'I can see that you've worked hard, but I want our friend upstairs to be comfortable. He'll need more pillows for a start, so you'd best take them off the boys' beds. They won't notice the difference.'

'I wouldn't bet on it.' Lily sniffed as she plumped up the bolster and laid it across the bed. 'I'll do it, but I'm not taking the blame when they find out.'

'Don't worry about that. I'll deal with them.' Matt strolled over to the window and tugged at one of the curtains, sending a shower of dust onto the windowsill and causing a jagged tear in the moth-eaten material. 'We must have something better than this.'

Lily smoothed the counterpane and straightened up, holding her hand to her aching back. 'That's Nell's department, Matt. You'll have to ask her.'

'I will, as soon as she gets home.' He turned to her with a grateful smile. 'You've done well, Lily. I know it's an almost impossible task, but saving young Labrosse might be the answer to all our problems.'

'What problems?' Lily stared at him nonplussed. 'You said that before. Can't you tell me what's wrong?'

'It's nothing for you to worry your head about, Lil. Let's just say that Labrosse's father is an important man, and I've just found out that he has shares in the dock company.'

'I don't understand. What has that to do with us?'

He was silent for a moment, eyeing her speculatively.

'If I tell you something will you promise not to mention a word of it to the others?'

'Cross my heart and hope to die,' Lily said, making the appropriate sign with her hand.

'This is strictly between the two of us, but I'm hoping that a word in the right quarter from an influential man like Labrosse's father might give us more time to find other accommodation.'

'What do you mean by that?' Shocked and startled, Lily stared at him in horror.

'Leave it at that, Lily. No one knows a thing about this, except Nell.'

'What don't they know? You're scaring me, Matt.'

'To put it in a nutshell, the dock company have given us notice to quit the house. I've only just found out about it myself, but they've written several times to Grandpa and he's ignored the letters. We've got until the end of the year and then we're out.'

'I don't understand. I thought that Grandpa had the house for the rest of his natural.'

'So did I, but it seems the new dockmaster isn't happy with his present accommodation and this house should be his by rights. The dock manager called me into his office, and it seems that the original arrangement with Grandpa, which he neglected to mention, was that he could have this house for a period of five years after his retirement. That time will be up at the end of December.'

Lily could hardly believe her ears. 'There must have been some mistake. Did you ask Grandpa?'

'Of course I did, but he went off in one of his rages

and denied ever receiving any letters from the dock company. He seemed to think that it was a plot by some unknown enemy to humiliate him. I'm afraid he's going a bit doolally.'

Lily sank down on the edge of the bed. 'I know he's a bit odd at times, but he's not out of his mind.'

'I think Pa's death affected him more than he would admit. I know he loves the old house but unless a miracle happens we'll have to leave. The dock manager made it perfectly clear that he wants us out, which is why I was hoping that Labrosse senior might be persuaded to put in a good word for us, and at least give me more time to find somewhere suitable for us to live.'

'And what if he can't or won't help us?'

'We can only hope that he'll be grateful to us for looking after his son, which is why we must put in every effort to pamper the fellow.'

'But if the worst happens, where will we go, Matt?'

'I'll find somewhere. If all else fails there are a couple of rooms to let above the shop next door to the fire station.' Matt moved swiftly to her side and ruffled her hair. 'Don't look like that, Lily. Your big brother will look after you. Now, I'm going to fetch Labrosse and we'll make him comfortable. I just hope that he won't remember anything about the attic when he is himself again.'

He hurried from the room and Lily sat for a moment, stunned by what she had just learned. She had been born in this house, as had all her brothers and sisters; it was the only home she had known. The thought of leaving in such a manner was horrible and quite terrifying. She had seen down and out people living beneath railway arches and curled up in shop doorways at night, roosting like pigeons. She rose slowly to her feet, the weight of the secret she must keep from the family resting heavily on her narrow shoulders. But Matt had taken her into his confidence and she must be proud of that. She must not let him down.

She could hear him moving about in the attic room above and she forced herself to take positive action by adding more coal to the fire. The orange and gold flames leapt up the chimney, forming glittering patterns as they ignited the soot on the fireback. It was ironic, she thought, that her brothers spent their working lives putting out fires and yet tonight they would grumble because there was no comforting blaze in the hearth. There was just enough fuel left in the coal shed to keep the kitchen range going and a modest fire in Grandpa's room, but the front parlour would remain cheerless and chilly until payday. Suddenly Lily's whole world seemed to have been turned upside down. Times had been hard in the past, but she had felt safe and secure until now; she realised with a heavy heart that if the dock company had their way, everything was about to change.

'Here he is,' Matt said, pushing the door open with the toe of his boot. He carried the semi-conscious man across to the bed and laid him down gently. 'He's been raving like a lunatic, so chances are he won't recall a thing. Make him comfortable, Lily, I've got work to do.'

'Where are you going?' Lily demanded anxiously. 'What do I do if he wakes up?'

Matt shrugged his shoulders. 'I don't know, Lil. Give him some more laudanum, I suppose, only don't overdo it. Just keep him quiet and Nell will see to him when she gets home. I've got to write up my report for the shipping agent, and he is going to contact Labrosse's father in Dieppe by telegraph.' Matt's serious expression melted into a grin. 'I dunno, Lil, but the wonders of modern science might save us yet.'

She did not feel much like smiling as he left the room. Downstairs she could hear Grandpa's bell clanging away with the insistence of a fire engine on a shout, and Armand was tossing about on the pillows, muttering feverishly. She braced herself to lift his head gently and hold a glass of water to his lips. This seemed to revive him a little and he opened his eyes. For a moment she thought that he smiled but then he began rambling again and she laid him back on the pillows while she mixed a small dose of laudanum and water. She stayed with him, stroking his hair back from his forehead and speaking softly as she might to a fractious child, until he lapsed into a deep sleep.

When she left the room she found that her legs were shaking. Looking after sick people seemed to come so easily to Nell, but for Lily it was an ordeal. Sympathy for the young Frenchman had overcome her qualms, but she would gladly relinquish her nursing duties to her eldest sister. She hurried downstairs to placate her grandfather who was interspersing the ringing of his bell with pleas for food.

*　　*　　*

Later that day, when Grandpa and Aggie were both having their afternoon nap, Lily returned to Armand's bedside armed with her sketching materials. Her fingers had been itching to capture his likeness on paper, and she knew that she had at least an hour undisturbed. Dr Macpherson had arrived at midday, hoping no doubt to sample some of Aggie's cooking, but she had not been in a generous mood and he had gone off in a huff, having glanced at the patient and said he was doing as well as could be expected.

Lily settled down to make sketches of the handsome Frenchman. It would have been much easier had he been awake, but perhaps it was better this way. While he slept he did not seem to suffer pain from his burns and his sprained ankle, and when she laid her hand on his forehead he felt cooler to the touch. That must be a good sign.

She worked feverishly, making sketch after sketch. If she had had her paints with her she could have added colour, bringing the drawings to life. She would just have to memorise the soft, thrush's wing sheen of his hair and the pale olive complexion that she found so fascinating.

She barely noticed the fading light, and she was so absorbed in her task that she did not hear the sound of approaching footsteps until it was too late. Molly burst into the room, causing Lily to drop her pencil and send sheets of paper fluttering to the floor.

'You'll cop it if Nell finds out. What d'you think you're doing anyway? Isn't it a bit odd sitting there making drawings of the poor bloke when he's unconscious?

I call it weird. And I don't know how you can see to draw in this poor light.'

Lily scrambled about on the floor, picking up her drawings. 'You won't tell on me, will you?'

'What's it worth?'

'Don't be mean, Moll. You know I haven't got anything worth trading.'

Molly tossed her head. 'You can let me take my turn sitting with Armand.' She sighed ecstatically. 'Isn't that the most wonderful name you've ever heard? And he's filthy rich so Aggie was telling me. His pa is a shipping magnate.'

Lily shuffled her sketches into a pile, rising to her feet and clutching them to her breast. 'I wouldn't get any ideas if I were you. Armand Labrosse wouldn't look twice at girls like us.'

Molly moved round the bed to sit on the chair that Lily had just vacated. 'We're as good as any of those rich society females. All they've got is money. We've got . . .' She paused, frowning.

'Well, you've got yellow hands today and a green splodge on your cheek. If he opens his eyes and sees you sitting there he'll probably die of fright, or think he's gone to hell.'

Molly jumped up to look in the mirror over the mantelshelf. 'I can't see a thing.' She lit a candle using a spill from the jar in the hearth and took a second look. 'Damn and blast! I wish I'd been apprenticed to a milliner or a dressmaker. I'm sick to death of coming home looking like a fright.' She hurried to the washstand and poured water into the bowl, scrubbing her face with her hands and reaching for the towel that Lily had placed there earlier.

'That was for Armand,' Lily protested. 'Now I'll have to fetch a clean towel, but you can empty the wash-bowl since you used the water.' She glanced over her sister's shoulder. 'And it's all green and yellow. If Nell sees that she'll know it was you.'

Molly seized the bowl and went to the window, throwing up the sash and tipping the contents into the tiny patch of garden below. 'There, that's the evidence gone. It's up to you to find a clean towel and a jug of fresh water.' She slammed the window, causing the glass to rattle. 'And if I'm not going to tell on you, I want one of those likenesses of Armand, and you can fetch me a cup of tea with two sugars.'

'You are so mean,' Lily retaliated. 'Sometimes I hate you, Molly.'

'And you'd better light the fire in the parlour,' Molly added, strolling over to the washstand and replacing the bowl. 'It's freezing down there and the others will be coming home from work soon.' She held her hand out. 'Let me see which one I want.'

Reluctantly, Lily handed over her sketches. 'Take one then, but don't show anyone. And I can't light the fire downstairs because I used the coal for the parlour fire to keep your precious Armand warm.'

Molly was examining the drawing in the candle-light, and she either did not hear Lily's last remark or she chose to ignore it. She looked up and there was genuine admiration in her eyes. 'I dunno much about art, Lil, but these are blooming marvellous. You must do his portrait when he wakes up, and I want the first copy.'

Lily felt herself blushing at this unexpected praise and her anger evaporated. 'Do you really?'

Molly selected one sketch and handed the rest back to Lily. 'I certainly do, and I won't breathe a word to Nell. You are a born artist, my girl. I wish I had half your talent. Now go and make me that cup of tea. I'm going to sit here and dream about being married to this gorgeous man. I can just see myself dripping in diamonds and wearing the latest Paris fashions. No more smelly dyes or listening to old man Jones scolding me.'

As Lily left the room, Molly was still rambling on about the life she would have with the handsome young Frenchman. Lily could well imagine vivacious, irrepressible Molly capturing Armand's heart. He had only to wake up and look into her sparkling green eyes and see her tumbling locks of flame-coloured hair to fall hopelessly in love. Lily knew that by comparison she was a pale copy of her elder sisters both in looks and in temperament. She had neither Molly's fire nor Nell's serene, dark beauty. She was just Lily, the youngest and least important member of a talented, argumentative, temperamental family, and now she was burdened by a dreadful secret which if it came to fruition would tear their lives apart.

That evening, much to Aggie's annoyance, Matt and Luke remained in the kitchen after supper, sitting at the table playing cards. Mark had braved the rain to go and see Flossie, and Nell had taken a bowl of broth up to the sickroom to try to tempt Armand to take a little sustenance. Molly and Lily were left to wash the dishes in the scullery. Having completed her part of the task, Molly said she did not want to spend the evening listening to Aggie's grumbles or watching her brothers gambling, using shirt buttons instead of money. She said she was going to bed early as it was the only way to get a little peace and keep reasonably warm, and she shot a warning glance at Lily as she left the kitchen. Translating this look into words, Lily knew that Molly was going to challenge Nell's right to be the first of the Larkin sisters Armand would see when the fever cleared from his brain.

Lily occupied herself by tidying the china on the dresser, and when that was done she went into the scullery to fetch her brothers' wet boots, which they had kicked off when they came home from the fire station. She stuffed the toes with old newspapers and put the boots in front of the fire to dry overnight. She took care not to disturb Aggie, who had fallen asleep with her several chins resting on her chest and her lips vibrating with occasional loud snores.

'Isn't it time for Grandpa's cocoa?' Matt said, looking up as Lily went past his chair. 'I'll have a cup if there's any to spare.'

'And me,' Luke added, throwing down his cards. 'You've got me beaten, Matt. It's lucky we're only playing for buttons. I'd be bankrupt if it was money.'

'And you can put those buttons back in the box when you've finished,' Lily said, ruffling his hair. 'They cost money and if you lose them you'll be going about with your shirts flapping open.'

Matt leaned back in his seat, grinning. 'You're a rotten card player, Luke. You're more likely to make a fortune making up silly rhymes than you would as a gambler.'

'He writes lovely poetry,' Lily said, leaping to Luke's defence. 'One day he'll be rich and famous, you'll see.'

Matt's smile faded into a frown. 'We can't wait that long.'

'What's up?' Luke demanded. 'You've been in a mood all evening, Matt.'

'Nothing for you to worry about.' Matt pushed back his chair and rose to his feet. 'Forget the cocoa, Lil. I'm going for a walk.'

'Why don't you wait until the rain stops? Stay in and have a nice hot cup of cocoa?' Lily said anxiously. She knew that Matt was worried, but getting soaked to the skin and risking pneumonia would not solve any of their problems.

'Ta, Lil, but I want some fresh air.' He stooped to pick up his boots and left the room, his stockinged feet padding softly on the floorboards.

'He's a moody devil,' Luke said sulkily. 'One moment he's fine and the next he's grumpy as hell.'

Lily took the cocoa tin from the mantelshelf. 'I expect he's got a lot on his mind,' she said, taking off the lid and inhaling the bitter-sweet chocolate scent. There was just enough cocoa powder to make two cups, but her brothers took precedence over everyone else in the house and she was used to going without. They were the breadwinners and without them the women would starve. That was the way of things. She had never thought to question it.

She served Luke first and then took a brimming cup to her grandfather's room. He was already in bed and looking distinctly cross. 'You're late with my cocoa. What've you been doing, girl?'

'It's the same time as usual, Grandpa,' Lily said patiently. 'It just seems later because the nights are drawing in.'

'I can tell the time, and you're ten minutes past the hour. If we'd run the docks in such a slapdash way there would have been chaos. You should take a leaf from my book, Lily.'

'Yes, Grandpa.'

'And you should stop filling your head with all that drawing nonsense or you'll go the same way as your mother. Be satisfied with learning to keep house and look after your family.'

'Yes, Grandpa,' Lily said, plumping up his pillows.

He eyed her suspiciously. 'And don't give me that blank look, Lily Larkin. There's no finer calling for a woman than to be a domestic angel. Your grandma was one such. She was a wonderful woman and it's a pity you don't take after her. Nell does, God bless her. But you and Molly . . .' He left the sentence hanging in the air, shaking his head.

'Goodnight, Grandpa,' Lily said, dropping a kiss on his grey head. She left him to drink his cocoa, closing the door softly behind her. She had grown accustomed to his constant harping on her failings, and she had learned to ignore it, treating it as the ramblings of an old man who was disappointed with life. Once, when she had been much younger, she had been upset by his criticisms, but now they rippled over her like the river water at ebb tide. She took her night candle from the table at the foot of the stairs. It cast long shadows that moved with her as she mounted the staircase, but she was not afraid of the dark. The old house seemed to wrap its arms protectively around her and the thought of having to move out was too horrible to contemplate. She had intended to go to her bedroom, but she could not resist taking a peek into Armand's room.

Seated one on either side of the bed, Molly and Nell faced each other and Lily could feel the air snapping with the tension between them. Despite their downcast faces, the tableau they presented in the glow of the firelight and flickering candles was one of touching concern for a sick man. It was ruined by Molly, who turned her head to glare at Lily. 'Shut the door, silly. You're causing a draught.'

'How is he?' Lily closed the door behind her and tiptoed over to the bed.

Nell put down her sewing, and Lily saw that she had been attempting to patch one of the curtains. 'He's a little better, I think. At least, he doesn't seem to be so hot and he's stopped rambling.'

'It's a pity he's been speaking French all the time,' Molly said, sighing. 'I'd love to know what he's been saying and Nell won't tell me, although I'm sure she understands.'

Nell shook her head. 'I can only pick out a few words,

and I think he was talking about the accident that grounded his ship. It didn't make much sense.'

'Look,' Molly cried excitedly. 'He's opening his eyes.' She leaned towards him. 'Hello, Armand. I'm Molly.'

Nell glared at her, raising her finger to her lips. 'Leave him alone, Molly. Let him come round in his own time.'

Lily moved closer to the bed. 'I think he's trying to say something.' She held her breath, willing Armand to look at her, but his gaze was fixed on Nell. Lily's heart sank; it was always the way. Men devoured Nell with their eyes; she could have had any number of suitors had she given them the slightest encouragement, but she had never shown the least interest in any of the young men who came knocking on their door. Nell's excuse was that she had too much responsibility at home to think about love and marriage, but looking at her sister now Lily suspected she might have had a change of heart. There was a delicate flush to Nell's cheeks, a light in her eyes and a tender curve to her lips as she leaned forward to lay her hand on Armand's brow.

'Well?' Molly demanded. 'Has the fever gone or not? Don't just sit there staring at him as if he was a slice of chocolate cake.'

Nell withdrew her hand, blushing furiously. 'Hush, Molly. What a thing to say.'

'Be quiet, both of you,' Lily said. 'He's trying to say something.'

There was a moment of silence as all three sisters stared at the injured man. Armand looked from one to the other and a slow smile spread across his sculpted features. 'Am I in heaven with the angels?'

Molly clasped her hands to her breast and with a sharp intake of breath her rosy lips formed a circle of delight. 'Oh, how sweet.'

Lily's heart fluttered against her ribcage, and she felt herself melting like ice cream on a warm day. She was lost for words as she gazed at Armand. His eyes were large, slightly almond-shaped, and the dark-rimmed irises shone like molten gold in the firelight. She was bereft of words.

Nell rose hastily to her feet. 'Monsieur Labrosse,' she began tentatively. 'H-how do you feel?'

He attempted to sit up, but fell back against the pillows with a groan. 'My head, it is a little hurt I think and my ankle too. Ladies, I fear I have given you much trouble.'

'Oh, no.'

Lily felt a sudden urge to giggle as she and her sisters spoke in unison.

Armand raised his hand and a smile played on his lips. 'You are too kind. But tell me, how long have I been like this?'

'Two days, monsieur,' Nell said, casting a warning look at Molly who was hovering near the bedhead with the look of a blackbird about to pounce on a juicy worm. 'You were brought here after the fire on board your ship.'

'Please, my name is Armand. I believe I owe you much and I am grateful.'

'Armand is a lovely name and it's a pleasure to have you here,' Molly said, leaning towards him with a smile that made her cheeks dimple. Lily had seen her sister practising this art in the mirror and Molly was now using it to good effect. Lily noted somewhat gloomily that the Frenchman was impressed, and she raised her hand to her own smooth cheek. No matter how hard she tried she could not compete with Molly's dimples or Nell's classic beauty.

'And you are Molly; you have already told me that.' Armand turned his head to look at Nell. 'And you, mademoiselle. May I know your name?'

'Helen,' Nell whispered. 'But everyone calls me Nell.'

'Nell.' He savoured the word, rolling it round his mouth so that it sounded delightfully foreign. 'It is a beautiful name and I must thank you for looking after me so well.'

Nell's blush deepened. 'You are too kind, but now I think you should rest.'

Lily had had enough of being ignored and she cleared her throat. 'I'm Lily and I found you and brought you home.' She met her sister's angry glances with a defensive lift of her chin. 'Well, I did.'

Armand held his hand out to her. 'Then I must thank you, Mademoiselle Lily. You saved my life, I think.'

Lily laid her hand in his and felt an arrow of desire shoot up her arm to target her heart. 'I'm so glad,' she murmured. 'I mean, I'm so glad you are getting better now, monsieur.'

'Armand,' he corrected, closing his eyes. 'Just Armand.'

'You must rest now,' Nell said, becoming brisk and businesslike. 'Lily will go downstairs and heat up some of the broth left from dinner, and Molly . . .' Nell lowered her voice. 'Just go away and leave the poor man in peace.'

'Shan't,' Molly hissed, leaning over the bed with her eyes narrowed like a cobra about to strike. 'You can't send me away, Nell. I've as much right to be here as you.'

'Very well,' Nell retorted coldly. 'Stay, but make yourself useful. Make up the fire and trim the candle wicks. We don't want our patient to choke on their smoke. Lily, what are you waiting for? Go and heat up some broth.'

Lily knew better than to argue with Nell when she was in a commanding mood and as she left the room she observed that, for once in her life, Molly was doing as she was told. Wonders would never cease, and all because of a handsome foreigner who had touched their hearts. Lily barely felt the ground beneath her feet as she flew downstairs to fetch sustenance for Armand. She was unaccountably light-headed and happy. She wanted to throw back her head and sing. She was in love.

But over the next few days it became even more apparent to Lily that both her sisters were equally smitten with Armand Labrosse; a fact which did not go unnoticed by their brothers and was the cause of much hilarity and a considerable amount of teasing. For the first time Lily found herself at an advantage over Nell and Molly who had of necessity to go out to work, leaving Lily in sole charge of the patient. Aggie was not best pleased, but Lily tried not to let her household tasks suffer by getting up an hour earlier in the morning and cleaning out the grates before anyone rose from their beds. On payday, Matt had replenished their stock of coal and candles, and Nell instructed Aggie to buy scrag-end of mutton to add to the vegetable stew that had become their staple diet. In the meantime, everyone waited anxiously for news from Paris as to when they might expect a visit from Armand's father.

In the afternoons, while Grandpa and Aggie took their naps, Lily was free to sit with Armand. He was allowed out of bed for longer periods each day, and she made him comfortable in a chair by the window so that he could look out and view the busy river traffic, the cranes at the wharves and the ships, barges, colliers and other small trading vessels loading and unloading their cargoes. At first, Lily was shy and their conversations were inclined to be one-sided, with Armand doing all the talking and Lily an avid listener, but gradually she became more relaxed in his company and began asking him questions about his life and work. She learned that he was the only son of Philippe Labrosse, whose father had been a man of humble origins and a brush maker by trade. Philippe had begun by peddling his father's wares on the streets of Paris and had branched out by renting a small shop where he sold hardware. He had been so successful that soon he had a chain of shops and had taken an interest in importing goods from abroad. This in turn had led him to invest in shipping and now, so Armand said with pride, the Labrosse family owned a fleet of merchant ships, trading worldwide.

Lily had listened awestruck. Her admiration for Armand knew no bounds, and very soon she found herself telling him about Ma and her talent as an artist, and then it was just a small step to admitting her own passion for drawing and painting. When Armand had asked to see her work Lily had been reluctant at first, but after gentle persuasion she had shown him her sketches and watercolour paintings of the London docks. His admiration and appreciation had been genuine and unstinting.

'Lily, you are an artist most certainly. You have a great talent and it should not be hidden under the bed.' He held one of her paintings up to the light. 'See how the water dances and gleams. You have captured the sunshine in a way that makes the picture spring into life.' He looked up at her with his dark eyes glowing. 'Do you do anything other than scenes of the river?'

'I like to do portraits, but I can't get anyone to sit for me,' Lily admitted shyly.

'But you have done some, have you not? Who was the fortunate sitter?'

Lily lowered her gaze as a bubble of laughter rose to her throat. 'You, Armand. Only you didn't know it at the time.'

'Let me see.'

She shook her head. 'They are not very good. You will laugh.'

'Allow me to be the judge of that, *ma chérie*.' Armand held out his hand. 'Please show them to me.'

It was a command that she could not disobey and Lily pulled the sketches from the bottom of the pile. 'They are very rough, Armand.' She held her breath while he examined them.

He laid them down, looking up at her with a serious expression. 'These are not good, Lily.'

She bit her lip, turning her head away. She would not cry. She would not allow him to see how his words had wounded her. She leapt to her feet. 'I have chores to do downstairs, Armand. I've wasted enough time.' She bundled up her sketches and hurried towards the door, but he called her back.

'Lily, wait.'

Chapter Five

'Come back, Lily.' Armand beckoned to her with a smile that sent a shiver of delight down her spine. 'You did not allow me to finish, *ma chérie*. I said they were not good and I meant it.'

Unable to resist the gently teasing tone of his voice, Lily was drawn to him as if in a trance. 'I don't understand.'

He gazed at her work, shaking his head. 'No, these are not good, they are superb. Who taught you to paint and draw like this?'

Her breath caught in her throat and she could hardly believe her ears. Such praise from a man like Armand was as thrilling as it was unexpected. 'I used to watch Ma when she painted, but that was a long time ago.'

'I would like to see her work. Have you any of her paintings, Lily?'

'Grandpa destroyed them all. We are not allowed to mention her name in front of him, and no one must know that I've done these. They are all afraid I will turn out to be wild like Ma.'

Armand threw back his head and laughed. 'What nonsense. I know you all a little now and you are a pure white lily, which in the romantic language of flowers is interpreted as youthful innocence. It is Molly who is the wild one with thorns like the dog rose, meaning pleasure and pain, and Nell is . . .' He broke off, shrugging his shoulders. 'Ah well, she is the rose without the thorn.'

'What does that mean?' Lily stared at him, intrigued by the unexpected romantic side to his nature.

'It means love at first sight. But we are not talking about your sisters, Lily. We are talking about you and your great talent, which must not be denied.'

'Oh, but it must,' Lily cried, coming back to earth with a bump. 'This is a secret you must keep, Armand. Please, for my sake, don't mention any of this to anyone. I am forbidden to paint and draw, and even if I have talent as you say it can get me nowhere. It is just something I have to do, but it is of no use to anyone else.'

Armand stared at her, frowning and shaking his head. 'My poor Lily, that is not true. You were born to create beautiful things; you must not deny your art.'

'I'm sorry I told you about it,' she murmured, backing towards the door. 'I should not have bothered you with my problems. Please forget what I said. We never had this conversation.' She left without giving him time to reply and she ran to her own room to hide the sketches under her bed. 'Language of flowers,' she muttered as she hurried down the stairs. 'If he had grown up here he wouldn't talk so soft.' She paused, startled by the unexpected sound of men's voices in the entrance hall. She recognised Matt's deep tones and when his companion responded it was with an accent so similar to Armand's that Lily knew it must be Monsieur Labrosse himself. She went down to meet them.

Matt looked up and greeted her with a smile. 'Lily, come and meet Armand's father, who has travelled all the way from Paris to see his son.'

She bobbed a curtsey. 'Hello, Mr – I mean, Monsieur Labrosse.'

He took her hand and raised it to his lips. 'Mademoiselle Lily.'

She felt the blood rush to her cheeks as she snatched her hand away, glancing anxiously at Matt but he was nodding furiously and frowning. She took this mime to mean that she must accept this foreign way of greeting and she swallowed hard. 'Thank you. I mean . . .' She floundered, not knowing quite what to say, but Armand's father seemed unperturbed and his smile never wavered.

'I have to thank you and your family for taking care of my son, but if I may I would like to see him now.'

'Of course,' Matt said. 'I'll take you to him right away. Lily will fetch you some refreshment and she will make up a bed for you. I assume you will be staying for one night at least?'

Monsieur Labrosse held up his hand, shaking his head. 'Thank you, no. I am the guest of the manager of the London Dock Company who is an old friend. I require nothing, other than to see Armand and satisfy myself that he is recovering after his ordeal. I plan to take him home to Paris as soon as I have finished my business in London, that is if I may trespass on your hospitality for a day or two longer.'

'Oh yes, please let him stay.' The thought that Armand might be spirited away so suddenly had not occurred to Lily until this moment and it was almost too painful to bear. They were staring at her and she realised that she had spoken the words out loud. 'He might not be strong enough to face the sea voyage.'

'It's entirely up to Monsieur Labrosse, Lily.' Matt mounted the stairs. 'Follow me, monsieur.'

Lily stood as if frozen to the spot. She had not thought as far as Armand's eventual recovery and return home. The realisation that she might never see him again sliced through her with an actual pain. He had admired her work and he had understood her love of art and now he was going to leave. He had likened her to a white lily with the innocence of youth, but the feelings she had been harbouring for him had been anything but innocent. He had stirred something within her that she had never experienced before; it was an entirely grown-up emotion and a physical desire. In the few short days that she had known Armand Labrosse, Lily realised that she had bridged the gulf between adolescence and womanhood. And yet, in her heart, she knew that her case was hopeless. Armand had left her in no doubt that it was Nell who had first claim on his affections. The winter sun might be slanting through the hall windows, but to Lily it felt as if it was snowing. She had fallen in love and realised that it was a lost cause all in the space of an hour. It was a bleak day indeed.

Later that evening Nell and Molly received the news in their different ways. Nell attempted a brave smile that did not reach her eyes; Molly burst into floods of tears and stormed out of the kitchen. There was silence in the room as the family listened to her thunderous footsteps reverberating on the stair treads followed by a loud crash as she slammed the bedroom door.

Aggie sighed and raised her eyes to heaven. 'She hasn't done that since she was fourteen. It's quite like old times.'

Matt pushed his chair back from the supper table and stood up. 'She'll just have to get over it. When Monsieur Labrosse saw how well Armand was doing he decided to return home tomorrow. They'll be sailing on the evening tide.'

'I have a lesson to prepare for the morning,' Nell said, rising to her feet. 'I'll be in the front parlour if anyone wants me.'

'Wouldn't you rather sit with Armand?' Lily asked tentatively. 'I mean, it is his last evening with us.'

Nell moved swiftly to the dresser where she had left a pile of books. She picked them up, clutching them protectively to her breast. 'We will never see him again,' she said softly.

'You've hardly touched your supper,' Aggie said crossly. 'All that good mutton stew going to waste.'

Mark reached for her plate. 'I'll eat it. The sheep might have died of old age but it's tasty.'

'You're a pig,' Luke said, pulling a face. 'You'll get fat and your Flossie will find another chap.'

'She loves me as I am,' Mark retorted, stuffing a whole potato into his mouth.

Matt flipped him round the head. 'You've certainly got the manners of a hog. Anyway, I'm going out.'

'Will you be late back?' Nell asked. 'I don't want to lock you out.'

'I've been summoned to a meeting with the manager of the London Docks.'

'At this time of night?' Nell said, angling her head. 'That sounds ominous, Matt.'

He uttered a humourless laugh. 'It's meant to be informal; a chat over a glass of wine or two and Labrosse will be there, so perhaps it's a pat on the back for looking after his son.'

'It's a pity they didn't invite all of us,' Luke said, getting up from the table. 'I'd like a chance to see how the rich folk live. Anyway, I'm going to the parlour. I hope you've lit the fire, Lily. That fellow upstairs has had all the attention lately. I shan't be sorry to see the back of him.' He strolled out of the room, holding the door open for Nell. 'Are you coming?'

'Yes, right away.' She paused in the doorway. 'Good luck, Matt.'

'What was all that about?' Mark demanded as the door closed on them. 'What did she mean?'

Lily held her breath, wondering if Matt was going to admit that they were in danger of being evicted from their home, but he shrugged on his jacket and his expression gave nothing away. 'It's something and nothing. It could be that Labrosse wants a bit more information about the cause of the fire. It's all in my report, but I'm not going to turn down the opportunity to enjoy a glass of good wine or two.' He turned to Lily, who had risen from her chair and was busy stoking the fire in the range. 'You'd best go upstairs and see if our guest needs anything, Lil. He might be leaving tomorrow but we want him to think kindly of us.' Matt plucked his cap off the hook behind the door and left the kitchen with Aggie staring after him.

'I dunno,' she said, puffing out her cheeks. 'There's something going on and I'd like to know what.'

Patting his full belly, Mark stood up. 'That was good grub. I say we ought to keep young Labrosse here for longer if we're to get meat every day.'

'Well, since you enjoyed your meal so much, you can help by stacking the dishes in the scullery,' Aggie said sternly. 'It's not fair to leave everything to Lily, and I doubt if we'll see young Molly again this evening. She could do with a good spanking if you ask me.'

Mark opened his mouth to say something, but Lily had seen the mischievous twinkle in his eyes and she sent him a warning glance. 'You'd best go now if you want to see Flossie. Mr Cobbold locks the shop door at nine o'clock and he won't open it for anyone.'

'You're a good little thing, Lil. I don't know what we'd do without you.' Mark patted her on the cheek as he made his way to the door.

Left alone with Aggie and a mountain of dirty crockery, Lily sighed. Was it always going to be like this? Much as she loved her family, she wished they would see her more as a person and less as an unpaid servant. Armand had made her feel like a woman and he had acknowledged her talent as an artist, but by this time tomorrow he would be gone from their lives forever. It seemed so unfair.

'Stop daydreaming,' Aggie said sharply. 'I hope

you're not going to start spouting poetry at me. I couldn't do with two of you with your heads in the clouds.'

Lily smiled reluctantly. 'You don't have to worry about me, Aggie. I couldn't make up a rhyme to save my life.'

'Then you must be in love like the other two, and I say it's a good thing that young man upstairs is leaving tomorrow. He's turned all your heads with his foreign ways.'

'I must go and see if he wants anything,' Lily said hastily. 'I won't be long, Aggie. You sit down and rest and I'll clear up in a minute.' Without giving her time to reply, she left the room.

Upstairs, she opened the door to Armand's room quietly in case he was taking a nap after his meal, but she withdrew when she realised that he was being entertained by Molly. The sound of their laughter echoed off the high ceilings and it seemed to Lily that her sister was living up to the wild rose's reputation for bringing pleasure; but perhaps the pain was yet to come. Lily returned to the kitchen with a heavy heart.

It was getting late by the time she finished the washing up and had dried and stacked the dishes on the dresser. Aggie had gone to bed in the small room off the kitchen, and the only sound in the house was the creaking of old timbers as they contracted in the cold night air. Lily doused the fire with damp tea leaves that had been used several times and would not stand another brew, and having satisfied herself that the back door was locked she made her way to the front parlour.

There was no sign of Luke or Nell and the fire had burnt to ashes. She left the room in darkness and looked into her grandfather's room to make sure that he had not fallen asleep with the candle still burning. He was getting very forgetful with advancing years and had almost set fire to the house a couple of times in the past few months. Having assured herself that all was well, she was about to go upstairs when the front door opened and Matt lurched into the hall. He carried his cap in his hand and the wind had ruffled his dark hair, causing him to look dishevelled and unkempt; quite unlike his normal self.

Lily went to meet him. 'Matt, are you drunk?'

'I might be a bit squiffy, Lil.'

'I've never seen you like this.'

He hooked his arm around her shoulders. 'It was that bastard dock manager, Lil.'

His voice rose in anger and she was afraid that he would wake the whole house.

'Come with me, Matt,' she said, taking him by the hand and leading him towards the kitchen. 'I'll make you a cup of tea. You've got to sober up and tell me what's happened.'

The heat had not gone completely from the fire and the kettle was still simmering on the hob. Lily made a pot of strong tea using fresh leaves. It was a reckless extravagance, but she would worry about that in the morning. There were more important matters to think about at this moment. Matt drew Aggie's chair closer to the range and sat down, staring moodily into the dying embers as he sipped his tea.

'It's no good, Lily,' he said at last. 'I thought – or rather I hoped – that Labrosse might be able to put in a good word for us.'

'What went on this evening? I've never seen you in such a state.'

He curled his lip into a cynical smile. 'It was all very jolly at the start. Labrosse was very grateful for what we'd done for his son, and the wine was flowing, but then he went off to bed saying he had a business meeting early in the morning. I was left with our friend the manager, and it seems they want the house much sooner than I thought. We've only got until the end of this month to find alternative accommodation. He gave me a long speech about how lucky we've been staying on since Grandpa retired but he said business is business and they aren't running a charity. He made me feel like a pauper, the smug bastard.'

Lily threw her arms around him. 'We'll be all right. You said we might be able to rent rooms next to the fire station. It doesn't matter if it's not what we're used to. As long as we're together, we'll be fine.'

'I wish I was as certain, ducks,' Matt said, shaking his head. 'It's not so bad for the boys and me. We're used to living over the shop when we're on night watch, but it's going to be tough on you girls, and then there's Grandpa. The shock might finish the old bloke off.'

'Not Grandpa,' Lily said with more confidence than she was feeling. 'He's tougher than that.'

'I dunno, Lil. I've done my best to keep the family together, but I've failed somewhere along the line. I always wanted Pa to be proud of me, but for the first time I'm glad he didn't live to see this day.'

'Don't say that. If Pa could see how hard you've worked to keep us all he would be more than proud. I know I am.'

'You're a poppet, Lily. Don't ever change.' Matt raised his hand to pat her on the cheek. 'Go to bed, there's a good girl. I'll sit here and smoke a pipe of baccy before I go up, and I'll finish the tea in the pot.'

'All right, Matt.' She made a move to go but he caught her by the hand.

'Best not mention any of this to the others. Not yet, anyway. I'll tell them when it's absolutely necessary, and in the meantime you can pray for a miracle.'

She left him sitting in semi-darkness, lighting his pipe with a spill from a glowing coal. She went slowly upstairs feeling as though she was in a living night-mare. The old house might be crumbling round their ears but it was home. All her childhood memories were encapsulated in its walls and she was not going to let it go without a fight. She went past her bedroom and headed for Armand's room, entering without both-ering to knock.

In the soft glow of the firelight she could see the shape of Armand's dark head silhouetted against the white cotton pillowcase. She thought at first that he was asleep but as she approached the bed he turned his face towards her. 'What is it, Lily?'

'Armand, I need your help.'

He raised himself up on one elbow. 'Of course, anything you want, within reason.'

She thought she saw the flicker of a smile in his eyes but in the poor light she could not be certain. She knotted her fingers together behind her back. 'The dock company are going to throw us out on the street at the end of the month.' The words tumbled from her lips.

He frowned. 'But why? Is it that you cannot pay your rent?'

'It's not that. They need the house for the present dock-master. Grandpa was allowed to stay on for a short time only, but he didn't tell us that. Matt was hoping that your father might put in a good word for us, but I don't think he was given the chance. Will you speak to him tomorrow? Please, Armand, it might not be too late.'

'I will do so, but to be honest with you, Lily, I don't think it will make much difference. My father owns some shares in the dock company it is true, but not enough to influence their decision in a matter such as this.'

'But he might be able to help. If not we'll be living in two poky rooms above the fire station in Cock Hill. Think of Nell, and Molly too.'

He reached across the counterpane to touch her hand. 'And you, Lily. What would you do without your drawing and painting?'

'I would survive. I have pictures in my head and in my heart. They will always be there when I close my eyes, or when I see the sun turning the ripples on the river into diamond necklaces, but it would be terrible for Grandpa to lose his home. His pride will suffer, and Matt thinks he has let us all down. You will help us, won't you, Armand?'

He squeezed her fingers. 'I will try, my little Lily. If only for your sake, I will do my best.'

'Thank you, Armand, thank you so much.' She raised his hand to her cheek for the briefest of moments and then let it fall back onto the faded satin coverlet that had once graced her parents' bed. She could still feel the imprint of his fingers as she hurried from the room. The blood was drumming in her ears with the insistence of a military band as she ran to her own room, stopping outside the door to take off her boots so that she did not wake her sisters as she made her way across the bare boards to her bed. Slipping off her print frock, she slid beneath the covers, shivering as her warm flesh met the iced glassiness of the starched cotton sheets. Lying on her back she looked up at the stars through the small windowpanes where fingers of frost glinted in the moonlight. She could still feel the heat of Armand's hand on her cheek and she touched it gently, closing her eyes and sending him a kiss in her thoughts. He might think of her as being little more than a green girl, but loving him had matured her into a woman. She drifted off to the place where dreams become reality, walking into his open arms and dancing the night away to the strains of a Viennese waltz.

Lily spent the next morning in a state of feverish anticipation. Nell had taken Armand's breakfast to him before she left for the school, and Molly had insisted on clearing out the grate in his room and had lit the fire. Lily had to wait until her brothers and sisters had gone to work before she had a chance to speak to him alone. In her dreams she had spent the night being held in his arms, but in broad daylight she felt suddenly shy in his company, and unusually tongue-tied.

'I haven't forgotten our conversation last night,' he said as she was about to take his breakfast tray downstairs. 'I will speak with my father when he visits me later today. Perhaps I can persuade him to delay our return to Paris. I want to be sure that you and your family are treated fairly.'

'Thank you,' she murmured. 'I knew I could rely on you, Armand.'

She took the tray back to the kitchen and found Aggie sitting at the table counting out piles of silver and brass coins. Aggie looked up, grinning broadly. 'What a windfall! We'll have roast beef for dinner tonight, or maybe a nice fat capon, seeing as how it's his nibs' last meal with us.'

Lily picked up a silver florin. 'Where did all this money come from?'

'Monsieur Labrosse gave it to Matt in payment for his son's board and lodging, and not before time if you ask me. Anyway, better late than never, and I'm off to market. I might even make a treacle pudding as a special treat.' She slid the money into a leather pouch.

In spite of everything, Lily had to smile. If Aggie had been a cat Lily was certain she would have been purring with satisfaction at the thought of having money to squander on luxuries. Perhaps in the circumstances she ought to have warned Aggie to be more prudent as hard times were coming, but Lily could not betray Matt's confidence and it seemed a shame to spoil Aggie's fun. She went instead to clear out the grate in her grandfather's room and light the fire. She turned a deaf ear to his grumbles, but she couldn't help wondering how he would react when faced with eviction from his beloved home. She could not imagine Grandpa existing away from the river, even such a short distance as Cock Hill. Without his spyglass and his view of the trading vessels plying the Thames day and night, she had a horrible feeling that he might wither and die like the sooty leaves on the roses that rambled over the portico in summer.

'So when is the young Frenchman leaving us?' Grandpa demanded as Lily hefted the bucket of cinders from the grate. 'I saw his pa come to the house yesterday but nobody thought to introduce us. I might as well be dead for all you lot care.'

'That's not true, Grandpa. We all love you.'

'I'm shut up here and forgotten. It's my house and the fellow ought to have paid his respects to me.'

'Monsieur Labrosse was in a hurry, Grandpa. He sent his compliments to you and asked to be excused, but he will come and see you today.' Lily eyed him warily to see if her improvisation had hit the right note. Unfortunately it was true that Grandpa did get overlooked occasionally, but it was hard to include him in their daily lives when he was so unpredictable. Sometimes he was completely rational, but if he was in one of his moods he might fly into a rage at the slightest provocation, and he had been known to order the odd unwary visitor out of the house. He had thrown a teapot at the vicar when he had chanced to call, and

97

that was the last time they had received the Reverend James Crisp. He had left the house with a large lump on his head and the beginnings of a black eye. It was no wonder that he had curtailed his visits, although Nell still attended church every Sunday without fail.

'Go on then, girl,' Grandpa said testily. 'Why are you standing there gawping at me like a codfish? I want my morning tea, and a slice of cake wouldn't go amiss.'

'Yes, Grandpa. I'll fetch it now.' Lily hurried from the room, hoping that her brothers had not devoured the last of Aggie's gingerbread. She was about to return to the kitchen when someone hammered on the front door. She put the bucket of cinders down and tugged at the door handle, but once again the wood had swollen with the damp and she had to exhort the visitor to give the door a push from the outside. It gave way suddenly, sending her staggering backwards as Monsieur Labrosse stumbled over the threshold.

He righted himself with a rueful smile. 'Your door, he does not want to open, mademoiselle.'

Lily righted her mobcap, which had slipped over one eye, hoping that her sooty fingers had not left a smudge on her forehead. 'Armand is expecting you, monsieur.'

'Thank you, I know the way. You have no need to trouble yourself, as I see that you are busy.' Taking off his top hat, Monsieur Labrosse crossed the hall in long strides, taking the stairs two at a time.

Lily was impressed. For an older man, who must be on the wrong side of forty-five, Monsieur Labrosse was quite sprightly. She would have liked to be present when Armand put their case to his father, but she would just have to wait and hope for the best. She hurried to the kitchen and fed the range with the cinders, and having done that she went into the scullery to wash her hands and face at the sink. She was drying herself on a scrap of towelling when a footstep behind her made her spin round to see Monsieur Labrosse standing so close to her that she could feel his breath on her face.

'Oh, sir, you made me jump. I didn't hear you come into the kitchen.'

He smiled and raised his hand to wipe a drop of moisture from her cheek with the tip of his finger. 'You are all alone?'

Lily took a step backwards and felt the cold stone sink press into her spine. 'I – our cook will be back soon, but I can make you a cup of tea if you would like one.'

He threw back his head and laughed. 'You English and your tea. No, I thank you, but I do not want tea.'

'How did you find your son, monsieur?' Lily asked breathlessly, hoping that the mention of Armand would make him remember his senior years. She did not like the way he was looking at her, and he was too close for comfort. She could feel the heat of his body through the thin cotton of her gown and he was pressing his knee between her legs in the most embarrassing and improper way.

'Armand is grateful to you all but he is eager to return home.' Monsieur Labrosse allowed his fingers to travel down her cheek, caressing the curve of her neck and cupping her breast with his hand. 'You are so young and fresh, and I have no doubt as pure and innocent as your name would suggest. Am I right?'

In desperation, Lily thought of calling out for her grandfather, but his room was too far away for him to hear now that he was getting a bit deaf. 'Did Armand tell you about our problem, sir?' she asked, forcing herself to sound calm when every instinct was urging her to cry for help.

'My son has told me of your family difficulties, *ma chérie*. I might, under certain circumstances, be able to come to your aid.'

She felt panic rising. She was beginning to understand him only too well, but she was on alien territory. She had no experience of dealing with unwelcome advances from an older man, or any man if it came to that. Growing up in a family with three brothers she had been as carefully guarded as the Crown jewels, and although she was aware of the admiring glances they received from local men, Lily was well aware that her sisters' would-be suitors had to run the gauntlet of Matt, Mark and even dreamy Luke, and most of them fell by the wayside. Molly had a string of admirers, but they stayed well away from Labour in Vain Street, and if they met Molly outside her place of work they only walked her part of the way home. Molly might be a rebel but she was mindful of her family obligations.

Lily wished with all her heart that Molly was here with her now. She would know what to do, but she herself was at a loss as to how to handle a practised philanderer like Monsieur Labrosse. He was smiling and speaking to her in gentle, persuasive tones such as he might have used to a spirited mare.

'You don't need to be frightened of me, Mademoiselle Lily. I could be very, very kind and generous to an enchanting young creature like you, and I could help your family if you are prepared to be – how do you say – nice, I think. If you will be nice to me I will be very good to you.' He slid his hand behind her head and drew her inexorably towards him.

'No, sir. Please, I beg of you do not . . .'

Chapter Six

His mouth clamped over hers and his tongue probed between her lips. Lily struggled in vain. His breath tasted shockingly of stale cigars and wine laced with a hint of garlic. She felt sick and faint and more frightened than she had ever been in her whole life.

'Papa!'

Armand's shocked tone brought about Lily's sudden release. Monsieur Labrosse thrust her away from him, turning his back on her to face his son. 'Armand, what are you doing? You should be resting.'

Lily slipped past Monsieur Labrosse with a stifled cry of sheer relief. She ran to Armand and was instantly more concerned for his wellbeing than for herself. 'You must not put weight on that injured ankle, Armand. Please sit down.'

He shook his head. 'I am all right, but what about you? Did he hurt you?'

Monsieur Labrosse muttered something beneath his breath as he pushed past his son. 'You know me better than that, I think. She is no more than a foolish child.'

'Where are you going, Papa?' Armand demanded angrily. 'I think Mademoiselle Lily deserves an apology.'

Monsieur Labrosse came to a halt in front of Lily,

glaring down at her. 'If you think I will help your family after this debacle then you are very much mistaken.' He turned to Armand. 'As you are on your feet you can come with me to Bell Wharf Stairs where our vessel is unloading. You will wait on board until this evening when we sail for home.'

Armand leaned on a chair for support, his hands curled into fists as they gripped the wood. 'Papa, I cannot leave these good people without a word of thanks.'

'Write them a letter. Come, I have business to complete and I am not leaving you here with these peasants.' Monsieur Labrosse made for the door, holding it open. 'Come now, Armand. I will not ask you a second time.'

Lily held her breath; for a moment she thought that Armand was going to stand up to his father, but he seemed to crumble. 'Very well. You win this time, Papa, but only because I am not in a position to argue.' He turned to her with an apologetic smile. 'I am so sorry, Lily. This is not how I wanted to leave you and your family.'

'You will come back one day, won't you, Armand?'

'Yes, that is a promise.' He took her hand and raised it to his lips. 'You will say goodbye to Nell for me? And the rest of your excellent family.'

'Of course.'

'And you will not neglect your art.'

She shook her head, at a loss for words.

'Very touching.' Monsieur Labrosse's caustic tone sliced through the air like a knife. 'I wait no longer. Come.'

Armand leaned closer to Lily, lowering his voice to a whisper. 'I will return.'

Lily spent the rest of the morning wondering how she was going to break the news to Nell. It was bad enough that her own heart was aching more painfully than a bad tooth, but she could not bear to think how Armand's seemingly cowardly defection would affect her eldest sister. Lily had never allowed herself to hope that a man like Armand might choose her over Nell, and when it seemed that Nell reciprocated his feelings Lily had tried to be happy for them both. But now she was to be the bearer of tidings that would surely dash Nell's hopes of a happy ending to her budding romance.

She had intended to wait until her sisters returned home from work, but Aggie had sensed that something was wrong when Lily did not take a tray of food to the sickroom at midday, and when she began preparing tea for her grandfather Aggie was downright suspicious.

'Isn't him upstairs having a cup of tea?' she asked with raised eyebrows. 'Has he taken a turn for the worse?'

'No, he is much better today.' Lily continued to cut slices from a loaf of bread, buttering them well to suit Grandpa's taste.

'So is he coming downstairs to join us for supper then? I'm curious to meet this chap.'

'He's gone, Aggie. Armand left with his father earlier today.'

Aggie almost dropped the bird she was plucking. 'That was a bit sudden, wasn't it?'

'Not really. Their ship sails on the evening tide. Monsieur Labrosse wanted to be certain that Armand was there in time.'

'Oh, well, that means there will be more of this nice fat capon for everyone else,' Aggie said, shrugging her ample shoulders. She resumed plucking the bird with renewed vigour. 'You'd best go upstairs and strip the bed, Lily. For all we know he might have brought bugs with him. You can't trust them foreigners.'

Lily had been putting off the moment when she had to go into Armand's room, but now she had no excuse. The fire had burned to ash hours ago and the room seemed cold and empty. She folded the counterpane and blankets, piling them neatly on the window seat, and then she stripped the sheets off the feather mattress. The indentation remained where Armand had lain, and the scent of him lingered in the sheets and pillowcases. Lily held them to her cheek, imagining her head resting on the pillow close to his. She lay down on the bed, closing her eyes and musing on what might have been, even though she knew in her heart that it was unlikely to become a reality. She lost track of time as she lay cocooned in the downy softness where Armand had so recently lain. She was neither asleep nor completely awake, but drifting in a dream-like state until the daylight faded into dusk and the street lamp outside flickered into life. She rose reluctantly and gathered up the soiled bedclothes, leaving them in the corner of the room ready for the washtub on Monday. It was on washday that Armand's ship had foundered and caught fire – from now on she would always associate Mondays with the young Frenchman who had visited them briefly but whose presence had made such an impact on their lives.

She took one last look around the room. She could remember when the house was filled with laughter. They must have been happy in love at first, she thought sadly, but then it ended in betrayal and bitterness. And now Armand had been taken from them and hearts would break yet again. She left the room, closing the door softly on the poignant memories.

In the kitchen Molly was taking off her bonnet and shawl with an aggrieved look on her face. 'Is it true, Lily? Has Armand left without so much as a goodbye and thank you?'

'No, it's not true,' Lily said wearily. 'Yes, he's gone but he was made to leave by his hateful father, and he asked me to make his apologies for his sudden departure, and to tell everyone how grateful he was for everything.'

Molly angled her head, a curious expression on her pert features. 'What do you mean, his hateful father? I thought that Monsieur Labrosse was supposed to be quite charming.'

Aggie thumped the saucepan lid back on a bubbling pan of potatoes. 'Don't take no notice of Lily. She's had her nose put out of joint and we all know who's to blame.'

'What are you talking about, Aggie?' Nell's voice from the doorway caused them all to turn their heads.

She looked from one face to another. 'Well, isn't anyone going to let me in on the secret?'

'Armand has gone and it's all her fault.' Molly pointed an accusing finger at Lily.

'But I thought his ship was sailing on the evening tide.' Nell's alabaster skin paled to ashen. 'Why would he leave so suddenly? Something terrible must have happened.'

Lily was desperate to reassure her. 'Armand had no choice, Nell. His father insisted that he went straight to the ship.'

'You must have said something to upset them both, Lily,' Molly said, tossing her bonnet and shawl onto the nearest chair. 'You can be so tactless at times. I could kill you, I really could.'

'I don't know what all the fuss is about,' Aggie muttered. 'He's paid for his keep and we're having a decent meal for a change.'

'All you think about is your stomach, Aggie.' Molly choked on an angry sob. 'Armand and I were just getting to know one another, and now he's gone. My life is ruined.'

'Don't be so melodramatic,' Nell said sharply. 'Lily, I want to know what went on here today.'

She was cornered and the only way out was to tell them the truth. She related the facts as simply and plainly as she could, despite frequent interruptions from Molly who liked to dramatise everything and could turn a simple nursery rhyme into a three-act tragic opera.

'It seems incredible that Monsieur Labrosse would

behave in such a way,' Nell said, staring at Lily in disbelief.

'But it's all true. I'm not lying.'

'What do you expect from a Frenchman?' Aggie said gloomily.

'Well, I think she must have encouraged him in some way.' Molly tossed her head. 'Lily is jealous because Armand fancies me.'

'If I was like you then it might be true,' Lily retaliated with spirit. 'But I was just standing at the sink, washing the dishes and minding my own business, when he came up behind me.'

'It's all right, Lily,' Nell said, moving swiftly to her side. She gave her a hug. 'Of course I believe you. Shame on you, Molly, for thinking such a thing of your sister.'

'Oh yes, I'm always in the wrong and Lily never puts a foot out of place. Well, she has now and she's made Armand go away. I'll never forgive you, Lil. Never!' Molly ran from the kitchen, slamming the door behind her.

'I pity the man who takes her on,' Aggie said, opening the oven door and prodding the capon with the tip of a knife. 'That little madam could do with a good spanking.'

'I still don't understand why Armand left without an argument,' Nell said softly.

'He really had no choice,' Lily whispered. 'Don't be too hard on him.'

'Good riddance, I say.' Aggie closed the oven door with an expressive thud. 'Supper will be ready in half an hour and those who don't turn up on time will just have to eat it cold. I'm not ruining a prime bird by overcooking it.'

'I don't think I can face food,' Nell said, holding her hands to her temples. 'I have a headache, Aggie. I think I'll go to my room.'

'That's all the thanks I get for my efforts,' Aggie grumbled. 'But your brothers will scoff everything, that's for sure.'

Ignoring this last remark, Lily ran after Nell and caught up with her in the hall. 'Armand's ship doesn't sail for another two hours. You could still say goodbye to him.'

Nell's dark eyes widened. 'I couldn't – could I? I mean, it wouldn't be a very ladylike thing to do.'

'Bother being ladylike. I'll come with you if you're scared to go on your own. The ship is moored alongside Bell Wharf Stairs; it's not far and you can't let this chance pass you by. If you love Armand, then you must tell him so.'

Nell shook her head. 'I couldn't do that. We've only known each other for such a short time. What if he doesn't feel the same way about me? I would feel so stupid.'

Lily took her by the shoulders and shook her. 'Don't be a goose. I've seen the way he looks as you. Give him a chance.'

'All right,' Nell said slowly. 'I'll go and see him, but you must understand it's just to say goodbye. I don't want you to come out with any embarrassing comments.'

'I won't utter a word. In fact, I won't even come on board. I'll just come with you for moral support.'

'Very well then, but we'll need our shawls. It's freezing outside.'

'Leave it to me. I'll sneak them out while Aggie is looking the other way. If we hurry we can be back in time for supper and no one will ever know.'

A hand clamped on Lily's shoulder, making her jump. She turned her head and found herself looking into Molly's green eyes.

'No one will ever know what?' Molly demanded. 'What are you two plotting?'

'It's nothing,' Lily said vaguely. 'We were just talking.'

'You can't fool me. I heard you say you'd be back in time for supper.'

'It's none of your business.' Lily sidestepped her sister but Molly was too quick for her and she barred her way.

'You two are going to see Armand, aren't you? You were going without me, you sneaky bitches.'

'Molly! Don't use that gutter language in this house,' Nell cried angrily. 'Yes, we were going to say goodbye to Armand, but I think after all it's a bad idea. I've changed my mind and I'm not going now.'

'Well, I am.' Molly made a move towards the front door and tugged at the handle. 'Bloody door, it's stuck again.'

'You can't go out like that,' Nell said anxiously. 'Don't be stupid, Moll.'

Molly put her foot against the door jamb and heaved,

almost falling flat on her back as it opened suddenly and Matt burst in on a blast of frost-spiked air.

'What's going on?' he demanded, staring from one to the other. 'Where do you think you're going, Molly?'

'Don't blame me,' Molly said, glaring at her sisters. 'They started it. They were going without me.'

'It was just a misunderstanding.' Nell shot a warning glance at Molly. 'We weren't going anywhere.'

'I thought you were on watch tonight, Matt,' Lily said in an attempt to divert his attention.

He turned to her and Lily was shocked by the bleak expression in his dark eyes. 'I've just had a visit from the dock company's solicitor. They want us out of the house by Friday. If we don't leave voluntarily, they'll send the bailiffs in.'

'But they can't do that,' Nell said dazedly. 'Why would they turn us out of our home?'

'It's a long story. I'll explain everything later, but I'm afraid we have no choice.'

'Oh, Matt, are you sure?' Nell's eyes filled with tears. 'I don't understand.'

'There's no doubt about it, I'm afraid.'

Molly let out a loud wail. 'They can't take our home away from us. It's not fair.'

'There must be a logical explanation,' Nell insisted. 'They can't just throw us out on the streets for nothing.'

Matt met Lily's anxious gaze with a slight shake of his head. 'As I said, I'll explain everything later, but as to the suddenness of it all, I think Labrosse may have had a hand in it. He was just leaving the office when I went in to see the dockmaster. He gave me a filthy look in passing, although for the life of me I can't think why.'

'I can,' Lily murmured. 'I think it may be my fault.'

'I don't see how, Lil,' Matt said, hooking his arm around her shoulders. 'We've got to move out and that's that.'

'You can't just stand by and see us thrown out on the streets,' Molly stormed. 'Where's your fighting spirit, Matt? If I was a man I wouldn't stand by and see my sisters evicted from their home. I'd biff old Labrosse on the nose for a start.'

Matt's lips set in a grim line. 'You don't know what you're talking about, Molly. Luckily the rooms over the shop next to the fire station are still to let. We're going to have to make the best of it and no arguments.'

'If there really is no other choice, we'll manage somehow,' Nell said gently. 'It might not be so bad, Molly.'

'And the boys won't have far to go to get to work,' Lily added, making an attempt to lighten the mood.

'That's not funny.' Molly choked back a sob and her lips trembled. 'We won't have room to swing a cat. It will be hell on earth.'

'There are plenty worse off than us,' Matt said severely. 'But Molly's right in one sense. The rooms are small so we won't be able to take much with us.' He turned to Nell. 'We've only got two days to organise ourselves, so I'm putting you in charge of packing, and you'd best tell Aggie what's going on before one of the boys blurts it out and upsets the old girl.'

'What about Grandpa?' Lily asked anxiously. 'He's going to be very unhappy.'

'He'll have to put up with it like the rest of us,' Matt said grimly.

Nell laid her hand on his arm. 'Would you like me to break it gently to him?'

'No, this is my job. Don't worry, Nell. I won't give the old boy a heart attack, even if I could cheerfully throttle him at times.' Matt strode across the hall and entered Grandpa's room without knocking.

'Oh, dear,' Nell said faintly. 'Poor Grandpa. He loves this old house.'

Molly gulped and sniffed. 'This is probably his fault. He must have upset the dock company.'

'That's not fair,' Lily cried angrily. 'Grandpa was a valued employee; he's just getting a bit forgetful in his old age.'

'Stop being so damned fair-minded, Lil. It drives me crazy.' Molly turned on her heel and flounced towards the staircase. 'I'm going to sort my things. Heaven knows I haven't got much but I'm not leaving anything that's mine. So there!' She paused at the foot of the stairs, glancing over her shoulder. 'You'll have to leave your paints and things here, Lily. There won't be anywhere to hide them now.' With an angry twitch of her shoulders, Molly raced up the stairs without giving Lily a chance to retaliate.

Lily glanced anxiously at Nell. 'I don't get them out until I've finished all my chores.'

'It doesn't seem to matter now,' Nell said, shaking her head. 'We've got more important things to worry about.'

As if to confirm her words, the door to Grandpa's

room flew open and Matt strode into the hall followed closely by their irate grandfather.

'I'll not be turned out of my house by anyone,' Grandpa raged. 'This is my home and no clodpole of a dock company manager is going to take it away from me. The river runs in my blood and the only way I'm leaving here is in a wooden box.' He retreated into his room, slamming the door and sending a shower of plaster floating down from the ceiling.

'That went well,' Matt said with a wry grin. 'I don't know what we're going to do with the old boy, but I'd sooner live with a caged tiger than share a bedroom with Grandpa.'

Nell bit her lip. 'Aggie is going to be just as difficult.'

Before joining his brothers on the night watch, Matt had obtained the key to the rooms they hoped to rent. It was still dark with at least two hours to go before dawn when Lily and Nell left the house next morning setting out to inspect their future accommodation. The move from their old home hung over them like a storm cloud, ominous and getting closer with each passing minute. They barely spoke as they made their way through the strangely silent streets. The denizens of the night had gone to earth, some of them sleeping off the excesses of their carousing and the effects of smoking opium as they huddled in doorways, apparently dead to the world. The day workers were just beginning to emerge from their homes, trudging wearily to their places of employment, shoulders hunched, heads down, and the only sound the clatter of their hobnail boots striking sparks off the cobble-stones.

Lily and Nell quickened their pace and their breath plumed into clouds around their heads in the ice-cold air. The rooms that Matt had found for them were above a tobacco shop, which was separated from the fire station by a narrow passageway leading to the stable yard at the rear. It was pitch dark in the alley with just a glimmer of light at both ends. They had to feel their way along the rough brick wall until they came to a doorway, which when unlocked opened onto a winding stair-case. Nell went first, stumbling over the splintered edges of the stair treads with Lily close on her heels.

At the top of the stairs they came to a small landing with two doors, each leading into an empty room, but in the dim light from the street lamp outside their worst fears were confirmed. The smell of ale from the former beer shop next door seemed to have permeated the fabric of the building and was mixed with the odour of the stables and a strong smell of tobacco from the shop below. The two rooms were reasonably large and each had a fireplace, although the only facility for cooking was a trivet and a hook from which a black-ened kettle hung over the empty grate in the front room. Festoons of cobwebs hung from the beamed ceiling and the skirting boards were pockmarked with mouse holes.

Lily shivered, wrapping her shawl closer around her body as she took in her surroundings. 'This is awful, Nell.'

'You're right, but at least it will put a roof over our heads and perhaps later on we can find a small house to rent cheaply.'

'It's not going to be easy,' Lily said, moving to the window and wiping away the grime to make a small circle of clear glass. She peered out at the street below. 'The only good thing is that we're next to the fire station. They boys won't have far to go.'

'You always look on the bright side,' Nell said, chuckling. 'We'll be all right, Lily. It will just take a bit of adjustment, but we'll get through this.'

'I can see Luke,' Lily cried, tapping on the window and waving. 'I think he's coming this way.' She hurried from the room and ran downstairs to open the outer door.

Holding a lantern in one hand and a steaming mug in the other, Luke came towards her, grinning broadly. 'It's not exactly Buckingham Palace, is it?'

Lily shook her head. 'It's dreadful.'

'I've brought you a cup of tea. Are you on your own, Lil?'

'No, Nell's here but we can share the tea. Ta, Luke, you're a brick.' She took the mug from him and made her way back up the stairs with Luke following her.

He stopped in the doorway, holding the lantern so that it shed a pale golden light around the empty room. He pulled a face. 'It's worse than I thought. You couldn't call it home from home.'

Nell squared her narrow shoulders with a determined lift of her chin. 'It will be when Lily and I have done with it, but I'd best be on my way now or I'll be late for work.'

'I hope you don't expect me to do this all on my own,' Lily protested.

'Of course not, but you can make a start and we'll come back this evening after supper and finish it off.' Nell turned to Luke. 'And you needn't grin like a fool, Luke Larkin. You can help by fetching some coal and kindling for the fire.'

Luke made a mock salute. 'Aye aye, captain.'

'When it's clean and we've got some of our furniture in here, I'm sure we'll be quite cosy,' Nell said hopefully. 'Now I really must be going or I'll be in Mr Sadler's bad books, and I want to ask him if I can have some time off tomorrow so that I can organise the move.' She made for the stairs, pausing in the doorway. 'I haven't even thought how we are going to transport our furniture.'

'Matt's arranging to borrow a cart from one of his mates,' Luke said cheerfully. 'And a couple of the blokes on day watch are going to give us a hand, providing there aren't any shouts. Don't worry, Nell. It will all go like clockwork.'

Lily smiled and nodded, but in her heart she was not so sure.

As Lily had feared, things did not go exactly as planned. The next morning, Grandpa locked himself in his room, shouting through the keyhole that he had no intention of leaving his home. Taking her cue from him, Aggie sat in her rocking chair by the kitchen range, refusing to budge.

'If he isn't leaving, then neither am I,' she said, gripping the wooden arms of the chair with the expression of a martyr about to be burnt at the stake.

Nell pleaded with Grandpa and then with Aggie, and finally, casting her eyes heavenwards, she threw up her hands. 'I give in,' she said as the clock on St Peter's church tower struck midday. 'We'll just have to leave them here and let the bailiffs deal with them.'

Lily sent a pleading look to Aggie. 'Please come with us, Aggie. We won't be in that place forever. We'll start looking for something more suitable straight away, but we have to leave here. If you go, then Grandpa will have to give up as there'll be no one to look after him.'

Aggie clenched her jaw and stared straight ahead. Her silence was more convincing than a hundred words.

'Thank goodness Molly had to go to work,' Lily said in a low voice. 'She would probably chain herself to the railings outside and then we would have the police involved.'

Nell shook her head. 'I haven't got time for all this, Lily. We must make sure that Matt and the others have loaded everything we need on that rickety old cart. I just pray that it gets to Cock Hill before it collapses or one of the wheels drops off.' She sighed heavily. 'Mr Sadler offered to help, but I hope he doesn't turn up. I wouldn't want him to witness this spectacle. It would be so mortifying.'

Lily cocked her head on one side, instantly diverted. 'I thought that Mr Sadler was a bit of an ogre, Nell. Does he fancy you?'

Nell's cheeks reddened. 'Of course not, Lily. What a thing to say. Mr Sadler is an excellent man, totally devoted to teaching underprivileged children and giving them a better start in life. He hardly knows that I exist, except for being an able assistant.'

'Then he's a fool,' Aggie said darkly. 'All men are numbskulls if you ask me.'

'I didn't,' Nell said, surprising Lily with the sharpness of her tone. She whisked out of the room leaving Lily and Aggie staring after her.

'Well,' Lily said, packing the last of their crockery and cutlery into a tea chest, 'it looks as if you will have to stay here on your own with Grandpa, Aggie. I'll miss you, but you know best.' Without waiting for an answer, she left the kitchen, making her way along the passage to stand outside her grandfather's door. 'Grandpa, can you hear me? It's Lily.'

'Go away, girl. I'm not leaving my house and that's that.'

'But Grandpa, you know they'll send the bailiffs in and they'll break the door down. They'll drag you out, and Aggie too. It will be awful.'

'They wouldn't dare.'

Lily was quick to hear a tremulous note in her grandfather's voice. 'They would, Grandpa.'

'I'm not going. They'll have to carry me out in a wooden box. This is my home. I've earned the right to live out my life here. I was an important man once.'

Lily could hear the frailty in his voice but she recognised the stubborn tone. An idea occurred to her and she ran out through the open front door, almost barging into Mark who was coming back to collect another load for the already groaning cart.

'Hey, look out,' he said, chuckling. 'Where's the fire?'

'Very funny,' Lily called over her shoulder. 'This is a real emergency.' She picked up her skirts and ran down the garden path and out into the street. There was just one person who might be able to persuade Grandpa Larkin to leave his old home, and she knew where to find him.

Chapter Seven

Lily found Bill Hawkins sitting in the taproom of the Prospect of Whitby, drinking a pint of porter.

'Bill, I need your help,' she said breathlessly.

He stood up, glancing anxiously round at the assemblage of dockers, sailors and warehousemen who had stopped drinking to stare curiously at Lily. 'You shouldn't be in a public house, Miss Lily. What would your grandpa say?'

'It's because of Grandpa that I'm here,' Lily said urgently. 'He won't leave the house, Bill. He's locked himself in his room and refuses to listen to anyone.'

He took her by the arm, propelling her through the crowded bar and out onto the quay wall. 'I'll come with you, but I doubt if there's anything I can say or do that will make him change his mind. He's a mite stubborn, if you'll excuse me saying so.'

'That's putting it mildly, Bill. But if anyone can persuade him to change his mind, it's you.' Without waiting for his answer she raced on ahead, crossing the bridge over the dock entrance at a run and arriving home with her bonnet hanging by its ribbons and her hair falling loose around her shoulders. She came to an abrupt halt at the sight of Nell standing outside the front door in conversation with a tall man dressed all in black. Although they had never been formally introduced, Lily had seen Mr Eugene Sadler, the headmaster of the Ragged School, on several occasions in the past, although only from a distance.

Nell turned and frowned as she took in Lily's dishevelled state. 'Where have you been, Lily? I thought you were looking after Grandpa.'

Lily glanced curiously at Mr Sadler, who was observing her with such a grave expression on his chiselled features that he reminded her of a parson about to deliver a sermon. 'I went to fetch Bill. He's the only one that Grandpa might listen to.'

Bill had caught up with her by now and he took off his cap, acknowledging Nell with a respectful inclination of his head. 'Miss Nell.'

'I would be very grateful if you would try to make Grandpa see sense, Bill,' Nell said with a tight little smile.

'I'll have a word with him, but the guvner has a mind of his own, miss.' Bill gave Mr Sadler a curt nod and disappeared into the house.

Nell turned to her companion. 'Mr Sadler, may I introduce you to my youngest sister, Lily?'

Mr Sadler doffed his top hat. 'How do you do, Miss Lily?'

'Very well, sir.' Slightly in awe of the stern-faced schoolmaster, Lily bobbed a curtsey.

'Will you excuse us a moment, Mr Sadler?' Nell said, taking Lily by the arm.

'Certainly, Miss Larkin.'

Nell drew Lily into the porch, speaking in a low

urgent voice. 'Mr Sadler closed the school early so that he could come here and talk to Grandpa. I'm so embarrassed and now I feel a complete fool. You should have waited here for me.'

'That's not fair. You said the schoolmaster might not turn up.' Lily shot a curious look at Mr Sadler's stern profile. 'Why has he come anyway? He doesn't know Grandpa.'

'Mr Sadler is a well-respected man, and he has some standing in the community.' Nell glanced anxiously over her shoulder. 'I don't know what to say to him.'

Lily followed her gaze and was struck once again by Mr Sadler's imposing appearance. The top hat made him look at least a foot taller than he was, and his erect carriage and serious demeanour would impress anyone. She was fired by a sudden inspiration. 'Why not ask your Mr Sadler to have a word with Aggie? If anyone can persuade her to be reasonable, I'm sure it would be your schoolmaster. He could easily be a preacher and you know how Aggie respects men of the cloth.'

Nell's eyes brightened. 'I'll speak to him now. Wait here and don't say anything to anyone. You have a habit of putting your foot in it.'

Half an hour later, Aggie and Grandpa were seated in Mr Sadler's dog cart and Bill was loading a wagon with Grandpa's bed and personal belongings. Mr Sadler handed Nell up onto the driver's seat and he turned to Lily, who was standing at his side. 'Are you travelling with us, Miss Larkin?'

She looked up into his grey eyes and was surprised by the warmth of his smile which softened the severe lines of his angular face, and the firm set of his lips. He was younger than she had at first supposed, and really quite human, she thought. She shook her head. 'Thank you, no, Mr Sadler. I'd better check everything in the house and make certain that nothing important has been left behind.'

He hesitated for a moment, as if struggling with a natural reticence. 'I am truly sorry to see you and your family put to so much trouble. If there is anything I can do to help . . .' His voice trailed off and a dull flush spread upwards from his starched white collar to flood his pale cheeks with colour. He cleared his throat and climbed up beside Nell, taking the whip and flicking it expertly just above the horse's ear. 'Trot on, Socrates.'

'Socrates! What an inspiring name for a horse.'

Nell's words floated to Lily on the stiff breeze as the vehicle lurched forward, picking up speed as the horse moved from a sedate walk to a brisk trot. Matt's friend who had kindly supplied the wagon urged his sturdy carthorse into action and drove off slowly, following the schoolmaster's vehicle. Lily watched the last of their belongings disappearing along Labour in Vain Street with a feeling of deep sadness. Part of her life had ended on this day, and what the future held was a matter of conjecture.

'Is there anything else I can do for you, Miss Lily?'

She spun round having quite forgotten that Bill was standing behind her, cap in hand, and looking so downcast that she wanted to hug him. 'You must come to

Cock Hill and visit Grandpa just as you've always done,' she said, smiling up at him. 'You are his only link with the past now, Bill, and he would miss you dreadfully if he didn't see you as often.'

A slow grin illuminated Bill's craggy features. 'D'you really think so?'

Lily laid her hand on his arm. 'You were the only person he would listen to today, Bill. Grandpa would still be locked in his room if it wasn't for you. I don't know what you said to him, but it worked.'

'It was between us men, Miss Lily. I'm sad to see the guvner leave his home, but I'm happy I was able to help.'

He loped off in the direction of the wharf, leaving Lily alone on the pavement outside the house. She went indoors, making for her bedroom where she took her drawing materials and sketches from beneath her bed, the only one left in the room as the other two had been dismantled and taken to Cock Hill. Tonight she would have to sleep top to toe with Molly and she was not looking forward to that. She tucked her treasured possessions into an old pillowcase that she had kept for the purpose. Taking one last look around the room that she had shared with her sisters for so many years, she went outside onto the landing, closing the door behind her.

She paused at the top of the stairs. The only sounds she could hear were the echoes in her head from long ago. If she closed her eyes, she could imagine the faint strains of Ma playing the piano and Pa's deep baritone rendition of a popular song. Ma's tinkling laughter had filled the house with joy, but her tears and tantrums had also left their mark. Lily remembered only too well the raised voices and bitter quarrels. There had been good times as well as hardships, and then Armand had come into their lives. Handsome, helpless and excitingly foreign, he had charmed them all. Lily sighed as she made her way down the curved staircase for the last time. Would they ever see him again? He had promised to return, but circumstances and a domineering father might prevent him from keeping his word. She must allow him to fade into the realm of her dreams. There was nothing for it but to get on with the business of living in the tough world of the East End outside the protective shell of the dock-master's house. From now on their lives would be quite different and undoubtedly much harder.

With the bulging pillowcase tucked beneath her arm, Lily left the home of her childhood and turned the key in the lock.

She arrived outside the tobacconist's shop to find Matt, Mark and Mr Sadler unloading crates, cardboard boxes and the parts of Grandpa's dismantled iron bedstead from the wagon. There was no sign of Nell, Grandpa or Aggie.

Matt thrust one of the smaller boxes into her hands. 'Where've you been, Lil? We need all the help we can get.'

She opened her mouth to explain but Mr Sadler took the box from her, frowning at Matt. 'That's too heavy for a girl. Allow me, Miss Larkin.' He balanced the

126

cardboard box on top of a crate containing crockery and hefted it into his arms. 'Perhaps you would be kind enough to lead the way?'

'Thank you,' Lily said with a grateful smile. In his shirtsleeves, Mr Sadler looked much more approachable. She led him along the narrow passage to the door, which had been wedged open for easy access. They found Nell upstairs in the main living room on her hands and knees in front of the grate coaxing flames from damp kindling and small nuggets of coal, while Grandpa and Aggie sat like bookends on either side of the window that overlooked the street.

'I'm not staying here,' Grandpa muttered. 'This is no place for a family like ours. We're used to better things.'

'Whose fault is it that we're in this pickle?' Aggie demanded. 'As I see it, old man, it was you who threw the letters from the dock company into the fire. Shame on you.'

'Don't speak to me like that, you old besom. You're forgetting your place, missis.'

'It's miss as you well know, and if I'm a servant I should expect to receive a wage for my labours. You haven't paid me anything for five years.'

'You get your bed and board, don't you? You have clothes on your back and shoes on your feet. You'd be out begging on the streets if we didn't look after you.'

Aggie thrust her chin out like an angry bulldog. 'Look after me? I'll have you know, old man, that I could get a position anywhere. There are folk crying out for a good cook-general.'

'Well, they wouldn't get one with you. Your pastry is like lead and your stews taste like dishwater.'

Nell sprang to her feet. 'Stop it, both of you. I won't stand for this childish behaviour. You're both old enough to know better.'

'Ahem.' Mr Sadler cleared his throat. 'Where would you like me to put these things, Miss Larkin?'

Nell spun round and her cheeks reddened with a blush. 'Oh, Mr Sadler, I didn't see you standing there, and you really shouldn't be carrying that heavy crate. My brothers ought to be doing the heavy work.'

He set his load down on the floor. 'It's nothing, Miss Larkin. I'm only too glad to be of assistance.'

Nell brushed a strand of hair back from her forehead, leaving a streak of soot on her pale skin. 'I'd offer you a cup of tea, but I'm afraid it will be some time before the kettle boils.'

He regarded her with a solemn expression. 'If I might make a suggestion, Miss Larkin?'

'Please do, Mr Sadler.'

'I'm not normally a drinking man, but perhaps a jug of hot buttered rum might help to alleviate the winter chills.' He turned to Grandpa Larkin. 'What do you say, sir?'

Grandpa sat upright in his chair, his eyes suddenly alert. 'That's the first sensible suggestion anyone has made today. I'd be obliged to you, sir.'

'And some bread and cheese would go down nicely,' Aggie added hopefully. 'Or a murphy oozing with butter.'

A slow smile lit Mr Sadler's grey eyes. 'I'll see what

I can do. Perhaps Miss Lily would care to come with me and help to carry the comestibles?'

'I don't want to put you to any trouble on our account, Mr Sadler,' Nell said, frowning. 'I'm sure you've done quite enough for us already.'

'It would be a privilege to help, Miss Larkin.' Mr Sadler moved to the door, beckoning to Lily. 'A basket would be useful if we are to transport hot potatoes from the stall at the corner of School Lane.'

Lily snatched up an empty wicker basket and followed him from the room. 'This is very good of you.'

He descended the staircase, flattening himself against the wall as Luke staggered past carrying part of the bedstead. When they reached the alleyway, Mr Sadler paused, turning a serious face to Lily. 'I have great respect for your sister. She is a fine woman and it grieves me to see her in such reduced circumstances. I'm more than happy to do this small service for her family.'

There was no mistaking the sincerity in his voice and Lily realised with something of a shock that Mr Sadler, who until today had been a faceless person known to the family by name only, was head over heels in love with her sister. She found herself looking at him with new eyes, and her heart went out to him. He was undoubtedly a fine man, and now she looked at him more closely she could see that he was good-looking in an unobtrusive sort of way, but he was on the wrong side of thirty which in Lily's opinion was verging on middle age. What chance did a schoolmaster have against a dashing fellow like Armand?

Clutching her basket, she followed him along Cock Hill to the street corner where a man was selling baked potatoes. The acrid smell of the coke brazier mingled with the delicious aroma of hot potato and melted butter. Lily's stomach rumbled in anticipation of tasty food. Retracing their steps, they called in at a public house where Mr Sadler purchased a jug of hot buttered rum. It was only a short distance then to the fire station, where two of the men from the day watch were busy polishing the brass on the steam-fired engine, and a third was checking the hosepipe. They waved to Lily and the most junior fireman sniffed the air, laughingly demanding a taste of the brew. Lily blew him a kiss and was immediately scolded by Matt, who had come to collect the last few items from the wagon.

'Behave yourself, Lil,' he said sternly. 'There's to be no flirting with the men. It's bad for discipline.'

'Don't be too hard on her,' Mr Sadler said gently. 'She's very young.'

Matt eyed him coldly. 'When I want advice on how to treat my sisters, I'll ask for it, schoolmaster.'

'Matt,' Lily said, shocked by his unfriendly tone. 'Mr Sadler has been very kind, and generous too.'

Matt had the grace to look slightly abashed. 'I'm sorry, mate. It's not a good day for being sociable.'

'I understand,' Mr Sadler said gravely. 'If there is anything I can do . . .?'

'You can take the toddy upstairs before it gets cold.' Matt's features relaxed into a shadow of a smile. 'I'll be up for my share in a moment.'

'It's probably been harder on Matt than any of us,' Lily said when they were out of earshot. 'He's taken responsibility for all of us since our father died.' She opened the door to their stairway, standing back to allow Mr Sadler to enter.

He paused on the threshold. 'I think I can understand how your brother must be feeling. The burden of responsibility must fall on his shoulders, but even so he is most fortunate to have a large family.'

Lily was intrigued. 'You sound almost envious.'

'Perhaps I am. I was the only child of older parents who died before I reached my majority. So you see, I am quite alone in the world and even if times are hard for you at the moment, at least you have each other. That is worth a king's ransom, Miss Lily.'

'You're right,' Lily said slowly. 'I hadn't really given it much thought before. Sometimes we squabble amongst ourselves, but I love my family even when they are being horrible.'

He smiled. 'We'd best get this food and drink to them before it gets cold, and maybe I could call again sometime. Do you think your sister would be agreeable to that?'

She thought of Armand and Nell together. She might wish it to be different, but she suspected that when Nell gave her heart it was forever. 'I'm sure she could have no possible objection,' Lily said tactfully.

'You said what?' Nell demanded.

Lily avoided meeting her angry gaze by tucking the sheet beneath the mattress on one of the four beds that had been set up in the back room. 'I don't know,' Lily muttered. 'What was I supposed to say when he'd been so kind to us?'

Nell yanked at the sheet from her side of the bed. 'I have a great deal of respect for Mr Sadler, but I don't want to give him the wrong impression.'

'I think he's lonely, Nell.'

'If he is then I'm very sorry, but I want to keep our relationship on a strictly professional basis.' Nell picked up a folded blanket and laid it across the bed. 'Don't stand there gawping at me, Lily. We've got three more beds to make up in here and three more in the living room.'

'He obviously likes you or he wouldn't have gone to so much trouble and expense today.'

'I can't help that. I've never given him any encouragement, and I really don't want to have him call here. This is hardly the place to entertain guests of any sort, let alone a fastidious man like Mr Sadler.'

A sound from the doorway made them both turn their heads to look at Molly, who had just arrived home from work.

'This is worse than I thought,' she cried, tearing off her bonnet with a dramatic gesture of despair. 'We can't live here, Nell. It's just awful.'

'Keep your voice down,' Nell said sharply. 'Don't set Grandpa and Aggie off again.'

'They're sound asleep in their chairs,' Molly retorted crossly. 'I don't know how they can do it, but they look peaceful enough.'

'They've done nothing but moan ever since they

arrived here,' Lily said with feeling. 'It is hateful, Moll, but there's nothing we can do about it.'

Molly tossed her head. 'I suppose our wonderful brothers are living like lords in the fire station while we're stuck here.'

'That's not fair and you know it,' Nell said sharply. 'They're doing the night watch and they're no better off next door than we are.'

'Well, I'm not sharing my bed with her,' Molly said, jerking her head in Lily's direction. 'I'm a working girl and I need a good night's sleep. I won't have her smelly feet on the pillow next to my face.'

Nell sighed, shaking her head. 'We've just got to put up with it, like it or not.'

'Well I don't like it and I'll not put up with it,' Molly cried passionately. 'You two make me sick. Where's your fighting spirit?' She flounced out of the room.

'She'll come round,' Lily said hastily, sensing that Nell was close to tears. 'I expect she'll see things in a different light when she's had some supper.'

Nell sniffed, and putting her hand in the pocket of her skirt she took out a shilling. 'Matt gave me some money to buy food. Take this and go to the grocer's shop on the corner, Lily. We need bread and milk for breakfast. Perhaps things won't seem so bad when we've had a good night's sleep.'

Lily slept in Aggie's chair by the window. Molly had kicked up such a fuss about sharing her bed that it seemed the easiest solution. They had managed to get Grandpa into bed in the back room. He had gone reasonably quietly and Lily could only guess that he was worn out by the events of the day. Then they had had to deal with Aggie, who was desperate for the privy in the back yard but refused to go on her own. In the end they all went, with Nell leading the way holding the lantern and the others clutching hands as they followed her down the stairs and out into the dark passageway. The privy was close to the stables and the horses whinnied and neighed as if calling out to them, perhaps hoping for a piece of cabbage stalk or a juicy carrot. Matt always said that the horses were fed and housed better than the firemen, and as she waited in the frosty yard for her turn in the evil-smelling privy Lily had to agree with him. After a cat's-lick of a wash at the outside pump, they scuttled back indoors as fast as they could when hampered by Aggie's rheumatics.

Now her sisters and Aggie were sound asleep and Lily tried in vain to make herself comfortable in the wooden rocking chair. There were no curtains at the window and she huddled beneath a blanket, looking down at the street. The frosty cobblestones glittered and sparkled in the yellow glow of the gaslights, and a hunter's moon hung like a silver shilling in the black velvet sky. Pinpricks of stars twinkled diamond-bright above the chimney tops and the roof tiles on the buildings opposite glistened with what Lily fondly imagined was stardust. Her artist's eye took in the scene and she felt her spirit soaring despite the discomfort of her situation. It was a harsh world down below on the pavements of Shadwell and Limehouse. She could see bare legs protruding from shop doorways, and hunched figures poorly clad against the cold making their way to destinations unknown. Maybe they had nowhere safe and warm to spend the bitter winter night, or perhaps they were returning to hovels with twenty or more people to one small room. Lily pulled the blanket up to her chin and tried to be grateful for what they had. Mr Sadler's words echoed in her brain as sleep claimed her. 'At least you have each other. That is worth a king's ransom.'

She was awakened suddenly by the most horrendous noise. There was much shouting, cries of distress, the urgent clanging of a bell, and all this followed by the thunder of horse's hooves and the rumble of cartwheels. Almost falling from her chair, Lily peered out of the window to see her brothers clinging to the fire engine as it was driven at speed along the street towards the docks. Her heart was beating so fast it made her breathless but there was no sound from her sisters or Aggie other than the occasional soft snore. She wondered how they could sleep through such a din, but none of them stirred. Lily settled back in the chair and dozed fitfully until just before dawn, when the clatter of the lamplighter's boots on the cobblestones below awakened her with a start. This time she could not go back to sleep and she rose from her chair to light the fire. By the time Nell and Molly awakened, Lily had the kettle dangling on the hook over the flames and was sitting cross-legged on the floor clutching a toasting fork with a slice of bread impaled on its prongs.

After breakfasting on tea and toast scraped with a little butter, Nell and Molly went off to work just as

Matt, Mark and Luke returned from night duty. The stench of soot and burning clung to them even though they had washed the worst of it off at the fire station. They went straight to their beds, too exhausted to speak, and Grandpa shuffled into the front room announcing that he had barely slept a wink. This was countered by Aggie who could always beat him in a verbal battle. Having given them tea and toast for their breakfast, Lily made her escape.

Wrapping her shawl around her head and shoulders she left the building with her shopping basket over her arm. Ostensibly she was on her way to market, but hidden in the bottom of the basket she had her sketching materials. There was little for her to do in the two rooms. Aggie had made it clear that she intended to claim them as her own domain; even without a kitchen range she decided that she would be able to make soup or boil meat in a pot over the fire. She insisted that she was perfectly capable of looking after Grandpa Larkin; and she would take pleasure in organising his daily routine. Lily had not stopped to find out what Grandpa thought of this plan. She was determined to take some time for herself and do what she wanted for a change. The move might have its compensations after all. There was no longer a large and dusty old house to keep clean, and for the first time in years Lily was liberated from the daily grind of housework. She intended to make the most of it.

The sun was shining from an azure sky so fresh and delicate that Lily's fingers itched to paint it using a wash of cobalt blue with just a hint of viridian. There was an ice-cold chill in the air, but there was no wind or even the slightest breeze to deliver the stench from the manufactories, chemical works or the tanneries. She made her way down Bell Wharf Lane and a short distance along Lower Shadwell Street to Bell Wharf Stairs. It was here that she loved to sit and make drawings of the busy river traffic and today was no exception. The tide was on the turn and the river sparkled in the sunlight, reflecting the blue of the sky. It flowed through the city like a satin ribbon in great loops of pure ultramarine. Lily committed the brilliant colours to memory. The dark reddish-brown of the brick warehouses, the pale grey of Portland stone, the rich tan of the Thames barge sails and the dark green lichen and waterweed that coated the stanchions and stone steps. The rainbow in her mind exploded with colour and light. She felt her spirit soaring to fly with the fluffy white clouds, scudding like spring lambs across the sky.

She was so busy looking upwards that she almost fell over a man sitting on the quay wall. 'Oh, I'm so sorry,' she apologised. 'I didn't see you there.'

He rested his sketching pad on his knees and squinting against the bright light he looked up at her. Lily found herself staring into the bluest pair of eyes she had ever seen. It was like gazing into the infinite blue of the sky and his eyes seemed to reflect the sunlight, sending it back to her with a smile. 'Hold on, there. Where's the fire? You nearly had me plummeting into the drink.'

'You're an artist,' Lily gasped, staring down at the deft strokes of charcoal on a white background. Even without a touch of colour the scene portrayed the very essence of the river. 'It's wonderful.'

He put down his sketchpad and scrambled to his feet, bowing over her hand with a courtly gesture that both thrilled and embarrassed her. 'I'm flattered, Miss . . .'

Feeling the blood rush to her cheeks, Lily withdrew her hand, glancing over her shoulder in case anyone who might know her was watching. She did not want such forward behaviour reported to any of her brothers, but the young man's smile was irresistible and his eyes danced with merriment. 'Lily Larkin,' she murmured shyly.

'Don't worry, Miss Larkin. No one will know that we are not old acquaintances meeting by chance on this glorious morning.'

'But I don't know who you are,' Lily said, making an effort to sound prim and proper as Nell would have wished, but his smile was infectious and her lips twitched. She stifled a nervous giggle.

'That's easily remedied. My name is Gabriel Faulkner and I am the ne'er-do-well son of a well-respected artist, whose talent has sadly bypassed me.'

'Oh, no, sir. You are quite brilliant,' Lily said sincerely. 'I wish I was half as good as you.'

'You are interested in art, Lily?'

She felt her blush deepen at his casual use of her Christian name. 'I like to draw and paint when I get the chance, but my family don't approve . . .' She paused, aware that she was in danger of blurting out the scandalous nature of her mother's behaviour and subsequent desertion.

'Well now, this is most interesting. What subjects do you favour, Lily? Flowers perhaps? Or landscapes?'

She was aware of the teasing note in his voice and she had read enough novels to know that young ladies of quality were expected to be accomplished in art and music. It must be obvious to him that she came from a quite different background. She found herself envying Molly's quick wit and ability to bandy words with the opposite sex. 'I draw the river,' she said simply. 'I was born and bred here. We live – I mean we used to live in the dockmaster's house. Grandpa says Thames water flows in our veins.'

Gabriel eyed her curiously. 'I would like to see some of your work.'

She hesitated. She had concealed most of her sketches at the bottom of the cedar chest where Nell kept the bedlinen, and which was one of the few items they had brought from their old home. 'I have an unfinished one here.' Taking a sheaf of paper from her basket, she selected the sketch she had made on this spot just days before the fire that had brought Armand into their lives. Her pulses were racing as she handed it to Gabriel. She waited, hardly daring to breathe, as he studied her work. She could not help noticing his hands as he held the flimsy sheet of paper. She had always romantically imagined that an artist would have long slender fingers, but Gabriel's were short and square-tipped. Workmanlike was the word that sprang to mind and she was vaguely disappointed. Clutching her basket tightly, she suppressed the urge to ask for his opinion. The suspense was terrible and yet it was thrilling. Here was a real artist with obvious talent, who would give her an honest evaluation of her work.

Gabriel looked up and his expression was grave.

'Y-you don't like it?' Lily felt as though the sky had fallen in and was crushing the life out of her. 'Is it that bad?'

Chapter Eight

'Where did you learn to draw like this?' Gabriel demanded. 'Who taught you?'

'No one,' Lily said, wishing that she had kept her sketch hidden from sight where it really belonged. She stared down at her shabby boots, unable to look him in the face.

'Come now, I find that hard to believe. You must have had an able tutor, or else this is someone else's work.'

This last remark made her raise her head and she tried to snatch the drawing from his fingers, but he held it above his head and out of reach. 'Give it back to me, please.'

'Not until you've told me about yourself. I want to know more about you, Lily.'

'There's nothing to know. I just make sketches to amuse myself and because . . .' A sob caught in her throat and she couldn't speak.

His smile faded and he laid his hand on her shoulder. 'You do it because it's a consuming passion,' he said gently. 'You have to express yourself and this is the only way you can speak from your heart.'

She raised her eyes to meet his and was startled to see understanding and compassion in their blue depths. She wanted to cry with sheer relief that someone understood her desperate need to create beauty and to reveal the world about her as she saw it. She nodded.

'I know it is so, Lily. I feel the same way, and so does every artist worth their salt. You have raw talent, my girl. You would benefit enormously from expert tuition but judging by this one sketch you show promise, and I'd love to see more of your work.'

'No, that's impossible,' Lily said, coming back to earth with a jolt. 'I'm glad you like my drawing, but it is just a pleasant pastime, no more.'

Gabriel's eyes widened and he cocked his head on one side. 'I don't believe you. I can recognise pure passion for art when I see it. Heaven knows I earn my bread and butter by giving drawing lessons to young ladies who would far rather be cavorting with their dancing masters, but you are different, Lily Larkin.'

Visions of her mother flitted through Lily's mind. A tumult of angry voices echoed in her head as she recalled the day that Ma had left home with her lover, and all in the name of art. 'I must go,' she murmured. 'I have things to do.' She turned and ran and it was only when she reached Cock Hill that she realised that Gabriel was still in possession of her drawing. She was out of breath and she slowed to a walk. It was silly to have panicked. What must he think of her? But on the other hand she knew she was on very dangerous ground. Her family, with perhaps the exception of Luke, would be horrified if they discovered her secret vice was indulging in the activity that had torn their family apart. The worst of it was to realise that she had been drawn to Gabriel Faulkner by the invisible thread that was their shared love of art. He was not her romantic ideal of a hero, as Armand had been, but there was something about him that was disturbing, unconventional and possibly dangerous.

From that day on, Lily avoided Bell Wharf Steps and she went further afield to make her sketches, sometimes walking as far as Kidney Stairs or Limehouse Cut entrance. Each time she left home she found herself glancing over her shoulder in case Gabriel had by some chance discovered her address. On one such occasion, about two weeks after their meeting, she was walking along Cock Hill when she saw a man wearing a wide-brimmed felt hat similar to the one she had seen on the ground beside Gabriel, and her heart did a somersault inside her breast. As he drew nearer she realised that he was a complete stranger and her initial relief quickly turned into a feeling of disappointment. She had been trying her hardest to forget Gabriel's words but they kept coming back to haunt her. It had been such a relief to learn that she was not a complete freak of nature in her love of colour, shape and form, and her innate desire to put what she saw on paper. Feelings of guilt assailed her each time she left the house with her sketching things concealed in her basket, but it was good to be out of their cramped living quarters, even in the worst weather. Grandpa was becoming more and more cantankerous with each passing day. Aggie was frustrated by the lack of cooking facilities in their rooms and had become even grumpier than usual. Nell went about pale-faced and uncomplaining, but Molly made up for her elder sister's silent suffering by voicing her discontent loudly and repetitively. Matt, Mark and Luke spent even more time in the fire station and Lily could hardly blame them. Life at home was becoming intolerable, and her only solace was to find a quiet spot in order to sketch and paint. The only difficulty was that the little pans of watercolour were now almost empty, despite Lily's frugal use of the precious pigments. Very soon she would have no colour to work with and no hope of finding the money to purchase more of the expensive art materials.

Two days before Christmas Nell was sitting at their old kitchen table, poring over the household accounts in the guttering light of a candle. She had just returned from school, and although it was only four o'clock in the afternoon it was almost pitch dark outside and a sleety rain was slapping the windowpanes. Lily had attempted to make their room look a little festive by making paper chains out of old newspaper which she and Molly had laboriously painted with red dye smuggled home from Molly's place of work. Grandpa was taking his afternoon nap in the back room and Aggie was huddled in her chair by the window with a shawl wrapped around her head and shoulders and a stone hot water bottle at her feet.

'If it gets any colder we'll all freeze to death,' she muttered just loud enough for Lily and Nell to hear.

Molly had not yet returned from work and Matt, Mark and Luke were on duty in the fire station.

'I wonder how much a goose will cost this year?' Nell mused, chewing the stub of her pencil.

'How do you expect me to cook a goose over that paltry fire?' Aggie demanded, suddenly alert. 'Or do we sit up all night holding it over a candle?'

'That's very funny,' Nell said lightly. 'But I was thinking perhaps we could take the bird to the baker's shop tomorrow and eat it cold on Friday.'

'Matt and the boys won't like that,' Aggie snapped. 'They love my roast with good gravy and plenty of vegetables.'

'We can boil potatoes and carrots,' Lily said, attempting to sound positive.

'And I suppose you expect me to boil plum pudding in the kettle?' Aggie buried her face in her shawl. 'What have we come to? How low can a family sink without actually living in the gutter?'

'That's enough, Aggie.' Matt had entered the room unseen by Aggie, who had her back to the door, and she looked round, flushing guiltily, but seemingly unrepentant.

'I was there when you was born, Matt Larkin. I wiped your snotty nose and bandaged your knees when you came in from school covered in cuts and bruises. I only spoke the truth and you know it.'

Lily hurried to her side and put her arm around Aggie's shoulders. 'Don't distress yourself, Aggie dear. We'll manage somehow, and I'm sure we'll soon find another house to rent with a proper kitchen and a washhouse with a copper. I used to grumble about doing the laundry, but anything is better than carting all the dirty clothes to the public washhouse.'

Matt shuffled his feet. 'I just came to say that we won't be in for supper. There's a big fire in a tobacco warehouse near Free Trade Wharf. We'll be gone all night, Nell, so don't wait up.'

Nell sprang to her feet. 'Oh, do take care, Matt.'

He hooked his arm around her shoulders and gave her a hug. 'Careful is my middle name, ducks.' He was about to leave the room but he paused in the doorway. 'There's a fellow downstairs asking about you, Lily. Said he's got something for you.'

'Who on earth could that be?' Nell mused, staring curiously at Lily. 'I hope you haven't been flirting with the butcher's boy, my girl.'

Lily felt her heart skip a beat, but common sense reasserted itself quickly and she decided it could not possibly be Gabriel. In any event, why would a sophisticated man like him come in search of an East End girl? 'Of course not,' she said, snatching up her shawl. 'It's probably a message from one of Grandpa's old cronies too shy to come and knock on the door.' She followed Matt out of the room and down the stairs. At least he was in too much of a hurry to pay attention to the person who had come calling on his youngest sister. Matt took his duties as head fireman of his watch very seriously indeed.

Lily emerged from the alleyway, peering through a curtain of sleety rain. At first she could not see anyone other than passers-by hurrying about their business, but then a male figure emerged from the shadows and came towards her.

'You're a hard person to track down, Lily Larkin.'

There was no mistaking the bantering tone of Gabriel's voice. 'How did you find me?' she asked breathlessly.

He drew her into the doorway of the tobacconist's shop. 'With great difficulty as it happens. You told me that you'd lived in the dockmaster's house and I went there, only to find the new occupants had no idea as to your whereabouts. I went back every day, questioning the men who worked on the wharves, and then I found your friend Bill. He took a bit of convincing that I was not a debt collector or something more sinister, but in the end I managed to persuade him that my intentions are entirely honourable and he gave me your address.' He plunged his hand inside his greatcoat and drew out a folded sheet of paper. 'I wanted to return your sketch.'

Lily took it with trembling fingers. 'Th-thank you, sir.'

'Gabriel,' he corrected softly. 'We are going to be friends, and I intend to see to it that your great talent is not wasted.'

'I don't understand. What are you saying?'

'I'm saying that I am sick and tired of teaching unwilling and untalented young women. I want you to be my pupil.'

'That's impossible. Even if I wanted to, my family wouldn't let me. I told you that before.'

'I can't accept that argument, at least not without a

good reason.' He took her by the shoulders, looking deeply into her eyes. 'You have a real talent, Lily. Why waste it?'

'It's out of the question. I'm flattered to have your good opinion, but I want you to promise not to take this any further. Now, I must go. Please don't try to see me again.' She broke away from him and ran out into the sleet, which was rapidly turning into a hailstorm.

'What was all that about?' Nell demanded when Lily burst into the living room shaking hailstones from her hair.

'It was just someone passing on the compliments of the season from Bill,' Lily lied desperately.

Nell frowned. 'That's odd. Why didn't Bill come in person?'

'I dunno.' Lily moved away to poke the fire, giving herself time to think. She realised then that it was a foolish lie, and one likely to be disproved when Bill came to see Grandpa on Christmas Day.

'I think she's got a fellah,' Aggie said. 'That's why she's always creeping out of the house when you're at the school, Nell. I think she's meeting a man. No good will come of it.'

'Is this true, Lily?' Nell demanded anxiously.

Lily was about to deny Aggie's accusation when a loud knocking on the outside door made them all jump.

Aggie peered out of the window. 'I can see the second engine being made ready to go. It looks like the other watch has been called out on this one, Nell. It must be a big fire.'

148

'Go and see who it is, Lily,' Nell said wearily. 'I must finish balancing the household accounts. Matt will want to see them in the morning.'

Lily was only too happy to oblige. She ran downstairs to open the door which led into the alleyway. Standing there with his helmet in his hands was Foster, one of the younger firemen from the day watch.

'We've been called out to the blaze in the tobacco factory, and we're a man down. Jones slipped on the icy pavement and we think he's broke his arm. Can Miss Nell come and take a look at him?'

'He should go to hospital,' Lily said cautiously. 'I don't think Nell could do much to help.'

'This is an emergency. If Miss Nell can just strap him up Jones could get a cab but the poor bloke is in agony and we've got to leave right away.'

Lily nodded her head. 'All right. I'll fetch her.'

The horse was ready and waiting in the shafts and the firemen had donned their helmets, but there was an uneasy silence as Lily and Nell made their way to the back of the building. They found Fireman Jones lying on a pallet, grey-faced and in obvious pain.

Ted Harris, the senior fireman, greeted them with a worried frown. 'Can you fix him up, Miss Nell?'

She went down on her knees regardless of the muddy floor that was soiling the skirt of her one good dress. 'Can you move your fingers, Mr Jones?'

He shook his head, biting his lip. 'No, miss. It's broke all right.'

'There's not much I can do for you other than to

strap it to your body,' Nell said apologetically. 'Could someone find me a length of cloth or webbing, please?'

Ted shook his head. 'We've nothing like that here, Miss Nell.'

'Then I'll just have to use my shawl.' Nell slipped the shawl off her shoulders. 'If you could just raise Mr Jones a little, I'll wrap this round him.'

Ted hoisted Jones none too gently into a sitting position causing the injured man to groan in a way that set Lily's teeth on edge. Nell worked quickly, tying the soft woollen cloth so that the arm was clamped to Jones' body. He slumped back onto the pallet with his eyes closed and beads of sweat standing out on his forehead.

'He must go to hospital straight away,' Nell said, rising to her feet.

'Foster,' Ted shouted to the fireman waiting by the cart. 'Go and find a cab. Jones has to go to hospital.'

'He'll need someone to accompany him,' Nell said anxiously. 'He might pass out from the pain.'

'I can't spare anyone, miss. We must leave right away and we're two men down now. Young Connor Reilly has been poorly all day and I let him off early just before we finished our shift. We're short of a driver now as well as the second fireman, and this is going to be an all-night job.'

'I can drive the wagon,' Lily said impulsively.

Ted stared at her as if she had gone mad. 'Out of the question, miss. We can't have a novice driving a machine like this, let alone a slip of a girl. It's against the rules and regulations.'

'I don't see why,' Lily said calmly. 'I can handle the reins as well as any of my brothers. They taught me to drive a cart when I was knee high to a grasshopper.'

Nell shook her head. 'Mr Harris is right. It's much too dangerous. Matt would never let you do such a thing, besides which I want you to help me get Mr Jones to hospital.'

'There's a cab waiting, chief,' Foster called from the entrance to the fire station. 'There was one passing by and he's ready to go.'

'Come here then and help this young lady get Jones into the cab.' Ted turned his head to give Nell a searching look. 'Are you sure you can handle this?'

'Of course.'

'And I can drive your fire engine,' Lily said eagerly. 'You could waive the rules and regulations in an emergency.'

He stared at her for a moment and then he nodded his head. 'Very well, but you leave the scene as soon as we get there. I can't allow a civilian's life to be put at risk.'

'Lily, no,' Nell said, catching her by the arm. 'I forbid this.'

Lily wriggled free. 'I'll be all right. Don't worry about me, Nell. I'll come straight home, I promise.'

'There's no time to waste,' Ted said urgently. 'We have to go now.' He strode off towards the fire engine and Fireman Foster hoisted Jones to his feet, hooking his good arm over his shoulder as he walked him out of the station to the waiting cab.

'You will be careful, Lily,' Nell said, giving her a quick hug.

Lily smiled and nodded. This was an experience she had never thought she might share with her brothers. It was going to be a great adventure. She picked up her skirts and ran to the engine. Ted tossed her unceremoniously up onto the driver's seat.

'There's a helmet and a jacket on a hook behind you, miss. Put them on quick and get going.' He climbed nimbly onto the cart with Foster and another fireman following suit. Shrugging on the jacket, which was several sizes too large, Lily rammed the helmet on her head and with a flick of the whip she encouraged the horse to a brisk trot. The cold night air almost took her breath away as she urged the animal to a canter. The sleety rain had stopped but the roads were still slippery and treacherous with huge puddles that spewed up volumes of spray as the wheels sliced through them. She stood up in the well of the cart, cracking the whip as she handled the reins with supreme confidence. She could smell smoke now, and to the east, in the direction of Limehouse, the sky had turned a dull red. She clanged the bell, shouting at drunken pedestrians weaving across the road seemingly oblivious to the danger of crossing a street in the path of an oncoming fire engine.

The scene that met her eyes above Free Trade Wharf was one that might have depicted the gates of hell. A warehouse fire had spread from one building to the next. Great tongues of flame leapt high into the sky sending showers of sparks cascading down like a mighty firework display. The acrid smell of burning filled the air and noxious plumes of black smoke drifted skywards. Silhouetted against the orange and crimson glow, Lily could see her brothers and their helpers vainly trying to contain the blaze. The men on her engine leapt into action and she found herself suddenly redundant and under strict instructions to go home. She took off the helmet and shook out her hair. She was fascinated to see it gleam in the light of the inferno as if it had absorbed the glow of the flames. She climbed down from the fire engine and was suddenly aware of a group of reporters standing round with notebooks in their hands. A photographer was bent over a camera on a tripod with his head hidden beneath a dark cloth. This very moment would be recorded and reproduced on the front pages of tomorrow's newspapers. She felt her stomach contract with a buzz of excitement. She was in the midst of a great drama and it was thrilling.

She was about to replace the helmet on the cart when one of the reporters broke away from the group and ran towards her. 'Excuse me, miss. Did I see you driving that contraption?'

Lily hesitated. She did not want Mr Harris to get into trouble for stretching the rules. 'Well, I, er . . .'

'Put the helmet on again, miss. This calls for a photograph.'

'Oh, no,' Lily protested, attempting to take off the telltale jacket. 'I don't think so.'

'Please keep it on, miss. What a scoop this will make. I can just see the headlines tomorrow – Young Girl Drives Fire Engine.' The reporter paused, frowning.

'No, that's not right.' He beckoned frantically to the photographer as he emerged from his cover. 'Franklin, come here. I want a picture of this girl.' He turned back to Lily. 'What's your name, ducks?'

'It's Lily, but I really don't want my photo taken, sir.'

'Lily,' he mused, tapping his teeth with his pencil. 'Lily Saves the Day. No, that's dreadful. Lily in the Smoke – nah.'

The photographer came up behind him, setting up his tripod. 'What are you on about, Christian?'

'Just thinking of a headline, old boy. This heroine is called Lily. I was trying to think of something that would appeal to the great British public.'

Franklin angled his head, staring at Lily. 'Look at that hair. It's the colour of the fire itself. What about – Lily in the Flames?'

Christian slapped him on the back with a loud guffaw. 'Splendid. What a headline. I should get a raise out of this.' He hurried to Lily's side, taking the helmet from her hand and placing it on her head. 'There you are, ducks. Stand still and smile if you can, but don't look too happy. Try to look like the heroine you are. Don't move a muscle, love. You'll go down in history.'

Next morning when her brothers returned exhausted, filthy and drained of energy from fighting the fire, Lily braced herself to face Matt's anger.

'What the hell were you thinking of, Lily?' He threw the newspaper down on the table with an exclamation of disgust. 'You've made us a laughing stock and brought the Metropolitan Fire Brigade into disrepute.

154

Poor old Harris will get a wigging for allowing a civilian to drive the fire engine, and a girl at that.'

'Aw, don't go on at her,' Mark said, his wide grin exposing a row of white teeth against his soot-blackened face. 'It's Christmas Eve and we're famous, brother. We've got our names in the newspapers.'

Luke put an arm around Lily, giving her a cuddle. 'I think she was very brave, and if you look at it from a practical point of view, Matt, she probably helped save our lives. The fire was getting out of hand and we would have been in a sorry state if Harris and the others hadn't turned up when they did.'

'It's all my fault,' Nell said, hanging her head. 'I should have stopped her, but I couldn't let poor Mr Jones go to hospital on his own.'

Matt's harsh expression softened. 'You did the right thing, Nell. It's young Lily who must take the blame for this. She might have been killed.'

Lily sensed that anxiety was behind her brother's anger and she managed a watery smile. 'I'm sorry, Matt. I'm really sorry.'

'Well don't you ever do a thing like that again,' he said gruffly.

'How about a nice cup of tea?' Aggie suggested, taking the teapot off the trivet in front of the fire. 'You boys look as though you could do with some breakfast. There's porridge in the Dutch oven that's been simmering gently all night.'

'I could eat a horse,' Matt said, rolling up his sleeves. 'A cup of tea and a bowl of porridge would go down a treat.'

'Not until you've washed off some of that soot,' Nell said with mock severity. 'You look like a trio of chimney sweeps and you smell terrible.'

'Aw, Nell, don't make us go out into the freezing yard,' Luke pleaded.

Matt took him by the shoulders and propelled him towards the door. 'Nell's right. We're not fit to sit down at the table. I know I stink of soot and worse and so do you. C'mon, Mark, that includes you.'

Aggie and Nell exchanged meaningful glances as the three brothers trooped out of the living room. 'It's not right,' Aggie muttered. 'They shouldn't have to wash themselves out there in the bitter cold.'

'I know,' Nell said, shaking her head. 'I've been looking for a house to rent ever since we moved in here, but the ones I've seen are either too small or too expensive.'

'I could go out and look for work,' Lily suggested tentatively. 'I mean, there's no need for me to stay at home now. Perhaps Molly could find me something at her place.'

'She was in a filthy mood this morning because I've got the day off and she hasn't. Let's hope she cheers up before tomorrow.' Nell regarded Lily with a thoughtful frown. 'But what would you do, Lily? More to the point, what could you do? You'd end up working in a factory or washing dishes in a chophouse.'

'Yes,' Aggie said, nodding her head sagely. 'And you can't expect me to heave water up and down those steep stairs, or bring coal up from the yard. I'm not as young as I used to be.'

Lily knew she was beaten. The sort of work she might expect to get would pay poorly and would make little difference to the family fortunes.

'Don't look so glum, ducks,' Aggie said, handing her a cup of tea. 'Drink this, and have a bowl of porridge before those greedy gannets eat the lot.'

'Thanks, Aggie, but I'm not very hungry.' Lily sipped the tea and went to sit by the window, leaving Nell and Aggie to discuss the preparations for Christmas Day. Sounds of movement were coming from the room next door which meant that Grandpa had awakened and would soon be demanding his breakfast. The events of last night were beginning to fade like the memory of a half-forgotten dream. Had she really driven the fire engine through the frosty streets, ringing the bell and shouting like a madwoman at anyone who got in her way? Had she really witnessed flames shooting almost as high as the stars? Had the sky been tinged crimson, vermilion and rose madder with streaks of orange and cadmium yellow? Her fingers itched to put the scene on paper and she wished, not for the first time, that she had the opportunity to use oil paints in order to get the depth and strength of colour she needed to recreate the dramatic scene.

'Where's me breakfast?' Grandpa Larkin burst into the room still wearing his nightcap and nightshirt. 'I'm faint from lack of nourishment. What's the use of keeping a pack of women if they won't look after a fellow?'

Nell leapt to her feet. 'Aggie will give you a cup of tea, Grandpa. But don't you think you should get dressed before breakfast? It's very cold and we don't want you catching a chill.'

'Bah! Nonsense. I'm as strong as an ox and I want me breakfast.' Grandpa eyed the Dutch oven with a malevolent sneer. 'And I don't want that pap. I want bread and cheese or a nice tasty bit of bacon, and a pint of porter would go down well.'

'You'll get what you're given, old man,' Aggie said, bristling. 'All hell's been let loose here since last night, and you've slept through the lot. No one has had the time to go to the bakery for bread, and a nice hot cup of tea will do you far more good than the devil's brew.'

'The devil's brew?' Grandpa cackled. 'There's nothing in the Good Book that says a man can't have a drink when he wants one.' He raised his hand as Aggie opened her mouth to argue. 'Didn't Jesus turn water into wine? He wouldn't have had any truck with those mealy-mouthed temperance folk.'

'Never mind that, Grandpa,' Nell said hastily. 'Lily will go to the baker's and there's a heel of cheese left from supper last night, but you'll have to make do with tea this morning.'

'But I can smell good ale,' Grandpa muttered. 'It comes out of the walls and up through the floorboards, even though the beer shop closed years ago.'

Lily jumped to her feet and as she did so she noticed that a small crowd had gathered in the street below. She craned her neck to get a better look and realised with a sinking heart that some of the men held note-books in their hands, and at least three of them were setting up cameras on tripods aimed at the fire station.

One of them looked up and caught sight of her. He raised his hand and pointed. She could see his lips working although she could not hear his words, but the upturned faces of the onlookers confirmed that she had been recognised. She backed away from the window, knocking a chair over in her haste.

'For Gawd's sake, what's wrong with the girl?' Grandpa demanded, wiping spilt tea from the front of his nightshirt. 'Look what you made me do, you silly thing.'

'What is it, Lily?' Nell moved towards the window but withdrew quickly. 'Oh, my goodness.'

'What's up?' Aggie demanded.

'It's the press,' Nell whispered. 'They're practically mobbing the place. We must keep out of sight and perhaps they'll go away.'

The words had hardly left her lips when a loud rapping on the outer door made them all jump.

'Open up. We know you're there, Miss Lily Larkin. You was seen at the window. We just want a few words from you. Open up.'

Chapter Nine

Someone in the passageway was hammering on the door so loudly that the whole building seemed to shake. There was a breathless hush in the room as they stared helplessly at each other. Grandpa Larkin was the first to speak and he put down his teacup with a thud. 'I'll go and sort the buggers out. I ain't having my breakfast spoiled by the likes of those rowdies.' His bare feet made soft padding noises as he strode across the room with his nightcap askew. Nell just managed to catch him before he reached the landing.

'You can't go downstairs like that, Grandpa. What will they think?'

'It doesn't matter what they think. I won't have this sort of behaviour.'

Lily hurried to Nell's aid. 'But Grandpa, supposing they take a photograph of you in your nightshirt, what would Bill and the others say if you were on the front page of the evening papers?'

He seemed to shrink inside his voluminous nightshirt like a candle flame extinguished under a snuffer. 'They wouldn't dare. I was a man of consequence.'

'They've no consciences,' Aggie said darkly. 'They just want blood.'

'Leave them to Matt.' Nell slipped her arm around

her grandfather's skinny shoulders. 'He'll soon put a stop to their little game.' She nudged him gently out onto the landing. 'Go and get dressed, Grandpa, and as soon as the newspaper men go away Lily will go to the shop and get fresh bread for your breakfast.'

He shot her a sideways glance. 'And a jug of porter?'

Nell nodded her head. 'All right. Just this once – after all, it is Christmas Eve.' She helped him into the back bedroom.

Left alone on the landing, Lily stood at the top of the stairs listening to the din in the passage, but a new sound added to the reporters' clamour: the clatter of booted feet and shouts from her brothers. There seemed to be a brief scuffle, with loud protests from the newsmen and a great deal of swearing on both sides, but the argument lasted less than a couple of minutes and appeared to end in retreat as the outer door opened and Matt strode in followed by Mark and Luke. They took the stairs two at a time and their faces were wreathed in triumphant grins.

'Don't go down there on any account, Lily,' Matt said sternly. 'They've left the alley but no doubt they'll hang about in the street for a while yet.'

Mark yawned and rubbed his eyes. 'I'm turning in as soon as I've had my breakfast and I guarantee I'll be asleep before my head hits the pillow.'

'It will soon be forgotten, ducks,' Luke said, giving Lily an affectionate hug. 'You're not to worry.'

After what seemed like an eternity to Lily, who had been watching anxiously from the window, the crowd

161

on the pavement below began to disperse as the reporters, having apparently decided that their blockade was not working, gave up and slouched off. Having given Lily strict instructions not to venture outside on any account, Nell and Aggie took the opportunity to slip out of the building unnoticed and Lily was left to do the housework while they went to market. Matt, Mark and Luke had retired to bed, and, to Lily's relief, Grandpa had eventually ceased complaining about his meagre breakfast and was snoozing in the chair by the window. She busied herself with the chores, but she had of necessity to go out into the back yard to empty the night soil from the chamber pots and to fetch water and coal. This entailed several trips and on the last, when she was hefting a heavy coal scuttle across the yard, she was accosted by Christian and Franklin, the reporter and photographer who had put her on the front page of the national newspapers.

'Good morning, Miss Lily,' Christian said, doffing his cap. 'How does it feel to be famous?'

They had placed themselves strategically so that she could not get into the building, leaving her no alternative but to stop and talk to them. She put the heavy coal scuttle down, wiping her hands on her apron. 'It will be forgotten by tomorrow, I've no doubt.'

'Ah, such is fame,' Franklin mused.

'But you have an interesting history,' Christian said slyly. 'I've done a bit of sleuthing, Miss Lily, and I've unearthed some fascinating facts about your family.'

Lily shivered as a tingle ran up her spine, but she

held her head high, feigning ignorance. 'I don't know what that could be, gentlemen. Now if you'd be kind enough to let me pass, I've got things to do.'

Christian folded his arms across his chest. 'This is all a bit of a comedown for your lot, isn't it, miss? I mean, your grandpa was the dockmaster for many years, living in that big house on the waterfront, and now you're stuck here in a couple of rented rooms above a tobacconist's shop. Not what you're used to, is it?'

'It's just temporary,' Lily said, attempting to sound confident. 'We're looking for something more suitable, but my brothers have to be near the fire station.'

'Yes, that leads me to another point. What did your brothers say when you bowled up in the middle of that huge conflagration? I can imagine that they were not best pleased; after all, you are just a girl. How old are you, miss?'

Lily decided that she did not like Christian with his mean ferret-face and insolent sneer. She looked round for a means of escape and saw that Franklin was setting up his camera. It was pointing directly at her. She picked up the coal scuttle. 'That's none of your business, sir. Now please let me pass. I've nothing more to say to you.'

'We can't let you go without giving us another picture, and I'd like to know how your mother will feel when she sees her daughter's face on the front page. I understand that she ran off with her art teacher, and she's now living in what might be called an unconventional style. You must have been quite a little girl when she abandoned you. How did you feel about that?'

'I've nothing to say.' Lily heard her voice break with emotion despite her attempts to remain calm. She must not let them see how much their callous snooping hurt and upset her.

'Look this way, miss.'

She turned her head to look at Franklin but when she realised he was about to take her picture she raised her hands to cover her face. 'I don't want this. Please go away and leave me alone.'

'Not a chance, ducks,' Christian said with a throaty chuckle. 'I'm not letting this story go. Is it true that your mother's lover is a famous artist now and keeps company with Mr Dante Gabriel Rossetti and the rest of the Brotherhood?'

'I don't know anything. Please let me pass. I want to go indoors.'

'You heard her.' Gabriel's voice reverberated off the walls in the narrow confines of the alley. He strode up to Franklin, snatching the cloth from the camera and tossing it onto the ground. 'Miss Larkin doesn't want her photograph taken, thanks, mate. Now push off.'

Christian took a menacing step towards him. 'You damage that valuable piece of equipment and you'll have to pay for it, cully.'

'You're trespassing,' Gabriel countered. 'And you're not welcome here. You heard the lady; she has nothing to say.'

Christian made a move towards him but Gabriel gave

him a shove that caught him off balance and sent him toppling onto the cobblestones.

'I'll have you in court for assault,' Christian roared, scrambling to his feet.

Ignoring him, Gabriel took the coal scuttle from Lily's hand. When they were safely inside he closed the door. 'Are you all right, Lily?'

It was only then that she realised she was trembling from head to foot but she nodded her head. 'Th-thank you. I'm fine.'

He eyed her with a quizzical smile. 'And now you're famous. That was a very brave thing you did last night.'

She mounted the stairs ahead of him. 'You've seen the papers?'

'I could hardly miss the story. You were headline news. Lily in the Flames – what a title for a photograph, or better still an oil painting – I wish I'd thought of it.' He followed her up the narrow flight of stairs, hesitating in the doorway of the living room. 'May I come in for a moment?'

'Yes, of course.' She was relieved to see that Grandpa still slept soundly and had not been disturbed by the rumpus outside. She watched as Gabriel placed the scuttle in the grate and she was suddenly embarrassed by her humble surroundings. She clasped her hands tightly in front of her as she tried to think of something to say.

'I'm afraid they'll be back,' Gabriel said in a matter-of-fact voice. 'The gentlemen of the press rarely live up to their name when they get the scent of a good story.'

'You heard what they said then? About my mother, I mean.'

'You mustn't take it to heart, Lily. There are always two sides to every story and I don't think your mother was entirely to blame for her actions.'

'How do you know so much about my family?' She was beginning to suspect that he knew more about her than she had thought possible.

'What makes you think I do?'

'Please don't answer a question with another question.' She realised that she had spoken sharply and she managed a rueful smile. 'I didn't mean to snap at you, Gabriel. It's just that I'm so tired of everyone treating me like a child. If you know something about Ma, please tell me.'

'Would you like to meet her, Lily?'

'There you go again, asking another question.'

'I do know her, as it happens, and she gave me a message for you.'

Lily's legs gave way beneath her and she sat down heavily on the nearest chair. To be in the company of someone who knew her mother was as shocking as it was exciting. 'She gave you a message for me?'

'She would like to see you, Lily. I showed her your sketch and she was most impressed.'

'I'm almost twenty, Gabriel. The last time I saw my mother I was just nine years old and now all of a sudden she wants to see me?'

'She thought you might feel like that and she understands. She said she would leave it to you and abide by your decision, but I can take you to her this minute, if you so wish.'

She shook her head, dazed by the sudden turn of events. 'Did she really say she wanted to see me?'

'She did, and I believe she was sincere.'

Lily pressed her hand to her brow as a multitude of conflicting emotions assailed her. When she was a child she had prayed for this moment, but suddenly and inexplicably she was afraid. 'After all this time,' she said softly. 'Are you absolutely certain, Gabriel?'

'I'm only passing on the message, Lily. I can see that you might not want to know her after what she did to you and your brothers and sisters, and I would understand if you said no.'

'Did she say she wanted to see them too?'

'No, Lily. Just you.'

Torn between the desire to see Ma again and loyalty to her family, Lily struggled with her conscience. 'No,' she said slowly. 'It wouldn't be fair on the others. If Ma doesn't want to see my brothers and sisters I can't go behind their backs. They would never forgive me, and I would never forgive myself. It would tear our family apart and there's been enough heartache in the past.'

He took her hand and held it, his eyes searching her face. 'Are you sure this is what you want?'

'No, of course it isn't.' She snatched her hand away to dash angry tears from her cheeks. 'Oh, I wish I'd never driven that stupid fire engine and had my picture plastered all over the front pages of the newspapers.'

'You're upset,' Gabriel said gently. 'I'll go now and leave you to think about your decision. If you change your mind, let me know.'

'I won't. It would be very wrong of me to sneak off without telling the others. If Ma wants to see us again she must make the first move.'

'I understand.' He produced a silver case from his breast pocket and took out a gilt-edged visiting card. 'But if you should change your mind, this is where you can contact me.'

She took the card and examined it closely. Printed in elegant copperplate, the address was in Gower Street, an area with which she was unfamiliar. 'I don't think I will ever have need of this, but thank you anyway. It was kind of you to come.'

'Now you make me feel like a guest at a tea party. I hope we can still be friends.'

'Of course.'

'And there's something I wanted to ask you.'

She was quick to hear the tentative note in his voice which sat at odds with his usual confident manner and she was intrigued. 'Ask away.'

'I mentioned it before and I was sincere in my offer. I'd like to take you on as my pupil. You have a great talent, Lily, and it would be a crime to suppress or ignore it.'

To be tutored by a professional would be a dream come true, but she was painfully aware that it was not for her. 'I'm sorry, but I can't afford lessons. I can't even afford to buy more paints to refill the box that Ma gave me all those years ago.'

'I would supply all the material you need, Lily. Is that the only reason?'

'No, it isn't, Gabriel. I have to find work so that I can contribute to the housekeeping. Nell is looking for a place to rent where we can be more comfortable.'

'There's more to it than that, I think.'

'It's hard to explain, and I doubt if you'd under-stand.'

'I think I do,' Gabriel said gently. 'But I can't bear to see a gift like yours wasted.'

'Maybe one day, when we are more settled, I could take you up on your offer.'

'Then we must hope that day comes soon, Lily. Perhaps I'll see you down in the docks when I go sketching?'

'It's possible,' she said, attempting a smile. He would never know how much it cost her to turn down such a generous offer, but she realised now that she had lived in a dream world for far too long.

He took her hand and raised it to his lips. 'Merry Christmas, Lily.'

'Merry Christmas, Gabriel.'

She stood there for some time after his footsteps had died away. Had she been wrong in refusing to see Ma? Her heart was telling her that she should have gone with Gabriel, but a small voice in her head insisted that she had been right to say no. The others would never have forgiven an act which they must consider to be treachery. She went to kneel by the bed she now shared with Molly and reached underneath for her paintbox. Opening it, she tucked Gabriel's calling card inside, heaving a despondent sigh at the sight of the small china pans now sparkling white having given up the last of their rainbow hues. Without the means to buy more paint she would have to limit her artistic output to sketching from now on. She tucked the box back in its hiding place and rose slowly to her feet.

In these dreary surroundings it didn't feel a bit like Christmas. She gazed sadly at the two iron bedsteads and the truckle bed where Aggie laid her head at night. They might not have lived like toffs in the dockmaster's house, but it had held all her childhood memories, both happy and sad. All that was left of their old home were their beds, the deal kitchen table, six bentwood kitchen chairs and the dresser containing what was left of Ma's prized dinner service. The two rocking chairs placed opposite each other in the window were from the old kitchen, and on the floor was a scattering of rag rugs, painstakingly made by Aggie, but they did little to disguise the fact that the floorboards were well worn and uneven. Despite Lily's attempts to scrub them clean, the dirt was ingrained. Nell had made an attempt to conceal the fact that the plaster was crumbling in large patches from the walls by hanging some of the pictures taken from their old home. The result was oddly depressing as most of the images were monochrome seascapes or sepia tints of sailing ships, reminders of Grandpa's early days as a seafarer. The paper chains, over which she and Molly had taken so much trouble, hung limply against the wallpaper with its much faded and almost indistinguishable pattern of cabbage roses. There was not much of a festive air about the place they were forced to call home. Deprived of light and colour, Lily felt sad and depressed and she had an urgent desire to escape to the place where she had always found inspiration and solace – the river.

Snatching her bonnet and shawl from the row of wooden pegs behind the door, she hurried downstairs and out into the alley, praying that the reporters had gone far away and that she would not bump into Nell and Aggie on their way home from market. It was a relief to find that there was no one waiting for her and she was able to merge with the crowds unnoticed. She threaded her way between horse-drawn vehicles to the far side of the street and almost without thinking she found herself heading towards Bell Wharf Stairs. Whether by subconscious design or sheer instinct, she was making her way back to the scene of the ship-wreck that had brought Armand into their lives. Nell never mentioned his name, but Molly often called out to him in her sleep. Lily had to tickle her feet in order to make Molly turn onto her side and lapse once more into deep and rhythmic breathing.

She found a quiet spot out of the bitter winter wind and she sat dangling her legs over the wooden parapet. She gazed up into the azure sky where wisps of white cloud floated like angels' wings. The sun was a pale golden globe suspended in a sea of blue, and its rays bounced off the ripples on the water as the unstoppable Thames made its way to the sea. It might be Christmas Eve but the river traffic was as busy as ever with wherries, lighters and barges plying their business in between the larger seagoing craft. A schooner was tied up alongside Bell Wharf and the cranes were swaying and dipping like wading birds feeding off the mud in the river bed. Their chains rattled and clanked; the scrape of metal against metal merging with the shouts of stevedores, seamen, ships' chandlers and agents. It was a symphony of noise accompanied by the deep bass of barrels rolling over cobblestones and waves slapping against wooden hulls. Seagulls mewed their mournful cries overhead and pigeons flapped their wings as they circled above her, keeping an eye out for food waste from the vessel's galley.

Lily closed her eyes for a moment, breathing in the familiar smells of her childhood that some might find distasteful, but to her the odour of river mud, engine oil and smoke evoked memories of home. She opened her eyes, blinking against the bright sunlight as she heard someone calling her name. Had she drifted off to sleep in those brief moments? Momentarily dazzled, she could just make out the silhouette of a tall man standing a little way from her, hat in hand.

'Lily, *ma chérie.*'

'Armand?' She clambered to her feet, hardly able to believe her eyes. 'Is it really you?'

He came slowly towards her and it was only then that she saw that he was limping and leaning heavily on a cane. He dropped his top hat and stick on the ground and took her hands in his, holding her at arm's length. 'My little Lily. Never had I thought that you would be waiting here for me on the shore.'

'But I wasn't,' Lily breathed. 'I didn't know you were coming. How could I?'

Armand drew her too him and kissed her first on one cheek and then the other. 'I hope you don't think me too bold, *ma chérie*, but I feel for you as my little sister – the sweet girl who rescued me from the fire.'

Torn between tears and laughter, Lily could have wished that he had addressed her as anything but his little sister, but her pleasure was undiminished. He was here and he was holding her hands, looking at her with such tenderness that her heart swelled with joy. 'It is so good to see you, Armand. And you are able to walk again.'

He released her hands and bent down to retrieve his hat and stick. He smiled ruefully. 'My leg, it is getting better, Lily, but yet I could not run a mile.'

'But what are you doing here, Armand? Tomorrow is Christmas Day and you are far away from home. Have you come on business?'

'I came partly on business but mainly to see you and your family again. I owe you all a debt of gratitude for looking after me, and also an apology for the way my father treated you.'

'That wasn't your fault, Armand.'

He frowned. 'I don't know what I could have done in the circumstances, but I have felt very bad for the way my father behaved. I would like to visit your home and make my apologies in person to your grandfather and all your family.'

Lily bit her lip. She would not have minded for herself, but she knew that Nell would be mortified if Armand were to find them living in such altered circumstances. 'That's a bit difficult at the moment,' she murmured. 'We had to leave the dockmaster's house.'

'*Mon Dieu!* I did not think it would come to that. I had hoped that Matt would be able to come to some arrangement with the manager of the dock company. I am so sorry, Lily.'

She raised her eyes to meet his troubled gaze. 'You really mustn't blame yourself, Armand.'

'But I do, Lily, and I know that my papa was unhelpful to say the least. I would like to come to your place of living now so that I may offer some assistance to your family. I do feel in some way responsible for your misfortune.'

Lily didn't know how to respond. She was certain that Nell would want to see Armand but she was not so sure about Matt. Molly still thought she was in love with him, but Lily suspected that the main attraction was Armand's wealth and position.

'You hesitate, Lily. Is there some reason why I should not pay my respects to your so excellent family?'

'I'm not sure how my brothers would react, but I know Nell would be very pleased to see you again, and Molly too.'

'Your brothers and grandfather, they blame me for what happened. Is that not so?'

'They've never said as much.'

'So it is even more important that I speak to them and put matters to rights. They not only saved my life, but Matt's report on the cause of the fire exonerated the ship's company from blame and we were able to collect the insurance monies. I want to help your family, Lily. It is a debt of honour.'

In the face of such persistence, Lily could hardly refuse, but when they arrived in Cock Hill she realised that they were attracting curious stares from passers-by. Casting a sideways look at Armand she could see that they must appear to be an ill-matched couple. In this part of London it was unusual to see a gentleman dressed in the height of fashion and with no expense spared, especially when accompanied by a girl in a shabby linsey-woolsey skirt over a red flannel petti-coat, with a much-darned woollen shawl wrapped around her shoulders and a bonnet on her head that had also seen better days. As they made their way along the narrow passage that led to their rooms Lily was even more conscious of their surroundings. She dreaded to think what Armand might be feeling as she led him up the stairs to the narrow landing. Aggie's strident tones could be heard through the closed door of the living room. Nell's responses were muffled, but loudest of all was Grandpa's querulous voice demanding to know why his midday meal was not ready.

Lily stole a look at Armand's face but he met her anxious gaze with a smile. 'Shall we go in? I can't wait to see Nell and pay my respects to Monsieur Larkin.'

Lily opened the door and ushered him into the room. Nell was at the table, slicing a loaf of bread, and Aggie was stooped over the fire poking the coals beneath the soot-blackened kettle.

'Never mind coddling your stomachs with tea,'

Grandpa said, thumping his hand on the arm of his chair. 'I want a man's drink with my bread and cheese, and a wally or some pickled onions would go down a treat.'

Nell opened her mouth to reply but on seeing Lily and Armand standing in the doorway she seemed to freeze.

'Look who has come to see us,' Lily said nervously.

Grandpa rose from his chair, glaring at Armand through narrowed eyes. 'If that's who I think it is, tell him he's not welcome here.'

'Grandpa,' Nell cried, blushing furiously. 'That's no way to speak to a guest.' She dropped the knife and hurried towards Armand, wiping her hands on her apron. 'This is a pleasant surprise, Monsieur Labrosse.'

Lily could only guess at the self-control that her sister must be exerting to look and sound outwardly calm. 'I was down by the river, Nell,' she said hastily, 'and we bumped into each other.'

Armand took Nell's hand and raised it to his lips, looking deeply into her eyes. 'I hope I have not inconvenienced you by arriving unannounced, Miss Nell.'

'You can just sling your hook, mister,' Aggie said, hurrying to Nell's side like a bulldog protecting its mistress. 'It's all because of you and your pa that we're forced to live in this midden.'

'Aggie, that's not true, and it was certainly uncalled for,' Nell said sternly.

'It has a ring of truth,' Armand admitted. 'You must excuse me, Miss Aggie, but I have come to offer my sincere apologies for the way in which my papa behaved. I have come to make amends for the suffering caused by his behaviour.'

'You don't know the half of it,' Aggie muttered with a meaningful glance in Lily's direction. 'Your pa should keep his wandering hands to hisself and not go propositioning young girls.'

Nell shooed Aggie out of the way. 'Perhaps you would like to finish slicing the loaf, Aggie. You are so much better at it than I.' She turned to Armand with an apologetic smile. 'You must excuse Aggie. She is very loyal to us, but she had no right to speak to you in that way.'

'I'd every right,' Aggie muttered beneath her breath, seizing the bread knife and attacking the loaf as if it were Monsieur Labrosse's neck on the guillotine. 'Perishing Frogs.'

'Hear, hear,' Grandpa said loudly. 'You've got a lot to make up for, young man.'

'Armand, you will stay for something to eat?' Nell said, casting a warning look at her grandfather. 'Grandpa and Aggie don't mean to be rude.'

'I know what I mean to say,' Grandpa shouted. 'And I say what I mean. We're here because Labrosse senior put the hard word on me with the manager of the dock company.'

'Perhaps I should leave,' Armand said in a low voice. 'I don't want to cause any more upset, Nell.'

Lily laid her hand on his arm. 'Please don't go, Armand.'

'She's right,' Nell said hastily. 'Please stay and share our luncheon. It's only bread and cheese, but . . .'

Armand patted Lily's hand, but his eyes were upon Nell. 'Bread and cheese would taste like manna from heaven in your company, but I am distressing your esteemed grandpapa and Miss Aggie. This is not what I intended.' He bowed to Grandpa, clicking his heels together in military fashion. 'My apologies to you, sir. I came with the best of intentions, and I hope you will allow me to make some reparation for the actions of my papa.'

'You can't get my home back for me, so don't bother,' Grandpa said sulkily.

'And you can't restore a young girl's faith in old men,' Aggie added, brandishing the bread knife in a most alarming manner.

Lily met Armand's anxious gaze with a shrug of her shoulders. 'It was a misunderstanding between your pa and me – that's all it was.'

'I beg you to forgive him. His shame is mine and I would cut off my right arm rather than upset or offend you or any member of your family.'

Grandpa hobbled towards Armand, shaking his fist. 'Get out of my home. We may have come down in the world but that don't mean you can come here and gloat over our misfortune. Now get out and don't come back.'

'Grandpa, please,' Nell cried, pale-faced and visibly trembling.

Lily put her arm around her sister's shoulders. 'It's all right, Nell. I'm sure Armand understands.'

'I will leave right away, Monsieur Larkin,' Armand said with a stiff bow from the waist. 'I came only to try to make amends but I see I am not welcome. I beg your forgiveness, sir.'

He left the room abruptly and Nell collapsed in Lily's arms, sobbing as if her heart would break.

178

Chapter Ten

Moments later, Matt burst into the living room demanding to know the reason for all the uproar. Nell rushed past him, but when Lily made to follow her he caught her by the arm. 'What's going on, Lily? What has happened to upset Nell?'

'I met Armand purely by chance and he wanted to come here to apologise for his pa's behaviour. You can ask Grandpa and Aggie what happened next, I'm going after Nell to make sure she's all right.' Without giving him a chance to question her further, Lily broke free of him and raced after her sister. She found Nell at the pump in the back yard, splashing cold water on her face.

'I'm so sorry, Nell. I would never have brought Armand home with me if I'd known what sort of reception he'd receive.'

'It's not your fault, Lily. But what Armand must think of us now, I can't imagine.'

'It's so unfair,' Lily said, shivering as a gust of wind whipped straw and dust into swirling eddies.

'They didn't give him a chance.' Nell's bottom lip quivered ominously.

'He's too fine a man to let them stand between him and the woman he loves,' Lily said gently. 'He came back for you, Nell. I'm certain of that.'

Nell was silent for a moment, staring into Lily's face with a startled look in her eyes. 'You love him too, don't you, Lily?'

'It doesn't make any difference, Nell. It's you he wants, I know it. He thinks of Molly and me as his sisters; he said as much.'

'Oh, Lily, I am so sorry. I keep forgetting that you're grown up now. I still think of you as my baby sister who must be looked after and protected from the world, but you're no longer that little girl grieving for her mother. You're a heroine – Lily in the Flames – that's what the newspapers called you, and you have feelings for Armand. What are we going to do now?'

'We're going to go indoors and carry on as usual,' Lily said with more certainty than she was feeling. 'There's nothing else we can do, Nell. Unless, of course, you feel you ought to go to Bell Wharf where Armand's ship is being unloaded.'

'And say what to him? We can't keep meeting simply to apologise for our relations, and I don't know how Armand feels about me.'

'I would have thought that was obvious.'

'Not to me.' Nell linked her hand through Lily's arm with a brave attempt at a smile. 'Come along, Lily. We'd best go in and soothe a few ruffled feathers. Then there's the goose to be plucked and taken to the bakery.'

'But what about Armand?'

'I doubt if we'll ever see him again after today. What man would put himself in such an embarrassing situation again?'

Lily squeezed her hand. 'A man in love, Nell. I'm sure he will return.'

Next morning Lily was awakened by cries of distress. Pushing Molly's feet away, Lily snapped upright in bed to see Nell standing by the cupboard where they kept their food. In her hands she held the carcase of the goose, stripped of all its flesh.

Lily leapt out of bed and padded across the bare boards, brushing her tangled locks back from her face. 'What happened to that?'

'Rats!' Nell said, dropping the bones back onto the plate. 'They've eaten the whole thing. We've no Christmas dinner, Lily. How am I going to tell the boys?'

'What's all the noise?' Molly cried, sitting up in bed and yawning widely. 'Can't a girl get her beauty sleep?'

'Merry Christmas,' Lily said, chuckling as the humour of the situation struck her. She could just imagine the faces of her brothers when the skeleton of the goose was placed before them for their Christmas dinner.

'I'm glad you think it's funny,' Nell said crossly. 'How am I supposed to feed the family now?'

'We'll just have to get pie and pease pudding from the shop in Broad Street. I didn't fancy cold goose anyway.' Lily went to kneel by the grate, riddling the grey ashes and sweeping them into a dustpan. 'I'll get the fire going, Nell. We'll feel better after a cup of tea and a slice of toast. That is if the rats haven't gnawed their way into the bread crock and eaten that too.'

'Don't joke about such a thing.' Nell hurried to the

dresser and lifted the lid of the earthenware crock, peering in and uttering a sigh of relief. 'The bread is all right, thank goodness. You had me worried for a minute.'

'Shut up and let me go back to sleep,' Molly moaned. 'It's not as if we have anything much to look forward to today.' She tugged at the rags tied around her hair, pulling them out one at a time. 'I can remember when we had lots of lovely presents and the sort of food that I can only dream about now.'

'At least the rats had a good blowout,' Lily said, crumpling yesterday's newspaper with her picture on the front page and stuffing it into the grate. 'We'll have to make do with tea and meat pie.'

Nell tipped the bare bones into the slop bucket. 'At least we have food and we have coal for the fire. We won't starve or freeze to death like some of the poor families who send their children to the Ragged School. And if we have to go without presents this year, then so be it.'

'If you say we have each other I'll scream and throw my boots at you,' Molly said with feeling. 'I'm going back to sleep but you can wake me when breakfast is ready. I'm going to enjoy my day off from slaving over vats of stinking dye. When I marry my rich gentleman I'm never going to work again.' She flung herself face down on the pillow.

Lily was quick to note the sad downturn of Nell's mouth and she could have shaken Molly for her selfish outburst. 'Don't take any notice of her, Nell. It's just Molly being her usual thoughtless self.'

'It's time she grew up and realised that there are other people in the world than her,' Nell said with unusual asperity.

'I heard that,' Molly muttered into the pillows. 'I hate living like this.'

Nell sighed, shaking her head. 'We all do, Molly, but we've just got to make the best of it. Anyway, it's time the boys were up. They're on duty this morning and they'll want a cup of tea before they start their watch.' She glanced at the truckle bed where a motionless hump beneath the coverlet indicated that Aggie was still sound asleep. 'Wake her up for me, Lily. I believe Aggie would sleep through anything.'

Later that morning, Nell and Aggie had gone to church leaving Lily and Molly to keep an eye on Grandpa, who had awakened in a crotchety mood made even worse when he discovered that the rats had devoured their Christmas dinner. He had eventually been placated by several cups of hot, sweet tea and slices of toast spread with the scrapings from the butter dish, which left none for Lily who had not yet had time to eat. She made do with a cup of tea and went down into the yard to fetch water, but when she returned minutes later she was faced with an angry Molly who had risen from her bed at last and was strutting around the room wearing her best frock and an angry scowl.

'Look at this, Lily,' she grumbled, holding out her skirts to display a brown scorch mark. 'How many times have I told you to use a cool iron? You've ruined my one and only decent gown. Can't you do anything right?'

Lily set the heavy bucket down on the floor biting back a sharp retort; after all it was Christmas Day. Peace and goodwill to all men – and she supposed that included sisters as well.

'I could do with a glass of hot toddy,' Grandpa muttered, eyeing Lily hopefully. 'A bit of Christmas cheer wouldn't go amiss, young lady.'

'Maybe later, Grandpa,' Lily said automatically. She doubted whether the family finances would run to such luxuries, but she was not going to be the one to dash Grandpa's hopes.

'I had a glass of negus at work yesterday,' Molly said, sitting on the edge of her bed and swinging her legs. 'Old man Jones was in a festive mood, but it's a pity he didn't think to give us extra wages instead of wine and a mince pie. If he had I might have been able to afford a new frock, since this one is only fit for the ragbag.'

'Ungrateful girl,' Grandpa said, shaking his finger at her. 'You'll come to no good, young Molly. You're flighty like your ma and look what happened to her.'

'What did happen to her, Grandpa?' Molly demanded sweetly. 'Tell us again.'

'You know very well what she did, bringing shame on us all. You're a bad girl to tease an old man.' Grandpa turned away to stare moodily out of the window. 'Charlotte Delamare was never good enough for my boy.'

Lily filled the kettle in silence and hung it on the

hook over the fire. She did not want to get involved in yet another family dispute. It was obvious that Molly had awakened in one of her moods and was intent on goading Grandpa as a way of enlivening her day. Lily prayed silently for some form of diversion and was surprised and startled when almost immediately the room echoed with the sound of someone knocking on the outer door.

'A visitor!' Molly cried, leaping off the bed and racing from the room as if her life depended upon it. She returned moments later clutching a large package wrapped in brown paper and tied with string and sealing wax. 'It's for you, Lil,' she said, thrusting it into Lily's hands. 'No one ever sends me presents.'

'For me?' Lily stared at the elegant copperplate. It was addressed to her but she did not recognise the handwriting. 'Who brought this, Molly?'

'I dunno,' Molly said, pouting. 'A boy: I didn't know him.'

'I wonder what it is.'

'There's only one way to find out,' Grandpa said testily. 'Open it for Gawd's sake and put us out of our misery.'

'Yes, open it,' Molly echoed. 'Maybe it's a big box of chocolates and we can all share it.'

'Or a box of cigars.' Grandpa brightened visibly. 'I haven't had a good cigar for – well, I can't remember the last time.'

Lily untied the string and was patiently peeling off the paper when Molly snatched the parcel from her hands and ripped it open, revealing a highly polished wooden box with a brass catch and a leather handle. She thrust it back at Lily. 'Hang it – it's not chocolates.'

Lily's fingers trembled as she lifted the catch. She opened it, letting out a gasp of delight and then closing it again with a snap.

'Well, girl, don't keep us in suspense,' Grandpa said, leaning forward in his chair. 'What is it?'

'Just a box,' Lily said hastily. 'Nothing very interesting; in fact I think there must be some mistake.'

Molly angled her head, eyeing Lily suspiciously. 'Is that what I think it is?'

Lily frowned. 'It's a box for keeping things in. If I can find a return address on the paper you tore up I'll send it back directly.'

Molly leaned closer, whispering in Lily's ear. 'It's a paintbox, isn't it? Who do you think sent you that? I think I can guess.'

'I don't know what you're talking about.'

'You can't fool me, miss. It was from that artist bloke, wasn't it? I found his card amongst your things when I was looking for a hair ribbon.'

'You shouldn't have been snooping, you wretch.'

Molly smiled triumphantly. 'You've got a gentleman friend, you sly cat. Well, I don't care because that means you can have him and I can have Armand. I'll keep your secret, Lil, if you promise to leave Armand to me.'

'What are you two whispering about?' Grandpa demanded. 'It's very rude. Speak up if you've something to say.'

Molly skipped across the floor to drop a kiss on his

forehead. 'We were just saying that Matt ought to treat you to a jug of hot toddy. It is Christmas Day after all and the blooming rats have eaten our dinner, so I think we all deserve a treat. I think I'll go down to the fire station now and put it to him.'

'Good girl, Molly,' Grandpa said, patting her on the shoulder. 'Thank God you don't take after your mother in every way. She was a selfish piece; never gave a thought to anyone other than herself.' As Molly made a move towards the door, he called her back. 'And tell Matt if I can't have hot toddy, I'll make do with mulled wine so long as they put plenty of brandy in it. Off you go, missy.'

With Grandpa sinking into a reverie with a rapt look on his face, which Lily could only assume was in anticipation of an alcoholic treat, she went to sit on her bed and opened the box once again to inspect the contents. It was twice the size of her old paintbox and contained several rows of china pans filled with solid pigment. She took out a small glass bottle that was obviously intended to hold water, marvelling at the craftsmanship that enabled her to slip it back in its snug compartment. Next to it was a china palette for mixing the colours and lying in a slot at the front of the box were six watercolour brushes of varying sizes. Their bristles were made of sable and so soft that she hardly felt them when brushed against her cheek; it was a wonderful present but it would have cost a small fortune. It would tear her apart to give it up, but she knew that she ought not to accept such an expensive gift. She would have to return it to Gabriel.

She sat for a while running the tip of her finger gently over the silky surface of the paints and visualising the wonderful array of colours they would make when transferred to paper. But it was not for her; it was a dream that was never going to come true. Only wealthy women could afford a box such as this. The cost of it would have kept her family in food for a week. She came back to earth as she heard footsteps outside the door and she slid off the bed, tucking the box beneath it and rising to her feet just as Aggie and Molly entered the room, followed by Nell and Mr Sadler.

Nell went straight to Grandpa, who had apparently dozed off, and she shook him by the shoulder. 'Grandpa, Mr Sadler has come to visit us.'

'Eh, what?' Grandpa shook himself and opened one eye and then the other, glaring over Nell's shoulder at Mr Sadler, who stood with his top hat tightly clutched in his hands.

Mr Sadler cleared his throat nervously. 'How do you do, sir? May I wish you the compliments of the season?'

'You can wish me whatever you like,' Grandpa said, scowling. 'What d'you want here, schoolmaster? The rats ate our dinner, so don't hope to fill your belly here.'

'Grandpa!' Nell said in a shocked tone. 'Mr Sadler has just come to pay his respects.'

'He's got something for you, you miserable old man,' Aggie said, pushing past Mr Sadler and making her way to warm her hands in front of the fire. 'It's blooming taters out there. Wouldn't be surprised if we had snow before nightfall.'

'What have you got then?' Grandpa demanded, his eyes brightening.

Mr Sadler took a step towards him, taking a small wooden box from his inside pocket. 'A few cigars, Mr Larkin. A small Christmas gift for you.'

Grandpa snatched the box and opened it, taking out a cigar and rolling it between his fingers as he held it under his nose, sniffing and inhaling the scent of Havana tobacco. 'The real thing,' he murmured. 'Lily, fetch me a lighted spill.'

Lily hurried to do his bidding, flashing a grateful smile at Mr Sadler. She thought he looked most uncomfortable in his Sunday-best suit, with a starched collar cutting into his thin cheeks and his shock of dark hair carefully combed and slicked with pomade. He was shifting from one foot to the other, and he reminded her of a stork she had once seen on a rare visit to the Zoological Gardens in Regent's Park.

'That was very kind of you, Mr Sadler,' Nell said, taking off her bonnet and mantle. 'May I offer you a cup of tea?'

'Thank you, that would be most acceptable, Miss Larkin.'

Lily waited patiently while Grandpa took a silver-plated cigar clipper from his waistcoat pocket, snipped the end off the fat cigar and pierced it with the point of the small instrument. He took the spill from her and warmed the cigar before lighting it with a beatific smile on his face. He extinguished the spill with a puff of blue smoke. 'Excellent cigar, schoolmaster. You've gone up a notch in my estimation.

Now all I need is that mulled wine or hot toddy and I'll be a happy man.'

'The demon drink,' Aggie said, shaking her head. 'The kettle has boiled and I'm making a pot of tea. Am I right in thinking you're a temperance man, Mr Sadler, sir?'

'Aggie,' Nell said sternly. 'That's none of your business.'

Lily was torn between an overwhelming desire to giggle and sympathy for Mr Sadler, who was looking more discomforted by the minute.

'I enjoy a glass of sherry wine on festive occasions,' he said after a moment's consideration. 'But I am not inclined to partake of strong spirits. Perhaps a little champagne at a wedding might be acceptable, or a fine wine with a good meal, but never hard liquor, which I believe has been the ruin of many a good man.'

'And woman.' Aggie poured boiling water onto the tea leaves in the china teapot, which was still perfect apart from a chipped spout that was inclined to send hot tea splashing in all directions.

'I would ask you to stay for luncheon, Mr Sadler,' Nell said apologetically, 'but I'm afraid we had a mishap with the goose.'

'The rats ate it,' Molly said with a wicked grin. 'We're overrun with them, Mr Sadler. I wouldn't stay if I were you.'

'I wouldn't dream of imposing upon your family, Miss Molly.' Mr Sadler's grim expression softened as he turned to Nell. 'Perhaps I could escort you to luncheon at a chophouse, Miss Larkin. That is if your family could spare you.'

'Thank you, but I can't accept your kind offer,' Nell said, blushing furiously. 'You must understand that I couldn't desert my family on this of all days.'

Lily was puzzled by Nell's refusal of such a generous offer, but Aggie was still going on about the Temperance Society and Grandpa was sitting in his chair puffing out smoke like an old steam engine. Lily decided that this was turning out to be a very odd Christmas. She was hardly surprised when a loud knocking on the front door interrupted Aggie in full flow.

'I'll go.' Glad of an excuse to leave the room, Lily hurried downstairs and opened the door to find both Gabriel and Armand standing in the alley. Gabriel was weighed down by a huge wicker basket filled with fruit and Armand's arms were filled with hothouse flowers. In his hat he had a sprig of mistletoe. Lily looked from one to the other in amazement.

'Merry Christmas, Lily,' Gabriel said, smiling. 'I've come to wish your family the compliments of the season.'

'As have I,' Armand countered. 'I left here under a cloud yesterday, Lily. I have come to make peace with your grandpapa.'

'I don't suppose the flowers are for him,' Lily said, unable to resist the temptation to tease Armand, who was glaring at Gabriel as if put out by the presence of a possible rival. 'You'd better come in, Armand.' She stood aside to allow him to enter and he made his way up the steep staircase, but when Gabriel stepped over the threshold, she barred his way. 'What do you think you're doing? I told you that I can't accept your offer.'

'I just want us to be friends, Lily. It is the season of goodwill after all.'

'Keep your voice down.' Lily glanced anxiously over her shoulder, but Armand had reached the top of the stairs and was out of earshot. 'You really shouldn't have come here. My family wouldn't approve of our friendship.'

'But we are friends, are we not?'

She nodded. 'I suppose so.'

'And did you receive the present, Lily?'

'So it was from you. I can't accept such a gift – it's much too expensive.'

'No, my dear Lily, you've got it all wrong. The paintbox was not from me, although God knows I wish I'd thought of it first. It was from Cara, your mother.'

'That can't be true. My mother was called Charlotte, and she left us years ago.'

He slapped his hand on his forehead with a self-deprecating smile. 'Of course, silly of me, I ought to have realised that you would know her only as Charlotte, but now she chooses to be called Cara. It is part of her bohemian lifestyle.'

'I don't understand why she has singled me out from my brothers and sisters.'

He took her hand and held it. 'She is deeply, deeply sorry for what happened ten years ago, Lily. She wishes more than anything in the world to make amends for deserting you especially, since you were such a child then, and perhaps she feels closest to you because of the talent you both share.'

'But why now? Why would she want to see me after all this time?'

'Only she can answer that, Lily. But your mother is an accomplished artist in her own right and she has many admirers in the art world. She begs you to come with me today.'

Looking into his eyes, she could see no hint of mockery in their depths and she knew that he was sincere, but she was shocked by his revelation. For years she had longed for this moment and had been certain that one day Ma would return to the bosom of her family, but this was not how she had expected it to happen.

'I can't, Gabriel,' she murmured, lowering her gaze. 'Not today of all days.'

'Why not?'

She pulled her hand free. 'I just can't, that's all. Maybe tomorrow.'

'Is that what I am to tell her, Lily? She will be very disappointed.'

'Will she?' Lily felt an angry lump knotting in her stomach. 'Well, perhaps Ma would like to think of the past ten Christmases when she didn't care about us at all. I want to see her, of course I do, but I can't and won't do anything to upset my family.'

Gabriel placed his arm around her shoulders. 'I understand, and I will try to make Cara see things from your point of view, but she's a stubborn woman and once she makes up her mind to something . . .'

His wry expression drew a gurgle of laughter from Lily. 'It runs in the family. You should take warning, Gabriel.'

'It's too late for that,' he said softly. 'I am involved more than you could possibly imagine.'

'I'd better go upstairs,' Lily said hastily. 'They'll wonder what's keeping me. Will you come and meet them? Armand will have told them that you're here.'

He shook his head, picking up the basket of fruit and thrusting it into her arms. 'I think not. I don't want to make things difficult for you today, but perhaps my gift might ease the way when I next call on you.'

'A bottle of rum would be even more likely to warm Grandpa's heart.'

Gabriel pinched her cheek so gently that it felt more like a kiss. 'You are a rebel at heart, I can tell.'

She shook her head. 'Not really. Well, perhaps just a little.'

He touched her hair, wrapping a lock around his forefinger. 'Such a colour – golden like the sun and yet with a hint of fire; no wonder they thought of you as the lily in the flames. I would like to paint you like that, with your hair streaming out in the wind and a background of burning buildings. Would you sit for me one day, Lily?'

She was about to answer when Molly appeared at the top of the stairs. 'Nell says you are to come up at once, Lily. And he is to go away. Grandpa says he won't have a strange young man turning up uninvited. I never said a word. Honest.'

'I'm coming.' Lily turned to Gabriel with an apologetic smile. 'I'm sorry about that.'

'It's all right. I understand, and if you were my granddaughter I would probably feel the same.'

He pulled a face that made her laugh out loud and put her instantly at her ease. 'I can't imagine you as a grumpy grandpa.'

'I would have to be a husband and father first.' Gabriel lifted her hand to his lips and brushed it with a kiss. 'I've never seen myself in that role, but I'm beginning to see the attraction of being a family man.'

'Lily!' Molly's voice rose to a crescendo. 'Come on up, or shall I send Aggie down to fetch you?'

'I must go,' Lily said, placing one foot on the bottom step. 'Merry Christmas, Gabriel.'

'Merry Christmas, Lily. Shall I call for you tomorrow so that I may take you to Keppel Street to see Cara?'

She hesitated for a heartbeat. She longed to accept, but she knew what her answer must be. 'Perhaps another time. I'm sorry. I really must go upstairs and join the family. Goodbye, Gabriel.'

He saluted her in mock military style. 'Until then, Lily.' He let himself out into the alley.

Molly leaned over the banister rail. 'He's gone at last. For heaven's sake hurry up, Lily, or we'll both be in trouble. You know how impatient Grandpa is.'

Hefting the heavy basket of fruit up the narrow staircase, Lily was already wondering if she had done the right thing. Her desire to see Ma had overcome her reservations and now she was set on a path of deception that might have disastrous consequences. She could only hope that Ma's wish to see her would evolve into the desire to embrace all her children. She went slowly up the stairs, battling with her conscience and comforting herself with the thought that hers could be the first step in reuniting their family.

There was a lull in the conversation as she followed Molly into the living room and placed the basket of fruit on the table.

'Well, I'm blowed,' Grandpa exclaimed, rising to his feet and hobbling over to examine the gift. 'I haven't seen fruit like this since I worked in the docks.' He held up a pineapple. 'When did we last taste one of these?'

'I can't remember,' Nell said, shaking her head. 'It's a generous gift and we ought to thank your friend, Lily. Who is he, and what does he do for a living?'

Molly grinned mischievously. 'He's an artist, isn't he, Lil? Tell them.'

Lily's worst fears were realised as she noted the shocked looks on all their faces. 'His name is Gabriel, but it doesn't matter because I won't be seeing him again.'

'I should hope not.' Grandpa dropped the pineapple as if it had burnt his finger. 'The fellow will be a wastrel like the rest of his ilk. I won't have him in the house and he can take his bleeding basket of fruit and toss it in the Thames for all I care.'

'Oh no, Grandpa,' Lily cried, rescuing the pineapple as it rolled across the floorboards. 'I mean, we can't waste good food. It would be a crime.'

'It would be a sin against God,' Aggie added, licking her lips as she fingered a ripe peach. 'I've not tasted one of these since I was a girl.' She turned to Grandpa with a fierce frown. 'The damage is done now, old man.

The gift has been accepted and hurling pineapples around the room isn't going to hurt anyone but the said piece of fruit. It certainly won't bother the young man who brought the present. We should honour the day, if not the deed.'

Molly snatched an orange and began peeling it. 'It's Christmas, Grandpa.'

'If I may make so bold, sir,' Mr Sadler said, clasping his hands together and steepling his fingers. 'It would seem a shame to dispose of such a handsome gift, but if you have no use for it I know many poor families who would be suitably grateful to receive such bounty.'

'Keep your thoughts to yourself, schoolmaster. I'm the head of this household and what I say goes. Eat the bloody rubbish if you must, you women, but save an orange to put in the mulled wine, if I ever get it.'

As he stomped back to his seat in the window, Lily couldn't help noticing that Grandpa had forgotten to limp. She tried not to smile as he threw himself down in his chair, sending it rocking to and fro like a metronome set to its fastest beat.

'I'm sorry if I spoke out of turn.' Spots of colour stood out on Mr Sadler's high cheekbones.

Nell laid her hand on his arm. 'Your sentiments were honourable, Mr Sadler, but perhaps a little misplaced in the circumstances.'

'Won't you call me Eugene, Miss Nell? After all, we are not in school now, and as your sister says, it is Christmas Day.'

Nell glanced anxiously at Armand, who had been standing silently watching and listening but keeping

197

out of the argument. He stepped forward, clearing his throat. 'May I make a suggestion?'

Lily held her breath as Molly sucked hard on the orange, making a noise that earned her a frown from Nell. Aggie spat out the peach stone, eyeing Mr Sadler with interest. He bridled, moving a step closer to Nell as if about to snatch her from his rival's grasp, but Nell was looking up at Armand with a tender smile. 'Please do, Armand. What would you like to say?'

'I would like you all to be my guests for dinner tonight. I am staying at the Prospect of Whitby, which may not be a hotel of the highest luxury but the food is good, and it is not too far away from here.'

'You can count me out,' Grandpa muttered. 'I can't even walk to the other side of the street on my rheumaticky pins, so I'll just have to stay here and starve.'

'Certainly not, Monsieur Larkin. I won't allow that. It would be my pleasure to send a cab to fetch you and one to bring you home again after we have dined.'

'That's a very generous offer, Armand,' Nell said, casting a warning look at her grandfather. 'I'm sure we would be most happy to accept.'

'I'll come gladly,' Molly said through a mouthful of orange. 'I can't remember the last time we ate out and I'm sick of pie and pease pudding.'

'Speak when you're spoken to, young lady,' Grandpa snapped. 'It's for me to say yea or nay, not you.'

Tossing her curls, Molly flounced over to her bed and sat down, turning her back on the assembled company.

'Spare the rod and spoil the child,' Grandpa said, shaking his fist.

Mr Sadler cleared his throat several times and his lips moved silently before he managed to get the words out. 'I – I had better leave now, Miss Larkin. I can see that my presence is *de trop*.'

'Ah, monsieur, you speak French,' Armand exclaimed, slapping Mr Sadler on the back.

'I am a schoolmaster, sir. I am an educated man.'

Armand bowed from the waist. 'Of course. My apologies. I meant no disrespect, and you would be most welcome to join us for dinner.'

'Thank you, no. I have other plans.' Mr Sadler turned to Nell, lowering his voice. 'I will leave now, Miss Larkin.'

'Please don't go, Eugene,' Nell said shyly, blushing as she enunciated his Christian name. 'Won't you stay and take a glass of mulled wine with us?'

'I'm still waiting for it,' Grandpa complained. 'Here, French fellow, make yourself useful and go to the pub across the road. A jug of mulled claret or buttered rum would go down a treat.'

'It would be my pleasure,' Armand said, releasing Nell's hand. 'Will you accompany me, Nell?'

Mr Sadler stepped in between them. 'A common tavern is no place for a young woman, monsieur. I don't know how you behave in your country but we do not allow ladies to enter public houses.'

Lily could tell by Armand's expression that he was baffled by this pronouncement and she could see a question forming on his lips. 'It's all right for us to dine in a private room,' she said hastily. 'It's just that only women of a certain kind frequent taprooms.'

Aggie almost choked on the second peach that she had sneaked from the basket. 'You shouldn't speak about things like that, Lily. It's not nice.'

'I'm dying of thirst here,' Grandpa muttered. 'Never mind the social niceties. You two men can go together and fetch a jug each. That would be fair.'

'I don't usually frequent public houses,' Mr Sadler said stiffly. 'Perhaps Miss Lily would be kind enough to point us in the right direction.'

Only too pleased to avert any further arguments, Lily snatched up her shawl. 'Come along then. I'll take you down to the street and show you where to go.'

With Armand and Mr Sadler following her, Lily led the way along Cock Hill to one of the more reputable public houses. She left them at the door and made her way back along the street, wrapping her shawl around her shoulders as large feathery flakes of snow began to fall from a leaden sky. She had her head down and did not at first see the man who stepped out of the alleyway in front of her.

Chapter Eleven

Through a lace curtain of snow, Lily recognised the reporter who had dubbed her Lily in the Flames. 'Oh,' she gasped. 'Not you again.'

'Christian Smith, journalist. We weren't properly introduced last time.' He doffed his bowler hat, sending a shower of snowflakes to join the frosting on the pavement. 'Merry Christmas, Miss Lily.'

Recovering a little from her fright, Lily eyed him curiously. 'Don't tell me that you're working on Christmas Day.'

'A good reporter is never off duty. I'd like a few words with you, but I suggest we go somewhere a good deal warmer than Cock Hill in a blizzard.'

'I've nothing to say to you, sir.'

He took her by the arm, propelling her towards one of the pubs that Lily had deemed to be too rough and ready for Armand and Mr Sadler to enter. She tried to dig her heels in, but the leather soles of her boots acted like skates on the slippery paving stones and she found herself being bundled into the taproom of the Old Rose. The fuggy atmosphere took her breath away and the thick haze of smoke from the blazing coal fire and countless clay pipes made her cough.

Christian steered her to a settle in the inglenook. 'What will you have to drink?'

'I don't want anything.' She made an attempt to rise but he pushed her down onto the hard wooden seat.

'Not so fast, young lady. You and I have business to discuss.' He signalled to the potman who was clearing a table close by. 'A large brandy, my good fellow, and one for yourself seeing as how it's Christmas Day.'

'Thank you, sir. Right away.' Grinning happily, the potman shuffled over to the bar counter.

'You can't keep me here against my will,' Lily said with more bravado than confidence. 'My brothers will come looking for me if I am gone for too long.'

Christian sat down beside her, edging her into the corner of the settle. 'Your brothers are on watch at the fire station, missy. I've checked. And anyway, this won't take long if you cooperate.'

She looked him in the eyes, and her first impression of him was confirmed. He had the face of a ferret and the cold eyes of a reptile. 'Say what you have to say and then I'm leaving.'

He threw back his head and laughed. 'By God, you're a cool one and no mistake. I like a woman with spirit and I like you, Lily Larkin.'

'The feeling isn't mutual,' Lily said, fighting fear with anger.

He leaned back in his seat with a smug smile. 'But I've got a lot to say to you, missy. I've stumbled across a story that will be of great interest to my readers.'

'It can't have anything to do with me then,' Lily said

defiantly. 'I'm an ordinary girl from a hard-working family.'

'But not an ordinary family, I think.' He angled his head with a calculating gleam in his eyes. 'I've got a nose for a good story and my instincts never let me down.'

'I don't know what you're talking about.'

'My dad used to work on the docks until your grandfather gave him the sack. I remember standing in the rain outside the dockmaster's house while my old man went inside to beg for his job. Old man Larkin sent him off with a flea in his ear. I'll never forget the look on Dad's face as he staggered out of that house, which was like a palace compared to the hovel we lived in. "We're done for, Christian," he says, clutching his chest and going grey in the face. "I'm finished." And with that he fell to the ground stone dead.'

'I'm very sorry,' Lily murmured. 'That's really dreadful, but what has that got to do with me? It must have been a long time ago and I'm sure my grandpa . . .'

'Don't make excuses for the old devil. He killed my dad as surely as if he'd stuck a knife in his poor old heart. It gave out because he'd worked hisself into the ground for the dock company and that was all the thanks he got for it.'

'It's very sad, but I still don't understand.'

'When I found out you were related to old Larkin, it rang bells in my head. I remembered the scandal when your ma ran off and left you all. That tickled my interest, especially when I found out that you'd had to leave the dockmaster's house and were living above a shop. Now that was poetic justice to my mind. Then when that toff stuck his oar in I knew I was on to a good story. When I found out who he was all the pieces of the puzzle slotted together.'

'Have you quite finished?' Lily demanded. 'It seems to me that you're making a story out of nothing, so you don't need anything further from me.'

Christian's hand shot out as she attempted to rise and he caught her by the wrist, forcing her to remain seated. 'But I do, missy. I want to meet your ma. She's quite a woman by all accounts, although I'd hesitate to call her a lady.'

'I haven't seen my mother since I was nine. I know nothing of her life now.'

'But you know Mr Gabriel Faulkner.'

It was a statement rather than a question and Lily said nothing. Christian's attention was momentarily diverted by the arrival of his drink and he tossed a coin at the potman, who caught it deftly in one hand. 'Keep the change, my good fellow.' He took a swig of his brandy. 'Ah, that's better. It warms the cockles of your heart; you should try some, my dear. It's all paid for by my newspaper – I have an expense account and I could be generous to a girl like you.'

Lily bit back a sharp retort. One look round the crowded taproom was enough to convince her that she would get short shrift if she made a fuss. The tough-looking customers propping up the bar were unlikely to be sympathetic to a girl in her position. In her shabby clothes and down at heel boots she might be mistaken for a dollymop; a servant girl out to boost her meagre wages by selling her favours.

Christian finished his drink, calling for another. 'Now then, girlie,' he said, exhaling brandy fumes into her face. 'It will interest my readers to know that you are stepping out with the son of your mother's fancy man. What have you got to say to that?'

'I – I don't know what you're talking about.'

'Are you really so innocent, or are you just pretending?' His intense gaze did not waver as he sipped his brandy. 'You must know something of the story.'

When she remained silent, Christian continued with obvious relish. 'Everard Faulkner, well-known painter and friend of Dante Rossetti and the Brotherhood, left his wife for your ma ten years ago. The poor lady died of relapsing fever shortly afterwards, although some say it was a broken heart that killed her. Her only child Gabriel, who was fifteen at the time, went to live with his grandmother until she passed away three years ago. According to my source he now resides in Gower Street, but is a frequent visitor to the house in Keppel Street, the love nest of your ma and her lover. Charlotte Delamare, who has reverted to her maiden name, is an artist in her own right and Everard Faulkner is even more famous. Some might call them notorious, although I wouldn't be so crass.'

Lily's first instinct was to call Christian's spiteful words into question, but there was a ring of truth in what he said. It fitted with the little that Gabriel had told her, although he had omitted to mention that he was related to the man who had torn the heart out of her family.

'I can see that my revelation is news to you, Lily,' Christian continued with a smug grin. 'Quite obviously the gentleman thought it best to keep the truth from you.'

She was not going to let him see how shaken she was by his disclosures. She met his gaze with a lift of her chin. 'You seem to know everything. I can't think what you want from me.'

'A statement will do for a start, ducks. A few well-chosen words for my readers, who will be most interested to know the reaction of Mrs Larkin's family.' Becoming suddenly businesslike, Christian pulled a notebook from his coat pocket and a pencil. 'Will you be visiting your ma in Keppel Street? And will the rest of your family follow suit? I can imagine it will be quite a reunion after such a long time, although I understand that your grandpa never approved of his son's choice of wife.' He leaned forward, his eyes narrowed in a basilisk stare. 'I'm going to rub the old man's nose in the dirt, and you're going to get me an interview with that mother of yours. I won't rest until I have the whole of the Larkin family scandal headline news.'

Lily leapt to her feet, pushing the table away with all her strength and sending the glass flying onto the flagstones where it shattered into tiny shards. 'I've had enough of this. You can make up anything you like but I'm not saying another word.'

There was a moment's silence as the other customers stopped chatting and turned their heads to stare at Lily and Christian. Pushing her way through the crowd, she stormed out of the pub, emerging into a swirling snowstorm and almost crashing into Armand and Eugene Sadler as they returned with the jugs of Christmas cheer.

'Lily!' Armand exclaimed. 'Did you just come out of that place?'

'Shame on you, Miss Lily,' Mr Sadler said gravely. 'I hope you have a suitable explanation. Your family would strongly disapprove of such behaviour.'

Looking at her closely, Armand slipped his free arm around Lily's shoulders. 'It doesn't matter, *ma chérie*. Let us take you home.' He thrust the jug of hot toddy he had been carrying into Mr Sadler's hands. 'There is no need for any of this to be mentioned, I think. Lily must have her reasons and it is really none of our concern.'

Mr Sadler looked as though he might argue and then appeared to change his mind. 'Very well, we will say no more about it, and I suggest we walk quickly or the festive cheer will have turned to ice.'

If Lily was unusually quiet when they reached home, no one seemed to notice. The hot toddy had a cheering effect on the company and the disaster with the goose was soon forgotten. Grandpa mellowed enough to accept Armand's invitation to dine at the pub, and when it was extended to include Aggie and Mr Sadler the atmosphere in the dreary room became quite convivial. Lily felt isolated and alone like a spectator at a play as she sat back and watched them all laughing and talking. Their world was about to be ripped apart for a second time by the malicious gossip-mongering of a man out for revenge, and she felt powerless to do anything to prevent disgrace and disaster. She was consumed with guilt. If she had not disobeyed the family by wilfully following her instinct to draw and paint she would never have met Gabriel, and she would have remained sublimely unaware of her mother's unconventional and shocking lifestyle. Her anger was largely directed at herself, but she was also furious with Gabriel for telling her half-truths. She was tempted to drag the paintbox from beneath the bed and vent her feelings by throwing it in the Thames, but deep down she knew she could never carry out such a deed. It would be sacrilege to destroy such a wonderful object, one which would, if she were allowed to make use of it, enable her to create colour and beauty enough to satisfy her soul.

That evening in a private room at the Prospect of Whitby, Lily barely tasted any of the hearty meal that Armand had ordered. The mulligatawny soup was undoubtedly delicious even if Aggie complained that she would suffer all night after such a rich dish. The roast turkey with all the accompaniments was eaten with relish and washed down with copious glasses of red wine, although her brothers chose ale for prefer- ence. The plum pudding was a triumph and was brought into the room ablaze with warmed brandy, but Lily only toyed with a mouthful. Matt, seated on her left, was only too willing to finish it for her, and only Luke, seated on her right, seemed to notice that she was not in the best of sorts.

'Are you all right, Lil?' he whispered. 'You've hardly eaten anything.'

'I'm fine,' she answered softly. 'Just a bit of a headache.'

'I'm not surprised with all this noise,' Luke said, casting a glance around the table at the laughing faces flushed with a surfeit of good food and fine wine. Mark was telling jokes that even made Grandpa chuckle and brought a smile to Aggie's lips, while Eugene and Armand vied for Nell's attention. Molly had chosen to sit next to Armand and she was assiduous in her attempts to divert his attention from her sister. Lily felt vaguely sorry for Nell, who had done nothing to invite the attention of either of the gentlemen at her side. She looked small and delicate as she sat between them, like a pale flower trapped between two strong saplings. Molly on the other hand was definitely a briar rose, throwing out thorny tendrils in her attempts to reach the sunlight, which in her case would be a smile from Armand.

Lily's fingers itched to sketch the scene; the faces pale and lustrous in the candlelight and the deep shadows in the corners of the room where the glow from the roaring log fire could not reach.

'A penny for them,' Luke said, chuckling. 'You've been somewhere else all evening, Lil.'

She turned to him, forcing her lips into a smile. 'I'm a bit tired. I think I'd like to go home.'

'Are you unwell?'

'No, I'll be perfectly fine in the morning.' She lowered her voice. 'I don't get much sleep thanks to Aggie's snoring and Molly's feet sticking in my ear.'

He squeezed her hand beneath the tablecloth. 'At least you don't have to listen to Grandpa wheezing and grunting all night. The cattle in Smithfield make less noise than he does.'

'You look tired, Lily,' Nell said, interrupting the flow of Eugene's oratory as he attempted to talk Armand down. 'Perhaps we should go home and leave the men to their port and cigars.'

Armand half rose to his feet. 'No, please stay, Miss Nell. We do not make our ladies leave the table in Paris. We value their company too much.'

'Gallantly said, sir,' Eugene said, flushing angrily. 'But if Miss Larkin wishes to go home, I will gladly escort her and her sisters.'

Nell stood up and both Armand and Eugene leapt to their feet. 'No, please,' she murmured, turning to Armand. 'Don't leave your own party. Luke will see us home.' She cast a meaningful look at her brother.

'I was going to offer.' Luke rose from the table. 'Lily's got a headache and I could do with an early night. We were on a shout in the early hours and I'm ready for bed.'

Aggie heaved her body from her chair, her face shining with perspiration and her cheeks flushed. 'Ta ever so for the dinner, Mr Armand. I haven't had a feast like that for a long time.'

'Get on home, woman,' Grandpa said, scowling. 'Don't show us up.'

Matt raised his glass to Armand. 'It was a splendid meal, but it's not over yet. Sit down, Armand, and you too, Eugene. The night is still young and Luke will see the girls safely home. It's still Christmas and I intend to make the most of it.'

'Are you sure you don't want me to accompany you, Miss Nell?' Armand asked in a tone that sounded more like a plea than a suggestion.

Molly jumped up, tossing her fiery curls. 'I'd like you to escort me, Armand. Never mind my ungrateful sister. Anyway, she's got the schoolmaster.'

'That's enough, Molly.' Nell's sharp retort made everyone stare at her in surprise, and she blushed rosily. 'I mean, we don't want to drag Armand out onto the icy pavements at this time of night. To fall on a recently recovered limb might do irreparable damage.'

Armand opened his mouth as if to protest but Eugene had snatched up Nell's shawl and was wrapping it around her shoulders. 'I must be going anyway. I have an early start in the morning.'

'The school is closed tomorrow and Sunday,' Molly snapped. 'There's no need for you to follow us like a lovesick puppy.'

Lily could see Matt's brow darken and Grandpa looked as though he would like to slap Molly for her cheek. Nell appeared close to tears and only Mark seemed oblivious to the storm of emotions in the room. He was cracking walnuts with his teeth and dropping them one by one into his glass of wine. 'Splendid meal, Armand old chap,' he said, looking up with a grin. 'What d'you say to a flagon of buttered rum to finish off with?'

That seemed to finish the argument as Armand was obliged to ring for the waiter. With a triumphant flourish, Eugene proffered his arm to Nell and they left the parlour followed somewhat reluctantly by Molly and Aggie.

Lily laid her hand on Luke's shoulder. 'I'll go with them,' she whispered. 'Mr Sadler will see us safely home. There's no need for you to come.'

All the way home Lily listened to Aggie grumbling that she would have liked to stay and sample the fine Stilton cheese that had been brought to the table, and Molly's constant carping on the fact that were it not for Mr Sadler's interference, Armand would have escorted them.

It had been a day fraught with emotion and Lily was glad to lie down in bed, even though Molly tossed and turned, pulling the coverlet up to her chin and exposing her feet as they rested on the pillow close to Lily's head. Aggie had fallen asleep as soon as her head touched the pillow, but Lily could tell by her soft breathing that Nell was wide awake. Most young women would be delighted to have captured the hearts of two eligible men. Molly would have crowed her triumph from the rooftops, but Nell was different. Lily knew that it was not in her nature to be flirtatious or to enjoy hurting the feelings of another person. Nell would have cut off her right arm rather than wound someone who loved her. Lily lay still, willing sleep to come and relieve her of her worries. She heard the distant chimes of the clock in St James's church tower strike midnight, then one and two, and her brothers stomped up the stairs not long afterwards, laughing and shushing each other in their tipsy attempts to keep quiet as they man-handled Grandpa into their room.

The building lapsed once again into a drowsy silence but sleep still evaded Lily. What worried her most was Christian Smith's threat to expose the family scandal in his newspaper. She dared not tell her brothers. Matt was a fair man but he had a temper when roused, as did the normally easy-going Mark. She knew instinctively that any attempts to suppress the story or threats on Christian's person would only make matters worse. Luke was the diplomat of the family, but she doubted whether his gentle nature would stand up to Christian's bullying ways. Drifting off to sleep eventually, she realised that there was only one course open to her. Gabriel had given her his card; tomorrow morning, when everyone went about their daily business or slept off the excesses of the previous night, she would visit Gower Street and hope to find him at home. He was a man of the world, and he might know how to put a stop to the story before it became public knowledge.

'This is a respectable house. I don't allow my gentlemen to entertain females on my premises.'

Lily shifted from one foot to the other as she stood on the doorstep of Gabriel's lodging house. It had taken much longer to walk to Gower Street than she had estimated, and the sky was heavy with the threat of more snow to come. The landlady, a tall thin woman with a face that showed traces of past good looks worn into lines by hard work and ill temper, barred the entrance like Cerberus at the gates of hell. Her tight-lipped cynical expression suggested that she viewed the whole world with distrust, and young unattached females in particular.

'If you please, ma'am,' Lily said humbly, 'could you ask Mr Faulkner to spare me a few minutes out here in the street? What I have to say to him won't take long.'

'I don't hold with artists and models. We all know what they get up to in private. I suppose you are one of them.' The emphasis on the word *them* was accompanied by a sarcastic sneer.

'I'm neither, ma'am. In fact I'm related to Mr Faulkner,' Lily said, adding truthfully, 'in a way.'

'They all say that. Mr Faulkner has sisters aplenty, and cousins too. Now be on your way before I call a constable.'

Lily glanced over her shoulder as she felt the eyes of passers-by boring into her back. She knew she was blushing but it was from embarrassment and not guilt. She could tell by the landlady's intractable stare that she was not going to get past her, but then she remembered Christian Smith and she was desperate. 'Gabriel,' she shouted. 'If you are in there please come out. It's Lily.'

'Well, I never,' the landlady exclaimed, bristling. 'The brass neck of the girl.' She was about to slam the door when Gabriel materialised beside her as if by magic.

'Lily, my dear little sister. I thought I recognised your voice.'

'Is this one of your tales, Mr Faulkner?'

Gabriel edged past her. 'Mrs Lovelace, would I lie to you?'

'Frequently, sir.'

'I'm mortified that you think so little of me.' Gabriel beckoned to Lily. 'Come inside out of the cold.'

Lily needed no second bidding, and she stepped into the entrance hall.

Mrs Lovelace regarded them with a quirk of her pencil-thin eyebrows. 'If this young person is your sister you may take her into the front parlour.'

'You are a wonderful woman, Mrs Lovelace,' Gabriel said, throwing the door open. 'Could I presume on your good nature a little further and request a tray of coffee? My sister looks perished.'

'If you insist.' Mrs Lovelace stalked off, the tilt of her head and twitch of her shoulders radiating disapproval as she disappeared into the dim recesses of the house. Lily entered the parlour, wrinkling her nose at the smell of camphor and lavender oil.

'It is a bit strong, isn't it?' Gabriel said, chuckling. 'Dear Mrs Lovelace has declared war on moths. Every piece of cloth in the house is soaked in camphor or lavender oil and sometimes both.' He pulled up a chair upholstered in green velvet, the colour, Lily noted, of the slime on the stone steps leading down to the river. She perched on the chair, blinking as her eyes grew accustomed to the gloomy interior of the room. Dark green velvet curtains were drawn across the windows and Lily found herself wondering if Mrs Lovelace had a dislike of daylight as well as moths, but even in the twilight room it was obvious that her devotion to cleanliness was carried out with religious fervour. The heavy furniture stood self-consciously on the polished floorboards like visitors to a museum standing before strange artefacts from foreign lands. The mantelshelf was heavily draped with matching velvet and crowded with ugly china ornaments. A fire was laid in the grate with the kindling set in a rigid pattern but it remained unlit, and the temperature in the room was little warmer than that outside.

Lily felt ill at ease but Gabriel seemed to sense her discomfort and he strode across the room to open the curtains, dodging the stiff-backed chairs and a whatnot crammed with figurines and topped with an aspidistra. A cold white light flooded the room, making it appear even chillier and less appealing than before. He moved swiftly to the fireplace and struck a vesta, igniting the tightly curled newspapers and sending flames licking round the kindling and lumps of shiny black coal. 'There, that will catch in a few minutes and make things more cheery.' He turned to Lily with eyebrows raised. 'What is it, Lily? Something dire must have occurred to bring you all the way to Gower Street.'

'Is it true?' Lily demanded. 'Are you Everard Faulkner's son?'

His lips twitched. 'It's no secret. We share the same name.'

'It's not funny, and you haven't answered my question.'

'I'm sorry. I didn't mean to offend you, and yes, it is true.'

'Why didn't you tell me that at the outset?'

He pulled up a chair and sat down beside her, leaning forward with his hands on his knees and a serious expression on his face. 'I didn't want to scare you off. I realised that you knew almost nothing about Charlotte's way of life, and I saw how her desertion had affected your whole family.'

'But you asked me to visit her all the same.'

'Perhaps I shouldn't have done that, and maybe I ought not to have told her that I'd met you by chance, but I believe she's sincere in her desire to make amends for leaving her family.'

Lily shook her head. 'I'm not sure that's possible, Gabriel. How did you come to terms with what happened?'

'I was upset at the time, and at first I would have nothing to do with my father or with Charlotte, but over the years I suppose I've grown accustomed to their unconventional lifestyle.'

'So what changed?'

'I grew up, and I realised that my parents had endured a loveless marriage. I stopped blaming my father for falling in love with another woman, and I accepted the fact that they were living their lives as they wanted, even though they were frowned on by society in general.'

She was silent for a moment as she considered this statement. Her own family had not been so generous and she herself had condemned her mother without ever wondering what had led her to abandon her family. She raised her eyes and found Gabriel staring at her with understanding and compassion, as though he could read her thoughts and sympathised with her dilemma.

'It's hard, isn't it?' he said softly. 'And you were obviously much younger than I when it all happened.' He laid his hand on her arm but withdrew it hastily as the door opened and a chubby-cheeked servant girl entered the room carrying a tray. He leapt to his feet and took it from her. 'Thank you, Mary.'

A rosy blush suffused her freckled face and she bobbed a curtsey. 'You're welcome, Mr Gabriel. Can I get you anything else?'

He glanced down at the white china coffee pot and matching cups and saucers. 'Some sugar perhaps, Mary. Or is Mrs Lovelace economising again?'

Mary stared up at him devotedly but blankly. 'I dunno what econo-whatever you said it was is, sir.'

'Never mind,' Gabriel said, setting the tray down on a spindly mahogany tea table. 'I'm sure we can do without.'

Mary cast a curious sidelong glance at Lily. 'Yes, sir.'

'That will be all then, thank you.' Gabriel held the coffee pot poised over a cup. 'You may go, Mary.'

She backed towards the doorway, blushing and grinning until she very nearly lost her footing as she encountered a stubborn chair. She bobbed another curtsey and fled from the room.

Lily held back her laughter until the door had closed on the unfortunate maid. 'She's gone spoons on you, Gabriel.'

He smiled modestly. 'I have that effect on all women, especially young girls fresh from the country like young Mary.'

'She'll learn,' Lily said, chuckling. 'One day she'll

see through your boyish charm and she'll fall in love with the milkman or the butcher's boy.'

'I certainly hope so. I wouldn't want to be responsible for breaking a young maiden's heart.' He held her gaze briefly as he handed her a cup of coffee. 'I'm sorry about the absence of sugar.'

'It's a luxury we often go without nowadays.' She bit her lip, wishing that she had held her tongue. She had not come here for sympathy or to underline their impoverished state. She changed the subject. 'I must go soon. No one knows that I came here today and I don't want them to find out.'

'There's something else bothering you, I can tell. You can trust me, Lily.'

She sipped her coffee, giving herself time to think. 'That reporter, the one who wrote about the fire.'

Gabriel angled his head. 'Lily in the Flames.'

'Yes, that's the one. His name is Smith, Christian Smith, although he doesn't behave in a very Christian way.'

'What's he done? If he's pestering you, Lily . . .'

The coffee cup jiggled on its saucer as her hand trembled. 'Hear me out, please, Gabriel.'

'I'm sorry, but I seem to remember sending him off with a flea in his ear.'

'Yes, you did, but he won't take no for an answer. He's determined to ruin my family and I don't know what to do.'

'Ruin you? I don't understand. You'd better start at the beginning.'

Placing her cup and saucer back on the tray, Lily struggled to regain her composure. She took a deep breath and began at the point when Christian had waylaid her in the snowstorm. Gabriel listened attentively. 'You must be careful, Lily,' he said when she came to the end of her narrative. 'Whatever you tell this man will be twisted to suit his own ends. You don't have to speak to him at all.'

'But if I refuse to cooperate he says he will write his story anyway, and he'll say awful things about my grandpa. I can't let him do that, and I daren't tell Matt or Mark because they'll be furious with me for disobeying them and it's all my fault anyway.' She bit back a sob and was fumbling for a handkerchief when Gabriel produced one from his pocket. He pressed it into her hand.

'How is it your fault? You've done nothing wrong.'

She blew her nose in the clean white cotton that smelt of expensive soap with a hint of gentlemen's spicy cologne. 'I h-have,' she sobbed, unable to stem the flow of tears. 'I've disobeyed my brothers and Nell by going out sketching and painting when I should have been working, and if I'd been doing what I should have then I wouldn't have tripped over you on the quay wall.' She mopped her eyes and sniffed as she struggled to control her emotions.

'Well, I for one am very glad that we met and it could have happened in any of a hundred different ways. Besides which, Lily, you are a grown woman, not a little girl. You don't have to do everything your family says. In fact I truly believe that you were right in defying their ridiculous edict.' He took her hand and held it in a firm grasp. 'You have talent and it would be a sin to deny that gift. You should nurture it, my dear girl, and not turn yourself into a drudge just to please your brothers and sisters. You are a person in your own right and you must always remember that.'

She met his earnest gaze with a reluctant smile. 'I love my brothers, especially Luke, but I wish Matt and Mark were more like you, Gabriel. I would be proud to have you as a brother.'

He pulled a face as he released her hand. 'I'm not sure if that's a compliment or not, but I'll take it as one. I'm more used to young ladies swooning at my feet than telling me I'm like a brother to them.'

His comic expression made her laugh and she shook her head. 'Now you're teasing me.'

'At least I've made you smile.'

'Yes, and I feel better for telling you my problems, but it's something I have to sort out for myself.' She rose to her feet, and realising that she was still clutching his hanky she offered it to him, but he shook his head.

'Keep it, I've got a dozen of the wretched things. I have an elderly aunt who gives them to me each year on my birthday.'

Lily smiled and tucked it away in her reticule. 'Thank you for listening so patiently but I really must go. It's a long walk to Cock Hill.'

He rose to his feet and went to the window. 'It's snowing again. You can't walk home in this, Lily. I'll go out and find a cab.' He paused, his attention seemingly caught by something on the far side of the street. 'Lily, come here. Is that who I think it is?'

Chapter Twelve

'Oh no,' Lily gasped. 'It's that dreadful man. He must have followed me here.'

'I'll sort him out,' Gabriel said angrily. 'Wait here, I won't be long.'

She caught him by the hand. 'No, please don't go out there. You'll only make things worse. He's a nasty, horrible person and means to ruin my family.'

Gabriel's eyes twinkled with merriment. 'I'm not afraid of nasty men and you mustn't be either. I'm your surrogate brother, don't forget, Lily, and brothers should protect their sisters. I don't speak from experience as I was an only child, but I won't allow him to upset you.'

'It's not for myself that I'm worried,' she insisted. 'Christian Smith wants to get his own back on my grandpa, and I truly believe he'll stop at nothing. Now I've made things worse by coming here and the next thing you know he'll be paying a call on Ma and your father.'

'My dear girl, they're used to dealing with the gentlemen of the press. They thrive on publicity because it sells paintings and they revel in being labelled bohemians.'

'I think he's seen us,' Lily said, hiding behind Gabriel

as Christian squinted at them through the driving snow. He made a move to cross the road and she tugged at Gabriel's arm. 'He's coming this way. What shall I do?'

'Keep calm and we'll slip out through the back door.' Gabriel propelled her gently towards the doorway and out into the hall. Taking her cloak from the hallstand he wrapped it around her shoulders. 'I'll see you home, Lily. I'm not letting you do this alone.' He snatched a greatcoat from its peg and shrugged it on. He took his hat and gloves and an umbrella, brandishing it with a boyish grin. 'If all else fails I'll impale the wretched fellow on the end of my gamp.'

Lily giggled in spite of her jangled nerves. 'That I would like to see.'

He took her by the arm. 'Come on then, Miss Larkin. Forward into battle, Christian soldiers go.'

'You are funny,' Lily said, giggling.

'Yes, I'm a laugh a minute. No one takes me seriously.' He led her through the house and down the back stairs, where at the end of a long narrow passageway a door opened into a small back garden. The sound of horses neighing and the smell of the stables emanated from the mews on the other side of a high brick wall, and Lily could see the roof of a private carriage with a coachman perched on the driver's seat. This, she thought, was a totally different place to the rough and tumble of Cock Hill. She clung to Gabriel's arm as they made their way carefully across the snow-covered grass, leaving a tell-tale trail of footprints like ugly blemishes on an otherwise porcelain complexion. He opened the gate. 'We'll cut through the back alleys. We'll be sure to find a cab in Tottenham Court Road.'

She hesitated, biting her lip. 'I think I'd rather walk.'

'It's still snowing. You'll be soaked to the skin and frozen before you've got halfway home.'

She did not want to admit that she could not afford the cab fare and she shook her head. 'Even so . . .'

'Naturally I'm coming with you. I said I'd see you safely home and I wouldn't dream of asking a lady to pay the cabby. It would make me look like a gigolo.'

Tempted almost irresistibly by the prospect of a comfortable ride in a hansom, Lily had a vision of Matt's face if she arrived home accompanied by Gabriel. Alone she might manage to slip into the building unnoticed, but stepping out of a cab would draw attention to herself and her companion. She realised that Gabriel was watching her intently but she still could not bring herself to admit the truth. 'I wouldn't want to risk your reputation,' she said, forcing her cold lips into a smile. 'Besides which I love the snow, and walking is good for the complexion.'

'Very well, I can't force your to come for a carriage ride with me, but I hope you're wearing a stout pair of boots.'

'Yes, I'm perfectly fine.' She was not going to admit that every step she took let in a little more icy water through gaping holes in the soles of her boots. She had intended to take them to the cobbler but there had simply been too much to do since their hasty departure from the dockmaster's house. 'Point me in the right direction, and I'll be home in no time at all.'

'I'll walk with you part of the way,' he said firmly. 'I need some fresh air.' He settled his top hat on his head with a firm pat and tucked her hand in the crook of his arm. He frowned. 'Where are your gloves, Lily? Did you leave them in my lodgings?'

'I forgot to wear any.' She omitted to say that Molly had borrowed her one and only pair and had not returned them.

He slipped off his fine kid gloves and slipped them over her fingers. 'My dear little sister, you need a nanny to look after you.'

Lily looked at her small hand swamped by the soft black leather and she laughed. 'I need a nanny with much smaller hands than yours.'

He peeled off his other glove and gave it to her. 'Never mind how it looks. You must look after those talented fingers, Lily. An artist is like a concert pianist when it comes to their hands.'

'An artist?' She looked up at him in amazement. 'Do you really think I'm good enough to warrant that title?'

He held her arm as they walked along the snowy pavements. 'I think that given the right tuition you could be an even better painter than your mother, and she is well respected in the art world.'

'Is she?' Lily cast him a sideways glance. 'I don't know, you see. No one ever speaks of her at home and anyway we don't move in those circles. Ma's family was said to be a cut above the Larkins, but they'd lost all their money when they fled from France. Grandpa said she was lucky to have married a man like Pa, who was prepared to work hard to keep his wife and children, but it didn't seem to be enough for her.'

Gabriel squeezed her fingers. 'That's just the way it goes sometimes, Lily. My parents were ill-matched like so many others who are forced to stay together either by convention or necessity. It makes me wary of entering into the marriage stakes. I've seen too much misery caused by that particular institution.'

Lily slipped and almost lost her footing on a particularly icy patch and she would have fallen if Gabriel had not caught her round the waist. He stopped, peering into the driving snow. 'This is ridiculous. I'm hailing a cab whether you like it or not. You'll break an arm or a leg if you try to walk all the way home in a snowstorm.' He raised his hand to attract the attention of a cabby but there was a passenger on board and the hansom tooled past at a surprisingly brisk pace considering the state of the road.

'There's no need really,' Lily said anxiously. 'I can find my way perfectly well and I must get home before I'm missed.'

'It must have taken you an hour or more to walk here. Didn't you tell anyone you were going out?'

'No, because they would have stopped me. It's taken me much longer than I thought it would, which makes it all the more important for me to leave now.'

'If you think I'm going to let you walk all that way in weather like this, then you're mistaken.' Gabriel hailed another cab and this one also drove past them. 'This is madness. Your teeth are chattering nineteen to the dozen and your nose is turning blue.' Without waiting for an answer he took her by the hand, walking on at a brisk pace.

'Where are we going?' Lily demanded breathlessly. 'Gabriel, I must go home.'

'You'll die of pneumonia if we don't get you dry and warm. It's not far to go and we'll kill two birds with one stone, so to speak.'

Breathless and having to concentrate on keeping upright in the slippery conditions, Lily had no alternative but to allow him to lead her through the streets. The snow was falling in earnest now, obliterating landmarks and swirling around them in dizzying circles increasing in intensity as a wind roared in with the tide. 'Where are we going, Gabriel? I don't recognise this place.'

'Save your breath, Lily, 'we're almost there.' He led her on for another hundred yards or so until he came to a halt outside one of the tall terraced houses in a well-to-do street. He knocked on the door, hooking his arm protectively around her shoulders in an attempt to shield her from the blizzard that howled around the houses like a screaming banshee.

'Who lives here?' Lily asked tentatively, although even before the door opened she knew the answer.

'Good day, Mr Gabriel.' A prim housemaid bobbed a curtsey, but her formal tone belied the cheeky grin on her pert face. 'Come in, sir.'

Ushering Lily in before him, Gabriel stepped into the entrance hall. 'Are they at home, Prissy?'

'Yes, sir. Shall I tell them you're here?'

'No, we'll surprise them.' Gabriel divested himself of his hat and greatcoat, placing them in the maid's outstretched hands. He helped Lily off with her cloak, taking his gloves from her cold fingers with a smile. 'Don't be afraid, little sister. They won't bite you.'

'I'm not ready for this,' Lily said in an undertone as she untied her bonnet.

'Let me take your wet things, miss,' Prissy said, smiling. 'I'll get Cook to hang them on the airer above the range.'

'Thank you, Prissy.' Gabriel moved towards the staircase that rose in an elegant curve to the first floor. He beckoned to Lily. 'You can sit in the hall if you wish, Lily, but I'm going upstairs to the drawing room.'

She moved slowly, like a sleepwalker. She wanted to turn and run, and yet she desired nothing more than to see her mother. The conflicting emotions made her knees feel as though they had turned to jelly, and she stumbled as she reached the foot of the stairs. She would have fallen but Gabriel caught her in his arms, setting her back on her feet with a sympathetic smile. 'Come on, be brave. It won't hurt, I promise.'

She allowed him to lead her up the thickly carpeted staircase. The walls were papered in fashionable William Morris prints that Lily had seen and admired in magazines. If she had not been so nervous she might have stopped to study the oil paintings in their heavy gilded frames, but they were little more than a colourful blur to her eyes.

'My father did most of these,' Gabriel said, as if sensing her unspoken question. 'Some of them are your

228

mother's, and there are many more in their studio on the top floor.'

'I'm not sure about this,' Lily whispered. 'I really should leave now.'

He paused as he reached the first floor landing. 'I'll send Perks with a message telling them not to worry.'

'They mustn't know I'm here.'

'Are you afraid of your brothers, Lily?'

'No, of course not, but they'll be hurt and angry. They'll think I've betrayed them.'

'That's ridiculous. You're entitled to see your own mother, and there's nothing they can do or say to alter the fact.' He crossed the floor in two strides and opened the door into the drawing room. 'Cara,' he proclaimed loudly, 'I have a visitor for you.'

Lily stood poised for flight. Her instinct was to run to her mother, but a small voice in her head warned her of the consequences, insisting that she should turn tail and retreat before she took a step that might tear her family apart for the second time.

'Lily.' Gabriel held the door open, beckoning to her.

Her heart was beating so fast that she felt quite dizzy as she entered the spacious room. Cold north light poured in through three tall windows and a coal fire blazed in the grate, but Lily was only dimly aware of her surroundings. She moved slowly to stand beside Gabriel, but her attention was fixed on the elegant figure reclining on a chaise longue. Even though she had not seen her mother for ten years, Lily could have picked her out in the midst of a crowd. Charlotte's abundant Titian hair was confined loosely by a green satin ribbon that almost exactly matched her eyes. Her long limbs were barely concealed by a velvet robe richly embroidered in gold thread, open to the waist to reveal a filmy gown, frilled and ruffled in a romantic style that was reminiscent of a bygone era.

'Mama. It's me, Lily.'

Everard Faulkner turned away from the window where he had been looking out into the snowstorm. A haze of cigar smoke wafted up towards the ceiling as he took a small black cheroot from his lips. He stared at Lily in amazement. 'By God, it's you all over again, Cara.'

Charlotte rose to her feet in one sinuous movement to glide across the Persian carpet with her arms outstretched and her garments flowing around her in a diaphanous cloud. 'My own darling Lily. My little girl.'

Before she had a chance to react, Lily found herself clasped in a fond embrace and a cloud of expensive perfume heavy with tuberose, bergamot and jasmine. 'Mama,' she murmured, at a loss for anything better to say.

Charlotte held her at arm's length, gazing at Lily as if she would like to eat her. 'My own little girl. How you've grown, my darling. You were a skinny little creature all spindly limbs and bright red curls when I was torn from the bosom of my family, and now look at you.'

'I say, steady on, old girl,' Everard protested. 'As I recall there wasn't too much tearing involved. As I recall you galloped off like a filly at the beginning of a race. You couldn't get away from that dreary house quick enough . . .'

'Oh shut up, Everard,' Charlotte said good-naturedly.

'It was a traumatic time for us all, and I shed copious amounts of tears on leaving my beloved children.'

'I didn't notice you being too upset when we left on the boat train for Paris,' Everard said with a wry smile.

'Darling, don't be horrid.' With one arm draped around Lily's shoulders, Charlotte blew him a kiss. 'I suffered in silence, if you must know.'

'Do you ever do anything in silence, Cara?' Gabriel asked with a mischievous twinkle in his eyes.

'Don't tease me, you bad boy.' Charlotte drew Lily over to the chaise longue and pressed her down on the seat. 'Everard, sweetheart, ring for Prissy and order some champagne. We must celebrate the reunion of mother and daughter. I might even make a painting of it, with myself as model of course and my dearest Lily sitting at my feet.'

'Gazing up at you with adoring eyes,' Gabriel added, winking at Lily.

She looked away, catching her breath on a sob. 'You broke my heart when you run off like that, Ma.'

'Ran off, darling. Don't you remember anything I taught you?'

'I remember how the house went quiet when you left. You took the laughter with you, and nothing was the same again.' Lily searched in her reticule for the handkerchief that Gabriel had given her. She blew her nose.

'Stop that at once, Lily,' Charlotte said, frowning. 'You'll make yourself look a perfect fright and you know I can't stand to look at ugly things.'

'Have a heart, dearest,' Everard said mildly. 'Can't you see the poor child is upset?'

'As am I, dearest.' Charlotte reached for a silver vinaigrette and flicked it open, wafting it beneath her nose. 'A mother's heart is a delicate thing and easily bruised if not broken. I think that will be the subject of my next painting, with myself as the bereaved mother, of course.'

Gabriel tugged at the bell pull. 'Heavens above, Cara. Can't you think of anyone but yourself? Lily is the injured party here.'

Charlotte dropped the vinaigrette; her lips trembled and teardrops sparkled on the tips of her long eyelashes. 'My poor baby girl.' She wrapped her arms around Lily, rubbing her cheek against her hair. She drew away with an exaggerated shudder. 'Good heavens, child, you smell like a chimney sweep's boy.'

Lily leapt to her feet, glaring at her mother as she tried desperately to control an alarming jumble of emotions. 'So would you if you lived above the fire station and a tobacconist's shop, and had no water to wash with because the pump in the stable yard was frozen solid.'

Charlotte recoiled visibly. 'There's no need to take that tone with me, Lily. I remember very well what it was like to live in that old ruin of a house so close to the river that it practically floated at high tide.'

'We don't live there any more,' Lily cried passionately. 'We were forced to leave, and now we live crammed into two miserable rooms.'

'That's unfortunate,' Everard said, clearing his throat. 'Bad show.'

Gabriel stared at Charlotte with a frown puckering his brow. 'You have no idea how your family have

232

been living, Cara. I've seen the place and you wouldn't house your pet pug dog in those dismal rooms.'

She clutched her head with both hands. 'Stop, stop. You're bringing on one of my heads.' She paused as someone rapped on the door. 'Enter.'

Prissy breezed into the room with a broad grin on her face. 'You rang, missis.'

'Ma'am,' Charlotte said wearily. 'How many times must I tell you that, you stupid country wench?'

'It's all right, Prissy.' Gabriel gave her an encouraging smile. 'Ask Cook to show you where to find the champagne and which glasses to bring.'

Prissy's full lips had trembled visibly at Charlotte's brusque tone but she smiled again and bobbed a curtsey. 'Yes, master. Right away. Toot sweet as me dad says.'

'Thank you, Prissy.' Gabriel closed the door behind her as she gambolled out of the room like an eager puppy. 'She means well, Cara. Have a little patience with the poor child. She's new to city ways.'

'Oh, heavens!' Charlotte reclined against the buttoned back of the chaise longue with a martyred expression. 'One cannot get good servants these days. I was just saying the very same thing to dear Effie Millais.'

Not wanting to incur another rebuke for being ignorant, Lily cast a questioning look in Gabriel's direction. He raised his eyebrows with a resigned sigh. 'Save your name-dropping for people who are easily impressed, Cara. Lily has had little chance to become acquainted with the art world, and the fact that she has pursued her talent at all is a great credit to her.'

'I'm sure I don't know what you mean,' Charlotte

said, pouting. 'I was simply speaking of a personal friend.' She leaned forward, gazing intently at Lily. 'Effie is the wife of John Everett Millais, a very well-respected artist and a personal friend. Everard and I move in exalted circles now, my dear. I was so very bored with firemen and the smell of the docks.'

'Your sons are firemen and proud of it,' Lily said sharply. 'Matt, Mark and Luke risk their lives daily to save others. They are brave and true and you shouldn't speak of them like that.'

'Dear Matt,' Charlotte mused. 'He must be quite grown up now. He was always such a serious boy, and then there was Mark who always made me laugh and poor Luke who as I recall cried rather a lot.'

Lily was incensed by this casual reference to her brothers. She loved them dearly even if their mother did not. 'My brothers are fine men, but you hurt them deeply, which is why I am forbidden to paint because they fear I will turn out like you.'

'I say, steady on, old thing.' Everard moved swiftly to Charlotte's side and clasped her hand in his. 'Your mother has had a shock today, seeing you again after all this time, Lily. Let's take things slowly so that you two can get to know each other again with no recriminations.'

'She has every right to feel as she does, Father,' Gabriel said, laying his hand on Lily's arm in a protective gesture. 'And as for you, Cara, you wanted me to bring her here, so I think you could be a little more sensitive to her feelings. She will have to face her family when she gets home and they won't make things easy for her.'

'It's all right, Gabriel,' Lily said with a grateful smile.

'I didn't want to come here today, but now I'm glad I did because it will make the separation from my mother easier to bear.'

Charlotte uttered a moan and closed her eyes. 'Tell her not to be so cruel, Everard.'

'I am not the one who is cruel, Ma. I didn't abandon my children to run off with a married man.'

'Now that's a bit harsh,' Everard protested.

Charlotte held up her hand. 'No, let her speak, dearest. I daresay some of what she says is warranted, and I admit that I may not be the best mother in the world, but I had my reasons.' She turned her lambent gaze on Lily. 'I followed my heart. One day you might know what it is to love a man to the exclusion of everything else in life, at least I hope you do, and then you will understand your mama and forgive her.' She covered her eyes with her hand. 'I feel faint.'

Everard threw himself down on the sofa to take her in his arms. 'My poor darling,' he crooned, rocking her like a baby. 'Don't cry, my love.'

'Crocodile tears, Cara,' Gabriel said angrily. 'Lily and her siblings are the ones who suffered as a result of your actions, and I think you owe them all an apology.'

'I am unwell,' Charlotte moaned. 'Are you going to allow your son to speak to me in that tone, Everard?'

'That was a bit harsh, old boy,' Everard murmured, casting a worried glance at his son. 'Say no more, please. Can't you see how hard this is for Cara?'

'I should go now,' Lily said, making for the door. 'You should never have sent for me, Ma. I would rather have kept my childish memories of you.'

'No, wait,' Charlotte cried, pushing Everard aside and leaping up from the chaise longue with amazing agility for one who moments before had professed faintness. She rushed over to Lily and enveloped her in a maternal hug. 'Don't leave like this, child. I did want to see you if only to tell you that you must not hide your talent from the world as I did for so many years.' She grasped Lily by the hand. 'You have inherited my gift and I want you to use it. Never mind your brothers and sisters. What do they know of art and literature and all the finer things in life? You are the only one who has inherited my talent, so don't waste it, Lily. I beg of you don't listen to Matt, who is his father all over again. Follow your heart, my dear girl.'

Breathless and almost swamped by her mother's passionate words and heady perfume, Lily was temporarily speechless. She looked mutely to Gabriel for help and he gently disengaged Charlotte's clutching hand and led her back to her seat. 'Perhaps I was wrong in reuniting you two,' he said softly. 'But I think it may prove to be a good thing in the end. I'll take Lily home now, Cara.'

'Yes, take her away. I'm quite exhausted with all this emotional turmoil,' Charlotte murmured, leaning her head on Everard's shoulder. 'Perhaps we will meet again in the fullness of time, Lily.'

Everard stroked her hair back from her forehead. 'There, there, sweetheart. You've been a brave darling and I'm sure that Lily will want to see her mama again very soon.' He stared at Lily with eyebrows raised as if willing her to answer in the affirmative.

'Yes, perhaps – I don't know.' Lily stumbled blindly towards the door. 'I must go now.'

'You're not walking home and that's for certain,' Gabriel said, barring her way. 'I'll send for the carriage and see you safely home. Perhaps I could explain to Matt . . .'

'No,' Lily cried hotly. 'You've done enough today, Gabriel. I don't know whether to thank you or to blame you, but you must keep away from my brothers for your own sake if not mine.'

She ran from the room, racing headlong down the staircase with Gabriel following close on her heels. He caught up with her at the foot of the stairs and swung her round to face him. 'I'm not letting you walk out into a snowstorm; it would be madness.' He glanced down at her shabby boots, exposed as she held up her skirts to avoid tripping over them. 'If I'd known what state your footwear was in I'd never have let you come this far.' He pressed her down onto a hall chair. 'Sit there and wait for me. I'm going to order the carriage and send Prissy to fetch your cloak.' Giving her a stern look, he strode off towards the stairs leading down to the basement kitchen.

Lily stared down at her boots and wriggled her toes. She could see one of her big toes peeking out through the leather upper where it had come apart from the sole. Her extremities were tingling painfully as the feeling returned to her frozen feet and fingers and the chilblains on her legs were burning fiercely. She knew she ought to refuse Gabriel's offer but the thought of walking several miles in such inclement weather was daunting and she was light-headed with hunger. It was a long time since breakfast and she had only eaten a slice of toast with a scraping of butter. She found herself thinking dreamily of the old days in the dockmaster's house when they had hot porridge for breakfast with molten pools of brown sugar to be spooned into her eager mouth. She could still taste Aggie's oxtail soup and the rich brawn made from a pig's head; boiled beef and carrots and scrag-end of lamb stew with caper sauce. All that good food had faded into memories since Aggie had lost the use of a kitchen range. Lily's stomach rumbled and she dragged her thoughts back to the present. The fact that Gabriel intended to see her home presented a problem. She decided to ask him to drop her at the top of the hill so that her brothers would not see them together. There was still the matter of thinking up a good excuse for her absence, but she would deal with that later. She stood up as Gabriel reappeared, holding her cloak. 'It's still a bit damp,' he said cheerfully. 'But we'll soon have you home and dry.'

Everard's carriage was old and the squabs were worn and shabby, but it was better than walking through the snow that had formed drifts against walls and in doorways, piling up around the bases of lamp posts and making it impossible to see where the pavements ended and the roads began. The trampling of horses' hooves and the constant traffic of carts, carriages, wagons and drays had made the roads passable but progress was slow, and dusk was falling by the time they reached Cock Hill.

'Set me down now, please,' Lily said, peering anxiously out of the window as familiar landmarks came into view.

Gabriel shook his head. 'I'm seeing you to the door, Lily.'

'No, you don't understand,' Lily said urgently. 'If Matt sees me with you I'll have to tell him everything and he'll be furious.'

'He'll be even more upset if you fall and break a bone or two.'

'I can manage. Please stop here.' She had seen light pouring from the open doors of the fire station and that must mean they were either on a shout or had just returned from one. She attempted to open the door, intending to leap out onto the road, but Gabriel caught her round her waist and drew her back onto the seat.

'Are you mad? You'll kill yourself, you silly girl.'

Lily opened her mouth to argue but the carriage had slowed down and come to a halt outside the fire station. Gabriel released her. 'I'm coming in with you and I'll explain everything to Matt.'

The door opened and Perks put the step down, holding his hand out to assist Lily to the snowy pavement where she almost collided with Matt. His face was streaked with soot and water dripped off his uniform jacket and helmet. His expression of astonishment changed into one of anger as he saw Gabriel alight from the carriage. 'What the hell is going on?' he demanded. 'Lily, I want an explanation and it had better be a good one.'

Chapter Thirteen

'I suggest we go inside,' Gabriel said in a low voice. 'Your sister is frozen and her boots leak. I'm surprised you allow her to go out in such a state.'

'Don't take that tone with me, mister. I've laid men out for less.'

'Please let me explain,' Lily said hastily, but Matt appeared not to hear her and he took a menacing step towards Gabriel, fisting his hands. 'I'll have you know that my sister is a respectable girl. Who the hell are you, anyway?'

Matt's raised voice brought Mark and Luke hurrying from the depths of the fire station. 'What's going on?' Mark came to a sudden halt as he spotted Lily. His relief was patent but was swiftly replaced by anger. 'Where've you been all day? Nell's out of her mind with worry.'

'Lily's home safe and that's all that matters.' Luke moved to her side, slipping his arm around her waist. 'Let's get you into the warm, love.'

'In a moment,' Lily said, smiling. Luke was always the comforter and the most thoughtful of her brothers but she did not want to leave Gabriel to face Matt's wrath. She turned to him with a pleading look. 'Please, Matt. It's really not what you think.'

With an obvious effort, he controlled his fiery temper. 'Go on then. Give me one good reason why I shouldn't fetch him one.'

'It's not Gabriel's fault. I went to see him . . .' Lily broke off. She could see that Matt was not listening to her.

'This is ridiculous,' Gabriel said, eyeing the brothers warily. 'Lily has done nothing wrong and neither have I. I suggest that we go indoors and discuss this like civilised human beings? I don't intend to get into a street brawl with men who bully their sisters.'

Matt grabbed him by the lapels, shaking him like a terrier with a rat. 'Say that again and I'll knock you down. You're the wrongdoer here and I've got my sister's reputation to think of.'

'Stop this, all of you,' Lily cried passionately as Mark stepped up to Matt's side, patently ready for a fight. 'I can speak for myself and it has nothing to do with Gabriel.'

'Do you deny you've been with this man all day?' Matt demanded.

'Yes. No, I mean I went to his lodgings . . .'

Mark let out a loud whistle. 'You admit that you went to a man's lodgings? What were you thinking of, Lil?'

She glanced upwards as a movement at the window caught her eye. She could see Grandpa and Aggie peering down at them. 'What was I thinking of?' Lily heard her voice rise above the sound of the traffic. 'I wanted to see Ma. There, that's the truth of it, and I went to Gabriel because he was the only one who knew where to find her.'

'You disobeyed me,' Matt roared. 'After everything that woman has done to our family you took it upon yourself to decide that it was time to forgive her.'

'You're a fool, Lily,' Mark said, shaking his head. 'Do you know what you've done?'

Luke laid his hand on Matt's shoulder. 'Come indoors, old chap. Let's talk this over quietly and sensibly.'

'Shut up,' Matt snapped. 'This is between Lily and me.'

'You can't blame her for wanting to see her mother,' Gabriel said calmly. 'And Charlotte wanted to see Lily.'

'Why don't you go away and mind your own bloody business?' Matt gave Gabriel a shove that sent him staggering back against the carriage door.

Perks cleared his throat nervously. 'Shall I send for a constable, Mr Faulkner?'

'I can handle this.' Gabriel squared up to Matt. 'Leave Lily alone and we'll have this out man to man.'

'Stop this.' Lily stepped between them. 'Gabriel has tried to help me. I wanted to see Ma again. I can't help myself, Matt. I have to paint and draw, it's in my heart and soul, and Ma is the only one who can truly understand how I feel.'

'Lily what on earth is going on?' The sound of Nell's voice made everyone turn their heads to look at her. She hurried towards them. 'Come inside, all of you. You're making a dreadful scene. People will talk.'

'And we can't let it get back to the schoolmaster or the Frenchie,' Matt said angrily. 'What's the matter with the women in my family? Are you all moon mad?'

Nell caught Lily by the hand. 'Come with me. I want

an explanation from you, miss. I've been sick with worry all day. How dare you run off without a word?'

'I'm not ten years old any more,' Lily cried, snatching her hand away. 'I'm a grown woman in case you haven't noticed. I've just explained to Matt and the boys that I wanted to see Ma, and Gabriel was the only one who could lead me to her. Is it a crime to want to see your own mother?'

Nell paled visibly. 'It is in this family, Lily. How could you be such a traitor?'

'That's just not fair, Miss Larkin,' Gabriel protested. 'I'm sure that Lily is sorry for upsetting you and for not telling you that she was coming to find me, but she's right. She's a free woman, and she knows her own mind.'

Matt pushed him aside. 'A free woman is she? Then take her with you, mate. I don't want a treacherous harlot in my house.'

'Matt,' Lily cried, scarcely able to believe her ears. 'Don't say such things.'

He eyed her coldly. 'If you want to be with Ma then you can go to her.' He thrust her into Gabriel's arms. 'And you, mister, can take her with my compliments.'

'No,' Luke cried passionately. 'This is all wrong. Lily's a good girl. She's done nothing wrong.'

'Leave it, brother,' Mark said, scowling. 'We've still got work to do. Let everyone calm down and we'll sort it out in the morning.' Casting a withering glance at Lily, he retreated into the fire station.

'Nell, say something, please,' Lily pleaded. 'Don't let him throw me out on the street.'

243

Nell was silent for a moment and then she shook her head. 'I think he's right this time, Lily. You've disobeyed us by pursuing your silly obsession with painting, and you've caused trouble ever since you accused Monsieur Labrosse of molesting you. We might still be in our old home if it weren't for you.'

'That's not fair, Nell. He did make improper advances to me and I never once encouraged him.'

'You've deceived us once too often. Why should I believe anything you say now?'

Matt nodded in agreement. 'You heard what your sister said, Lily. You wanted to be with Ma so you can go to her and see how you like living with people who have no respect for morals or decency.'

'But you can't just turn me out like this.' Lily gazed up into his angry face with a feeling close to despair. This was not the Matt she knew and loved. The furious white-lipped man was a stranger to her. She made a move towards him but he pushed her away.

'I've never struck a woman, but you're tempting me sorely. Nell's right, you've caused us too much grief to forgive you this time. You're no longer part of our family, Lily. You've chosen your side and you must stick to it.' He turned to Gabriel. 'You shouldn't have interfered with my family, mister. Now it's up to you. Take her and good luck to you.' Turning his back on them, he strode into the fire station.

Luke wrapped his arms around Lily. 'He'll get over it, Lil. Best do as he says for now and I'll try to smooth things over when he's calmed down.' He gave her a hug and hurried after Matt. The double doors of the fire station swung shut with an ominous clang.

'You will take care of her, Gabriel?' Nell said urgently. 'I can't condone what Lily has done, but I wouldn't want to think of her alone and homeless.'

'This can't be happening,' Lily murmured. 'You can't all turn against me like this.' She held her hands out to Nell in a plea for understanding and forgiveness, but her sister's face remained cold and aloof.

'Your wayward ways caused this rift. Perhaps you belong with Ma after all.' Nell walked away, disappearing into the darkness of the alleyway and leaving Lily standing on the pavement with Gabriel at her side.

Perks opened the carriage door. 'Where to, sir?'

'Keppel Street, Perks.' Gabriel helped Lily into the carriage. 'Don't worry. Cara will have forgotten your little contretemps by now. She'll be overjoyed to see you again.'

They entered the house in Keppel Street to find Charlotte dressed in her finery and Everard immaculate in an evening suit with silk-faced collar and lapels. 'Ah,' he said, smiling. 'You've arrived just in time; I was going to send Prissy for a cab.' He took his top hat and opera cloak from the maid with a nod of his head. 'Run out and tell Perks to wait. We won't be a moment.'

Bobbing a curtsey, Prissy hurried past Gabriel and Lily and ran out onto the pavement, calling to Perks. A blast of cold air was quickly eliminated as she returned immediately and closed the door.

'Fetch my mantle, Prissy,' Charlotte called over her shoulder. 'The one trimmed with sable. I must look my very best tonight.' She primped in front of a wall mirror, angling her head as she examined every detail of her elaborate coiffure. Her fiery curls were interspersed with pearls and sparkling gems, feathers and hothouse gardenias. Diamond earrings glittered with each movement of her head and a solitaire diamond gleamed from a heart-shaped gold locket hung on a black velvet ribbon around her slender throat. Lily stared in awe at her mother's magnificent gown of green watered silk with its extravagantly draped skirts emphasising her tiny waist, and a décolletage that showed off her voluptuous bosom to perfection. The candlelight softened the inevitable lines of age, and if her lips were suspiciously red and her cheeks owed some of their glow to the rouge pot, there was no denying that Charlotte Delamare Larkin was still a handsome woman.

She turned her head with a coquettish smile, having apparently forgotten everything other than the need to be admired. 'How do I look, Lily? Do you think we could pass for sisters?'

'I'd be flattered if anyone thought I looked like you, Ma,' Lily said sincerely. 'You're so beautiful.'

Charlotte held her arms out with a delighted smile curving her lips. 'My darling girl, of course you take after me.' She kissed the air close to Lily's cheek and then gently pushed her away. 'Don't crease my gown, dearest. This silk cost five and six a yard.'

'And the total cost including the bill from your

mama's dressmaker would keep a poor clerk's family for a month,' Everard said indulgently. 'But,' he added hastily as Charlotte's lips formed a moue, 'worth every penny of it as far as I am concerned.'

Charlotte blew him a kiss. 'You know you adore it when I receive compliments.' Taking her fan from the gilded table beneath the mirror she unfurled it with a flourish, holding it to cover the lower part of her face so that just her eyes were seen. She fluttered her eyelashes. 'He becomes quite jealous when I am the centre of attention, and I'm constantly being asked to pose as a model for his friends. Am I not, Everard?'

'Yes, my love. You are much in demand.'

Gabriel cleared his throat. 'This is all very well, but neither of you has thought to ask why I have brought Lily here this evening.'

Charlotte lowered her fan, closing it with a snap. 'I'm afraid we're otherwise engaged this evening, Gabriel. Perhaps another time, Lily?'

'You don't understand, Cara,' Gabriel said patiently. 'Lily needs somewhere to stay. It seems that your son Matt took exception to the fact that she came to see you today.'

'Dear Matt,' Charlotte mused. 'Always the hothead.'

'He threw her out, Cara.'

'How very like him. He, of course, takes after his father.' She turned to Prissy who had come running downstairs with a fur-trimmed mantle draped over her arm. 'Yes, that's the one. Hold it up so that I may put it on.' She made exasperated tut-tutting sounds as Prissy held the expensive garment out like a matador

247

tormenting a bull. 'Really, Everard, could we not afford a proper lady's maid for me? The child has obviously been used to dressing scarecrows.'

Prissy blushed scarlet as she fumbled with the heavy garment. 'Sorry, missis.'

'Ma'am, you silly girl. Don't you ever learn?'

Taking pity on Prissy's struggles, Lily stepped forward to assist her mother into the tight-fitting garment. 'There, you look stunning, Ma.'

'Thank you, darling, but you must learn not to use vulgar parlance if you are going to reside in Keppel Street. We don't use the language of the docks here.' She swept past Lily. 'Door, Prissy.'

Prissy ran to open it, tripping over her feet in her haste.

Everard put his top hat on at a rakish angle. 'We'll be off then. I take it you'll be toddling back to your lodgings, my boy? We don't want to cause an unnecessary scandal with an unmarried young lady all alone in the house, now do we?'

Gabriel threw back his head and laughed. 'That's rich, Father. Have you forgotten your own unconventional arrangements?'

'I have not, my boy, and it's for that reason that we must protect Lily's good name.' Everard swung his opera cloak around his shoulders with a flourish before following Charlotte out into the snowy night.

'Are you all right, Lily?' Gabriel eyed her anxiously. 'I'll stay for supper and then I must be on my way.'

She came back to earth with a start. For a moment she had been swept up in her mother's self-centred world of extravagance and hedonism, but now reality was closing in on her and she was forced to face the truth. She had been banished from home and family, and it was obvious that she mattered less to her mother than the pursuit of pleasure. She realised slowly and painfully that the reunion which she had dreamed of and longed for since childhood meant nothing to the one person who should have loved and cherished her. She was unwanted and unloved. Gabriel was waiting for an answer and she made a valiant effort to sound normal. 'I'm fine, thank you, just a little tired.'

'And wet through judging by the state of your boots and skirt,' Prissy said severely. 'You'll catch your death, miss.'

Lily turned to find the girl watching her with a concerned frown puckering her smooth brow. 'I've nothing to change into,' she said slowly as the magnitude of her position threatened to crush her. 'I came away with nothing.'

'D'you know, that's just like how I was.' Prissy put her arm around Lily's shoulders and gave her a hug. 'When me dad threw me out on the street 'cos I ate too much and weren't bringing in any money, I was quite at a loss. Our old cow had died, you see, and the hens was took by the fox. Then the harvest failed due to the rain and we was all facing starvation. I knows just how you feels, ducks.'

'Then perhaps you'd like to get a room ready for Miss Lily,' Gabriel said gently. 'And if Cook could make us some supper.'

'I'm not hungry,' Lily murmured, trying hard not to

break down and cry in front of Gabriel who had been so kind and patient all day. 'Perhaps you'd better do as your pa said and go home.'

'I'll look after her, sir,' Prissy said firmly. 'There's a fire in Mr Everard's study. He goes there to smoke a cigar or two after dinner, and have a few nips of brandy in peace and quiet without the missis nagging him.' She clapped her hand over her mouth, eyeing Gabriel warily. 'I shouldn't have let the cat out of the bag.'

He patted her on the shoulder. 'Don't worry, Prissy. I'm used to my father's little ways and I won't say a word.'

'Thank you, sir. You're a toff.' Prissy hurried to open the door. 'Shall I go out and call a cab, sir?'

'Certainly not, or you'll be the one to catch your death of cold. It's not snowing now and the walk will do me good.' Gabriel leaned over to kiss Lily lightly on the cheek. 'I'll leave you in good hands, my dear, and I'll come round first thing in the morning. We'll sort things out between us, never fear.'

'Thank you.' Lily almost choked on the words. She watched him leave the house with a feeling close to relief. At this moment all she wanted was to curl up in a warm place and go to sleep. Maybe in the morning she would find herself back in her own bed with Molly's feet on the pillow beside her as they slept top to toe. The two rooms in Cock Hill were slums when compared to this grand house, but they were home. She wondered if she would ever be welcome there again.

Prissy closed the front door. 'Now, miss, come with

me. I'll settle you down by the fire and what you need is a hot, sweet cup of tea and a bite to eat. While you're having your supper I'll light a fire in the guest room and find you one of your ma's nightgowns. Heaven knows, she's got more clothes than the Queen herself. You won't go without nothing in this house. I can promise you that.'

Lily found herself in a comfortable room lined with bookshelves. A fire burned brightly in the grate and a wingback chair was strategically placed so that the occupant could rest his feet on the brass fender. A mahogany desk was set beneath the window, but its tooled leather top was unencumbered by papers or anything to suggest that the master of the house did any serious work here. Heavy velvet curtains in a deep shade of russet kept out the cold and dark, and the scent of Havana cigars and brandy hung like a faint memory in the air. As she waited for Prissy to return Lily had time to look around. She was fascinated by the rows of books that seemed to have been chosen more for their matched leather bindings than as random purchases bought for their literary contents. She found herself thinking that Nell would love to be ensconced in a room like this with time on her own to immerse herself in all this book learning. Sighing, Lily sat down to wait for Prissy to bring her supper. She felt as though she had stepped into a dream, arriving in a world that was far removed from her own. She took a seat by the fire and sat warming her toes, watching the steam rise from her damp skirt and petticoats.

The door opened and she looked up, startled out of

her reverie by the arrival of Prissy carrying a heavily laden tray.

'There's tea and bread and butter and a slice of steak pie. Cook says it's not what she would have served to the master and mistress, but as they're dining out she thought as how you might like to share what we have for our supper.'

'Thank you, I'm sure it looks very nice but I'm not really hungry.' Lily's appetite had deserted her and the thought of food was nauseating, but she could tell by the stubborn set of Prissy's jaw that she was not going to give in easily.

'You must eat, miss. You're all skin and bone as it is and you'll fade away if you don't get some vittles inside you.' She stood with her arms folded across her chest until Lily picked up a fork and nibbled at a piece of pie. She managed to eat a little but her throat felt swollen and it was difficult to swallow. The steak pie was delicious and it reminded her of the ones that Aggie used to make for the family. The memory of meals around the kitchen table in the dockmaster's house brought tears to her eyes and created a painful ache in her heart.

'That's better,' Prissy said. 'I'll leave you to finish your meal while I go upstairs and make the room ready for you. I expect to see a clean plate when I come back.'

When she returned some time later, she scolded Lily for her lack of appetite, but when she had satisfied herself that her charge could not eat another morsel she hustled Lily out of the study and up three flights of stairs to a room on the third floor, which she assured her was the best guest room. 'There are more,' she said proudly, 'but I give you the biggest and most comfortable. I think the chimney needs sweeping in the blue room and the one at the back looks out onto the mews with all them cheeky stable boys waving and pulling faces every time a girl looks out of the window, and there are damp patches on the wall around the windows. I told the master but he said I shouldn't worry my head about such things.'

'Thank you, Prissy,' Lily said tiredly. 'I'm sure this is a lovely room and will suit me very well.'

Prissy bustled over to the fireplace and added a few more lumps of coal to the blaze. 'I've run the warming pan between the sheets. They're clean ones from the linen cupboard. The missis is very particular about bedding and you won't find no bed bugs or fleas in this house. Lord, I can remember a time when me and me brothers and sisters was nippers and our beds were alive with the little devils.'

Tiredness was sweeping over Lily in a hazy wash so that Prissy's voice seemed far away and her surroundings were a blur. All she wanted to do now was to crawl into bed and escape into a deep sleep. She must have yawned without realising it, as Prissy became suddenly businesslike. She helped her to undress, clucking and clicking her tongue against her teeth at the state of Lily's much-darned petticoats and stays with whalebones showing through their casings. 'Lord love us, miss. I got better duds than you and that's saying something. Are you very poor, miss? It don't seem right that your ma has all this and you go around like a ragbag.'

253

Lily was too exhausted to put Prissy in her place. 'I'm very tired. I think I'll go straight to bed.'

Prissy plucked a white cotton nightdress lavishly trimmed with broderie anglaise from the chair by the fire where it had been left to warm. 'This should be nice and cosy now. Lift your arms, there's a good girl.'

It was like being a child all over again but Lily had not the energy to argue. The lace-trimmed gown with voluminous sleeves and high neck was soft and warm, and obeying Prissy's instructions Lily perched on the edge of the bed while her boots and stockings were removed. Prissy dropped them on the floor with an expression of distaste. 'They can go in the dustbin,' she said severely. 'I'll go through the mistress's things as soon as you're settled in your bed. She has shoes by the dozen and drawers bursting with undergarments and silk stockings, as if she had as many legs and feet as a spider.' She chafed Lily's cold feet. 'You could do with a mustard bath for them tootsies. That's what Ma used to do for us when we was chilled to the marrow.'

'Do you miss your family, Prissy?'

'Sometimes, miss. But mostly I'm too busy and I know I'm bettering meself by living in a big house with three good meals a day and two new frocks a year. Add to that the money I save and send home and I think I'm doing pretty well.'

'You're a good girl, Prissy,' Lily murmured as she lay down on the bed, sinking into the softness of the feather mattress.

Prissy pulled the covers up to Lily's chin with a cheerful smile. 'There, look at you now, all cosy and warm. Goodnight, miss, sweet repose. Lie on your back and you won't hurt your nose. That's what Ma used to say to us when she tucked us in.'

'Your mother sounds lovely,' Lily said sleepily.

'She's an angel now. Up in heaven with the good Lord and St Peter and all that lot. She took sick and died two year ago come Lammas. We was sad at the time but we knew she wouldn't get beat no more. Me dad has a foul temper when he's a bit swipey, but then most men are like that so it seems, except for Mr Everard. Now there's a lovely gent if ever there was one.' So saying, Prissy blew out the candle on the wash-stand and crept out of the room.

Lily stared into the fire, watching the flames lick up the chimney. The sudden silence after Prissy's departure was all-encompassing. In the street below the sound of horses' hooves and the rumble of wheels was dulled by the hard-packed snow, and the bed was warm. All her life Lily had shared a room with her sisters and sleeping on her own was a new experience. Thoughts of her family and Matt's furious rejection were uppermost in her mind. She did not think she would ever sleep again. She closed her eyes.

It was still dark when the sound of someone raking the cinders in the grate awakened Lily. She snapped into a sitting position thinking that Nell was cleaning out the ashes and it should have been her turn to do so.

'Sorry, miss. I didn't mean to wake you.'

As Lily's eyes grew accustomed to the dim light of

the street lamp filtering through the window she saw Prissy kneeling in front of the hearth. 'What time is it?'

'Six o'clock, miss. I done all the other fires and left yours till last but one. I never go into the master's room until later. The mistress likes to lie abed all morning unless she's got an appointment elsewhere and she don't like to be disturbed by my noise.'

'I see.' Lily shivered and pulled the coverlet up to her chin. 'Are my clothes dry yet?'

'Your duds is in the dustbin; Mistress's orders when she come in last night. Very merry she was too, and the master. I think they had a good time judging by the noise they made going up to bed. I wonder they didn't wake you.'

Lily did not want to hear the details of her mother's private life. She changed the subject hastily. 'What am I to wear then, Prissy? I can't go about in the night-gown all day.'

Prissy's merry laughter echoed round the room. 'Oh Lor', you are a one, miss.'

'Yes, maybe, but I do need something to wear. If all else fails you must get my clothes out of the dustbin.'

Prissy turned her attention to the fire, leaning forward and puffing out her cheeks as she blew on the kindling. 'Leave it to me, miss,' she said in between breaths. 'I'll just get the fire going and then I'll fetch you a nice cup of tea. You can't get dressed until the room warms up anyway.' She scrambled to her feet, picking up the bucket filled with ashes. 'I'll be back in two shakes of a lamb's tail.'

*   *   *

Half an hour later, Lily was sitting in bed propped up on a pile of pillows while she ate her breakfast off a tray. Cook had provided two boiled eggs, a silver rack filled with triangles of toast and cut glass dishes filled with butter, strawberry preserve and orange marmalade. A separate tray with a pot of coffee and another filled with hot chocolate was set on the washstand. Unused to such luxury and finding that her appetite had returned, Lily tucked into her meal while Prissy sat in the chair by the fire sewing furiously. The silver needle seemed to fly as she stitched away at a gown belonging to Charlotte that had been discarded as being outmoded, but to Lily looked the height of elegance.

'Are you certain that Ma doesn't mind me having it?' Lily ventured, swallowing the last morsel of toast and jam. 'There looks to be years of wear left in that gown.'

Prissy snipped the thread with a satisfied smile. She held up the garment for Lily to see. 'That ain't half bad even if I say so meself. I was used to making clothes for the family so doing a few tucks ain't nothing to me.'

'You're very clever,' Lily acknowledged. 'I was never very good with a needle, whereas my sister Nell can darn so that you can hardly tell the difference and Molly is good at trimming bonnets. The only thing I'm passably good at is drawing.'

'Then you're an artist like your ma,' Prissy said with a wise nod of her head. 'I could tell you was an artist by the shape of your hands. I may not be educated like you but I got an eye for things.'

Lily put the tray aside, wiping her lips on the linen table napkin. 'I'd best get up then if the dress is ready. I'm not used to idling about in bed.'

Prissy rose from the chair and laid the dress out on the foot of the bed. 'Well, miss, there's nothing doing in this house until midday at least. The master might get up earlier but the missis sometimes don't rise until mid-afternoon. It all depends on how much they've drunk or if they've been at the laudanum or that other stuff – chloral or whatever it's called.'

'What are you saying, Prissy?'

'Nothing, miss. Maybe I was mistaken. Cook says that all them artistic types drink too much and take drugs, but I can see you don't know nothing about it and I should learn to keep me mouth shut. Talking too much is me big failing, so Cook says. I'm sorry, miss.'

Lily swung her legs over the side of the bed. 'I must get dressed now, Prissy. I have things to do and I must speak to my mother as soon as she is up and about. You will tell me when she wakes, won't you?'

'Of course I will. I'll see that you're all right, miss. You can trust me.'

Lily fingered the cotton lawn chemise that Prissy had selected for her and a pair of stays that looked brand new. She found it almost impossible to believe than anyone could possess such fine garments and not wear them. Prissy laced the stays, tugging hard and exclaiming with pride at the smallness of Lily's waist.

'Them fine ladies will be green with envy when they see you,' she said triumphantly. 'A hand's span, that's what you got, miss. I shall have to take the other gowns in several inches if they're to fit.'

'No, I can't take any more of my mother's clothes,' Lily said firmly. 'This gown is far too fine for me but I must wear something, and as my old clothes are thrown out I've little choice.' She gazed into the pier glass as Prissy endeavoured to fasten the tiny buttons down the back of the pale green silk gown. The sight that met her eyes was astounding and at first she thought she was looking at a stranger.

Prissy looked over her shoulder and grinned. 'It's true, miss. Fine feathers make fine birds as my mum used to say. You look every inch a lady and that colour don't half suit you. Mrs Stone, the mistress's dressmaker, calls it reseda. It's all the rage, so she said, and it matches your eyes a treat.'

Lily gulped and swallowed hard. That creature was not her. She was masquerading as a young lady when it was far from the truth. Molly would enjoy such a farce but she felt uncomfortable and desperately out of place. Her discomfiture seemed to have bypassed Prissy who was bursting with pride, as if she had created a princess out of a common street girl.

'Now all I got to do is find you a pair of shoes that fit and you're fit to be presented to the Queen,' Prissy said proudly. 'I'll show you downstairs to the morning parlour, miss. That's what Cook told me that young ladies do. They sit in the parlour and wait for callers, although I don't suppose anyone knows you're here apart from Mr Gabriel. Anyway, I'm sure he'll be round soon and then you can plan your day. I feel quite excited for you.'

'Thank you, Prissy.' Lily could think of nothing else to say.

The feeling of unreality persisted and continued even as she perched on the edge of a chair by the fire in the morning parlour. She felt ill at ease, as if waiting for something cataclysmic to happen although she knew not what it might be. She kept looking at the ormolu clock which was part of an ornate garniture on the mantelshelf, but the hands seemed to be stuck at half past nine. Nell would be teaching her pupils and Molly was probably up to her elbows in dye at the workshop. Matt, Mark and Luke would be asleep, having been on duty all night, and Aggie would be setting off to market, leaving Grandpa ensconced in his chair and gazing out at the street scene below. They all had their lives, but hers had been snatched from her by a cruel twist of fate. She wriggled her toes, hoping that Prissy would find a pair of stout boots so that she could walk round to Gabriel's lodging house. She could think of no one else who might be able to help her out of her present dilemma. One thing about which she was certain was that she could not remain in Keppel Street. Ma's lifestyle was not one into which she fitted with ease. Everard was a kind man but she could not expect him to support her as he might a daughter. She must find a way in which to earn her own living. It was not going to be easy.

The hands on the clock face seemed not to have moved at all. Lily rose to her feet and listened, but the inexorable tick-tock assured her that time had not come to a standstill. She paced the floor anxiously. Should she ring the bell for Prissy? It seemed a bit of a liberty to do so in someone else's house. She waited for another five minutes and then, in desperation, she was about to tug the embroidered bell-pull when the door flew open and Prissy burst into the room, her rosy cheeks a deeper shade of pink and her eyes sparkling with excitement. 'Oh, miss. You've got visitors. A pretty young lady and a handsome foreign gentleman with a limp. Shall I let them in?'

Lily was out through the door before Prissy had finished her sentence. She ran down the carpeted passage to the entrance hall to fling her arms around her sister. 'Oh, Molly, has Matt forgiven me? Have you come to take me home?'

Chapter Fourteen

'No, he hasn't, and I haven't come to take you home. For heaven's sake, Lily, let me go,' Molly cried, pushing her away. 'You're crushing me.'

Lily took a step backwards, her elation evaporating. Molly's expression was not encouraging. 'How did you know where to find me?'

'I remembered the address on that card Gabriel gave you. We went to his lodgings and asked him where you were living.' Molly cast an envious glance around the spacious entrance hall with its opulent crystal chandeliers, gilded furniture and the richly carpeted staircase sweeping upwards in an elegant arc. 'You're not exactly out on the streets, are you?'

Prissy stepped forward holding her hands out to Armand. 'Give us your hat and coat, sir, and I'll hang it on the peg.'

His worried expression melted into an amused smile as he took off his hat and gloves, handing them to Prissy while he divested himself of his overcoat. '*Merci, mademoiselle.*'

'Well I never did,' Prissy murmured, bobbing a curtsey. 'A foreigner.'

'We're not staying,' Molly said, frowning. 'It seems

we had a wasted journey, and to think that I was actually feeling sorry for you, Lily.'

'I'm glad you came.' Lily managed a tremulous smile. 'I didn't want things to turn out this way.'

'Shall I take your things then, miss?' Prissy asked, seemingly unabashed by Molly's sharp tone. 'You won't feel the benefit when you go out into the cold.'

'When I want your opinion I'll ask for it,' Molly snapped. 'Go about your business, girl.'

Lily felt the blood rush to her cheeks as she saw Prissy's bottom lip tremble ominously. 'Thank you, Prissy. I'm sure my sister didn't mean to raise her voice to you.'

'You're too soft,' Molly muttered. 'Give the girl an inch and she'll take a mile.'

Armand took Lily's hand and raised it to his lips. 'We are relieved to find you in such comfortable circumstances, Mademoiselle Lily. Molly was worried about you.'

'Unnecessarily, it seems,' Molly said with an irritated toss of her head. 'I wouldn't have come here if Luke hadn't convinced me that you would be huddled in a doorway, freezing to death. He didn't think that Ma would take you in, but obviously he was wrong.' She looked Lily up and down with a disapproving frown. 'It didn't take you long to get your feet under the table. I doubt if she'd make me as welcome, let alone dress me up like some fancy doll. You were always her favourite.'

'That's just not true,' Lily protested. 'I think Ma is genuinely sorry that she left us, and I'm sure she would be overjoyed to see you.'

'I haven't got your cheek. I work hard to earn my living. I don't play with paints and paper and pretend to be an artist. Maybe Matt was right when he said you were the cause of all our troubles.' Molly slipped her hand through the crook of Armand's arm. 'I think we'd best leave now, Armand. We've done our duty.'

'Come, come, that's not fair, Molly, *ma chérie*,' Armand said gently. 'Lily is here because she had no other choice. I feel responsible in some way for that.'

'Don't be ridiculous. How could it possibly be your fault?'

'My father is a man of passion. He allowed his admiration for so beautiful a young lady to carry him away, and for that I am ashamed and regretful.'

'You can't blame yourself for anything your father did,' Lily said, wishing that Armand had not raised the subject which was both embarrassing and painful to her. 'It wasn't your fault.'

'I was a guest in your home, Lily. I brought the trouble to your door, so to speak, and now I wish to make amends.' He winced as an awkward movement seemed to cause him pain from his injured leg.

'Are you going to keep us standing in the hall?' Molly demanded. 'If we're not leaving right away then you might ask us in. Anyway, Armand shouldn't be putting too much strain on his bad leg.'

'Yes, what am I thinking of?' Lily turned to find Prissy taking her time arranging Armand's coat on the hallstand as she listened to their exchanges with an expression of avid interest. 'Would it be possible to bring some refreshments to the morning parlour,

Prissy? My sister and Monsieur Labrosse have come a long way to see me.'

'You don't ask her,' Molly hissed. 'She's a servant. You give her orders.'

Prissy beamed at Lily. 'That's right, miss. I'm here to look after you. What shall it be? Sherry wine, tea or coffee perhaps?'

Lily was at a loss. She gazed helplessly at Armand, but Molly seemed determined to have her say. 'We'd like coffee and cake. Be quick about it.' She dismissed Prissy with an airy wave of her hand. 'There, you see, that wasn't too difficult, was it, Lily? You have to know how to handle servants or they'll take advantage of you.'

'Prissy has been very kind to me,' Lily protested. 'She's a nice girl and I don't think you should speak to her like that.'

'Never mind her. I'm fed up with standing in this draughty hallway. Besides which I want to see more of Ma's house since it's probably the only chance I'll ever get.'

Helpless in the face of her sister's determination, Lily pointed in the general direction of the morning parlour. 'The second doorway on your left.'

'Come on then. Don't stand there like a couple of wet ducks in a thunderstorm.' Molly stalked off towards the morning parlour, pausing to examine one of the many oil paintings that adorned the walls, but apparently unimpressed, she moved on, entering the room without a backwards glance.

Armand hesitated. 'Are you sure we will be welcome

in this house, Lily? I don't want to make things difficult for you with your mama.'

'She isn't an ogre, Armand. Whatever Molly thinks,
Mama has welcomed me as she would all her family.
I believe she is truly sorry for the way things turned
out. I'd like you to meet her and Everard too.'

'I'm glad for your sake, and maybe good will come
out of bad,' he said softly. 'You have broken the ice, as
you English say, and perhaps because of it your family
will now be reconciled.'

'I do hope so, Armand. I can't bear to think that I
am unwelcome in my own home.'

Molly popped her head round the door. 'What are
you two going on about? Didn't your ma ever tell you
it's rude to whisper, Armand Labrosse?'

Lily glanced anxiously at Armand and was relieved
to see that he did not seem to have taken exception to
Molly's sharp words. He smiled indulgently. 'The little
briar rose is growing impatient. Come, Lily, lead me
to the parlour and we will sit down and talk. I think
I may have a solution to your problems.'

'I heard what you said and I am not a briar rose,'
Molly said sulkily as they joined her in the morning
parlour. She flounced over to a chair by the fire,
throwing off her cape and sitting down to peel off her
gloves. 'I think it's horrid of you to call me that,
Armand. It makes me sound wild and full of thorns.'

'It is part of your charm, *ma chérie*,' Armand said
smoothly. 'But now if you will be patient for a few
moments longer, I will tell you my plan.' He paused
as the door was pushed open and Prissy entered,

266

carrying a tray which she placed on a table by the window. 'Coffee,' she said importantly. 'And some of Cook's best Madeira cake.' She glanced over her shoulder at Lily. 'Shall I pour, miss?'

'It's all right, Prissy,' Lily said, hurrying to rescue the heavy silver coffee pot held precariously in Prissy's small hand. 'I'll do it, and thank you.'

'No trouble, miss.' Prissy shot a darkling look at Molly. 'Let me know if she gets above herself and I'll stand up for you. I met her sort afore.'

'Yes, thank you,' Lily said hastily. 'I'll ring if I need anything else.'

Prissy winked at her and sashayed slowly past Molly, eyeing her as if she had plenty to say but was holding her tongue with difficulty. She left the room, closing the door firmly behind her.

'You must keep her at arm's length,' Molly said severely as Lily handed her a cup of coffee. 'Put her firmly in her place.'

Pushed beyond endurance, Lily glared at her sister. 'Since when did you know all about handling staff?'

'Well, there's Aggie. She's a servant.'

An image of Aggie's indignant face flashed into Lily's mind, forcing a reluctant smile. 'Don't ever let her hear you say that, Molly. She'd box your ears for less. Aggie is one of the family and you know it.'

Molly dismissed this with a careless shrug of her shoulders. She turned a sulky face to Armand. 'Are you going to put us out of our misery and tell us your grand plan, or do I have to sit here and take insults from my sister?'

'I'm sorry, Armand,' Lily said, handing him a brimming cup of coffee. 'Here we are bickering like schoolgirls and you have something important to tell us.'

'As I said, I feel partly to blame for everything that has happened to your family recently. If it weren't for you I might have died on the foreshore during that terrible fire.'

'It was nothing,' Lily murmured, sensing Molly's annoyance that she had had no part in the events of that fateful day.

'No, you are wrong, Lily,' Armand declared passionately. 'You took me into your home and you and your sister nursed me back to good health.'

'I was there too,' Molly said crossly. 'Don't I get any credit for your speedy recovery?'

'Of course, *ma chérie*. You were all ministering angels and for that I will be eternally grateful. But for your prompt actions and excellent nursing I might have died of pneumonia, so the doctor informed me.'

'Well, he's an old toper at the best of times,' Molly muttered, selecting a large slice of cake from the plate proffered by her sister. 'Go on, Armand, don't keep us in suspense.'

'I know that my papa was partly to blame for your family being evicted from the dockmaster's house. Your leaving there was inevitable in the circumstances, but he made it happen more quickly and that was unforgivable. I think he also had something to do with the fact that your brother had to pay a considerable amount to the dock company for alleged neglect of the property.'

'What?' Lily and Molly demanded in unison.

Armand put his cup and saucer down on a rose-wood sofa table. 'You did not know this?'

'Nobody tells us anything,' Molly said bitterly.

'That explains why we are so hard up.' Lily frowned as she remembered Nell poring over her housekeeping accounts. 'Nell never said a word about it.'

'She wouldn't,' Armand agreed. 'Nell is a saint if ever there was one. She did not want to worry you with her problems, but did you never wonder why you were living in such straitened circumstances?'

Lily shook her head. 'It all happened so quickly.'

'Nell treats us like babies,' Molly said, pouting. 'I thought she was just being mean.'

'I only found out recently.' Armand shook his head as Lily offered him a slice of cake. 'No, thank you.'

'So how did it come about?' Molly demanded. 'Come on, Armand. You can't tell us half a story and leave it there.' She put her cup and saucer down, eyeing the Madeira cake and licking her lips. 'I'll have another slice, Lily.'

Lily cut the cake and slipped it onto Molly's plate, but her attention was fixed on Armand. 'Please go on.'

'My papa has put me in charge of the London office.'

'Does that mean you'll be living in London perma-nently?' Molly asked eagerly.

'I will divide my time between London and Paris.'

'Nell will be so happy.' The words had tumbled in-advertently from Lily's lips but the look on Molly's face made her wish them unsaid.

'It will please us all.'

Molly's clipped tones made Lily flinch but Armand seemed happily oblivious to the heightened tension in the room. He sipped his coffee. 'This is excellent. It is so hard to get good coffee in London.'

'Never mind that,' Molly said through a mouthful of cake. 'Tell us your blooming plan and how you found out about the money that we had to pay the dock company.'

'As I said, my papa has put me in charge of the London office as he wants to devote more time to business at home. It was there I came across a letter from the manager of the dock company to my papa, confirming that he had taken action against your family and the rate at which the monies were to be repaid. It was not an insignificant amount and I realised that it would bring you close to bankruptcy.'

'I wish Nell and Matt had told us,' Lily said with feeling. 'I feel even worse now.'

'There is no need. I made it my business to settle matters with the dock company. There is now no debt and your family will be able to live as they once did, although sadly not in your old home. But,' he added, holding up his hand as Molly opened her mouth to interrupt, 'I have a property which I think is eminently suitable.'

'Oh, Armand, how wonderful.' Lily clasped her hands to her bosom, restraining the urge to give him a hearty hug.

'Where? Is it somewhere fashionable, Armand?' Molly's eyes shone and her unconcealed delight brought a smile to Armand's lips.

'Not exactly, but I think your esteemed *grand-père* will be more than happy with my choice. The house is close to Pelican Stairs and it overlooks the waterfront. It was once our counting house but the premises became too small and we moved to our warehouse on Bell Wharf. Since then the property has been empty and it will need some renovation, but I think it will make a comfortable home.'

Lily sighed. 'I wish I could see it.'

'It will be your home too,' Armand said with conviction.

Molly selected another slice of cake. 'I wouldn't be so sure about that. Matt is furious with Lily. He's not going to forgive her easily for what she did.'

Lily bowed her head. She knew that Molly only spoke the truth, but it was not what she wanted to hear. 'Perhaps if you put in a good word for me, Armand?'

'Of course I will do anything I can, but for now I think Molly is right. You are better off here with your mama. Matt will come round in time, I think.'

'I'd swap places with you.' Molly licked her fingers, eyeing the remains of the cake as if she would like to gobble it up, but she put her plate down and rose to her feet. She strolled around the room examining its contents as if she were assessing the value of each porcelain figurine and cut glass vase. 'Old what's-his-name must be worth a fortune,' she murmured appreciatively. 'He must have sold a few paintings to pay for all this.' She paused as the sound of the door-bell was followed by the patter of feet on the marble tiles. 'Visitors,' she said eagerly. 'I wonder if it's anyone famous.'

Lily listened to the sound of an interchange in the hall and she recognised Gabriel's voice. 'I'm afraid you're going to be disappointed, Molly. It's only Gabriel.'

'Oh him.' Molly's tone was disdainful. 'He admitted that it was his father who Ma ran off with. It was a bad day when you met Gabriel Faulkner.'

'That's not fair. It wasn't his fault any more than it was mine, or yours for that matter.'

'No, the real culprit is Ma, and that's why Matt won't forgive you for siding with her.' Molly snatched up her cloak and bonnet that she had discarded carelessly on a chair by the door. 'I think we'd better leave, Armand. I don't want anything to do with the Faulkners. Like father like son.' She clapped her hand over her mouth. 'I didn't mean to include you in that, of course.'

Armand rose to his feet. 'Perhaps it would be best if we leave now, Lily. I have nothing against the young man, but I have to respect Molly's delicate feelings.'

'Yes,' Molly said, swinging her cloak so that it swirled dramatically around her shoulders. 'I have delicate feelings. D'you hear that, Lily? Not that my family ever acknowledged the fact, but I'm highly sensitive. It's my artistic nature, although I'm nothing like Ma. You're her child through and through, Lily, and you'll have to suffer that for the rest of your life.' Molly made a move towards the door as it opened to admit Prissy.

'Mr Gabriel for you, Miss Lily,' she said loudly. 'Come this way, mister.'

'We meet again, Miss Molly,' Gabriel said, inclining his head in a semblance of a courtly bow. He held his hand out to Armand. 'I'm glad to see that you decided to come and see Lily. I'm sure it means a lot to her.'

'We were just leaving,' Molly said with a haughty tilt of her head. 'You haven't done her any favours, Gabriel Faulkner. I hope you realise that no decent man is going to look at my sister now.'

'Come, *ma chérie*, I think it is time we departed,' Armand said, ushering her gently from the room. 'My coachman will waiting for us and we don't want the poor fellow to freeze to death in the snow.'

'Goodbye, Lily,' Molly called over her shoulder. 'I'll tell Nell that you're doing very well without us.'

'Wait for me,' Prissy cried, scurrying after them. 'I got to open the front door. It's the law here in London.'

The room seemed suddenly quiet and Lily felt as if her last tie with home had been cruelly severed.

Gabriel put his arm around her shoulders. 'I don't think she understands at all.'

'No, how could she?' Lily said with a reluctant smile. 'No one has ever refused Molly anything, but she can't help the way she is; none of us can.'

'Wise words indeed.' Gabriel released her as Prissy returned carrying a velvet mantle and a matching bonnet in a fetching shade of blue. 'Good girl, Prissy,' he said approvingly. 'And I think Miss Lily will need some gloves or a fur muff. Perhaps you could find something suitable.'

'Certainly, Mr Gabriel.' Prissy grinned and winked

at Lily. 'He's a good 'un, miss. He'll look after you all right.'

She was gone again before Lily had gathered her wits enough to demand an explanation. Gabriel held out the mantle with an encouraging smile. 'Let's see if this fits, Miss Larkin. You and I have an important appointment this morning.'

Obediently, Lily slipped her arms into the luxurious garment. It was soft to the touch, light and yet deliciously warm. She could not resist stroking the velvet as if it were a living thing. 'It's beautiful,' she breathed. 'But it must belong to Ma. Won't she mind?'

'Of course not, little sister. Cara has more clothes than most ladies own in a lifetime. Fashion is her weakness – well, if I tell the truth just one of many – but meanness is not her besetting sin. Even if this were her one and only garment she would not begrudge her daughter wearing it on a cold and frosty day like today.' He perched the bonnet on Lily's loose hair. 'Don't ever put your hair up, my dear. You should always wear it framing your face, which is a perfect oval. Has no one ever told you that you are beautiful, Miss Lily Larkin?'

'No, I'm the plain one in the family,' Lily said earnestly. 'Nell is the beauty and Molly is the pretty one.'

'They both have their merits, but I see you with the eyes of an artist.'

The warm look in his eyes sent a shiver down Lily's spine and she felt the blood rush to her cheeks. Taking the ribbons from him, she turned away to fasten them in a bow beneath her chin, checking her appearance in one of the many gilt-framed mirrors that adorned the walls. 'Where are we going, Gabriel? Are you taking me home?'

'This is your home for now, Lily. I'm taking you to my lodgings and I am going to give you your very first lesson in art.'

She spun round to face him, hardly able to believe her ears. 'You're going to teach me to draw and paint?'

'Exactly so. We have the ideal opportunity, and I'm not going to let you miss it.'

'But Ma will wonder where I've gone.'

'We'll leave a message with Prissy. You must stop worrying, Lily. I'm looking after you now.' He ushered her out of the parlour as Prissy came running down-stairs carrying a large fur muff.

'Is this what you wanted, Mr Gabriel?'

'Thank you, Prissy.' He took it from her with an appreciative smile. 'We must look after those little hands, Lily. They will make your fortune one day, of that I have no doubt at all.'

Mrs Lovelace showed her disapproval of a young woman being entertained in a gentleman's room with a sniff and a twitch of her thin shoulders.

'It is an art lesson, Mrs Lovelace dear,' Gabriel said, flashing a smile in her direction. 'Miss Larkin is my pupil.'

'I've heard it called a lot of things,' Mrs Lovelace said stonily, 'but art lessons are a new one on me.'

'No, really,' Lily protested. 'Gabriel is my step-brother, missis. It's all perfectly above board. He is going to teach me.'

'I don't doubt it, but leave the door open. I don't allow usually allow young ladies in my gents' rooms, but if you're related by marriage then I suppose it's quite respectable.'

Truthful to the last, Lily opened her mouth to put her right on that point but Gabriel seemed to know what she was going to say and he took her by the arm, propelling her gently towards the staircase. 'The door will be left ajar, Mrs Lovelace. You may enter at any time you please.'

'I'll be checking on you,' Mrs Lovelace called after them as they ascended the steep stairs. 'Don't think I won't.'

Gabriel led the way to his room on the third floor, situated at the back of the house. A single iron bedstead was pushed against the wall on one side of the room and the covers were in considerable disarray, as if he had only just got out of bed. He moved swiftly to pull the coverlet over the tumbled bedding. 'I'm not a particularly tidy man,' he said apologetically.

Lily glanced round at the clothes scattered haphazardly on a wingback chair by the fireplace and odd shoes lurking beneath a table where the remnants of last night's meal were congealing on a dinner plate. 'I can see that,' she said. 'I've three brothers so it's nothing new to me, but doesn't your landlady clean the room?'

Gabriel moved to the table and began piling empty cups and plates, a wine glass and bottle on a tray. 'Mrs Lovelace doesn't soil her hands with cleaning. She has a maid for that and my room is done twice weekly. For the rest of the time I manage on my own.' He lifted the tray and set it down outside the door. 'Now then, take a seat by the window in front of my easel. I want you to sketch the view of the rooftops and chimney-pots. How do you feel about that, Lily?'

Her fingers trembled as she took off her bonnet and mantle. 'Nervous, Gabriel. I've only ever drawn and painted for my own pleasure.'

'Then let's see what you can do.' He flicked through a pile of canvases, some already painted and others white as the virgin snow on the rooftops. He placed a small one on the easel and handed Lily a piece of charcoal. 'Take your time, little sister. We have all day.'

Lily studied the scene through the window and began to sketch, quickly and with growing confidence, while Gabriel raked the dying embers of the fire into life, adding several lumps of coal and working a pair of bellows until a blaze roared up the chimney. Absorbed in her task, she did not realise he was standing behind her until he leaned over her shoulder. She looked up with a start. 'What's wrong? Have I made a mistake?'

'Not exactly, but your perspective is a little off.' He took the charcoal from her and with a couple of deft strokes transformed the scene.

'That's amazing,' Lily breathed. 'Such a small thing and yet it looks as though I could walk into the picture and disappear into its depths.'

'You would need wings on your feet, considering we are three storeys from street level, but you can see what I'm getting at, I think.'

She glanced up into his smiling face and a warm feeling washed over her. 'Thank you, Gabriel.'

'For what? We've only just begun.'

'For caring enough to teach me things I could never learn on my own.'

He moved away, taking a seat in the chair by the fire and putting his feet up on the fender. 'Let's just say it amuses me, and I hate to see talent going to waste.'

Lily was not fooled for a moment. She had known him for a short time only but she sensed that beneath the casual, carefree face he showed to the world Gabriel Faulkner was passionate about his art. 'I'd like to see some of your work,' she said shyly. 'If you'd let me.'

'Of course, but my ability pales in comparison to that of my father. He is the famous artist and I doubt if I'll ever be fit for anything other than to pass on my scant knowledge to students.'

Lily leaned forward to soften a shadow with the tip of her finger. 'Is that how you support yourself? If so, then you should charge me for my lessons.'

'Absolutely not, Lily. I wouldn't hear of it.'

'But you have to pay rent and feed yourself. How do you manage?'

'My mother left me some money. It allows me to live modestly and I keep telling myself that one day I will paint a masterpiece and make my fortune. Although I know it is unlikely to prove true.'

Lily replaced the charcoal neatly in its box. 'There, what do you think?' She held the canvas up for him to see. 'Have I passed my first test?'

'My dear, you've only just begun, but it's a good start. Tomorrow you will do some more sketches, and you will do them again and again until you can get the perspective absolutely right at the first attempt.'

'But may I not paint this picture now?'

'All in good time.' He rose to his feet. 'I think we will go out for a light luncheon and then call in at the National Gallery. I assume you've been there, Lily?'

She shook her head.

'That is easily remedied. We'll eat first and then we'll spend a most pleasant afternoon studying the old masters.'

They lunched at Verrey's in Regent Street, although Lily was overawed and frankly terrified by the starchy waiters in their black tailcoats and shiny shoes. She allowed Gabriel to order their food but she was uncertain which items of cutlery to use and had to watch him closely, following his every move, which seemed to amuse him greatly, although he refrained from making any comment on her ignorance of etiquette. Casting covert glances at the other diners, Lily was thankful that Ma had been a stickler for table manners, as had Aggie, who had begun her working life in service with a wealthy family up West. When they were smaller, Aggie had been deft with the use of a wooden spoon when it came to handing out punishment for eating with one's mouth open, speaking when it was filled with food, or resting one's elbows on the table.

Lily managed to eat her meal, although she was so nervous that she barely tasted the delicious turbot in dill sauce or the jugged hare, but the sparkling champagne jelly slipped sweetly down her throat and she managed to toy with a little blancmange studded with crystallised violets and rose petals. She sipped a glass of white wine but she would have much preferred a cup of tea, although she did not dare say so in case she offended the august waiter, who looked so important she thought that she ought to be the one waiting on him. Gabriel tried to amuse her with witty anecdotes, but she mostly missed the point as she concentrated on minding her manners. She was relieved when he finally called for the bill, paid it with a flourish and, having left a generous tip, escorted her out into the street. The pavements had been swept clear of snow in the West End and Lily was both fascinated and impressed by the well-dressed people who passed them by. Elegant private carriages vied for road space with commercial vehicles and cabs, and crossing sweepers appeared as if from nowhere to clear the road of dung and detritus so that they might get to the other side without soiling their shoes.

They walked the short distance to Trafalgar Square with Lily clutching Gabriel's arm and exclaiming in delight at everything she saw. He chuckled at her enthusiasm for the fountains and the recently placed lions designed by Sir Edwin Landseer that stood guard over Nelson's Column. Gabriel seemed to be enjoying himself as much as she was. When they entered the grand portals of the National Gallery Lily was immediately lost in the wonder of great art. An hour passed and then two and all too soon it was time to leave. She was in a daze as they stepped outside into the cold and darkness. She felt drunk with beauty and humbled by the great works she had just seen. Her own talent seemed minimal by comparison. Gabriel summoned a hansom and gave the driver instructions to go directly to Keppel Street. Lily sat back against the squabs, too overcome by her new experiences to speak, and he seemed to understand, making no demands on her and allowing her to dream.

There were lights in all the windows of the house as the cab drew up outside the house in Keppel Street. Gabriel helped her down onto the pavement and while he settled with the cabby Lily stood transfixed, her mind far away in lands created by artists long dead. Her imagination took her far away from the city with its cold smoky air and the underlying odour of putrid drains. Dimly she felt a hand on her arm and she turned, expecting to see Gabriel, but she did not instantly recognise the dark figure with a hat pulled down over his eyes. She opened her mouth to cry out in alarm but he laid a finger on her lips. 'Shh – it's me.'

Chapter Fifteen

'Luke.' Lily breathed a sigh of relief as he took off his hat and she saw her brother's much-loved face. 'You gave me a terrible fright.'

He grinned sheepishly. The light of the street lamp glinted on his hair turning it into molten copper. 'Sorry, Lil. I've been waiting for ages and I'm frozen stiff.'

She rapped on the doorknocker. 'You'd best come inside and get warm.'

'No, I don't think that's a good idea. I'll be in enough trouble if Matt finds out I've come to see you.'

'What's this?' Gabriel joined them as the cab pulled away from the kerb and drove off at a smart pace. 'Luke? What brings you here?'

'I was just asking the same,' Lily said, giving the knocker another smart tap. 'He's been standing in the snow for hours and he's chilled to the bone.'

The door opened and Prissy's face broke into a wide welcoming smile. 'You're home, miss. I was wondering where you'd got to.'

'I'd best go,' Luke said, backing into the shadows. He thrust a box into Lily's hands. 'Here, take this. It belongs to you and I thought you might want it above anything else.'

Lily took the paintbox with trembling hands. 'Oh,

Luke. I thought I'd never see it again. You're the best brother anyone ever had.'

'Come inside, old chap,' Gabriel said, patting him on the shoulder. 'There's no sense standing out here on the pavement.'

'Yes, please come in even if it's just for a few minutes,' Lily pleaded.

Prissy settled matters by stepping outside and taking Luke by the hand. 'C'mon, mister. Come indoors before we all catches our deaths of cold.' She dragged him over the threshold with surprising strength for one so small. 'I'm used to dealing with stubborn creatures,' she said, snatching Luke's hat from his hands and tossing it onto the hallstand with a deadly aim. 'I weren't raised on a farm for nothing.'

Lily followed them in, giggling at the sight of her big brother being manhandled by a tiny girl. He stood there looking bemused and blinking as his eyes became accustomed to the gaslight.

Gabriel closed the front door, shrugging off his great-coat and hanging up his hat. 'Well done, Prissy. I'm proud of you.'

Prissy blushed and shuffled her feet. 'It weren't nothing, Mr Gabriel. Shall I fetch you some beer or brandy? There's a fire in the morning parlour. The missis told me to keep it going for Miss Lily when she got home.'

'Where is she, Prissy?' Lily asked, keeping a wary eye on Luke in case he decided to make a bolt for it. He was looking distinctly uncomfortable and she could only guess that he was thinking of what Matt would say if he found out that his younger brother had disobeyed his orders.

'They've gone to the opera, but the missis said I was to lay up in the dining room for you and Mr Gabriel when you come home. Cook's done lamb collops and braised partridges because she knows that they're Mr Gabriel's favourites, and there's apple pie and some of the jelly left over from last night's dinner. Oh, yes, now I come to think of it there's that smelly old cheese that the master likes so much, although it ain't half as nice as the cream cheese Ma used to make when the milk went sour.'

'Yes, thank you, Prissy,' Gabriel said, taking her by the shoulders and propelling her towards the back stairs. 'Go and tell Cook that we'll eat in half an hour, and Mr Larkin will be joining us for dinner.'

'Oh no,' Luke said hastily. 'I dunno about that, Gabriel.'

Lily gave him a stern look. 'I won't hear of you going home without eating something. I expect you walked all the way here and intend to do the same on the return journey, so you must have some food inside you.' She began undoing the buttons on his pea jacket, which looked even shabbier compared to the elegant tweed overcoat with a fur collar that Gabriel had worn.

'All right, you win.' Luke took off his jacket and gave it to her. 'I suppose I might as well be hung for a sheep as a lamb.'

'You might indeed.' Gabriel led the way to the morning parlour. 'At least you can tell that brother of yours that you didn't consort with the enemy, and by that I mean my father.' He threw the door open and ushered Luke and Lily into the room where, as Prissy had said, the fire burned brightly and the gasolier had been lit creating a warm glow.

Lily pressed her brother into the chair by the fire. 'I expect your feet are wet. Why don't you take your boots off? No one will mind.'

He shook his head. 'I got me work boots on, Lily. They're pretty stout and kept me feet dry. I'm just cold.'

Gabriel moved swiftly to a side table laden with cut crystal decanters and he poured some amber liquid into a brandy glass. 'Here you are, old chap,' he said, passing it to Luke. 'Drink this, and then you can tell Lily how things are at home. I know she's been pining secretly even though she's not said a word to me.'

'I miss you all,' Lily murmured, unable to prevent her voice from breaking with emotion. 'Molly was here this morning, but she didn't tell me much.'

Luke sipped the brandy and almost immediately the colour flared in his pale cheeks. 'This is good. Only the best for Ma, eh?'

Lily glanced anxiously at Gabriel and he gave her a reassuring smile. 'It's good to see you, Luke,' he said, steering the conversation to safer ground. 'I suppose Molly told you where to find us?'

'Yes. She was as mad as fire when she came home. She couldn't get over the fact that Lily was living in luxury while she had to sleep in the same room as Nell and Aggie. Armand didn't say much, but I get the impression he felt that he was in some way to blame for everything.'

'He's a decent fellow,' Gabriel said, adding with a

wry smile, 'for a Frenchman.' He poured a small tot of brandy for Lily and pressed the glass into her hand. 'You're pale as the proverbial lily, my pet. Sip this slowly.'

The fiery spirit took her breath away but sent a warm glow through Lily's veins. She took a seat opposite Luke. 'Tell me about everyone at home. How are they all? Has Armand taken Nell to see the new house?' She hesitated, realising by the look on his face that Luke knew nothing of Armand's plans for the family. 'I mean, I thought Nell would have told you by now.'

Luke tossed back the drink and held his glass out to Gabriel. 'I think I need another, if you please.'

'I thought it would be common knowledge in the family,' Lily said, floundering. 'I mean, it would be wonderful for you all to have a proper home again.' She turned to Gabriel with a silent plea for help.

He refilled Luke's glass. 'I expect you were on duty in the fire station when Armand discussed the matter with the others.'

'Very likely, but no one tells me anything.'

Lily was shocked by the bitterness in Luke's voice. It was so unlike him as normally he was the most good-natured fellow and she loved him dearly. His head might be filled with dreams and rhymes but she had always felt closer to him than fiery Matt or easy-going Mark, who never took anything seriously. She leaned forward to pat him on the knee. 'Don't be angry. I'm sure Nell is dying to tell you.'

'I expect you're right, but I hate all this secrecy and upset. I want everything to be the way it was. I want you to come home, Lily.'

'You know that's impossible,' she said sadly. 'Matt has turned against me and so has Nell. I didn't mean it to be this way, but maybe in time . . .'

'It's still wrong. We should all stick together, not turn on each other like a pack of wolves.'

Placing her glass on the drum table at the side of her chair, Lily slid onto her knees, taking Luke's free hand in hers and holding it to her cheek. 'You and I are still friends, and Molly came here with the best of intentions. The others will come round, but until then I have to remain here with Ma and Everard. They've been kind to me and I know Ma would love to see you too.'

'Dinner's on the table,' Prissy announced, having barged into the room without knocking. She paused, casting an anxious glance at Gabriel. 'I done that wrong, didn't I?

He shrugged his shoulders and smiled. 'It could have been done with a little more finesse but we get the point, Prissy.' He held his hand out to Lily. 'Shall we?'

She rose to her feet. 'Come on, Luke. Let's enjoy a meal together and put all the squabbling aside. We can't help what the others think but we can stay friends, and maybe one day you can forgive Ma enough to give her a second chance.'

A reluctant smile banished Luke's frown and he was once again the brother she knew and loved. 'You always were the peacemaker, Lil. It's not the same at home without you, but we won't let it come between us.' He stood up and enveloped her in a great bear hug. 'I love you, little sister, and always will.'

Prissy muffled a sob. 'Ain't that just lovely? You

come again, mister. I can see you're good for my mate. We're the best of friends, ain't we, Lily?'

Gabriel shooed her out of the room. 'Don't let the mistress hear you talking like that, Prissy, or I'm afraid you'll be back on the farm in the blink of an eye.'

There was an awed silence in the dining room as Luke and Lily took their places at the table which could comfortably have seated twenty. Its gleaming mahogany vastness was complemented by matching chairs in the style of Thomas Chippendale, although Gabriel assured them they were reproductions and not genuine antiques. If he was trying to make them feel less uncomfortable it was not working. Lily had so far eaten her meals from a tray in the morning parlour or in her room, and this was the first time she had entered the opulent dining room with its heavily embossed wallpaper, ornate plaster coving and ceiling rose from which a brass gasolier with rose-tinted glass shades was suspended. The majestic wooden fireplace was carved in the latest fashion with plant-like fronds and exotic blooms which were replicated in the tiled insets and hearth. The air was heavy with scent from the hothouse flowers in vases strategically placed to bring a hint of summer into a winter room. Set on the table in between silver candelabra an epergne was filled with golden lilies and hung with bunches of black grapes. The mahogany sideboard groaned beneath the weight of silver serving dishes and salvers, and the moss-green velvet curtains were drawn to shut out the cold night.

Prissy hurried about doing her best to serve the

food, although when she spilt artichoke soup over Luke's hand Gabriel suggested that it would be best to leave the dishes on the table and they would help themselves. Prissy hesitated, looked doubtful, but was eventually persuaded to return to the kitchen and help Cook serve the remove.

Luke had licked the soup off his hand, but when Lily frowned at him, indicating the stiffly starched white table napkin, he shot an apologetic glance in Gabriel's direction. 'I'm sorry,' he said humbly. 'I didn't want to dirty it.'

'That's what they are there for, old chap,' Gabriel said easily. 'Our soiled linen keeps the laundress in employment, so who are we to cheat a poor woman of work?'

Luke did not look convinced and Lily hastily changed the subject. 'The soup is good. I wish we could share it with the others.' She bit her lip, glancing anxiously at Gabriel. 'I don't mean to sound ungrateful, but I hate to think of Grandpa and the rest of them living as they do, and me being fed like a princess and living in luxury.'

'I say enjoy it while you can,' Luke said, swallowing the last spoonful of soup with an appreciative smacking of his lips. His pale skin flushed scarlet as he caught Gabriel's eye. 'That weren't right, I can tell from your expression. What did I do wrong this time?'

'Nothing, I can assure you. In some countries I believe it is good manners to show appreciation of the cook's culinary efforts in that way, although polite society is extremely boring and stuffy and generally it's best not to make mouth noises at table.' Gabriel replaced his soup spoon at a right angle and Lily followed suit. She had observed the diners at Verrey's and table manner were obviously of great importance to the toffs. She wondered if she would ever be able to fit in with Ma's set, and she gave Luke a sympathetic smile, but to her surprise he seemed to have taken Gabriel's advice in good part.

'I'd like to learn all this etiquette business,' he said earnestly. 'I don't intend to stay a fireman all my life. As soon as I get my poems published I'm going to give up work and concentrate on being a poet. I want to be like Ma's friend Mr Rossetti and his sister. I'd give anything to meet them.'

'Then you shall, my darling.'

Lily turned her head to see their mother standing in the open doorway, her lissom figure silhouetted against the oak panels as she struck a dramatic pose. Illuminated by the combination of gaslight and candlelight, she glittered from head to foot. Her hair was piled on top of her head and her fiery curls were threaded with strings of imitation gems. A matching necklace which could have been real diamonds, or an extremely clever copy in paste, enhanced her slender throat and neck, plunging spectacularly into her décolletage. Her gown of white silk taffeta shot with palest blue and trimmed with cobwebs of fine lace gave the impression of moonbeams glimmering with each sinuous movement of her body. Lily caught her breath in a gasp of pure admiration, thinking that Ma knew how to make an entrance; judging by the expressions on Gabriel's and Luke's faces she held her audience spellbound.

Charlotte held out her arms. 'My darling boy. How wonderful of you to come and visit your mama.'

Luke rose to his feet, conflicting emotions evident on his boyish countenance. 'I didn't,' he said baldly. 'I come to see my sister.'

'Came, darling,' Charlotte corrected, smiling and holding her arms out to him. 'You came for whatever reason, but you are here and that's all that matters to your loving mama. I've missed you, my dear boy.'

Luke stood statue-still. 'Not enough to come and see us though, Ma.'

'Ahem.' Everard appeared behind Charlotte, clearing his throat and eyeing Luke with a certain amount of apprehension. 'Luke, my boy. You've grown up a lot since we last met.'

'I was thirteen when you run off with Ma.'

Gabriel pulled out a chair. 'Would you like to join us, Cara? We've only just begun supper.'

'I thought you were going to the opera,' Lily said warily. 'We weren't expecting you back so soon.'

'It was such a bore,' Charlotte said languidly. 'Carlotta Carcopino was supposed to be the prima donna but she has a sore throat and cannot sing. I refuse to sit for hours listening to someone's understudy, so we came away before the performance began.'

'But not before your mama was seen and admired by countless genuine opera lovers,' Everard said mischievously. 'You were the star tonight, *ma belle*. You turn heads wherever you go.'

Charlotte bestowed a brilliant smile on him with a modest flutter of her sweeping eyelashes. 'You always know what to say to flatter me, dearest. But this evening I am happy to be a devoted mama once again.' She surged forward in a cloud of bergamot and gardenia fragrances and enveloped Luke in an embrace, although she had to stretch in order to place her arms around his neck. 'My, how you've grown, Luke. You were such a little boy when I last saw you.'

Luke gave her a brief hug before pushing her away. 'I'm a man now, Ma. I'm twenty-three, too old to be cuddled like a nipper.'

'Darling, how cruel you are.' Charlotte collapsed into the chair held for her by Gabriel. 'I'd hoped we could forget the sordid past.'

'Yes, why don't we sit down and enjoy the rest of supper,' Everard suggested. 'We didn't have time to eat before the theatre and I must confess I could do justice to Cook's braised partridge.'

'I couldn't eat a morsel,' Charlotte said, eyeing a silver basket of bread rolls. 'Pass them to me, Lily. I might toy with a little soup if the servants haven't demolished it already. Ring for Prissy, Everard, and let's sit down like civilised people.' She turned to Luke. 'Tell me all about yourself, darling. Do you like being a fireman?'

Lily caught her breath. How could Ma be so unfeeling? She was speaking to her son as though he were a stranger she had met at one of her fashionable soirées. Lily glanced anxiously at Luke and her heart sank as she saw the hurt in his eyes. He backed towards the doorway.

'I can't put up with this tonight. I'm sorry, Lily, but all this ain't for me. I'm a plain sort of fellow and my poetry comes from my heart. I don't belong here and neither do you.'

'Don't go like this,' Lily pleaded. 'Stay and finish your supper.'

'Yes, there's no sense in rushing off before you've eaten,' Gabriel added with a persuasive smile. 'And Perks can drive you home afterwards. Isn't that so, Pa?'

'Certainly.' Everard nodded his head. 'Do stay, my boy. Don't distress your mother by leaving before she's had time to get to know you again.'

Lily cast an appealing glance to her brother. She hated to think that he felt unwelcome, especially as she was beginning to feel at home here.

Luke looked from one face to another and his jawline hardened. Lily recognised the Larkin stubborn streak with a resigned sigh.

'No, I've said my piece,' he said slowly. 'I shouldn't have come but for Lily, and I've done what I set out to do. So I'll be off now. No need to send for the carriage. I'd rather walk.' He took a step towards the door but Charlotte rose to her feet with a rustle of silk.

'Sit down, Luke. I won't have this childish behaviour at table.'

There was a stunned silence as all eyes were upon her. The languid manner had vanished and her eyes flashed dangerously. Luke glanced at Lily. 'I want to go home,' he murmured plaintively.

Charlotte waved her hand at Gabriel. 'Ring for Prissy.

We will sit down and eat our meal and Luke will behave like a man instead of a sulky little boy.'

'Yes, my boy,' Everard said pleasantly. 'I'd be very interested to hear some of your poems. Maybe after dinner you would give us a rendition?'

'I dunno.' Luke shifted from one foot to the other. 'Everyone at home thinks my writing is a joke.'

'Not everyone,' Lily insisted. 'I love your poems, and one day we'll write a book together. You can do the poetry and I'll illustrate it.'

'Now there's a thought.' Everard guided Luke back to his seat. 'I have some friends in publishing. Maybe I can introduce you to the right people.'

Reluctantly, Luke sat down and Gabriel rang for Prissy.

Lily breathed a sigh of relief. Maybe things were going to turn out well after all.

It was late evening when Luke and Gabriel took their leave of the party, which had grown lively under the influence of wine from Everard's well-stocked cellar. Luke, unused to drinking anything other than beer, had lost his normal reticence and had become quite animated. It had not taken much persuasion from his mother to encourage him to recite several of his poems and he left promising to return, bringing his work for them to peruse at their leisure. Lily had agreed to visit Gabriel next day to resume her lessons, and now that she was in possession of her precious paintbox she was even more eager to accept his offer. She had gone to bed that night feeling happier than she had for a long time. If Luke had come round, and if Molly was on her side, then it was just a matter of time before Matt, Mark and Nell understood her dilemma and forgave. She went to sleep clutching the hope that soon the whole family would be reunited.

Next day and every day for a month, Lily attended Gabriel's lodgings for tuition. Mrs Lovelace made her disapproval clear, but as Gabriel paid his rent regularly and was otherwise a model tenant, she allowed Lily to continue her visits. Even so, she insisted that the door was to be kept open at all times, and at least once an hour they heard her firm tread on the stairs and saw her thin figure walk slowly past as she glared into the room. This made Lily giggle but Gabriel simply shrugged and continued working away at his easel. He would not allow Lily to look at his painting, but she was aware that he was studying her and that she must be the model for whatever image he was creating on the large canvas. She was burning with curiosity, but every day at the end of their session Gabriel covered his work with a cloth and she was not allowed a single peek.

He always took her out for luncheon and they dined royally, or so it seemed to a girl brought up as frugally as Lily. In the afternoons they visited art galleries and exhibitions and as a cold and snowy January came to an end a thaw set in, sending rivulets of melting ice water tumbling along the gutters and overflowing from blocked drains. Everard had one of his paintings in the Royal Academy Winter Exhibition and Lily was so proud to know the artist that she had great difficulty in containing her excitement when she saw his painting displayed amongst those of the famous artists with whom he and Charlotte claimed acquaintance. She wanted to proclaim their relationships to all those around her who were studying his work, but she managed to restrain herself. Her boundless enthusiasm caused Gabriel much amusement. He teased her mercilessly, but took her out to tea at Brown's Hotel by way of an apology for laughing at her childish naïveté. They ended the day on a happy note and he escorted her home in a hansom cab, although he declined her invitation to accompany her in as he said he had business elsewhere. Lily stood on the pavement watching the vehicle until it turned the corner and disappeared from view. She felt slightly hurt and let down after an enjoyable day. She had become used to having Gabriel's undivided attention, and this was the first time he had gone off without revealing his destination. As she mounted the steps to the front door she wondered if he had an assignation with a young lady. Somehow the thought did not please her. She rang the doorbell.

Just as Prissy was about to let her in a shout from the pavement made Lily hesitate and glance over her shoulder.

'Hold on there just a second.' A burly man leapt off a butcher's cart, flinging the reins to one of the shabbily dressed, barefoot children who wandered the streets offering to hold horses for gentlemen or tradesmen for whatever sum of money they felt inclined to give. 'Watch me wagon.' The butcher rolled his sleeves up and took the steps two at a time, shoving his booted foot over the threshold as Prissy attempted to close the door. 'Not so fast, young woman.'

'Tradesmen's entrance is round the back,' Prissy said, banging the door against his boot.

'I ain't going round nowhere,' the man roared. 'I'm sick of being fobbed off by the cook. I wants to see the master of the house, or the missis.'

'They're out.' Prissy tried again to close the door but this time it was blocked by a muscular arm.

'I wants me money and I ain't going nowhere until I'm paid in full. Three months' meat and game I've supplied, and not got a penny piece in payment.'

'That ain't my problem,' Prissy insisted. 'Go round the back like I said.'

Lily could see that this was going nowhere and she nudged Prissy out of the way. 'Can I help, mister? Surely there's been some mistake?'

The man's face flushed to the colour of the brickwork on the exterior of the house. 'Mistake? I'll say there's been a mistake. It was not paying Jeb Colley, that's the mistake. I want me rightful dues.'

'I'm sure it's an oversight,' Lily said, attempting a smile to hide the fact that she was a little scared of him. 'And they are out at present. If you'd like to call back later . . .'

'You don't get me with that 'un. I'm too long in the tooth to fall for that tale. I ain't budging from this spot until I get all or part of the money owing.' He folded his arms across his chest and leaned against the doorpost, his florid countenance ill-matched by ginger mutton chop whiskers and a quivering moustache.

Lily thought quickly. She had five and three in her purse, which Gabriel had insisted she kept in case of emergencies. 'How much, mister?'

'Ten pound four and sevenpence three farthings. Not a penny more nor a penny less.'

It was a princely sum and Lily could hardly believe that anyone could spend that much on meat and game in a year, let alone in three months. 'Surely not.'

''Tis true, miss. I can prove it in court if necessary, or I'll take it in kind if you'll let me in.'

'Don't listen to him, miss,' Prissy cried, tugging at Lily's hand. 'Tell him to sling his hook. Don't let him in whatever you do.'

'I'm sorry but I don't have that kind of money,' Lily said, trying to sound firm but reasonable. 'Please come back later. I'm sure that Mr Faulkner can sort this out.'

'Not likely. I'm staying right here.'

'Slam the door, miss,' Prissy said urgently. 'He'll get fed up soon enough.'

'I heard that,' Jeb Colley shouted, moving his foot so that it was impossible to close the door without severing his lower limb.

Lily was at a complete loss now and growing desperate. A small crowd had gathered and Jeb was relating his story to them and receiving sympathetic acknowledgement that he had a just cause.

'Send for the bailiffs,' a man suggested.

'Or a copper.' The woman at his side shook her fist at Lily. 'Toffs, they think they can do as they please and us poor folk have to suffer.'

Lily backed away. She had never been classed with

the toffs before and in this instance she resented the implication that she might have anything to do with the butcher's dilemma. If she were to be honest, she was in complete sympathy with him should he be telling the truth. She turned to Prissy. 'What shall I do?'

'Stamp on his toes, miss. That works sometimes.'

'Do you mean this has happened before?'

'Many times, miss. I lost count.'

Lily was shocked. She could hardly believe that her mother or Everard would be party to what amounted to theft from honest working people, especially as they lived in such style. The silver alone must be worth a fortune, and if Ma's jewels were real she could pay the butcher with ease. The situation was turning nasty and Lily was growing more anxious by the minute when a hackney carriage drew up, scattering the onlookers as they leapt to safety. The driver climbed down, shooing the rest of the bystanders out of the way as he helped Charlotte to alight. In her hands she held bandboxes bearing the names of large West End stores that Lily had heard of but had never visited: Derry and Toms, Peter Robinson and Lilley and Skinner.

'Make way for the lady,' the cabby said, gathering up even more packages from the interior of the cab.

Charlotte smiled and acknowledged the crowd as though they were an admiring group of art lovers. She mounted the steps, coming face to face with an angry Jeb Colley.

'Excuse me, sir, but you are preventing me from entering my house.'

'So it's yours, is it, missis? Well then you can pay me what you owe.'

'Don't be ridiculous, man. The tradesmen's entrance is where you will be dealt with.' Charlotte attempted to walk past him but Jeb caught her by the arm.

'Not so fast, missis. If you got money to pay for them expensive duds then you can settle up with the likes of an honest hard-working butcher.'

'I don't carry cash on my person,' Charlotte said haughtily. 'Unhand me, sir, or I'll be forced to send for a constable.'

'You heard the lady,' the cabby said belligerently. 'Let her go, cully.'

'Not until I get me money.'

Lily flung the door wide open. 'Come inside, Ma. Don't let him bully you.'

'He won't let me go.' Charlotte's lips trembled. 'Do you think it brave to terrorise innocent women, sir?'

'Innocent my foot. You got ten pound four and seven-pence three farthings' worth of meat and game off me, and I want me money. If you can afford to go on a spending spree, then you can stump up the reddies.'

'Let her go, you big brute.' Prissy charged past Lily and butted the butcher in the stomach.

The air rushed out of his lungs in a loud bellow, raising a cheer from someone in the crowd. Jeb Colley released Charlotte's arm as he doubled over, gasping for breath. Prissy seized the opportunity to yank her mistress unceremoniously over the threshold and Lily took the packages from the cabby. Doffing his cap to Charlotte he sauntered down the steps amidst boos from the bystanders, who made it obvious that they resented his partisan attitude which they suspected had been secured by a generous tip from his erstwhile passenger.

Lily slammed the door before the butcher had time to recover. She leaned against it breathing heavily. 'What was all that about, Ma? Do you really owe him that much money?'

Charlotte thrust her purchases into Prissy's hands. 'Take these to my room and unpack them, carefully. I don't want any sticky fingerprints on my new gowns or my satin shoes, and if I find a bent feather on any of my hats you'll be in trouble.'

'Yes'm.' Prissy bobbed a curtsey and hurried off as fast as she could when hampered by a pile of band-boxes and packages.

'I need sustenance.' Charlotte made her way to the morning parlour with Lily following close on her heels.

'Ma, did you hear what I said?'

'Darling, don't bother your head with tradesmen,' Charlotte said, flinging her mantle onto the nearest chair and snatching a decanter from the side table. She poured a large measure of brandy into a glass and drank deeply. 'Pass me a cigarillo, darling girl. They're in the silver box on my escritoire.' She refreshed her drink and took another mouthful.

Lily eyed her in astonishment. She had never seen a woman toss back alcohol in such a practised manner. She gazed helplessly round the room, wondering what an escritoire might be when it was at home, but a silver box gleamed at her from the top of what appeared to be a small desk. She fetched it obediently and handed it to her mother, watching in awe as Charlotte flicked it open and selected a small black cigar which she lit with a spill from the fire. Inhaling deeply and then exhaling with a satisfied sigh, she shot a challenging look at Lily. 'What are you staring at? Haven't you ever seen a woman smoke a cigarillo?'

'No, Ma. I'm seeing and hearing things today that I never thought I'd witness.'

'Oh, you mean the little man who sells meat. He's of no account. Don't worry your head about him.' Charlotte drained the last drop of brandy in her glass and held it out to Lily with an appealing smile. 'Pour me another, sweet child. Mama has had a frightful experience with that horrid little man.'

'You owe him money, Ma. He has to make a living like the rest of us.'

'You've a lot to learn, darling. Don't be such a little bourgeoise.'

'I dunno what that means, but today I was ashamed of you, and if that makes me one of them things, then I'm glad.'

Charlotte's amused smile froze into an expression of contempt. 'You are your father's daughter after all. I can see the Larkin common streak coming out. And I thought you were pure Delamare.' She hurled the glass at Lily's head but it missed and shattered harmlessly against the wall in a glittering shower of crystal shards. 'Get out of my sight,' she screamed. 'Go to your room. I can't bear to look at you a moment longer.'

Chapter Sixteen

In her room Lily perched on the edge of her bed, shaken to the core by what had just occurred. The image she had long cherished of her mother had been dashed into pieces like the glass that had just been hurled at her with such venom. Her dreams of a loving gentle Madonna had been tarnished by the revelation of her mother's attitude to the tradesman, who was only claiming what was due to him, even if he had gone about it in the wrong manner. And then, before her eyes, Ma had changed into a screaming vitriolic harpy filled with hatred for her own daughter. Lily had seen Matt in a temper and Grandpa was always cross about something, but Nell would never have behaved like that, and even Molly at her worst was more temperate. Lily jumped as someone tapped on her door.

'Can I come in, miss?' Prissy opened it a little way and peered at her with an anxious smile. 'I brung you a cup of tea.'

This simple act of kindness brought tears to Lily's eyes. She had been too shocked and angry to cry until now, but her lips trembled uncontrollably and Prissy hurried into the room. 'Oh lawks, don't cry, miss. You'll start me off.' She placed the cup on the washstand and flung herself down beside Lily, wrapping her arms around her. 'There, there, ducks. You'll be all right. She's a silly old besom. We heard the noise in the kitchen and Cook sent me up with the dustpan and brush. It ain't the first time this has happened.'

Lily sniffed and wiped her eyes on Prissy's apron. 'It isn't?'

'Lawks no, miss. The mistress has often thrown a vase or something similar at the master when she's having one of her tantrums. I'd like a tanner for every time I've cleared up the broken glass or china. It's a wonder there are any ornaments left in the parlour.'

'She hates me, Prissy.'

'No she don't, miss. That's the brandy talking and that there stuff she sips from the brown bottle. She's always having a crafty nip and sometimes it makes her happy and other times it makes her spiky as a holly leaf.'

'What's in that bottle? Is it medicine for some dreadful illness?'

Prissy threw back her head and laughed. 'Heavens, miss. I thought I was the simple girl just up from the country. No, it's laudanum. Cook says that both the master and the missis and most of their arty friends are into taking things that make them go a bit mad. If my sainted ma knew I'd come to a house where they smoke cigars and enjoy strong drink, not to mention the drug-taking, she'd be spinning in her grave like a top, poor soul.'

'Does Mr Gabriel do these things?' The question had left her lips before Lily had time to consider whether it was appropriate to interrogate a servant about family matters.

'I don't think so. Cook says that's why he left home when he did. She's got a lot of time for Mr Gabriel.' Prissy slid off the bed and went to the washstand to retrieve the cup of tea. She handed it to Lily with an encouraging smile. 'Here, drink this and it'll make you feel better. I'll fetch a jug of warm water and you can wash your face. You don't want to go down to dinner looking as though you've been crying your eyes out, now do you?'

Lily sipped the tea. It was lukewarm but it was sweet and comforting. She managed a watery smile. 'I think I'll eat in my room. I don't think I'll be welcome downstairs.'

'She'll have forgotten all about it by the time she's had a bath and changed into one of them fine gowns she's just bought and not paid for.'

Prissy made to leave the room but Lily called her back. 'Wait a moment, Prissy. What do you mean – not paid for?'

'She's got an account at all them big departmental stores up West. Don't you know nothing, miss?'

'Obviously not,' Lily murmured as the door closed on Prissy. She sipped her tea. Why was life so complicated? Why was nothing as it seemed? She wished she could go to Nell and pour out her troubles, but Nell was as angry with her as Ma had been. Perhaps it was she herself who was at fault. Maybe she said and did the wrong things without knowing what she was doing. Lily shivered. The fire had burned down to glowing embers and the coal scuttle was empty. She raised herself to put the cup and saucer back on the washstand and went to sit on the hearthrug, wrapping her arms around her knees. What she would do and where she would go were problems that loomed over her like thunder-clouds. It was obvious that she could not remain here forever, nor could she go home. She did not even know where home was now, as the family might already have moved to the house that Armand had found them. A pang of regret speared her heart at the thought of the handsome Frenchman. She had long given up hope of anything romantic developing between them, but she still harboured tender feelings for him. She sighed, wishing that Gabriel had not gone off on his mysterious errand. She could do with his friendship now more than ever. Thinking about him now, and with the possibility that he had a sweetheart somewhere, only made her feel more lonely and alienated from all those for whom she cared. She closed her eyes and must have drifted off to an uneasy sleep as she was awakened by the door opening and Prissy staggering in with a bucket of coal in one hand and a jug of hot water in the other.

'Get up off the floor, miss. I'll get the fire going and then I'll help you wash and dress for dinner.'

Reluctantly, Lily scrambled to her feet. 'I told you, I don't want to go downstairs. I'll eat here in my room.'

'Stuff and nonsense. You ain't going to let them get you down, are you?' Prissy set the bucket down in the hearth, and taking the jug to the washstand she filled the china bowl with warm water. 'Where's your fighting spirit, miss?'

Lily smiled. 'I don't know, Prissy. I think it's deserted me.'

'You'll go downstairs and act like you own the place, that's what you'll do,' Prissy said with a determined toss of her head. 'You and me is out of place here, but we'll beat 'em yet. Now wash your hands and face like a good girl, and when I come back from filling her ladyship's bathtub I'll put your hair up just like them women what comes here for their dinners. You should see them all draped in furs and sparkling with jewels and I bet none of it's paid for. But that's how the arty people live, so Cook says, and I believe her.' Prissy tipped the coal into the scuttle, and having tossed a few shiny black nuggets onto the fire she left the room, promising a speedy return.

Not wanting to upset Prissy by ignoring her well-meaning advice, Lily stripped off her morning gown and splashed the rapidly cooling water on her face. She had barely noticed the light fading, but it was dark outside now, and the only light in the room came from the fire and the soft glow of the street lamp. Everard might have had gas put in the downstairs rooms but on the upper floors they had to rely on candles. As she lit the candles with a spill, the scent of warm wax reminded her of happier times in the dockmaster's house. They might not have had money to spare, but they had enjoyed a comfortable standard of living. There had been laughter as well as tears in the family home, but it was, she thought sadly, impossible to turn back time. She must hold on to what was good in her life at the moment, and that was her art lessons with Gabriel. He had said she was improving every day and she clung to that like a drowning woman holding on to a spar.

She glanced over her shoulder as Prissy entered the room.

'Look at you, miss, standing there in your shift. You'll catch a chill if you ain't careful.' Prissy held up a gown of shimmering emerald-green barège. 'The missis has had her bath and she's quite forgot your little spat. She sent this for you to wear tonight. She was throwing it out anyway since she's bought new ones today, but it was always too small for her. She only wore it once and then I had to lace her in so tight that she fainted away afore she got to the bedroom door. Still, as my ma used to say, "pride feels no pain". Anyhow, it'll fit you a treat and bring out the colour of your eyes.'

Before Lily had a chance to protest, Prissy had bundled her into the elegant garment and was busy doing up the tiny fabric-covered buttons down the back. 'What did I say? It's a perfect fit and you won't swoon every time you eat more than a pea. The missis is always swooning, mainly because she don't eat enough to keep a sparrow alive, but sometimes I think she does it to get out of an argument with the master. I has to keep the sal volatile handy and we're forever picking her up off the floor.'

With this new vision of her mother in her mind's eye, Lily went downstairs wearing the almost new gown, and her hair piled high on her head in an elaborate coiffure. Despite being raised on a farm, Prissy had a natural talent as a coiffeuse, and as Lily had no jewellery to adorn her Prissy had snipped a few white camellias from one of the floral arrangements in the drawing room and pinned them in her hair. Lily felt grand enough to attend a ball but she was apprehensive despite Prissy's insistence that all was well with the missis now. She had reached the first floor landing and almost bumped into her mother as she glided out of the drawing room on Everard's arm.

Charlotte gave her a dazzling smile. 'Darling girl, how fine you look.' She shot a look at Everard beneath her lashes. 'Doesn't my baby girl look pretty, dearest?'

Everard patted her hand as it lay in the crook of his arm. 'Splendid, my love. Lily is a credit to you.'

'We're going out,' Charlotte said with an airy wave of her hand. 'We're dining with dear Gabriel.'

Lily's heart gave an uncomfortable leap inside her breast. So that was why he had been so mysterious, and yet he could have told her that he was entertaining his father and stepmother. 'In Gower Street?' she said faintly.

'Gower Street?' Charlotte's delicate eyebrows rose in twin arcs of astonishment. 'Oh, I see. No, my sweet, not that Gabriel. We're dining with the famous artist Dante Gabriel Rossetti who is known to his friends as Gabriel, and after whom Everard's naughty son is named.'

Lily stared at her mother, slightly nonplussed by this change in attitude. Charlotte's eyes were suspiciously bright and her smile a little too dreamy; her pupils were dilated and Lily realised that what Prissy had said was true. Ma was not only slightly tipsy, but she had taken something that made her appear relaxed to the point of languor and had apparently obliterated all memory of their recent unpleasant encounter.

Charlotte leaned forward to tap Lily on the arm with her tightly furled fan. 'You must come with us one day, my sweet daughter. I want dear John Millais to meet you and maybe he will ask you to be a model for one of his paintings. Then there is Effie, his wife, and my bosom friend. We share so much in common, darling. We are both scarlet women according to stuffy polite society, although of course I was widowed when I married Everard, and Effie divorced Ruskin, her first husband. You've heard of him, no doubt. It was a complete and utter scandal, but I'll tell you about it when I have more time. Now we must go. Do hurry up, Everard, or we'll be late.'

'Yes, dear,' Everard said patiently. He guided her towards the staircase. 'Slowly does it, old girl. We don't want you to take a tumble on the stairs and spoil that nice new gown.'

'It was frightfully expensive,' Charlotte said happily. 'I hope you sell that painting in the Winter Exhibition, darling, or we'll end up in Carey Street.'

'Hush now, poppet. Don't worry your pretty head about such matters.'

Lily watched them progress slowly down the stairs, with Charlotte laughing and chattering like a school-girl and Everard helping her down each step. Lily did not know whom to blame the most, her mother for refusing to acknowledge that they were living well above their income or Everard for encouraging her in her folly. They were, she decided, equally at fault and she could only hope that the painting in the Royal Academy would do well enough to save them from the bankruptcy that seemed to be looming over their heads.

She followed them downstairs at a sober rate. It looked as though she would be dining alone tonight but she seemed to have lost her appetite. She waited in the hallway while Prissy helped Ma into a sapphire-blue velvet opera cloak with a scarlet satin lining, and Everard donned a cashmere overcoat with a black velvet collar and a top hat. He glanced over his shoulder with an apologetic smile. 'Sorry to leave you alone yet again, my dear. We'll make it up to you another time.'

Lily had heard this before. In the weeks that she had been living in Keppel Street she could count on her fingers the nights when they had dined as a family, and even then Ma and Everard had gone out afterwards or had entertained friends who came to drink and play cards. They had been artists and writers all unknown to Lily, and she suspected now that they were also little known in the world of art, but they talked a lot, drank even more and smoked cigars and cigarillos until the atmosphere in the drawing room resembled a London particular. On these occasions Lily had slipped away to her room early, unnoticed by anyone. Gabriel, when she had told him of these soirées, had warned her to steer clear of the louche society entertained by his father and stepmother. 'That's another reason I left home,' he had said. 'They're a worthless lot with little or no talent, but they think they're the next big thing. You have more artistic flair in your little finger than most of them have in their whole body. Avoid them if you can. Don't get sucked in by their big talk and impossible dreams.'

She recalled his words now. They had meant little to her at the time, but she realised that in many small ways Gabriel had tried to warn her about the bohemian lifestyle favoured by those who clung to the fringes of the Pre-Raphaelite Brotherhood. They were mere hangers-on, unaccepted by the great men and women of the art world.

'Go outside and see if Perks has brought the carriage to the door,' Everard said, checking his appearance in the wall mirror. 'Where is that boy? If he's late we'll have to go without him, Cara.'

Lily's attention was dragged back to the present. She thought for a moment that he meant Gabriel, although common sense told her that this was unlikely, and when Prissy opened the door Lily gave an involuntary gasp as she saw her brother framed in the doorway. 'Luke.'

He stepped inside, looking ungainly and awkward in an ill-fitting suit that Lily did not recognise as belonging to any of her brothers. The sleeves were too short, exposing frayed cuffs and bony wrists, and the trousers, equally lacking in length, had caught in the tops of his boots. Lily could see that he had attempted to put a shine on the leather but it was too scuffed to make any difference. Luke's fair complexion was already flushed with the cold and his colour deepened as he gazed at Charlotte and Everard in their evening clothes. In his hand he clutched one of Mr Cobbold's old ledgers. Lily recognised it instantly as the one in which he wrote all his poems and her heart went out

312

to him. 'Lily,' he said, his face brightening at the sight of her. 'You look absolutely splendid. I hardly recognised you.'

'We must go, old chap,' Everard said hastily. 'Come, my dear, we don't want to keep our illustrious host waiting.'

Charlotte grasped his arm to steady herself. 'Dear me, no. That would never do.' She waved vaguely to Luke. 'I see you've brought your work, my dear boy. This might be your one big chance. All manner of writers, poets and publishers are going to be there this evening.'

'Ma,' Lily exclaimed. 'What are you doing?'

Charlotte blinked as she attempted to focus her eyes on her daughter. 'What's the matter, darling?'

'Why are you taking him to one of those places? Luke won't fit in with the sort of people you know.'

'Of course he will,' Charlotte protested. 'He's a poet, and a good one too. Don't be so stuffy, Lily.'

'I'll be fine, Lil,' Luke said cheerfully. 'It's just this blooming suit that's making me uncomfortable. I got it from the dollyshop but I think the last person who wore it might have not been travelling alone, if you get my meaning.' He scratched beneath his arm, causing Charlotte to utter a faint moan.

'Never mind that now,' Everard shooed him out of the door. 'No time to change. Can't be too late. Frightfully bad manners.' With his arm looped around Charlotte's waist, and with Prissy's help, he assisted her down the steps to the waiting carriage.

'Don't go with them, Luke,' Lily cried anxiously. 'They're not our sort of people.'

He grinned cheerfully. 'Don't worry about me, Lil. My poems speak for me, so no one will notice that I'm a bit on the rough side. Ma says it's part of my charm.' He hurried out of the house, leaping the steps and jumping into the carriage after Everard.

Lily clutched the newel post, dizzy with anxiety. She had seen enough of her mother's so-called friends to fear that Luke's optimism was sadly misplaced.

'Well, they've gone,' Prissy said as she ran back into the house, closing the door behind her. 'They'll be more than a bit squiffy by the time they get home. I hope that good-looking brother of yours has a strong head for drink. Anyway, it looks like you're eating alone, miss. Shall I tell Cook to serve dinner now?'

'I'm not very hungry, Prissy. Perhaps some on a tray in the morning parlour, or in my room. To tell the truth I have a bit of a headache.'

'And you dressed up so fine,' Prissy said, shaking her head. 'You should be going to a ball or one of the eating places up West, not sitting by the fire in the parlour all on your own. It ain't right.'

Lily opened her mouth to placate Prissy but the sound of someone rapping on the doorknocker made them both turn with a start.

'They'll have forgotten something,' Prissy muttered, bustling off to investigate.

Lily crossed her fingers, hoping that Luke had listened to her warning and changed his mind, but when Prissy opened the door it was not Luke who stood on the threshold but Gabriel and Armand.

'It's like a blooming railway station,' Prissy exclaimed.

'Comings and goings all the time.' She stood aside ushering them in. 'Come in then if you're coming. It's taters out there.'

Gabriel stood back to allow Armand to enter first. He strode towards Lily with his hands outstretched. '*Ma chère* Lily, how beautiful you look. Are you otherwise engaged?'

Lily shook her head. 'No, I thought I was dining with Ma and Everard but they've gone out and they've taken Luke with them. I'm so worried about him.'

Gabriel joined them. 'Luke's a big boy now. I'm sure he can take care of himself. Where have they gone, as a matter of interest?'

'To Mr Rossetti's house, I think. But you know what Ma's friends are like, Gabriel; they'll gobble Luke up and spit him out when they tire of him.'

'Not if he gets noticed by the great and the good,' Gabriel said, smiling. 'I agree that some of the lesser beings in the set are a waste of time, but should Rossetti himself or any of the genuine Brotherhood take to Luke, it could be the making of him.'

'Alas, I do not move in those circles, nor am I a great lover of art,' Armand admitted. 'But Gabriel is right, Lily. Your brother is a man now and he must make his own mistakes, as we all do.'

'Is the French toff staying for dinner?' Prissy demanded, eyeing Armand with suspicion. 'We ain't got no frog's legs, mister. No snails neither.'

Lily shot her a warning glance. 'It's all right, thank you, Prissy. I doubt if Monsieur Labrosse is staying for

315

dinner, or Mr Gabriel for that matter.' She turned to Gabriel. 'Why are you here?'

'Allow me to answer that question,' Armand said before Gabriel had a chance to reply. 'We would like to take you somewhere special this evening, Lily. Gabriel and I arranged it as a surprise for you.'

'Yes, fetch Miss Larkin's mantle, please, Prissy,' Gabriel said firmly. 'We have a carriage waiting outside.'

Prissy stood her ground. 'And you'll bring her back safe and sound?'

Gabriel's lips twitched. 'I promise to have her home before midnight.'

Apparently satisfied, Prissy hurried upstairs.

'Where are you taking me?' Lily could barely contain her excitement, all her worries temporarily forgotten. 'Do tell me.'

'No, you must wait.' Gabriel and Armand exchanged conspiratorial grins.

As they alighted from the carriage in Wapping Wall, Lily thought that they might be dining at the Prospect of Whitby, and she wondered why Armand and Gabriel would have chosen a pub here of all places, when they might dine in style and comfort much closer to home. But as they emerged from the passage that led to Pelican Stairs and walked past the pub, she realised that the surprise was even greater than she had anticipated. Wedged between a builder's yard and a warehouse on the marble wharf stood what looked like an ancient hostelry. The name of the inn had been obliterated by years of dirt and the ravages of the weather, but the metal-studded oak door in its half-timbered frontage might once have opened to welcome sailors, stevedores and travellers. The bow windows leaned at a dangerous angle over the narrow wharf and Lily caught her breath as she recognised her grandfather's bewhiskered face peering out at her from one of the ground floor windows. It was too dark to make out his expression but she sensed that he was smiling at her, or perhaps it was wishful thinking. 'Are you sure I'm welcome?' she asked, turning an anxious face to Gabriel.

'We didn't bring you here just to look at the outside,' he said, grinning.

'Am I to stay?' The words tumbled from her lips more in hope than certainty.

'One thing at a time, Lily,' Gabriel said, tugging at the bell rope.

'I shouldn't have come. Matt will be furious.' Seized by panic, Lily backed away but Armand caught her by the hand.

'Do not worry, *ma chérie*, Matt and Mark are on duty at the fire station.'

Lily felt herself go weak at the knees as the door opened and she saw Nell's neat figure silhouetted against the light. 'Come in.'

It was all the invitation that Lily needed and she rushed forward to fling her arms around her sister. 'Oh, Nell, I'm so happy to see you.'

Nell gave her a brief hug and then extricated herself with a shadow of a smile. 'It was Armand's idea, and

Gabriel's too. I'd rather not do this behind Matt's back.'

'Oh, let her in for goodness' sake.' Molly popped her head round a door to the right of the narrow flag-stoned passage.

Somewhat reluctantly, Lily thought, Nell stood aside to allow Lily to pass.

Molly beckoned to them. 'Come into the parlour. It's the only room we have a fire apart from the kitchen. The chimneys smoke something terrible and they're either clogged with soot or birds' nests, we don't know which.' She gave Lily a peremptory hug. 'Good to see you, girl. Make yourself at home.' She gasped as Lily shed her cloak. 'My God, look at you.'

'Molly, don't blaspheme,' Nell scolded.

'Just look at that gown though.' Molly's eyes widened and her mouth turned down at the corners. 'It's enough to make a saint swear. It must have cost the earth.'

'It was Ma's,' Lily said hastily. 'She gave it to me.'

Molly tossed her head. 'Well aren't you the lucky one. We have to wear calico and cotton and you're dressed like the blooming Queen.'

'Come now, ladies,' Gabriel said, taking off his hat and gloves. 'No squabbling please. This is meant to be a happy family reunion. It's not Lily's fault if Charlotte gives her things. I daresay she'd be just as generous to you, Molly, and you also, Nell, if you would put this feud behind you.'

'Thank you, but I don't need you to tell me how to behave,' Nell said stiffly.

Lily could feel the tension in the air and not for the first time that evening she wished that Armand and Gabriel had warned her of their intentions. She would have come, of course, but she would have worn something simpler and been more prepared to face her sisters. Molly was glaring enviously at their mother's cast-off gown and Nell looked distinctly uncomfortable. Lily felt a wave of sympathy for her elder sister; poor Nell, always trying to do the right thing and forever battling with her conscience.

'Well, you'd best sit down and make yourselves at home,' Nell said with an obvious effort. 'I'll tell Grandpa you're here.'

'No need. I ain't deaf and I ain't senile.' Grandpa Larkin had entered the room unnoticed. There was a moment of expectant silence as everyone waited for his reaction. He held out his arms. 'Come here, girl. Give your old grandpa a kiss.'

Lily stumbled in her haste to reach him and she flung her arms around his neck. 'Oh, Grandpa, I've missed you. I've missed you all.'

He patted her back. 'There, there, girl. Don't squeeze the life out of me.' He held her at arm's length. 'My, don't you look grand. I hardly recognised you when I looked out of the window. Who's that? I says to meself.'

'It's me, Grandpa. I'm still your little Lily. I haven't changed.'

He shook his head. 'That little girl's gone for good, I think. You look all grown up, Lily, and quite the lady.'

Before Lily had a chance to argue, the kitchen door

opened and a waft of fragrant cooking smells preceded
Aggie as she burst into the room. She stopped short,
arms akimbo. 'Well I never. So it is you, Lily. I thought
I heard your voice.'

Lily eyed her warily, uncertain of her welcome.
'Aggie, it's good to see you.'

Aggie waddled across the floor to envelop her in a
hug. 'It's been too long. I didn't hold with any of the
nonsense spouted by the rest of them.'

'That's not what you said at the time, you old war-
horse,' Grandpa said irritably. 'You blamed Lily for
going to her ma just as loudly as the rest.'

'And it's time to put all that behind us,' Aggie
retorted. 'The girl has come home and here she should
stay.'

'Oh, may I?' Lily clasped her hands to her breast,
looking from Grandpa to Nell. 'Am I forgiven?'

Armand cleared his throat. 'Surely there is nothing
to forgive. Wasn't it only natural that a girl would want
to know her mama?'

'Yes,' Gabriel agreed with an emphatic nod of his
head. 'Come on, Nell. You must have some feelings
left for Cara.'

'Cara.' Nell wrinkled her nose in distaste. 'So that's
what she's calling herself these days. No, Gabriel, I feel
nothing for the mother who deserted us so callously.
She left me to bring up the younger ones when I was
still a girl. I had to shoulder the responsibility for housekeeping as well as teaching at the Ragged School. She
robbed me of my youth.'

'You are still young and, if I may be so bold, *très*

belle.' Armand took Nell's hand and raised it to his lips.

Molly let out a sound halfway between a sigh and a hiss. 'Oh for goodness' sake stop pandering to Nell. I say that Lily is one of us and should stay. I've missed her and she's the only one who knows how much starch to put in my petticoats.'

'It's not up to us,' Nell said quietly. 'Matt is still the head of the house.'

'And I suppose I'm just a wooden figurehead,' Grandpa grumbled. 'I'm the senior man and I say she should stay.'

'You've spoken sense, for once,' Aggie said, nodding. 'We've got the room now, even if the place is crumbling round our ears.' She glanced anxiously at Armand. 'No offence meant, mister.'

He smiled indulgently. 'I am not offended, *chère mademoiselle*. The building is old, as you say, but I will do everything in my power to make it more habitable. It just takes time.'

Lily cast a questioning look at Nell. She could see that her sister was wavering but she also understood that Matt was a force to be reckoned with. His anger and resentment towards their mother had never abated; if anything, it had deepened with the passing years. She could barely imagine his reaction if he discovered the truth about the household in Keppel Street. Perhaps it would be better if the family remained in ignorance of their mother's lifestyle. Lily slipped her hand into Gabriel's and received a reassuring squeeze. 'I'd love to come home, more than anything, but perhaps this isn't the best time. I don't want to upset Matt and Mark.'

'Luke is on your side,' Molly said defiantly. 'I say we should stand up to Matt. We're all grown up now and have minds of our own.'

'How about a nice cup of tea and a slice of my seed cake? I've got a proper range now and I can bake to my heart's content.' Aggie beckoned to Lily. 'Come and see my kitchen.'

'Never mind coddling your insides with tea and cake, I think something stronger is called for,' Grandpa said sternly. 'Let's go to the pub.'

'Capital idea.' Gabriel looked to Armand. 'What d'you say, old chap?'

'I agree.' Armand proffered his arm to Nell. 'May I escort you to the so excellent hostelry next door, Mademoiselle Nell?'

For a moment Lily thought that Nell was going to refuse, but a reluctant smile curved her lips, transforming her face into a picture of serene beauty. Lily could see that Armand was impressed and she tried hard not to envy her sister. Nell did nothing to attract men, but when she smiled she seemed to enslave them forever. Lily wished that she had that gift. She realised that Gabriel was eyeing her with raised brows and a questioning look. 'Are you coming, Lily?'

'Yes, of course.'

'I'll fetch my shawl,' Molly said, pushing past Lily and heading out of the room.

'I suppose I'm included in this, or do I have to keep

my place?' Aggie glared at Grandpa Larkin and he shrugged his shoulders.

'Come if you must, old woman. No one is going to stop you, but you can buy your own ale.'

Armand shook his head. 'It is my treat – isn't that what you say? Please come with us, Mademoiselle Aggie. It would not be the same without you.'

'Well then, there's one gentleman present at least.' Aggie stomped into the kitchen returning seconds later with her shawl. 'Come on then. What are we waiting for?'

The atmosphere in the pub taproom was smoky and noisy. After a jug or two of mulled wine and several pints of ale, mostly drunk by Grandpa, everyone began to relax, even Nell. Molly was less inhibited and she wanted to know every detail of life in Keppel Street. Lily was careful only to relate the best aspects. She was in the middle of describing some of Ma's more exotic outfits when Nell's expression changed to one of alarm and Molly held her finger to her lips in a warning gesture. Lily, whose back was to the outer door, turned her head slowly and found herself looking in Matt's angry face.

Chapter Seventeen

'I came looking for Luke,' Matt said furiously. 'What do I find but my sisters drinking in a taproom like common dollymops?'

Nell's hand flew to her mouth stifling a gasp of dismay, and following her sister's gaze, Lily saw Eugene Sadler standing behind Matt.

'I'm shocked, Miss Nell,' Eugene said gravely. 'This is no place for you.'

Matt seized Lily by the arm, dragging her to her feet. 'I blame you for this. It hasn't taken long for you to become corrupted by the bohemian way of living.'

'Matt, you're hurting me.' Lily stared into his face, terrified by the angry stranger who seemed to inhabit her brother's body.

'Let her go,' Gabriel said, leaping to her defence. 'This isn't Lily's fault.'

'I suppose you're to blame then. Like father, like son.' Matt released Lily, taking a step towards Gabriel with a pugnacious outthrust of his chin. 'Step outside and we'll settle this like men.'

A cheer rumbled through the curious onlookers in the bar. 'Sort him out, Larkin,' someone called loudly. 'Put the toff's lights out.'

The landlord strode towards them, rolling up his

sleeves. 'You'll take the whole thing outside, mate. I'm not having a brawl in my pub.'

Aggie helped Grandpa to his feet and Molly seized Lily's hand, dragging her out of the taproom to stand shivering in the rain which had begun to fall in a steady drenching shower. The others followed in quick succession. Eugene took off his overcoat and wrapped it around Nell's shoulders. 'Allow me to escort you home, Miss Nell.'

She cast an anxious glance at Matt, who was still arguing with Gabriel while Armand attempted to mediate.

'They won't come to any harm,' Eugene said patiently. 'It's men's business.'

'Well, I'm going home,' Molly announced loudly. 'Stay if you want to get soaked to the skin and catch lung fever.' She marched off along the quay wall with Aggie and Grandpa hurrying after her.

Lily hesitated, oblivious to the rain and wind. The evening had taken on a nightmarish quality with Matt and Gabriel bellowing insults and Armand speaking volubly in his own language.

'Come, Miss Lily.'

She looked round to see Eugene holding out his hand. 'Come away and let them sort it out between them.'

'Yes, Lily. Come with us,' Nell urged. 'You won't do any good here.'

Armand threw up his hands and walked away from the quarrel. He proffered his arm to Lily. 'Your sister is right, Lily. Come with me.'

325

'They'll hurt each other,' Lily murmured anxiously.

'No, they won't. It's just words.' He patted her hand. 'Come.'

There seemed little that Lily could do other than follow the rest of the party back to the house.

Inside it was warm and dry and everyone huddled round the fire with the exception of Aggie who was bustling about in the kitchen. Lily could see her through the open door as she arranged cups and saucers on a wooden tray. If things had been different, she would have been delighted to see Aggie in her element once again; queen of the kitchen and mistress of the range. She sighed and turned her attention to her grandfather, who had produced a bottle of brandy from behind the cushions on his favourite chair.

'Fetch glasses, Molly. I'm sure young Armand will appreciate a good cognac. You too, schoolmaster, if you've a stomach for it.'

'Thank you, sir,' Eugene said, acknowledging the offer with a nod of his head. 'I have been known to imbibe strong drink when the situation demands.'

'And none more so than now,' Grandpa agreed. 'I can't say that Matt was wrong in putting the blame on young Faulkner, but he should have waited until we'd finished our drinks. Making a scene in public ain't the way to behave.'

'Quite so.' Eugene nodded in agreement. 'And the taproom of a public house is no place for ladies.'

'We've been there before, even if it was in a private room,' Molly said over her shoulder as she searched the dresser for glasses.

Grandpa eased himself into his chair. 'And we was there to look after our women, so I don't see the need for all the fuss. Pour the brandy, Molly. Me hands is too stiff with rheumatics to hold the glasses steady.'

Nell slipped Eugene's coat off her shoulders and handed it to him. 'I'm obliged to you, Mr Sadler.'

'Must we be so formal, Miss Nell? Out of the school-room I think we agreed that you could address me by my Christian name.'

Nell shrugged her shoulders in an apparent show of indifference, but Lily was quick to see the colour flood to her sister's pale cheeks.

'What brings you to Pelican Wharf, Eugene?' Nell asked, casting him a shy glance beneath her lashes. 'What was it that couldn't wait until morning?'

It was his turn to look embarrassed and for a moment Lily felt quite sorry for him. She had been away from the family for over a month and it was becoming apparent to her that things had changed in that time. She had always suspected that Eugene Sadler was in love with her sister, but it was obvious now that his feelings ran deep indeed, which was unfortunate for him as Nell only had eyes for Armand. She barely seemed aware of the emotions she aroused in the schoolmaster's breast. Lily studied Armand's face as he smiled indulgently at Molly, who had sampled the brandy before handing him the glass with a coquet-tish sidelong glance. There seemed to be a degree of intimacy between them that had not existed a month ago and Lily was confused; she had thought that he was in love with her beautiful elder sister, but now she

was not so sure. Her own feelings were equally complicated. Armand was like a knight from the stories about
King Arthur that their mother used to read to them on
cold winter evenings when they sat round the fire. He
was everything that Lily had dreamed of, but had
seemed as unobtainable as those chivalrous romantic
figures from the past. Now, quite suddenly, something
had changed, although she could not quite decide what.
She moved to the window, peering out through the
small leaded panes in the hope of seeing Matt and
Gabriel reconciled and coming home, if not arm in arm,
then at least not at each other's throats. Her hand flew
to her throat as she saw Matt striding purposefully
towards the house. He was alone. Ignoring the others
she ran from the room to open the front door.

'Where's Gabriel?' she demanded anxiously. 'Is he
all right?'

'He's waiting for you in a hackney at the end of
Pelican Passage.'

'You didn't hit him, did you, Matt?'

He shook his head. 'No, but he deserved it for introducing you to that woman. Now Luke has gone the
same way and you are to blame, Lily.'

'Why? He's not a child. If he wants to see Ma then
it's up to him.'

'You encouraged him to write his stupid poems
instead of living in the real world. He should have
been on duty with us tonight but instead he chose to
wander off to spend the evening with her and that
libertine who turned her silly head.'

'Matt, you're not being fair. Everard is a nice, kind

man and he adores Ma. She loves him and they're happy together.'

'Are you telling me that it's all roses living in Keppel Street?' He took her by the shoulders, staring deeply into her eyes. 'I know you too well, Lily. You've seen the way they live and I don't think you like it one little bit.'

'How do you know what goes on behind closed doors?' Lily challenged. 'What right have you to sit in judgement on other people?'

'I made it my business to find out a long time ago. Do you really believe that the past left me unscarred? I was eighteen when Ma left us and I saw what it did to Pa. You were too young to understand but I knew it broke his heart and left him a shell of a man. After he was killed in that fire I went to see Ma and she was in such a state that she barely recognised me. God alone knows what she'd taken but I could hardly get any sense out of her. Then Faulkner came into the room and made up some excuse about her being out of her mind with grief.'

'Perhaps she was, Matt. Maybe she felt guilty for leaving us all.'

'I waited outside the house all that day, and in the evening I saw them drive off in a private carriage dressed to the nines, laughing and chatting as if nothing had happened. They were going out for the evening. Our pa was barely cold in his grave and you want me to believe that she has a heart.'

Lily stared at him in dismay. 'Why have you never told us all this?'

'I didn't want to remember it but you've brought it all back by your selfish ambition to be an artist just like her. You've chosen your path, and you are welcome to it. Now go, before I say something I'll regret.'

He snatched her damp cloak from the peg where she had hung it next to Nell's shabby mantle. 'There, take your velvet and fur and go back to the false life in Keppel Street. If you see Luke you can tell him he's lost his job. Let him earn his living by scribbling silly rhymes if he can.'

'No, Matt, please . . .' Lily held her hand out to him but he opened the door and taking her by the shoulders, pushed her out onto the wet cobblestones.

'Best hurry or he might not wait for you. Don't be fooled by his gentlemanly ways, Lily. He's got bad blood, just like his old man.'

The door slammed behind her and Lily found herself standing alone in the pouring rain. She pulled the cloak about her shoulders but she could not move from the spot. It was as if she had been turned to stone as she peered through the window at the achingly familiar family scene. Nell was seated by the fire in a high-backed Windsor chair drinking tea with Eugene standing by her side. In his hand he held a glass of brandy from which he took small sips, but his full attention was devoted to Nell. Viewing as an onlooker, Lily realised that for him at least there was only one person in the room. Nell seemed to inspire unconditional devotion, and yet again Lily felt a pang of envy for her eldest sister. She turned her attention to Molly, who was flirting openly with Armand, but he seemed preoccupied and seized upon Matt as he entered the room. They appeared to be deep in conversation. She wished she could hear what they were saying.

'What are you doing standing out here in the rain?'

Lily spun round to see Gabriel standing behind her. Rainwater was dripping from the brim of his felt hat and soaking his overcoat. 'Matt turned me out,' Lily whispered. 'I can't really blame him. He just doesn't understand.'

Gabriel slipped his arm around her shoulders. 'You're soaked to the skin. Let's get you home.'

'I have no home,' Lily said sadly. 'I don't really belong in Keppel Street, and no one wants me here.'

'You're talking nonsense.' He led her through the curtain of rain towards Pelican Passage. 'Of course you have a home with your mother and my pa. They love you, Lily.'

She shook her head. 'They've been kind to me, but I don't fit in with the way they live.'

'You sound as though you disapprove of them.' Gabriel's tone was light but Lily's heightened senses detected concern beneath his smile.

'I don't think that drinking to excess and taking drugs is a good thing,' she said choosing her words carefully. 'But it's not just that. Did you know that they owe money left, right and centre?'

'No one pays their creditors until they have to. It's just the way things are done in London.'

'No, it's more serious,' Lily insisted, stepping into a deep puddle and shivering as she felt the water ooze through the stitching on Ma's fashionable boots.

'Nothing in the house seems to have been paid for. Prissy tells me . . .'

'Never listen to servants' gossip, my love.' They had reached the end of the narrow passageway and Gabriel handed her into the waiting carriage. 'Keppel Street, please, cabby.' He climbed in beside her and reached out to clasp her hand. 'You're cold as ice. I hope you haven't caught a chill.'

Lily shook her head but said nothing. The ice was in her heart as Matt's harsh words repeated in her head over and over again. Gabriel was being kind but he could not be expected to understand how she was feeling. She leaned against him, shivering violently as the cold numbed her body if not her mind. She closed her eyes, allowing the motion of the carriage and the drumming of the horse's hooves to lull her into a dreamlike state. Gabriel held her hand, seeming to understand her need for silence.

When they reached the house in Keppel Street he handed Lily over to Prissy who put her to bed, clucking over her like a mother hen. She placed a stone hot water bottle wrapped in a piece of towelling at Lily's feet, and warmed Lily's cotton lawn nightgown by the fire before slipping it over her head. Lily suffered these ministrations in silence and meekly accepted a cup of hot beef tea which she sipped dutifully, although she would have much preferred a cup of ordinary tea, strong and sweet just like Aggie used to make.

Prissy gathered up Lily's wet garments, tut-tutting over the muddied hem of her skirt and the sad state of the velvet cloak. 'I dunno if this will ever be the same again. What was Mr Gabriel thinking of, allowing you to go out in a rainstorm? I'll have a few words to say to him when I sees him next.' She tossed the clothes over her arm and blew out the candles on the mantelshelf and the washstand. 'Now you go to sleep like a good girl. I'll bring you a cup of tea first thing in the morning, but if you should feel poorly in the night just ring the bell and I'll come running.'

'You're too good to me,' Lily murmured, snuggling down beneath the warm coverlet. In spite of everything, she smiled to herself. It was almost like being at home again with Aggie fussing over her, but not quite.

Next morning Lily awoke to uproar. The sound of raised voices echoed throughout the house and she snapped into a sitting position. It was not quite light but Prissy must have done her work as a fire burned merrily in the grate and the curtains had been drawn back to allow the first light of dawn to filter into the room. Lily sprang out of bed and opened the door, cocking her head on one side to listen. She could make out Prissy's high-pitched voice and that of Parsons, Charlotte's personal maid, but they were drowned out by male voices demanding to be admitted. Lily snatched up her wrap and was still struggling into it as she ran downstairs to the landing on the second floor, where she almost bumped into Everard. He looked only half awake as he attempted to tie the sash of his brocade robe, padding barefoot down the stairs ahead of her.

'What's going on?' Lily cried anxiously.

'Go back to bed,' he said shortly. 'This doesn't concern you.'

But of course it did, and Lily was not going to return to her room until she discovered what the fuss was about. She thought for a moment that it might be Matt and Mark come to make trouble, and when she saw Luke emerging from one of the guest rooms wearing a nightshirt that was too short for him and a nightcap askew on his copper mane, her worst fears seemed to be confirmed. 'What are you doing here, Luke? Didn't you know you were supposed to be on duty last night?'

He ran his hand through his hair. 'Don't shout, Lily. I've a terrible headache and I feel sick.'

'You've been drinking,' she said, sniffing suspiciously. 'What happened last night?'

'More to the point, what's going on now?' He leaned over the banisters, peering into the hall below. 'By God, I think it's the bailiffs, Lil.'

She breathed a sigh of relief. 'I thought it was Matt and Mark.'

'I wish it was them,' he murmured. 'I think this is serious.'

Lily moved to his side, craning her neck to catch a glimpse of the scene below.

'You have until midday to pay the monies owing, sir. If the due sum is not received we are empowered to seize goods to that value. This is your last warning.'

'But you don't understand,' Everard protested. 'I can't lay my hands on that sum at such short notice. I need more time.'

'Seems to me you was given plenty of time, sir. I'm

334

afraid you'll be facing the debtors' jail if you can't settle the matter to the creditors' satisfaction.'

Lily exchanged a worried glance with Luke. 'I knew things were bad, but I had no idea it was so serious.'

'I'd best go home,' Luke said in a low voice. 'I shouldn't have got so drunk last night but I had the best of times, Lily. You can't imagine how good it was to be with people who understand me and who listen to my poems without making a joke of the whole thing. Everard's friends said I've got a real gift for writing, and I should follow my dreams and give up working as a fireman.'

'I think that decision's been taken out of your hands. Matt was furious with you and he said you'd lost your job.'

'When did you see him?'

'Last night. It's a long story.' Lily moved away from the banisters. 'Everard's coming upstairs. I don't want him to think we've been spying on him.' She tugged at Luke's sleeve. 'You'd best get dressed. I'll see you at breakfast.'

He paled visibly. 'Don't mention food. I'm feeling a bit queasy.'

'I'll see you later.' Lily hurried up the stairs to her room and dressed hastily in a plain navy-blue merino skirt and a white cambric blouse. She sat in front of the dressing table and was brushing her hair when Prissy burst into the room. Lily swivelled round to look at her. 'What's the matter?'

'They're going to send the master to prison,' Prissy said breathlessly. 'Cook and Parsons are in a panic downstairs. They say we'll be out on the street afore the day's out.'

'Nonsense,' Lily said with more conviction than she was feeling. 'The master will sort things out. It's probably just a misunderstanding with the tradesmen.'

'No, miss. It's worse than that. We know that the bills haven't been paid for months. Cook says she'll go to her brother's house in Southwark, although she don't get on with his missis, and Parsons is in her room packing even as we speak.'

Lily's fingers trembled as she attempted to put her hair up and a lock of hair escaped.

Prissy hurried to her side, taking the brush from her hand. 'Lord, miss. How will you manage without me?' With a few deft strokes and the aid of ribbon and pins, she coiled Lily's long hair into a coronet. 'There you are, now you look a real bobby-dazzler.' Prissy's smile faded as she met Lily's eyes in the mirror. 'But where will we go, miss? I ain't leaving you, even if we has to sleep in the Thames Tunnel with the tramps.'

'It won't come to that,' Lily said firmly. 'Go downstairs and try to calm Cook and Parsons.'

'And the tweeny and the scullery maid. Then there's Perks too. He'll have heard the din from the mews.'

'Tell everyone to wait until the master has sorted everything out. I'm sure it's not as bad as it seems.'

Lily went downstairs to the dining room with her fingers crossed. She found Luke sitting at the table sipping a cup of coffee. He looked up hopefully. 'Any news, Lil?' His expression changed as Everard followed Lily into the room. Luke rose to his feet. 'I'm sorry, sir. We couldn't help overhearing what was said.'

Everard's normally cheerful face seemed to have creased suddenly into a maze of worry lines. 'I expect it'll be all round London by now. Bad news travels fast.'

'Is it that serious?' Lily asked anxiously. 'Is there anything I can do?'

'Only if you can perform miracles, my dear.' Everard slumped down in his chair at the head of the table. He looked round at the trappings of wealth that adorned the room. 'I can't pay,' he said simply. 'We've been living above our means for so long that it's become a way of life. I pinned all my hopes on selling my latest work at a price that would satisfy all my creditors, but it was not to be.'

'You can't just give up,' Lily cried passionately. 'Can't you sell some of the silver?'

'It's rented,' Everard said, shaking his head. 'Most of the furniture is rented and the bailiffs are returning at midday. It doesn't give me time to raise the money, and I've exhausted all the sources from whom I might get a loan.'

Luke rose somewhat unsteadily to his feet. 'I think I'd best leave now, sir. Thank you for introducing me to your friends.'

'I doubt if they'll be speaking to me when I'm in Cold Bath Fields Prison,' Everard said with a glint of his old humour. 'You've got talent, Luke. Don't waste it.'

Lily was tempted to beg her brother to stay but she managed to restrain herself. 'What will you do now, Luke? Will you go home?'

337

'I don't know, but I've nowhere else to go and maybe Matt will be a bit more reasonable this morning. I'll grovel if necessary.'

'Don't stop writing,' Everard called after him as Luke left the room. 'Good luck, my boy.'

Lily saw Luke out of the house. 'Keep in touch,' she called as he loped off along the street. He gave her a cheerful wave before disappearing around the corner. She returned to the dining room and found Everard still sitting at the table with his food untouched. He looked suddenly much older and smaller, as if he had shrunk to half his normal size. She knelt at his side. 'There must be something we can do to keep the creditors happy until you sell your painting. What about Ma's jewellery? That must be worth a small fortune. I could take it to the pawnshop . . .'

Everard met her eyes with an attempt at a smile. 'You are a good girl, Lily. But Cara's jewels are all paste. They would fetch very little and she would never forgive me if I took them from her.'

'But she loves you,' Lily protested. 'She would do anything to save you from jail. Does she know how serious things are?'

'She is an innocent in such matters,' Everard said fondly. 'I love to spoil her and indulge her every whim just to see that beautiful smile of hers. I fear this will break her heart.'

Lily rose to her feet. Suddenly she was angry, both with her mother for being so utterly selfish and with Everard for turning a grown woman into an over-indulged child. 'And you are just going to sit there

338

feeling sorry for yourself? Are you going to walk into prison without even trying to do something to prevent such a disaster?'

Everard shook his head. 'I'm tired, Lily. You can't begin to understand what a difficult life I lead. I'm a third-rate artist clinging to the fringes of those who have real talent, but it is all I know. I have no other profession and no head for business. I love luxury and beauty and I fear that without them I will shrivel and die.' He buried his face in his hands, rocking to and fro in his chair.

Her anger dissolved into pity for this frail person who seemed to have given up on life itself. Lily had lost her appetite, but she was not going to give in as easily as her stepfather. She left the room and marched upstairs to her mother's boudoir, entering without knocking. The odour of stale perfume, alcohol and cigar smoke was nauseating. The room was stuffy and airless. Lily went to the window, drew back the curtains and flung up the sash. 'Ma, wake up.'

A muffled groan from the depths of the four-poster was the only answer Lily received. She moved swiftly to the bedside and drew back the curtains. Charlotte blinked and pulled the pillow over her head, but Lily was having none of this, and she snatched it away. 'Ma, wake up. There's trouble.'

Charlotte raised herself on one elbow, blinking and shielding her eyes from the light. 'What's the matter?'

'The bailiffs, Ma. They're going to seize your property if Everard can't pay up by midday and he's likely to end up in jail.' There was no easy way to put things and even though her instinct was to sympathise, Lily chose not to let her mother down lightly. She pulled the covers back as her mother attempted to slide further down the bed. 'You're not getting away so easily, Ma. Everard needs you. He's in a bad way.'

'Oh, darling, don't nag me,' Charlotte whimpered. 'Send for Parsons. I need a seltzer and a cup of hot chocolate before I can even begin to think.'

Lily hesitated, staring at her mother in dismay. What, she wondered, would it take to make Ma face reality?

'Ring the bell, please,' Charlotte moaned. 'My head is splitting.'

Lily could imagine the state of chaos in the servants' quarters and she doubted if anyone would answer the summons, but she tugged at the bell pull anyway and murmuring an excuse she left the room.

Downstairs in the basement kitchen there was, as Lily had anticipated, an atmosphere of near panic. Cook was nowhere to be seen but there were thumps and muttered swearing emanating from the small room where she slept at night. The scullery maid was sitting on a stool with her apron over her head while Parsons strode up and down, wringing her hands. The tweeny had her hat and coat on and announced that she was going home to her parents in Limehouse before the bailiffs came and clapped her in jail. Seemingly oblivious to the situation, Prissy was in the scullery washing the breakfast dishes.

'Cook's busy packing,' Prissy said in answer to Lily's enquiry. 'Miss Parsons, you'll do yourself a mischief if you keep going on like that,' she added, frowning.

Parsons threw up her hands. 'The disgrace will ruin me,' she moaned. 'Who will take on a lady's maid from a discredited family? My reputation will be tarnished forever.'

'I'm sure it's not as bad as that,' Lily said, making an effort to sound confident, although secretly she thought that Parsons was right. 'Mr Everard will think of something, I'm sure of that.'

'I wish I had your confidence in him,' Parsons snapped. 'I had my doubts about taking the position with Mrs Faulkner and heaven knows my friends told me not to consider throwing my lot in with artists. I wish I'd taken their advice. What is to become of me?'

'Mrs Faulkner would like a cup of hot chocolate,' Lily said tentatively.

'Let her come down here and make it herself then. I'm going to pack my bag and escape from this madhouse.' Parsons stormed out of the room, slamming the door behind her.

'I'll make the chocolate,' Prissy volunteered. 'You go on up and comfort the poor lady. I'll bring it to her room when it's ready.'

The scullery maid gave a loud moan. 'Me dad will kill me. There are fifteen mouths to feed at our house and he'll give me the strap for losing me job.'

Lily stared helplessly at the girl whose head was still covered with the grubby apron.

'Pay no heed to her,' Prissy said, shaking her head. 'She's not got all her buttons, if you get my meaning. Too many cuffs around the head have left her a bit simple, but don't worry, miss. I'll get the cleaning woman to take her in; she's a good sort and has taken quite a shine to poor Minnie.'

'Thank you, Prissy. I'll go and find Mr Everard and see if we can't sort something out before the bailiffs return at noon.' Lily left Prissy in charge of the kitchen and went in search of Everard. She found him in his study, sitting at his desk staring into space. She took a seat opposite him. 'There must be something we can do.'

He shook his head, pointing to a sheaf of bills tied with red tape. 'We would have to rob a bank to pay off our creditors. I hadn't realised that things had gone so far.'

'Is there no way you could raise even some of the money?'

'Sadly no. I've borrowed from friends as it is and I can't repay them. That hurts even more than my debts to the tradesmen.'

'Perhaps they might take some of your paintings?' Lily suggested hopefully. 'The ones hanging on the staircase are really good and I'm sure they must be worth a lot of money.'

'You're too kind, Lily. I'm afraid the art critics don't agree with you. They call my work daubs, and they have been less kind to my beloved Carla. One of them said her latest work could have been done by a blind baboon, which was particularly cruel and totally uncalled for.'

'What will you do?' Lily's heart ached for him and she wished she could do something to help, but she was powerless as well as penniless. It seemed to her at that moment that the whole world was against them.

Everard raised his head to look at her and she saw defeat in his eyes.

'There's nothing I can do but wait for the inevitable, Lily. It's all my fault, of course. I should have been firmer with your mother and I should have kept track of our income and outgoings.'

Lily leapt to her feet, casting her gaze around the room. 'There must be something you could pawn. We could go through all your valuables right now, and I'll take them to the nearest pop-shop.' She fingered a silver and cut glass inkstand. 'This would raise a bob or two.'

Everard shrugged his shoulders. 'That fortunately is bought and paid for. Take it, Lily, but as to the rest, I'm afraid you're wasting your time.'

'Don't say that,' Lily cried passionately. 'Leave it to me. I'll do what I can.' She went round the room picking items up and then replacing them when Everard shook his head. Having exhausted the options in the study, Lily raced upstairs to demand help from her mother, but Charlotte refused to give up any of her jewels, laughing at the notion that they were clever imitations. 'You're being hysterical, my darling,' she said, sitting up in bed to sip her hot chocolate. 'Everard will send the bailiffs away with a flea in their big ugly ears. Now go away and allow your mama to get dressed. Oh, and ring the bell for Parsons on your way out.'

Lily tugged at the bell pull, knowing full well that Parsons would not respond. She was saddened by her mother's intransigent attitude, but she realised that Ma was living in a world of make-believe. Lily dreaded to

343

think what would happen when the world created for her mother by a doting Everard came tumbling down around their heads.

Taking the few items she could find of value, Lily enlisted Prissy's help in locating a pawnshop. They went together and Lily bargained hard to get a good price for the valuables, coming away satisfied with her efforts but worried that the sum they had raised would not be enough to buy off the creditors even temporarily.

It was midday when they returned to Keppel Street breathless and panting, having run the last few hundred yards. The front door was open and Lily paused on the top step, her heart racing inside her breast. She could hear her mother's hysterical sobs and shrieks even before she entered the house.

Prissy squeezed her hand. 'Best hurry with the money.'

It was good advice and Lily hurried to the morning parlour where she could hear raised voices. Just as she reached the door, Everard emerged handcuffed to a burly police constable. The bailiff's men were close on their heels.

'Everard, I've got the money,' Lily gasped. 'Please, constable, let him go. I can pay something towards the debt.'

One of the bailiffs held out his hand to take the purse from Lily. Without bothering to open it, he weighed it in his hand. 'No hope, miss.' He tossed it back to her. 'Keep it to buy the old bloke privileges when you visit him in the debtors' jail.'

Chapter Eighteen

The bailiffs cleared the house of everything that had belonged to Charlotte and Everard. Most of the furnishings were the property of the landlord, and the rented silver and china were quickly reclaimed by their owner. The paintings were stripped from the wall despite Lily's protests, and taken off to a gallery to be valued and auctioned at a later date. Charlotte was distraught and hysterical and it took all Lily's efforts plus a hefty dose of laudanum to calm her down. Leaving her mother lying in a drugged sleep with her flame-coloured hair spilling over the pillow reminiscent of one of the paintings she so admired, Lily went slowly downstairs. Silence echoed through the empty house and bare patches on the walls, once adorned by Everard's paintings, bore testament to the thoroughness of the bailiffs' work.

In the dining room the mahogany credenza had been stripped of the silver and the cut glass decanters. The epergne was gone from the centre of the dining table and the mantelshelf was bare of ornaments. The room had the sad and empty look of an unloved house put up for sale; the same was true of the morning parlour and Everard's study. The books had gone from the shelves and there was a space in the corner where the grandfather clock had ticked away the minutes, chiming the quarters and hours in sonorous tones.

Lily made her way downstairs to find the kitchen deserted except for Prissy, who was stirring a pan on the range. She looked up at the sound of Lily's footsteps on the flagstones and she grinned. 'I managed to save the stew, but the greedy vultures rifled through the larder snatching everything they could and filling their pockets as well as their greedy gobs. They'd have took the soup but it was too hot to handle.'

'Where is Cook?'

'She's gone, and so has Parsons. They've all scarpered except for me and I ain't going nowhere without you, miss.'

'You're a good girl, Prissy,' Lily said with feeling. 'But I can't pay you, and when they force us to leave this house I've nowhere to go.'

'Something will turn up,' Prissy said confidently. 'Sit down and I'll serve the soup, unless you'd like me to bring your grub to the dining room. You can't let your standards slip just because of a little upset.'

Lily smiled, shaking her head. Prissy had sounded just like Aggie, but the memory of last night with the family was still fresh in her mind and even more painful in the light of day. She could not go home; she had no home. She sat down at the table as her knees threatened to give way beneath her and the enormity of their situation hit her with full force. In between her attempts at raising money to pay off the bailiffs and dealing with her mother's hysterics she had not until now had time to think about the future.

Prissy placed a bowl of soup on the table in front of Lily. 'There you are, I wants to see that all gone. Shall I take some up to the missis?'

'No, let her sleep. She can have something to eat when she wakes.' Lily stared at the vegetables swimming in beef stock. The aroma was tempting but her stomach revolted at the sight of food and she pushed the plate away. 'I'm sorry, Prissy, but I'm not very hungry.'

Prissy stood over her like a small but determined terrier. 'You must eat, miss. You got to keep your strength up.'

Lily shook her head mutely.

'Just a spoonful, there's a good girl,' Prissy said, using a tone she might have used to cajole a small child. 'Just to please me, miss.'

Too emotionally exhausted to refuse, Lily picked up the spoon and took a mouthful.

Prissy nodded and smiled, taking a seat opposite Lily. 'You'll feel better with some vittles inside you. We got to have a plan, miss. They'll be back afore long and we'll be turned out on the street. I seen it happen no end of times in the village.'

Lily paused with the spoon halfway to her lips. 'You must go home, Prissy. The money we had from the pawnbroker won't go very far, and I can't pay your wages. You should go back to your family.'

'Not likely. You need looking after, and then there's the missis; how will you manage her without me to help you?'

'I don't know, and that's the honest truth.'

'Well, first thing you do when you've eaten all your dinner is go round to see Mr Gabriel. You got to tell him what's happened. He's your stepbrother so he's bound to help.'

'He rents one room in a lodging house, Prissy. We can't go there.'

'Then it's up to him to find a place for you and your ma. That's all there is to it.' Sounding supremely confident, Prissy mopped up the last of her soup with a crust of bread and popped it into her mouth.

Lily knew what Prissy had said made sense but she was reluctant to go cap in hand to Gabriel. A marriage contract between Ma and Everard might make her related to Gabriel in law, but that did not make her his responsibility. She would not and could not in all conscience impose on his good nature.

'So are you going round to Gower Street then?'

Lily looked up with a start as Prissy's voice intruded on her thoughts. 'To Gower Street?'

'To Mr Gabriel's lodgings,' Prissy said patiently. 'He's got to know what's happened to his old man, even if you're too proud to ask for his help.'

'That's not true,' Lily began but Prissy silenced her with a frown.

'Ain't it? I seen the look on your face when I mentioned his name. What else are you going to do? I doubt if that family of yours will be rushing round to help.'

Lily was about to protest when one of the bells rang to summon a servant.

'That's your Ma's room,' Prissy said unnecessarily. 'I'd best go to her and see what she wants.'

'No, I will.' Lily leapt to her feet as the bell continued to jangle with such violence that it seemed in danger of breaking the spring. The sound echoed in Lily's head, bringing back memories of the fire station and her brothers racing into danger in order to save lives. She ran from the room and lifting her skirts above her knees she took the stairs two at a time, half expecting to find her mother prepared to leap from the window or in a drug-induced stupor, having drunk the whole bottle of laudanum. Flinging the bedroom door open, Lily found her sprawled on the bed tugging at the bell pull.

'Is that you, Parsons?' Charlotte peered anxiously at Lily as if trying to focus her gaze.

'It's Lily, Ma.'

'I must get up and go to the prison. I want to be with Everard.' Charlotte raised herself on her elbow only to collapse again. 'My head is spinning.'

Uncertain whether she wanted to laugh at her own folly or to cry with relief, Lily went over to the bed and eased the embroidered bell pull from her mother's grasp. 'It's the laudanum making you drowsy, Ma. You've had a shock, and you need to rest.'

'They'll release him soon,' Charlotte mused dazedly. 'We must get the best lawyer in town.'

'Yes, of course we will.' Lily filled a glass with water and added a few drops of laudanum. 'Sip this and you'll feel better.'

Charlotte dashed the glass from Lily's hand. 'No, I

won't take the stuff. I need a clear head. Ring for Parsons, I want to get dressed.'

'Parsons has left, and so have the other servants. They've all gone except for Prissy.'

'Then send her to me. I must go to Everard, although I doubt if they'll let me see him, but I must try.'

'You're his wife, Ma. They let families live in the debtors' jail, but that's not for you and Everard wouldn't want you to see him in such a sorry state.'

'We're not married,' Charlotte moaned. 'At least not legally. We pledged our vows to each other in the moonlight on Hampstead Heath with our friends dancing beneath the stars. The wine flowed and a fiddler played a merry tune. It was so romantic.'

Lily stared at her in astonishment. 'You're not married?'

'In the eyes of God we are man and wife; we just never thought to have our union blessed by the Church or acknowledged in law.'

'Then Gabriel is not my stepbrother?'

Charlotte gazed at Lily with bleary eyes. 'What are you talking about? What difference does it make?'

'None,' Lily said hastily. 'Lie still and rest, Ma. We'll visit Everard, but not today.'

'Why not? I want to see him.'

'The bailiffs will be back with a court order evicting us from the property,' Lily explained patiently. 'I need to find somewhere for us to live before we start thinking about lawyers and visiting Everard in jail.'

'Give me some laudanum,' Charlotte moaned. 'And a glass of Madeira or brandy. I don't mind which.'

Lily refilled the glass with water and added more laudanum. 'Drink this and I'll see what I can find.'

Charlotte took the glass and drained it in one gulp. 'This isn't happening to me. It's a nightmare and I'll wake up soon and find everything back to normal.' She closed her eyes.

Lily crept out of the room and made her way slowly downstairs. Her mother's revelation had shocked her. She was aware that the artistic set adopted a bohemian style of living, but she had been brought up to follow Aggie's strict moral code and the fear of hellfire preached at Sunday school. She trembled to think how Nell and Matt would take the news that their mother had been living in sin all these years. Molly and Mark were the rebels, who either slept through church services or managed to slip away unnoticed before the sermon began. They would probably think that Ma was a modern woman and extremely daring. Luke would simply shrug his broad shoulders and think it romantic; he would probably write a few verses on the subject and then forget it as another inspiration filled his head. Lily paused halfway down the staircase, thinking of the brother to whom she felt the closest. She wondered if Luke had managed to persuade Matt to give him back his job, and if he had been allowed to remain in the family home. She hoped so for his sake.

She had just reached the bottom stair when someone hammered on the door. Her heart gave an uncomfortable leap in her chest. It must be the bailiffs returning and that meant they would be forced to leave the house right away. Her instinct was to ignore the person rapping on the knocker. She wanted to shoot the bolts and lock the windows to keep out intruders, but she knew it would be useless. She opened the door, peering out into the winter sunlight.

'Lily, I've just heard the news.' Gabriel brushed past her, entering the house on a gust of cold air. 'Perks came to see me and luckily found me at home. He says the bailiffs have taken everything including the horse and the carriage. Is it true?'

Her throat constricted and suddenly she wanted to cry, but she resisted the temptation to throw herself into Gabriel's arms and weep into the soft cashmere of his overcoat. She nodded her head, unable to speak. He took her by the shoulders, looking anxiously into her eyes. 'You poor dear, are you all right? It must have been a dreadful shock.'

She nodded again.

He put his arm around her shoulders, leading her to the morning parlour and uttering an exclamation of surprise and horror to see it cold and bare, stripped of all its finery. 'The bastards,' he breathed. 'Have they done this to all the rooms?'

'I – I think so. I haven't been to my bedchamber, but they've taken everything that doesn't belong to the landlord. They've arrested your pa and taken him to Cold Bath Fields Prison.'

'The devil they have.' Gabriel took off his hat and gloves, setting them down on one of the remaining chairs. 'This is a bad show. How has Cara taken it?'

'It's Charlotte. I can't stand all this silly pretence and

affectation. Ma's name is Charlotte and she's not even married to your pa, Gabriel. She's Charlotte Larkin and she's lying on her bed drugged with laudanum. I don't know what I'm going to do with her, or where we'll live. All the servants have gone except for Prissy, and the bailiffs will be coming back with a court order to turn us out onto the streets.' It had all come out in a rush and Lily stopped for breath, biting her lip. 'I'm sorry, I didn't mean to fling it all at you like that.'

He pressed her gently down onto the sofa. 'My dear girl, I'm so sorry. If only I'd been here I might have done something to help.'

Lily fished in her pocket for a handkerchief and, finding none, she sniffed. 'There's nothing you could have done. I tried to raise some money in the pawnshop but it wasn't enough. It will buy us a room for the next few nights but after that I just don't know what we'll do.'

Gabriel sat down beside her, taking a clean handkerchief from his pocket and pressing it into her hand. 'Wipe your eyes, Lily. I'm here to help my little sister. This is all my father's fault and I'll do my best to look after you and Car— I mean Charlotte.'

'I'm not your sister,' Lily muttered into the fold of the hanky.

'And I'm very glad we're not related,' Gabriel said, chuckling. 'No, don't glare at me like that, Lily. I mean it kindly. I'd much rather be your very good friend than your brother.'

'Don't joke,' Lily said crossly. 'It's no laughing matter.'

'Mrs Lovelace would certainly agree with you on that.' He rose to his feet and went to stand with his back to the empty grate. 'I'm afraid we are both homeless, Lily. The old girl's given me my marching orders, having overhead Perks announcing the fact that my pa has been arrested for debt and flung in jail. She said she runs a respectable lodging house and can't have people like me bringing discredit to her business. So you see, my dear, we're both in the same boat, and we'll look after each other.'

'I can't go anywhere without Ma, and Prissy refuses to leave me.'

'There's room for everyone. As a matter of fact I've been thinking about a move for some time and this has just brought matters to a head. It's not ideal but I know of a house in Cock and Hoop Yard, Spitalfields. It's not the most salubrious of areas but the rent is cheap and there is room enough for us all. I met the owner in a pub; he seems like a decent sort of chap, if a bit eccentric. I think you'll like him, Lily.'

'What sort of house is it, and what is the area like? Ma won't want to live in a slum.'

'Charlotte has no say in this, Lily. She can go and live with my father in the debtors' jail if she objects to my choice. I love her dearly, but I'm not putting up with her megrims. She'll have to earn her living like the rest of us.'

'But that's not fair, Gabriel. What can she do – and for that matter what can I do – to earn money?'

'I'm thinking of starting up an art school, but we'll work it out as we go along. My income is sufficient to

354

keep us from the poorhouse for the time being at least, and if my plans work out we'll be comfortably off, and we may be able to move to a better part of town. What do you say?'

The move to Cock and Hoop Yard took place that evening under the cover of darkness. The bailiffs had given Charlotte and Lily until next day to remove themselves from the house in Keppel Street, but neither Lily nor Gabriel thought it a good idea to wait until they were officially made homeless. With a mixture of what appeared to Lily to be luck combined with dogged determination, Gabriel had made all the arrangements for their move, including hiring two hackney carriages to take them to their new home. Gabriel, Charlotte and Lily travelled in the first cab, with Prissy and their luggage following in the second vehicle.

Lily was unfamiliar with Spitalfields and the area around the East India Depot, but she had vague recollections of the Minories and the Tower of London, which she had once visited on a family outing before the fatal day when Ma had left home never to return. Glancing at her mother slumped in the corner of the carriage, Lily felt nothing but pity. All the anger and resentment had faded as she had begun to understand her mother's love for Everard and her desperate need to express herself in art. This, coupled with a yearning to be surrounded by beautiful things, had led ultimately to her downfall. Until this moment Lily had not fully understood why Matt and Nell had tried so hard to keep her from fulfilling her desire to paint and draw, but now she could see something of herself in their mother, and suddenly everything became clear. She might disagree with their intransigent attitude but she could sympathise with their wish to keep her safe from temptation.

She had had plenty of time to think since she had been forced to leave her family in Cock Hill, and she realised that all their current troubles had begun with the fire at Bell Wharf. The arrival of the injured Frenchman in their midst had started a chain of events that had led them to the dire straits in which they now found themselves, and from which it seemed there was no happy ending. She had fallen headlong in love with Armand, but so had Nell and Molly. If he were to choose her above her sisters there would be even more heartache and sorrow heaped upon her suffering family. She closed her eyes, conjuring up a vision of herself and Armand, arm in arm, walking down the aisle with Nell and Molly as her bridesmaids. The church was cold and the light subdued but as they stepped outside into the sunshine and she looked up into her new husband's face – it was not Armand looking down at her with an adoring expression. Her breath caught in her throat and she opened her eyes with a start. She glanced anxiously at Gabriel but his attention was fixed on keeping Charlotte from slipping off the seat as the carriage swung into Houndsditch.

Lily turned her head to stare out of the window in an attempt to clear her mind of disturbing thoughts and visions. She loved Armand; of course she did. She could not be so fickle in her feelings that she had given her heart to another man. Could she? She took deep breaths, inhaling the familiar scents of the Orient, the Spice Islands and the West Indies that wafted from the warehouses through the open carriage window. She knew now that they were close to the river. She had grown up with the aroma of exotic spices, rum and molasses and the toffee-like smell of raw tobacco emanating from the ships tied up alongside the wharves. The fragrances, then as now, were adulterated by chimney smoke, soot, sewage and stinking river mud. Like all her memories of the past, this one was bittersweet but achingly familiar, and made her yearn for days gone by when life had seemed so simple.

The pounding of the horse's hooves slowed and came to a halt. Lily could see a tall building shored up with wooden struts and she hoped that this was not the haven that Gabriel had promised them, but then, with a feeling of relief, she realised that it was the back of a pub and the sign above the door bore the legend The Nag's Head.

'We're here,' Gabriel said, opening the door and stepping out onto the pavement. Having helped Lily alight from the carriage, he produced a large iron key from his jacket pocket and handed it to her. 'It's the first house on the left; the one with the gas lamp on the wall.'

She paused for a moment, taking in her surroundings. Her first impression was of loud noise emanating from the pub. She could hear the scraping of a bow across the strings of a fiddle, and someone bawling the words of a popular song as they attempted to make themselves heard above the din of raised voices, laughter and the clink of glasses and pewter tankards. A burly sailor lurched out of the door on a gust of warm air laden with the smell of ale, strong liquor and tobacco smoke. He staggered past Lily, touching his cap as he made his unsteady way towards the docks.

Following the direction that Gabriel had indicated, Lily realised that the house in Cock and Hoop Yard was the first in a terrace of three-storey dwellings set around a narrow courtyard. The gaslight mounted on the end wall of what was to be their new home illuminated a neat frontage with a mansard roof and a door facing the street painted green to match the shutters on the downstairs window. The house looked small and friendly despite the raffish neighbourhood. Lily put the key in the lock and it groaned and grated, refusing at first to turn, but with a little effort she managed to open the door. It was dark inside and she caught her breath as the stale smell of dust, soot and cold cooking fat assailed her nostrils. A spider's web brushed her face and caught on the brim of her bonnet like a veil. With a shudder she brushed it away, hoping that the spider was not lurking somewhere in its depths. She stood aside as Gabriel carried Charlotte into the house.

'Too much laudanum, I think,' he said cheerfully. 'At least she's quiet now.'

'I can't see a thing,' Lily whispered. She was afraid to speak loudly in case her voice summoned up the ghost of some past occupant who resented their intrusion.

'Feel in my pocket,' Gabriel said, shifting Charlotte so that she was draped over his shoulder. 'I've some vestas and a couple of candles which I thought might come in useful.'

Lily found what she was looking for and lit one of the candles, holding it above her head as she took in her new surroundings. Charlotte moaned and made a vague movement of her hands as if protesting at being held upside down, although she was not fully conscious.

'Lead the way upstairs,' Gabriel said softly. 'I checked with the landlord and the rooms are furnished after a fashion, but at least there are beds, and Prissy is following with the bedding.'

'I'm here,' Prissy called from the doorway. 'The cabby is helping me in with the things but he wants paying afore you disappear.'

Gabriel turned to Lily with a grin. 'My pocket again, Lily. The other side this time.'

Lily found the leather pouch, which was reassuringly heavy, and she gave Prissy enough to pay the cab fare with a generous tip. Leaving her capable young maid to organise the luggage, Lily led the way upstairs. Their footsteps echoed loudly on the bare treads, creating the impression that the small house was filled with a marching band of ghostly entities. Lily shivered. It seemed even colder inside than out. Something furry ran across her feet, and she stifled a scream, but she continued upwards determined not to be beaten by the cold and dark. In the morning things would look much better, she thought, hopefully. Tomorrow she would laugh at her unfounded fears. She reached the first landing. 'Which room, Gabriel?'

'I don't know, try the door opposite. There are only two bedrooms on this floor but there is another one in the attic.'

Lily opened the door and a cry of terror was ripped from her throat as she saw what appeared to be a small man slumped face down on the floor.

'What's the matter?' Gabriel demanded, pushing past her.

'It's a tiny man. I think he's dead.' Lily could barely frame the words.

Gabriel's laughter ricocheted off the ceiling, coming back to taunt him. 'Heavens no, Lily. Can't you see? It's a marionette?' He crossed the bare boards to move the object with the toe of his shoe.

Lily uttered a squeak of dismay, unconvinced until she saw the gaping wooden mouth and staring glass eyes of the puppet, and the strings that dangled from each of its limbs. 'What is it doing here?'

'Didn't I tell you? The landlord is a magician and a puppeteer. He used to live here but he owns the house next door and when the last tenant moved out Magnus the Magnificent moved in.'

'I've never seen one of these before,' Lily said, breathing a sigh of relief.

'Well, you have now.' Gabriel stepped over the grinning and slightly grisly-looking wooden caricature of a man and carried Charlotte to the bed, where he laid her down. 'We'll return his property first thing in the morning. I suggest we unpack only what we need for tonight, and I'll go to the pie and eel shop in Houndsditch and get us some supper.'

Lily stepped over the lifeless puppet and went to the bed. She brushed a lock of hair back from her mother's damp forehead with a sigh. 'I hope she'll feel better in the morning. She's lost without Everard.'

Gabriel paused in the doorway. 'I gave this address to the prison officials, but I plan to go there first thing tomorrow to make sure my father is being treated properly, and to find out how much it will take to gain his release.' He stepped outside onto the small landing, calling to Prissy. 'Bring a coverlet for Mrs Faulkner, please, Prissy. We don't want her to catch a chill.'

'Thank you,' Lily whispered to his shadowy form as he descended the stairs. 'Thank you for everything, Gabriel.'

That night Lily and Prissy shared the back bedroom. Lily took the single iron bedstead and Prissy curled up on the truckle bed. Despite the noise from the pub Lily fell into a deep sleep. When she awakened next morning she thought for a moment she was back in Cock Hill, but as she stretched and her eyes became accustomed to the gloom she realised that the person snoring in the other bed was Prissy and not Molly. It was bitterly cold in the room and she realised how spoilt she had been in Keppel Street with a fire lit before she awakened and clean clothes laid out ready for her. She reached for her wrap and slipped it about her shoulders before swinging her legs over the side of the bed. She shivered as her bare feet touched the ice-cold oilcloth that covered the floorboards. There were no warm slippers or a cup of hot chocolate to keep her going until breakfast, but she had been brought up without such luxuries and she could manage perfectly well without them.

Taking care not to awaken Prissy, Lily lifted the latch on the door and crossed the narrow landing to her mother's room. Charlotte's bedcovers were in disarray as if she had tossed and turned all night, but she seemed peaceful enough now, and for that Lily was grateful. She tiptoed out of the room and was halfway down the stairs when she was startled by a loud rapping on the front door. Outside in the street she could hear the steady tramp of hobnail boots as men trudged to work on the docks and wharves. The clatter of horses' hooves was accompanied by the rumbling of cartwheels and the shouts of coster-mongers as they hauled their barrows towards the market in Petticoat Lane.

'Oy, open up in there,' a man's voice demanded as he thumped again on the door.

Lily hurried to answer his summons before he woke the whole house. She opened the door a crack, peering out anxiously. 'Who's there?'

'It's me, Magnus, your landlord. Open up, young lady.'

Clutching her wrap around her, Lily stood aside as he entered the hallway, filling it with his bulk. He took off his bowler hat revealing a bald head somewhat at variance with his luxuriant set of mutton chop whiskers and curling black moustache. 'Good morning, miss. Magnus the Magnificent at your service.'

'Good morning, Mr Magnus,' Lily murmured, eyeing him warily. 'What can I do for you?'

'I apologise for the early morning call, my dear. But I left something of mine in the house and I have an early start today. We, my little friends and I, are travelling to Chelsea this morning. We are giving a performance at Cremorne Gardens.'

'Oh, you mean the puppet. I thought for a moment it was a tiny man lying dead on the floor.' Lily's giggle died on her lips as she realised that she had said the wrong thing.

Magnus glared at her, wide-eyed with affront. 'Do not speak about my children in that disparaging tone, my good woman. Where is my boy?'

'I'm sorry, I mean, I thought . . .'

'My little friends are real to me, miss. How else would I create a world in which others can believe if I myself were not wholly sincere?'

Lily made a move towards the front parlour where Gabriel had left the puppet dangling from the mantelshelf. 'I'll fetch it, I mean him, if you'll give me a moment.'

But Magnus did not seem to be in a patient mood and he strode past Lily, entering the parlour and uttering a cry of dismay. 'My poor boy, Charlie. What have they done to you?' Stepping over the pile of boxes and baggage that had been brought from Keppel Street, Magnus lifted the dangling puppet from the mantelshelf as tenderly as if it were a living thing. 'There, there, Charlie. My poor little fellow, did you think your pa had abandoned you?'

'I've heard about Cremorne Gardens,' Lily said in an attempt to steer the conversation away from the marionette. 'It must be a splendid place.'

Cradling the puppet in his arm, Magnus turned to her and his expression softened. He twirled his waxed moustache with the tip of his thumb and forefinger. 'We are frequently asked to entertain there. You must come and see my act. I will tell your brother that he must bring you one evening.'

Lily did not bother to correct him. She sensed that their new landlord would not take kindly to her sharing the house with a man to whom she was not related. 'Thank you, I'd like that.'

'Just mention my name at the gate,' Magnus said airily. 'If they don't let you in for nothing I'll eat my hat.' He swanned out of the room, setting his bowler back on his head with a dramatic gesture. 'I'll take my leave of you now, miss. The rent is due on Friday.' He let himself out of the house, murmuring apologies to Charlie for abandoning him to people who did not know how to treat an artiste of his calibre. Lily hurried to lock the door, but just as she was about to turn the key, someone outside crashed on the knocker. Thinking it was Magnus she opened the door to find a policeman standing on the pavement.

'Is this the residence of Mr Faulkner?'

Lily's mouth went dry. His serious expression frightened her and her heart began to race.

Chapter Nineteen

Had they taken something from the house in Keppel Street that did not belong to them? It would have been easy to make a mistake during their hurried departure. Lily eyed the young constable warily. 'Is something wrong?'

He took a notebook from his pocket and flipped through the pages. 'I'm looking for Mr Gabriel Faulkner, miss. Does he or does he not reside at this address?'

Lily hesitated. If Gabriel was in some kind of trouble she ought to warn him, but she could see by his set expression that the policeman was not going to be fobbed off easily. The sound of footsteps on the stairs made her turn her head. Gabriel's smile faded as he saw the police officer standing on the doorstep. 'Is there anything wrong, constable?'

'May I come in, sir?' The policeman took his helmet off and tucked it under his arm, stepping over the threshold as Gabriel motioned him to enter.

Lily closed the door. Something bad had happened; she sensed trouble. The police never turned up on a person's doorstep bearing good tidings.

The constable cleared his throat. 'Are you Mr Gabriel Faulkner, sir?'

'I am he.'

'Then I've got some bad news for you, sir. Perhaps we could speak in private?' He shot a meaningful glance in Lily's direction.

'Why don't you go upstairs and put something warm on?' Gabriel said, taking Lily by the shoulders and pointing her towards the stairs. 'Come into the kitchen, officer.'

Frustrated and frightened, Lily was about to go up to her room, but curiosity got the better of her and she tiptoed along the hall to stand outside the kitchen with her ear close to the keyhole. The constable was speaking in a low voice and she could not make out the words, but then Gabriel uttered an agonised cry. 'My father's dead? You must have it wrong, constable. He wouldn't have taken his own life.'

Forgetting her state of undress, Lily pushed the door open and rushed into the room. 'Gabriel.' She flung her arms around him. 'It can't be true. There must be some mistake.'

He did not respond to her touch. The colour had drained from his face and his lips moved but no sound came from them.

In desperation, Lily turned to the young policeman, who was looking thoroughly discomforted. 'It can't be Everard. He wouldn't do such a thing.'

'I'm sorry, miss. I just came to bring the message. I don't know nothing more. Mr Faulkner must accompany me to the prison to formally identify the body.'

'Speak to me.' Lily gave Gabriel a gentle shake. 'Please say something.' She gazed anxiously into his

face but still he did not respond. At the sound of footsteps pattering across the flagstone floor, Lily looked
round to see Prissy hurrying towards her.

'It's all right, miss. I heard it all from upstairs. Just
leave Mr Gabriel to me.' Gently disengaging Lily's
arms from around Gabriel's neck, Prissy gave her a
hug. 'Go upstairs and get dressed or you'll be next on
the slab.'

'Oh, Prissy. It can't be true. Everard was the kindest
person I've ever met. He can't be dead.'

'How'd he do it, constable?' Prissy demanded. 'Or
was he done in?'

'Hanged hisself, miss.' The constable's face flushed
a deep shade of red. 'I'm sorry to tell you so, but you
did ask. I can't say no more, and I'm directed to bring
Mr Faulkner to the prison as soon as you like.'

'I'm so sorry, Gabriel,' Lily said softly. 'Perhaps
there's been a tragic mix-up and it's not your pa.'

Her voice seemed to penetrate somewhere deep in
Gabriel's mind and he blinked, dashing his hand across
his eyes. 'I must go with the constable.'

'You'll go nowhere until you've had a nice hot cup
of tea,' Prissy said firmly. 'And you too, officer. You
look worse than him.' She shooed Lily towards the
door. 'Upstairs I said. Now.'

Gabriel had been gone all morning. Lily had wanted
to tell her mother straight away but Prissy suggested
it would be better to wait for Gabriel's return. If it was
a case of mistaken identity they would have upset the
missis for nothing, she said, nodding her head sagely.

It would be best all round to let her rest and regain her strength before she had to hear the tragic news. Lily knew she was being cowardly, but she took Prissy's advice, and making an effort to appear as if nothing untoward had happened she took her mother's hot chocolate to her.

Charlotte opened her eyes, blinking owlishly at her daughter. 'Where am I, Lily? This isn't my room.'

'We had to leave Keppel Street, Ma,' Lily said gently. 'Don't you remember?'

Charlotte's face contorted with pain. 'My poor darling Everard.' She closed her eyes and tears seeped from beneath her lids to run unchecked down her cheeks. 'I'll never be able to hold my head up in public again. We'll be ruined if this gets out.'

Lily plumped the pillows and made her mother comfortable. 'Don't upset yourself, Ma. Everard wouldn't want you to make your face all blotchy with crying.'

'How will we manage, Lily?' Charlotte glanced round the room with a shudder. 'I can't live like a pauper. I'll die in this dreadful place.'

Lily placed the cup of hot chocolate in her hands. 'You won't die, Ma. Drink this and you'll feel better.'

'My poor darling will be drinking filthy water and eating gruel for breakfast. We must find a good solicitor straight away. I don't care what it costs.'

Lily knew there was no point in arguing. Ma was refusing to accept the fact that they were virtually bankrupt. How she would take the news of Everard's suicide was too terrible to contemplate. She took the brown-glass medicine bottle from the mantelshelf and poured a few drops of laudanum into a glass of water.

Charlotte handed her the empty cup. 'I'll have my medicine now, Lily. Then you may tell Prissy to run my bath, and ask her to lay out my lilac watered silk morning gown. I must look my best when I visit Everard. He likes to see me turned out well.'

'Yes, Ma.'

Charlotte drained the mixture of laudanum and water, sinking back against the pillows with a sigh. 'I think I'll take a little nap. Wake me when my bath is ready, darling.'

Lily nodded her head. If she spoke now she knew she would break down and cry. She hurried from the room, satisfied that Ma would have a few more hours of peace before she had to face the news that would inevitably break her heart.

Downstairs, Lily found Prissy in the kitchen talking to a strange-looking woman who appeared to be wearing the costume of a milkmaid from a past century. The odd garments sat incongruously on her skinny limbs. She was neither young nor beautiful and her grizzled grey hair hung about her head in tight corkscrew curls. Her cheeks were rouged and her eyebrows blackened with soot so that they looked like two hairy caterpillars resting above her china-blue eyes.

'This here is Mrs Magnificent,' Prissy said by way of explanation. 'We was just about to have a cup of tea.'

'Mad Mary they call me.' The woman bobbed a curtsey. Her wide smile revealed bare gums except for one large top tooth which stuck out like a blanched almond. 'Mad Mary Preston. Me old man is Magnus the Magnificent and he said I should call and make meself known to you, seeing as how we're neighbours and you are our new tenants.'

'Pleased to make your acquaintance.' Lily was unsure how to treat this extraordinary creature and looked to Prissy for inspiration.

Mad Mary did not seem aware that she presented a comic figure. Her bodice was cut low, exposing rather too much of her wrinkled prune-like flesh. She wore a kirtle looped to expose a scarlet flannel petticoat which ended just above her twig-like ankles, and her over-large feet were encased in black patent-leather shoes with enormous silver buckles.

Without waiting to be invited, Mad Mary took a seat by the range. Producing a clay pipe and a tobacco pouch from somewhere about her person, she proceeded to smoke while speaking at length about the act that she and her husband performed onstage. When at last she came to an end, having drunk several cups of tea and puffed on her pipe until she had created a fug, she rose to her feet and announced that she must hurry if she were to catch the midday boat to Cremorne Gardens. 'Good day to you, ladies,' she said airily. 'I'm glad to be the first to welcome you to Cock and Hoop Yard. You'll find us a friendly lot, but don't let Silly Sally into the house. She's not all there, but there's no real harm in her.'

She left the room and Prissy ran to open the window even though it was raining heavily. 'That'll wash some of the paint off her face,' she said, chuckling. 'Seems to me they're all a bit mad round here, but at least she made you smile, miss. So she ain't all bad.'

'I shouldn't be laughing,' Lily said, hanging her head. 'I feel like crying but I keep hoping that Gabriel will come home and tell us it's all a mistake, and some other poor man has taken his own life. Although I know that's a wicked thing to say.'

'You think a deal too much,' Prissy said severely. 'Now you listen to me. I found your paintbox amongst Mr Gabriel's bags when I was unpacking and putting things away. I suggest you go in the front parlour and do what you like doing best. It'll take your mind off you-know-what.'

'But I can't,' Lily protested. 'What if Ma wakes up and calls out?'

'Lor' love you, ducks. This house is so small you could hear a mouse sneeze. If she calls out I'll be up them stairs in a flash. Now go on and do us a pretty picture to hang on the wall. This place could do with a bit of cheering up.'

Lily went into the front parlour and found her paint-box laid out waiting for her with a stick of charcoal and a sheet of paper. Her feelings of guilt vanished as she set about sketching the view from the window. The houses opposite were identical to the one they now occupied, and although they were somewhat rundown in appearance, the green shutters and doors gave them a certain raffish charm. A woman with a small child was standing at the pump on the corner, and there were slightly older children chasing each other in a game of tag. They were shabbily dressed but looked reasonably well fed and healthy, if slightly grubby. Lily found herself sketching away as if her life depended upon it. Lost in a creative world of her own, she barely touched the slice of bread and scrape that Prissy put beside her for her midday meal with the promise of something more substantial later.

'I should go upstairs and check on Ma,' she murmured, half rising from the wooden stool placed in front of the window.

'No need. I went up just now and she's sleeping like a baby. Best leave her like that until we know for certain.'

Lily nodded in agreement. She prayed silently that Gabriel would return and tell them that Everard was alive and well, but she knew it was a slim hope and her fears were confirmed later that afternoon. She had just finished painting a slender girl in a blue cotton gown that was far too flimsy for the winter weather. Seemingly oblivious to the cold, the girl danced about the yard holding her skirts out and kicking her bare legs up in the air. Her flaxen hair was matted and soaked by the falling rain but she appeared to be enjoying every moment. It had to be Silly Sally, Lily thought, feeling almost envious of the girl in her simple state of mind where nothing appeared to matter. The fact that her feet and lower limbs were almost as blue as her stained gown did not seem to worry her, and she might look as though she had never had a square meal in her short life but she was laughing, and her lips moved as though she was singing. Lily was tempted to rush outside and give Sally the untouched food on her plate, but she was distracted by the sound of someone knocking on the front door. She emerged from the parlour to find Gabriel standing in the narrow hallway shaking raindrops from his hat, while Prissy fussed around him demanding that he take off his sodden overcoat. His grim expression confirmed Lily's worst fears.

'He's gone,' he said simply. 'Poor Father, it was all too much for him to bear. He couldn't face the disgrace of bankruptcy and what it would do to Charlotte. If only I'd been a better son I might have done something to prevent this terrible thing happening.'

Lily's hand flew to her mouth. 'Don't say that, Gabriel. It wasn't your fault.'

'Of course it weren't,' Prissy said firmly. 'Mr Everard was a grown man and he and the missis lived like lords even though they hadn't the means. If Mr Everard chose to take his own life then it was his decision and his alone.'

A scream from the top of the staircase made them all look up in horror as Charlotte swayed and made a grab for the banister rail. 'Tell me it isn't true.'

Lily and Gabriel exchanged agonised glances. He was the first to speak. 'I'm afraid it is only too true. I am so sorry.'

'Catch her, Gabriel,' Lily cried as her mother crumpled slowly to the floor in a flutter of silk and Brussels lace.

Gabriel leapt forward as Charlotte tumbled head

over heels, bumping painfully off each tread until he caught her in his arms just before she hit the stone floor.

'Is she dead?' The girl Lily had seen dancing in the rain had entered the house unnoticed. Silly Sally came to a halt in front of Gabriel. She cocked her head on one side, eyeing Charlotte's limp form without any apparent emotion other than curiosity. 'I saw a dead cat the other day. It looked all limp and floppy, just like her.' She reached out to finger the material of Charlotte's elegant peignoir. 'It's lovely. Is she a bride? Did she marry you, sir?'

'Get her out of here,' Lily cried, unable to bear it any longer. 'Please, go away, girl.'

Prissy moved swiftly to take Sally by the hand. 'She's not dead, love. The lady took a tumble and she's not very well. You go home, there's a good girl.'

Sally smiled happily. 'I'm glad the lady ain't dead. Things smell something awful when they go off. I'd like her dress if she don't need it no longer.'

Gabriel jerked his head in the direction of the doorway. 'Take her home, Prissy. Maybe one of the neighbours knows where we could get hold of a doctor.'

'Don't worry, guv. I'll fetch a pill-pusher even if I has to drag him by the hair.'

'I know where the doctor lives,' Sally said dreamily. 'I'll take you there, missis. Come on. Don't dilly-dally.' Without waiting for an answer, she dragged Prissy outside into the rain.

'Help me get Charlotte into bed,' Gabriel said gently. 'She'll be all right, Lily. I don't think she hurt herself when she fell, but we'll get the doctor to look her over anyway.'

Lily followed him upstairs as he carried Charlotte back to her room.

Ever resourceful, Prissy returned twenty minutes later with a doctor who tut-tutted over Charlotte's hysterical condition. There were no bones broken, he said after a cursory examination, just bruising from the fall which would fade in time. He prescribed arnica for the bruises and laudanum to sedate the patient, and having charged a fee of half a crown for his professional services he departed.

Drugged and semi-comatose, Charlotte lay in her bed staring at the ceiling, but Lily knew it was just a shell of a woman lying there like a corpse. Charlotte's heart and soul were somewhere else, searching for the man she loved more than life itself. Lily had never before witnessed such heartbreak and she felt completely helpless in the face of her mother's agonising grief. She wished she could take some of the pain on herself, but she knew that this was a journey her mother must make alone.

Gabriel was also suffering and Lily wanted to help him but did not quite know how. She managed to catch him alone the next day after he had returned from the prison with his father's few possessions. Prissy had gone out to the market to buy food and Charlotte was sleeping, sedated by laudanum. 'You look tired,' Lily said, pouring tea into Gabriel's cup. 'When are they releasing your father's body for burial? I need to know so that I can prepare Ma well in advance.'

Gabriel stared down at his fingers as they tapped nervously on the scrubbed pine tabletop. 'It's not that easy, Lily. Father's suicide has made it difficult for me to find a clergyman who would be willing to perform the ceremony, let alone allow him to be buried in the churchyard. Even then the interment must take place at night, between nine and midnight.'

'That's terrible,' Lily said with feeling. 'Everard was a good man at heart.'

'I know, Lily. My father was just weak and foolish with money. But the laws regarding suicides are very clear. Even if there was anything left after his creditors took their share, his estate would be forfeit. All his paintings, everything, will go. Charlotte won't inherit a penny.'

Lily laid her hand over his. 'I am so sorry, Gabriel.'

'It's all come as a bit of a shock.'

She squeezed his fingers gently. 'If there's anything I can do to help . . .'

'Look after Charlotte. She meant a lot to my father. I don't think I ever realised quite what they were to each other until it was too late.'

Lost in her world of suffering, Charlotte remained in bed for several days, refusing to eat or take anything other than sips of water laced with laudanum. Lily was at a loss as to how best to help her mother and she was afraid that Ma would simply pine away. She nursed her devotedly, spending long hours sitting by her mother's bedside in case she awakened and found herself alone and abandoned to her grief. She relied more and more on Prissy, who had taken over the housekeeping duties and had proved to be an excellent plain cook. She made the small house as comfortable as was possible with limited means, making forays into the street markets and auction houses and returning with the odd chair or rug.

Every evening there was a hot meal ready and waiting for Gabriel when he returned tired and dispirited having failed to make any headway with arrangements for his father's funeral. After supper, he would retire to the attic room where he had set up his easel. Lily understood that he drew comfort and solace from his art and that working on his portrait of her was a way of escaping from the problems that beset him. She was not allowed to see the painting, but she sat for him when required and at other times she left him to his own devices.

On the morning of the fourth day, when Charlotte still refused to rouse herself from her stupor, Lily realised that she must do something more than just sympathise with Ma. On her own she was powerless to prevent her mother from simply wasting away, but she hoped and prayed that the family would rally round their mother in her hour of need. Lily put on her cloak and bonnet and let herself out of the house. As usual, Silly Sally was loitering on the corner of the street. She made a beeline for Lily. 'Going for a walk, miss? Can I come with you?'

'No, Sally. I'm going to Pelican Stairs to see my family. Perhaps another day.' In no mood to be charitable, Lily hurried on.

Luke let her in, almost crushing the life out of her in a fond embrace. 'It's good to see you, Lil. I've been meaning to come to Keppel Street with my manuscript. Everard said he would present it to some of his literary friends.'

Lily could not bring herself to give him the sad news and she changed the subject. 'Are things all right between you and Matt?'

Luke pulled a face. 'He gave me a wigging but they were short-handed at the fire station so he took me back into the fold. He'd do the same for you if you'd meet him halfway.' He stepped aside, ushering her into the narrow passage. 'Come into the parlour and have a warm by the fire.'

Lily smiled in spite of everything. It was good to find Luke back with the family, particularly after his falling out with Matt which could have ended in a permanent rift. If only she could be reinstated so easily. 'Where is everyone?'

He moved closer to the fire, warming his hands. 'Grandpa's in his room. Aggie's in the kitchen as usual and Nell has gone to church with Eugene. Mark's paying court to Flossie and I dunno where Matt and Molly are.'

'So you've come to see us, Lily. Have you come to gloat or are you tired of living with fops and loafers?'

Lily jumped at the sound of Matt's voice. He emerged from the kitchen, followed by Aggie who pushed past him to rush over and hug her. 'Take no notice of him, ducks. You will stay and eat with us, won't you? I've roasted a couple of fowls and there's plenty to go round.'

Lily kissed Aggie's leathery cheek. 'There's something important I have to tell the family.'

'So we're part of your family now, are we?' Matt glowered at her. 'Very convenient when you want something, Lily. I thought you were living in luxury with that woman and her lover.'

Lily flinched at the harsh tone in her brother's voice. 'There's something you should know, but I wanted to Nell to be here and Grandpa too.'

'That's easy,' Aggie said. 'I'll go and fetch the old devil. He's probably supping his secret supply of ale. I knew no good would come of living next door to a pub.'

'And Nell's just walked past the window with Eugene,' Luke added. 'I think there's going to be an engagement there one day.'

Lily stared at him in astonishment. 'No, I can't believe it. Not the schoolmaster?'

'Who knows where the heart will lead us?' Luke mused. 'I've written a poem about young love. D'you want to hear it, Lily?'

'No she doesn't and neither do I.' Matt threw himself down on a chair by the fire. 'I blame you for encouraging him in this folly, Lily. He was a reasonably sensible fellow until you introduced him to those wasters who gather in Keppel Street like maggots on a rotting carcase.'

'That's not fair,' Luke protested. 'Lily had nothing to do with it. I went to see Ma of my own accord.'

'Can't we have one day without fighting?' Nell stood in the doorway, frowning. 'It's Sunday, the Lord's day.

Surely we can get on with each other for just a few hours?'

Matt shifted uncomfortably in his seat, and had the grace to look slightly abashed. 'I suppose so. Tell us why you've graced our humble abode with your presence then, Lily.'

'Matt, that's not what I meant and you know it.' Nell turned a serious face to Lily. 'I am pleased to see you, but I can tell by your face that there's something wrong. You didn't come here just for the pleasure of being scolded by Matt. What is it?' She took off her bonnet and moved aside to let Grandpa and Aggie into the room, closely followed by Eugene.

'Yes, spit it out, girl,' Grandpa said, hobbling over to Lily and giving her a peck on the cheek. 'I don't hold with family feuds, so I'm glad to see you.'

'And I too.' Aggie glared at Matt as if daring him to argue.

Eugene said nothing, but he smiled at Lily and she was struck by the genuine warmth in his expression. She glanced at Luke and he gave her an encouraging nod. 'Say what you came to say, Lil, and then we can eat. I'm starving.'

She took a deep breath. 'There's no easy way to put this. Everard got into debt and couldn't pay his creditors. He was arrested and taken to the debtors' jail where he hanged himself. Ma won't eat or rouse herself from her bed. I think she wants to die too and I'm scared.'

'That's terrible news,' Nell said, shaking her head. 'I'm truly sorry, but I don't see what we can do about it.'

Lily looked from one to the other with a sinking heart. She saw very little compassion in their faces. 'She's just given up. I'm afraid she'll just fade away and die.'

'Serve her right,' Grandpa said tersely. 'She never gave a thought to her children when she ran off with the artist chap. She was living in style while we were turned out of our home and living in two rooms. Let her stew in her own juice, I say.'

'Shut up, old man,' Aggie said angrily. 'She weren't all bad, and she's still their ma. Let Nell make up her own mind.'

'Don't speak to Grandpa like that.' Matt turned on Aggie, scowling angrily. 'Get back to the kitchen if you can't keep a civil tongue in your head.'

Aggie's bottom lip trembled and she recoiled as if he had slapped her across the face. 'Is this all the thanks I get for raising you and your brothers and sisters? I'm part of this family too, or will you put throw me out like you did your sister?'

'Stop, stop,' Nell cried passionately. 'This is all wrong.'

Eugene laid his hand on her arm. 'Don't distress yourself, Nell. I'm sure this can all be sorted out if we take it calmly and don't lose our tempers.' He cast a warning look at Matt, who threw up his hands in disgust.

'I'm the head of this household, schoolmaster. Not you.'

'No,' Grandpa bellowed. 'I'm the head of the house, and I say shut up. Shut your trap, Matt Larkin, and let someone else speak for a change.'

Matt stared at his grandfather in amazement. 'Grandpa – I . . .'

Grandpa Larkin held us his hand for silence. 'I say let Nell go and see her mother. This is woman's work and she's the one with the most common sense in this sorry family.'

Nell nodded her head slowly. 'Perhaps I should go with you, Lily, although I'm not sure I can do anything more than you've already done.'

'You'll have your dinner first,' Aggie said sternly. 'Lily looks fit to drop and you need a good meal inside you if you're to walk all the way to Bloomsbury, Nell.'

'We're nearer than that,' Lily said hastily. 'We had to leave Keppel Street. Gabriel has rented a small house in Cock and Hoop Yard, Houndsditch.'

'Well, it's still a fair step,' Aggie conceded. 'You'll eat before you go.' She waddled into the kitchen, casting a warning glance at Matt as she went as if challenging him to disagree with her.

He shrugged his shoulders. 'Go and see her, if you must, Nell. But don't expect me to run round after that woman. Not after what she did to us.'

'Nell must follow her conscience,' Eugene said sternly.

'This has nothing to do with you, schoolmaster,' Matt growled. 'I'd be obliged if you'd keep your nose out of our affairs.'

Lily could see a battle of wills rearing its ugly head and once again she attempted to steer the conversation to safer ground. 'Perhaps Molly ought to come with us, Nell. Where is she, anyway?'

Nell glanced round the room as if surprised by her younger sister's absence. 'I don't know where she is. Molly was here when we left for church, wasn't she, Eugene?'

He nodded his head. 'She was.'

'She went out soon after you'd left,' Luke volunteered. 'Said she was going to see Armand.'

'If you ask me she's been seeing a great deal too much of the Frenchie,' Grandpa said with a disapproving sniff.

'What d'you mean by that?' Matt demanded. 'Are you suggesting that there's something going on between them, Grandpa?'

'I ain't suggesting nothing. I'm telling you that flighty chit has set her cap at the Frenchie and none of you has taken the slightest bit of notice.'

'I thought they smelt of roses,' Luke mused. 'You can always tell.'

Lily struggled to suppress a nervous giggle at the sight of Matt's contemptuous expression. It seemed to her that the whole world had turned upside down. She had long given up romantic ideas concerning Armand, but she had never until now associated him with Molly. 'You must be mistaken,' she murmured.

'I bloody well hope so,' Matt said angrily. 'He'll have me to answer to if he's been taking advantage of my stupid sister.'

Eugene cleared his throat. 'Come now, Larkin. Aren't you jumping to conclusions?'

Matt opened his mouth to respond, but Lily had just seen Molly walk past the window. 'It's all right, Matt,' she said hastily. 'She's come home.'

'I'll have a few words to say to that young lady.' Matt rose from his chair just as Molly breezed into the room.

'Lily. What are you doing here?' She rushed across the floor to give her a hug. 'You're just in time to hear my good news.' She peeled the glove off her left hand, waving it around so that the large diamond ring flashed in the firelight. 'Look everyone, I'm engaged to be married. Isn't that wonderful?'

'Wonderful?' Matt grabbed her by the wrist. 'What sort of fellow gives a girl a ring like this without asking permission from her guardian, who in this instance is me?'

Chapter Twenty

Nell sat down suddenly as if her legs had given way beneath her. 'Who is it, Molly?'

'You can look as green as you like, miss,' Molly said, tossing her head. 'I know you fancied yourself in love with him too, but it's me that Armand wants for his wife. Me, Molly Larkin – soon to be Madame Labrosse.'

Matt fisted his hands, and his face paled beneath his tan. 'Over my dead body. Have you forgotten what that fellow's father did to Lily? I'll not allow you to marry a foreigner, especially one who hasn't the pluck or manners to come to me first.'

'That's not fair,' Nell protested. 'Armand was just as disgusted with his father as anyone else, and he's our landlord now. He let us have this house at a pepper-corn rent, and we'd still be living above the shop in Cock Hill if it wasn't for him.'

'Yes, thank you for reminding me that I'm a poor provider for my family,' Matt said angrily. 'I had to swallow every scrap of pride to accept his charity.'

'I knew you'd make a fuss,' Molly said, pouting. 'But it's too late. I've said yes and I'm wearing his ring. I'm twenty-one and you can't tell me what to do.'

'I can and I will.' Matt moved towards her with a martial gleam in his eyes. 'You're a silly little fool if you think a man in his position will marry a penniless girl from Shadwell.'

'Armand loves me and you can go to hell, Matt.'

'He's toying with your affections. He'll have his way with you and then he'll toss you aside and move on to the next gullible female. They say the apple doesn't fall far from the tree.'

'You're hateful,' Molly screamed. 'He truly loves me and he's proved it.'

Matt's brow darkened ominously. 'And what do you mean by that? Have you allowed him to take liberties with you?'

'Yes, we're lovers if that's what you mean. He'll have to marry me to make an honest woman of me.'

Matt raised his hand as if to strike Molly, but Lily threw herself between them. 'She's lying, Matt. She's just saying these things to get her own way.'

'But it could be true,' Molly teased. 'You'll never know, will you, brother?'

'That's enough,' Nell cried passionately. 'Stop this, both of you.'

'Yes,' Lily said, seizing Molly by the shoulders and shaking her. 'This isn't the time for a row. Something dreadful has happened.'

Molly's petulant expression faded into one of curiosity. 'Why are you here anyway? I thought you weren't allowed over the threshold by that tyrant we call our brother.'

'Tell her, Lily. Tell the selfish little cow that her mother is dying and see if she cares.' Matt strode across the room to snatch his overcoat from its peg.

'Where are you going?' Molly screeched. 'If you hurt Armand I'll – I'll never speak to you again as long as I live.'

Matt shrugged on his coat. 'I'm not going to hurt him. I'm going to kill him.' He slammed out of the room and out of the house. He strode past the window, ramming his cap on his head.

Molly uttered a shriek and threw herself into Luke's arms. 'Stop him, Luke. For the love of God go after him, or I'll be a widow before I'm a wife.'

'Technically that's impossible, old girl,' Luke said, setting her back on her feet. 'And I don't think he'll listen to me. He never has and probably never will.'

Nell turned a worried face to Eugene. 'He might listen to you.'

'I doubt it, but I'll try.' He retrieved his top hat and gloves from the table where he had placed them. 'Don't worry, Nell. I'll do what I can.' He left the room at his usual measured pace.

Lily sank down on the chair that Matt had recently vacated. 'Did you hear what Matt said, Molly? Our mother is in desperate need. Don't you care?'

'Don't all look at me like that,' Molly muttered. 'Why should I bother about her? She's never given a thought to any of us since she ran off with the painter.'

'She needs us now,' Lily cried passionately. 'She's lost the love of her life. Surely you can understand that, Molly?'

'She had her time in the sun and now I'm going to take mine.' Molly's tone was defiant. 'You should all be happy for me. Armand is handsome and wealthy and I never thought I'd get a chance like this.'

Nell moved swiftly to her side and slipped her arm around Molly's shoulders. 'But there are ways of doing things, dear. Matt is only trying to look after you and to protect our good name.'

'Good name, that's rich,' Grandpa snorted. 'Charlotte Delamare ruined that when she ran off with the man who was too cowardly to take his punishment and topped hisself.'

Molly's mouth opened and then closed. For once she seemed to have nothing to say.

'It's true, Moll,' Lily said softly. 'Everard hanged himself in prison and Ma's taken it badly. She won't eat and I think she's willing herself to die so that she can be with him.'

'How romantic,' Molly breathed, clasping her hands to her bosom. 'I think I might do the same if Matt won't allow me to marry Armand.'

'All my eye and Betty Martin,' Grandpa snapped. 'You've got the appetite of a horse, young lady. You've never given up anything in your whole life, nor have you spared a thought for anyone else.'

'That just not true.' Molly's green eyes filled with tears and her mouth drooped at the corners. 'You're being horrid, Grandpa.'

Nell patted her hand. 'Don't cry, dear. I daresay Grandpa didn't mean it exactly like that.'

'I did,' Grandpa muttered. 'Where's me dinner? I'm faint from lack of nourishment.' He rose from his chair and hobbled into the kitchen, calling for Aggie.

Lily and Nell exchanged despairing glances. 'What will we do?' Lily asked tentatively. 'Ma needs us, Nell.'

'And what about me?' Molly demanded angrily. 'Don't I count in this house? My fiancé might be murdered by our brother and all you can think about is Ma. She was always good at getting her own way.'

'Hush, Molly.' Nell frowned thoughtfully. 'I'll come with you, Lily. We'll eat first and then we'll go to see Ma.' She turned to Luke with a persuasive smile. 'You'll come too, won't you, Luke? You were always Ma's favourite son.'

He nodded emphatically. 'I'll bring my manuscript and read her some of my poems. That should cheer her up and she might put me in touch with the publisher that Everard mentioned.' He caught Lily's shocked glance and his cheeks flushed. 'God rest his soul, of course.'

'Well, I'm not coming.' Molly stood up, shaking out her crumpled skirts. 'I'm going to wait here for Armand.'

'You'll come with us if I have to drag you all the way,' Nell said firmly. 'You are so like Ma, and she doted on you for some reason I'll never understand. You always were a spoilt brat, Molly, but this time you're going to do something for someone else.'

The tiny bedroom in Cock and Hoop Yard seemed even smaller to Lily as her brother and sisters crowded around Ma's bed. Charlotte opened her eyes and blinked at the faces hovering above her. She reached out her hand. 'Molly, is that really you?'

Flashing a smug smile in Nell's direction, Molly leaned over to clasp her mother's hand. 'Yes, it's me, Ma. How are you?'

'Not well, darling, but all the better for seeing you.' Charlotte held her other hand out to Luke with a wan smile. 'And my darling boy, Luke. You came to see your poor afflicted mother.'

'Yes, Ma, of course I did. I'd have come sooner if I'd known about . . .' Luke's voice tailed off as he cast an agonised look at Lily.

'We're all here, except for Matt and Mark,' Lily said hastily. 'I'm certain they would have come if they'd known you were unwell.'

Charlotte's hands fluttered down onto the coverlet like two white butterflies. She sighed deeply. 'Matt will never forgive me, and I can't say I blame him. I was a bad mother to you all.' She acknowledged their denials with a wave of her hand. 'No, I was wrong to leave you as I did, but it was all for love.' Her voice trailed off and she closed her eyes. Tears seeped beneath her copper lashes and ran down her cheeks.

'Don't upset yourself, Ma.' Nell reached out to touch her mother's hand. 'It's all in the past and you have to be strong. I think Everard would be mortified if he saw you like this. I know I've been hard on you, and perhaps I didn't understand then how a woman can love a man to the exclusion of all others, but I'm older now and I feel for you.'

Charlotte opened one eye, staring at Nell. 'You've found someone?'

Lily held her breath as she watched a slow blush

rise from Nell's slender neck to suffuse her cheeks with colour. She had been convinced that Nell loved Armand, but it seemed she had been wrong, and this was confirmed by a snort from Molly.

'She's in love with a boring old schoolmaster, Ma. Now as for me, you'll be proud of me because I'm engaged to a wealthy Frenchman. I'm soon to be Madame Labrosse.'

Charlotte raised herself on one elbow. 'What's this? Who is this man? Do you know his family?'

Lily reached for the laudanum and the glass of water on the washstand. She measured a dose, holding it out to her mother. 'You mustn't overexcite yourself, Ma. You'd best take some of your medicine.'

Charlotte waved it away. 'Later, Lily. I want to keep a clear head while I listen to what my daughter has to say.'

'Since when have you cared what any of us did or didn't do?' Molly snapped. 'I've had as much as I can stand of my family today; first Matt and now you, Ma. You of all people should understand my feelings. I love Armand and I'm going to marry him.'

'Oh, what have I done?' Charlotte fell back against her pillows. 'I see myself in you, Molly. Stop and think before you rush into marriage.'

'You're all jealous of me, that's what it is,' Molly cried passionately. 'And you are a fraud, Ma. There's nothing wrong with you, so get up and stop wallowing in self-pity.' With a rebellious shrug of her shoulders, she stalked out of the room.

'She's just upset,' Nell murmured, biting her lip. 'Don't take any notice of her, Ma.'

'I think we should go now,' Luke said, taking the sheaf of papers from his inside pocket and laying them on the coverlet. 'Perhaps you could give these to your publisher friend when you feel more the thing, Ma.'

'That's enough, Luke. You shouldn't have bothered her at a time like this.' Catching him by the sleeve, Nell drew him towards the doorway. 'We're leaving, but we'll come again soon.'

'I think you should rest now,' Lily said anxiously. 'Please take your medicine, Ma.'

Charlotte snatched the glass and hurled it at the far wall where it shattered into shards and its contents trickled down the wall to pool on the floor. 'I'm getting up,' she said, swinging her legs over the side of the bed, but as she attempted to stand she swayed and fell back onto the bed. 'Perhaps I'll leave it until morning, but you can tell Molly that I haven't finished with her, and I'll have a few words to say to Matt when I see him.'

'Yes, Ma. Of course.' Lily hurried from the room, catching up with Nell as she was about to follow Molly and Luke out into the street. 'Thank you for coming,' she said breathlessly. 'I know it must have been difficult for you.'

Nell clasped Lily's hands. 'You were right to make us come here today, Lily. Seeing Ma like that has made me realise what's important in life, and in a strange way it's made me see things more clearly.'

'Like your feelings for the schoolmaster?'

'Don't call him that. His name is Eugene as you well know.'

Lily suppressed a smile. Nell had always maintained an outward display of serenity and rarely lost her temper. She had seemed almost saintly to Lily as she had struggled through the emotional turmoil of the in-between years when she was neither child nor woman. Now, all of a sudden, Nell's cast-iron self-control had slipped to reveal a woman with hopes and desire just like anyone else.

'He's a good man,' Lily said gently. 'But I thought it was Armand you loved.'

'So did I.' Nell smiled ruefully. 'I suppose you could call it infatuation. I think we were all a little in love with the romantic stranger who turned our lives upside down.'

'You and I have learned better,' Lily whispered. 'Perhaps Molly will come to her senses.'

'What are you two talking about?' Molly stuck her head round the door. 'Hurry up, Nell. It's getting colder by the minute and I think it's going to rain. I want to go home.'

'Coming.' Nell brushed Lily's cheek with a kiss. 'It might be better if Ma didn't come to call on us until the business with Armand is sorted. She'll only make matters worse if she tries to influence Matt.'

'We're going now,' Molly called impatiently. 'You can walk home alone if you don't come right away.'

Lily watched her sisters and brother disappear into the gathering gloom with mixed feelings. She was an outsider once again, just like Ma.

Prissy had come up behind her and Lily jumped as she felt a hand on her shoulder. 'Come and have a nice hot cup of tea,' Prissy said cheerfully. 'I've taken one upstairs to the missis, and she's sitting up in bed with a shawl wrapped round her shoulders sipping tea like her old self. I think she's on the mend.'

'Her heart is broken,' Lily said sadly. 'I don't suppose she'll ever get over Everard's death, but I think seeing Nell and the others might have helped a little. I just wish Matt would find it in himself to forgive Ma.'

Prissy sniffed. 'He needs a good sorting out, does that brother of yours. It sounds to me as if he's had his own way for far too long.'

'That's not fair,' Lily protested. 'Matt had to look after us all after Pa died in the fire. He took on a lot of responsibility.'

'He needs a woman, if you ask me. It ain't natural for a man of his age to be without a wife.' Prissy marched off, leaving Lily staring after her.

Perhaps she was right. Lily had never given a thought to Matt's emotional life. She had washed his clothes, darned his socks and made his bed for him ever since she was old enough to fill the copper and turn the mangle, but suddenly she was seeing him through a stranger's eyes. She followed Prissy into the kitchen, which was filled with the savoury smell of boiling mutton and onions. 'How do you know so much about people?' Lily asked as she took a seat at the table. 'What makes you so wise when you are so young?'

'I ain't that young,' Prissy said, pouring tea into a cup and handing it to Lily. 'I'll be seventeen next birthday, and I've had to earn me keep since I was a nipper. I had to work on the farm and take the eggs and butter to market. I looked after me younger brothers and sisters and nursed 'em through all their childish ailments. I suppose you pick up bits and pieces of know-how here and there, like gleaning in the fields at harvest time. There's a pattern to life in the country.'

Lily sipped her tea, watching Prissy as she bustled about the kitchen, preparing the evening meal. She had the sudden urge to sketch her as she worked, making drawings of those capable little hands and the strong line of Prissy's profile. Lily flexed her fingers. 'I think I'll do some painting before supper,' she said, rising to her feet. 'Or is there anything I can do to help you?'

Prissy turned to her with a grin of approval. 'No, miss. Go and rest your brain doing something you enjoy. We'll wait for Mr Gabriel to come home afore we eat.'

Lily suffered a pang of guilt. It was already dark and she had been too busy to give Gabriel a second thought. 'He's very late. He should be home by now.'

'He can take care of hisself. He'll be back when his belly's empty,' Prissy said firmly. 'You go and do your scribbling. Oh, and you'd best light the fire. I laid it first thing this morning so all it needs is a match to get it going. I don't want to come in later and find you froze to death.'

Taking a lighted candle, Lily went into the parlour and set about making herself comfortable. The fire responded to a match, flames licking greedily at the dry kindling and lapping hungrily around the blue-black coals. She pulled her chair close to the blaze but as she reached for the charcoal she found the box empty. With an exasperated sigh, she picked up the candlestick and made her way up to the top floor. She entered Gabriel's room, shielding the candle flame with her hand as a draught from a cracked windowpane almost extinguished it. Holding the candlestick higher, she stifled a gasp of surprise as she came face to face with a likeness of herself so vivid and alive that she might almost have been staring into a mirror.

On an easel facing her was the painting on which Gabriel had spent so much of his time, refusing to allow her even the smallest peek. Lily had instantly recognised herself, but on closer scrutiny the girl in the portrait was strikingly beautiful, determined and yet ethereal. Gabriel had captured a hint of vulnerability in her eyes, and an innocence which seemed at odds with the background of a conflagration that blazed against a black velvet sky. With her hair flying out behind her and glowing as bright as the heart of the fire, she stood in the well of the firemen's wagon, holding the reins like a modern Boadicea. It was a picture alive with colour and drama. The firefighters were in the background but that did not detract from their heroic efforts to contain the blaze. Lily caught her breath. She could almost feel the heat; hear the crackling and crashing of burning timbers, the shouts of her brothers and the men who formed a human chain taking water from the river, and the hiss of steam as it evaporated in the intense heat. The scene could have been the gateway to hell's inferno and the pale-faced girl an angel from heaven caught up in a tussle with the devil himself. It was, by any standards, a master-piece. Lily felt tears running down her cheeks as she was caught up in the emotion of the painting.

'You weren't supposed to look.' Gabriel's voice made Lily turn with a start.

'I didn't hear you coming.'

'It's finished. What do you think of it?'

Lily's hands fluttered in front of her face as she struggled to put her feelings into words. 'It's wonderful. I didn't know you were such a brilliant artist.'

He smiled, shrugging modestly. 'I was inspired by my subject.'

She studied the painting, stepping backwards so that she was standing side by side with Gabriel. 'You've captured the ferocity of the fire so well. It's as if you could warm your hands by just holding them close to the canvas. You might have been there yourself, it's so real. How could you have known what it was like? I don't understand.'

'Perhaps I felt it through you, Lily. The fire in the warehouse was not my inspiration, it was you.' His eyes held her for a moment and then he looked away. 'I've named it *Lily in the Flames*.'

'That was what that horrible reporter called me,' Lily said, grimacing at the memory of Christian Smith's unscrupulous attempts to grab the headlines.

'I don't think he'll bother you again.'

'What do you mean, Gabriel? Have you seen him recently? I thought he'd given up trying to get a story out of us.'

'I wasn't going to tell you, but he's got a nose like

397

a bloodhound. He knew about my father's suicide, God knows how, but he was snooping around the prison and we came face to face. In the end, we sorted it out like gentlemen.'

'You didn't fight him, did you? A broken hand would end your career.'

He took her hand and curled his fingers around hers. 'No, my love, I wouldn't resort to fisticuffs with a bruiser like Smith. I know I'd lose, so I paid him off.'

'Oh, you didn't. If you gave him money he'll come back again and again. He'll bleed you dry.'

'I made it worth his while to keep silent, and he understood that if he broke our agreement he would risk losing his job. I made it clear that I'd go straight to his editor if he tried to extort money from me, or if he came anywhere near my family.'

'I suppose that includes me, although it's not strictly true.' Lily raised his hand to her cheek. 'You have been like a brother to me, but we are not related in any way. Ma wasn't legally married to your father and we aren't your responsibility. I can't and won't allow you to support us, Gabriel. It wouldn't be fair.'

'That's nonsense, Lily. Do you really think I would abandon you now?'

'Well, not at this precise moment.' She made an attempt at a smile but her lips trembled and her eyes filled with tears. She flicked them away with a quick movement of her head. 'We won't talk about this now. It's getting late and we're both tired. Things will become clearer in the morning.'

She was about to walk away but Gabriel held on to

her hand, looking deeply into her eyes. 'My feelings won't have changed tomorrow, or forever after that. I won't abandon you or your mother. We belong together, Lily.'

'I love you for saying that, but you mustn't let us hold you back.' She laid her finger on his lips as she sensed he was about to protest. 'You are a great artist, Gabriel. I think this painting will make you famous, and you'll mix with the toffs. You're already one of them and we aren't. It's as simple as that.'

'Never let me hear you say anything of that nature again.' He hesitated, frowning. 'There's something I want to ask you, but this isn't the right time or place. Be certain of one thing, Lily, I'm not going to desert you, even if I have to put up with that cheeky girl Prissy for the rest of my life. You may not be my sister but that doesn't affect my feelings for you. Do you understand what I'm saying?'

The look in his eyes made her heart miss a beat. Until recently she had thought of him as a brother, but something had changed subtly and it was disturbing. At a loss for words and overcome by emotion, she reached up to brush his cheek with a kiss, and leaving him no time to respond, she left the room and hurried downstairs to the kitchen.

Prissy was dishing up the boiled mutton. 'What's up with you?' she demanded. 'You look all of a dither.'

Before Lily could think of a plausible explanation for something that she did not quite understand herself, Gabriel followed her into the room and took his seat at the table.

'That smells good,' he said appreciatively. 'I haven't eaten all day and I'm ravenous.'

'So did you sort out the funeral arrangements?' Prissy filled his plate to the brim and set it in front of him. 'Eat up, there's plenty more where that came from.'

Gabriel paused with his spoon at his lips. 'That's just it, I'm afraid. We'll have to be careful with the house-keeping for a while. I had some unexpected expenses today.'

'I suppose you had to bribe the vicar,' Prissy said knowingly. 'It happens all the time in our village. They're all at it, from the verger to the parson, taking tuppence out of the collection here and there for their own ends, and charging folks a fortune if their love child dies at birth and needs a Christian burial. Lizzie Manners drowned herself in the duck pond when her lover went off with someone else. Her pa was the local wheelwright and they say it cost him dear to have her buried in the churchyard, and that were in the dead of night and no hymns nor bells. It weren't right and it was the talk of the village for months.'

Lily knew that Gabriel was referring to the money he had given Christian Smith and not whatever it had cost him to pay for his father's funeral. She glanced at him, but to her relief he did not seem upset by Prissy's ramblings. 'Is it all arranged?' she asked tentatively.

'Yes, tomorrow night at ten o'clock, but I think it's probably for the best if we don't tell Charlotte.'

Lily thought for a moment. 'No. I think Ma ought to be able to say goodbye to Everard. She really did love him, and I don't think she would forgive us if we kept it from her.'

It was bitterly cold in the graveyard, and as if on cue the rain began to fall the moment the coffin was laid in the gaping black hole. By the light of a lantern, the vicar murmured the words of the burial ceremony, and the wind moaned through the yew trees like a ghostly choir accompanying his melancholy voice. Charlotte's sobs were muffled as she leaned against Lily, but she had held up well so far with none of the histrionics that Lily had feared. Prissy stood at Charlotte's side with her head bowed and her hands clasped in front of her. Lily glanced at Gabriel's strong profile, etched against the darkness by the faint glow of the gas lamps on the other side of the stone wall which separated the churchyard from the street. On a bitterly cold winter's night there was little traffic in this part of Shadwell, the nearest place that Gabriel could find where the vicar was willing to perform the interment.

The last words were uttered and clods of wet earth dropped onto the coffin, echoing eerily around the empty graveyard. Lily reached out to touch Gabriel's hand, closing her fingers around his and giving them a gentle squeeze. He turned to her and she could see that his dark eyelashes were moist with tears. 'He was a good man for all his faults,' Gabriel murmured. 'We had our differences but I did love him.'

Lily's arms ached to hold him and whisper words of comfort, but Charlotte had spotted the sexton and his helper as they arrived with spades. They were about to fill the grave with soil when she broke away from Lily, and with a loud scream she threw herself into the hole, falling with a thud on top of Everard's coffin. The vicar had walked off but he rushed back with his vestments flying about him like the wings of a demented seagull. 'What happened?'

The sexton leaned over the yawning chasm, holding up a lantern. 'She's fallen in, vicar.'

'She jumped,' Prissy said, shaking her head. 'Someone had better go down and heave her out.'

Hysterical sobs emanated from the grave and Lily clutched Gabriel's arm as a wave of dizziness swept over her. It was, she thought, a living nightmare. The anxious faces of the men leaning over the hole in the ground were made ghoulish by the flickering light of their lanterns. Charlotte's heartrending sobs were accompanied somewhat bizarrely by the sweet song of a nightingale somewhere in the bushes, and in the distance a dog barked.

Gabriel slipped his arm around Lily's shoulders. 'We'll get her out, don't worry. Go and wait in the cab with Prissy.'

She opened her mouth to protest but Prissy took her by the hand. 'We can't do no good here, miss. Come with me and wait in the warm. There's no point you catching your death of cold in the rain just because she's taken it into her head to bury herself along with him.'

The words might not have been sympathetic but they brought Lily back to reality and she held on to Prissy as they made their way through the dark graveyard, stepping over stone slabs and feeling their way along the wall to the lychgate. The cabby had been paid to wait and his horse pawed the cobblestones, snorting and champing impatiently at the bit.

It seemed like hours to Lily but she knew by the hands on the clock in the church tower that it was little more than ten minutes before Gabriel lifted a semi-conscious Charlotte into the cab. She was covered in mud and her clothes were sodden. Even in the dim light, Lily could see that her mother's face was turning blue and her breathing was shallow. 'We must get her warm and dry quickly,' she said anxiously.

'It'll take a good half hour to get home,' Prissy muttered. 'She could be dead by then judging by the colour of her face.'

'We must take her to Pelican Stairs,' Lily said in desperation. 'Prissy's right, Gabriel. She's cold as ice and barely breathing. We must take her home.'

Chapter Twenty-one

It was getting on for midnight by the time they reached the house on the wharf. Gabriel had paid off the cabby and he carried Charlotte all the way along the narrow passage to Pelican Stairs. She lay in his arms like a broken doll despite Lily's attempts to revive her.

'They'll probably all be in bed,' Prissy muttered.

Lily hurried on ahead. No matter if the family were sound asleep, she was determined to wake them, but as she approached the old inn she saw to her relief that there were lights in the windows. She rapped on the knocker, calling for Nell, but it was Grandpa who opened the door. He did not look pleased. 'Is that you, Lily? What d'you think you're doing roaming the streets in the dead of night?'

'I'm not alone, Grandpa. Let us in, please.'

He stood aside and his eyes narrowed as Gabriel carried Charlotte into the house. 'What's up with her?'

'Brandy, Grandpa. Is there any in the house? Ma had an accident and she's frozen stiff.' Lily hurried into the parlour and almost bumped into Nell in the doorway. Even in the dim light she could see that her sister had been crying. 'What's the matter? Are you ill?'

Nell shook her head. 'It's Molly. She eloped with Armand. Matt and the boys are on a shout and it will be too late to do anything about it by the time they come off watch.'

For a moment Lily almost forgot their mother's plight. She could see that Nell was deeply distressed and her first reaction was of anger towards Molly; selfish, thoughtless, wilful Molly, who must be the centre of attention at all times.

'I'm afraid I'll drop her if I don't put her down soon,' Gabriel complained, pushing past Lily and Nell and carrying Charlotte into the parlour. He set her down on the rocking chair by the fire.

'What happened?' Nell rushed to her mother's side, taking her limp hand and chafing it. 'She's soaked to the skin and covered in mud. How did she get in this state?'

'She had a bit of an accident,' Lily said, sending a warning glance to Gabriel.

'She's nothing but trouble,' Grandpa muttered. 'Always was and always will be.'

Prissy turned on him. 'That sort of talk don't help one bit. Where d'you keep the brandy, mister?'

He recoiled, staring at her as if faced by a dangerous animal. 'Who are you?'

Ignoring them, Lily went to the dresser and after a brief search found the bottle of brandy hidden behind a dented pewter tankard. She took a glass and poured a generous tot, taking it to her mother and holding it to her lips. Charlotte swallowed, coughed and opened her eyes. She looked dazedly round the room and uttered a low moan. 'Let me die. I don't want to go on without him.'

'What nonsense,' Nell said briskly. She turned to Prissy. 'You, girl, whatever your name is, go into the kitchen and make a pot of tea. You'll find everything you need in the pantry.'

Prissy stood her ground. 'Me name is Prissy, and I don't take orders from no one but Miss Lily.'

'It seems you can still afford to keep a servant,' Nell said, frowning.

Lily opened her mouth to protest but Gabriel answered for her. 'Prissy stayed on out of loyalty. I don't know what we would have done without her.'

'I'm sorry,' Nell murmured. 'I didn't mean to speak out of turn, it's just that I'm exhausted and worried sick about Molly, and now Ma is here in a dreadful state and what Matt will make of all this I dread to think.'

'No hard feelings, miss,' Prissy said graciously. 'Show me where the kitchen is and I'll make the tea.'

'That door,' Nell said, pointing her finger in the general direction of the kitchen.

Lily nodded to Prissy. 'A cup of hot, sweet tea would do Ma the world of good.'

'Certainly, miss.' Prissy walked sedately into the kitchen.

When she was out of earshot, Nell turned to Lily. 'So what happened tonight?'

Briefly, and succinctly, Lily told them about the events in the churchyard. Charlotte uttered a loud moan and fell back in her seat, clutching her hands to her breast. 'Everard, my love. How will I live without you?'

'There, there, Ma,' Nell said, gently. 'I'm sorry. I didn't know.' She glanced at Lily with an attempt at a smile. 'You did right to bring her here. I'm sure Matt will agree when he knows the full story.'

'You look like you could do with a snifter, mate,' Grandpa said, addressing Gabriel. 'The women get all the attention but you just buried your old man, so let's raise a glass to him, wherever he's gone.' He took two glasses from the dresser and poured a tot of brandy in each, handing one to Gabriel. 'Best put the past behind us now. What's done is done, and we've got other things to worry about.'

Gabriel downed the brandy in one swallow. 'Thanks, Mr Larkin. That was generous of you considering what my father put your family through.'

'And her,' Grandpa said, jerking his head in Charlotte's direction. 'She's the one who ran off. She's a flighty piece just like her daughter. Now we'll have old man Labrosse coming down on us like a ton of bricks, and quite possibly turning us out on the street. I've no doubt he had other ideas for his son than for him to wed a silly chit like young Molly with not a penny to her name.'

'Grandpa,' Nell cautioned. 'You don't know that for certain. Monsieur Labrosse might be happy to see Armand settled with a wife who loves him.'

'With a wife who loves money and pretty gewgaws,' Grandpa muttered. 'Just like that creature over there. Give her a slap, that'll bring her round better than all this mollycoddling.'

'You don't mean that,' Lily cried, her nerves stretched

407

to breaking point. 'She's sick and she needs looking after.'

'She needs a slap,' Grandpa repeated, refilling his glass. 'If my boy had been firmer with her she might not have strayed like she did. Anyway, I'm going to me bed. I'll leave you to sort her out, and as to young Molly, well I wouldn't want to be around when Matt finds out what she's done.' He saluted Gabriel with his glass as he left the room.

'Ma should be in bed with a hot brick at her feet,' Lily said anxiously.

Nell bent down to take off her mother's wet satin slippers. 'Only Ma would go to a funeral in midwinter with dancing shoes on. She can have Molly's bed for the night since she won't be needing it.'

'I'll carry her upstairs.' Gabriel leaned over Charlotte, taking her hand. 'Let's get you to bed, Cara my dear.'

Nell managed a tight little smile. 'Thank you, Gabriel. I realise that we weren't the only ones to suffer from our parents' affair, and I'm sorry if I misjudged you.'

Prissy opened the kitchen door. 'Who wants a nice hot cup of tea?'

Gabriel lifted Charlotte in his arms, ignoring her groans and muttered protests. 'Come along, Cara. Let's get you settled and Prissy will bring you a hot drink and maybe a warm brick wrapped in a flannel for your feet.'

'I want to die,' Charlotte moaned faintly.

'You'll feel better in the morning,' Lily said, following them from the room as Nell led the way upstairs. 'Everything will look better after a good night's sleep.'

Having sent Gabriel downstairs to drink his tea, Nell and Lily set about undressing their mother and getting her into bed, which was no easy task as Charlotte went as limp as a rag doll, refusing to cooperate. Nell tut-tutted in annoyance. 'She's worse than a two-year-old.'

'She's had a terrible shock,' Lily said mildly. 'She adored Everard and I have to admit that he was a good, kind man. I liked him a lot.'

'That doesn't excuse what they did.' Nell slipped a cotton nightgown over their mother's head. 'They lived off other people's money with no hope of repaying them. I call that stealing and I can't condone it under any circumstances.'

Lily struggled to get Charlotte's arms into the night-gown. 'Please, Ma. Help us a bit, there's a good girl.'

Charlotte sighed, but she allowed them to get her into bed just as Prissy arrived with the hot brick and a cup of tea. 'I've put a drop of brandy in it,' she whispered to Lily. 'She might not be able to sleep without the laudanum.'

Overhearing the last remark, Nell shook her head. 'She must get used to doing without it or she'll end up an addict. I've seen women in the streets who would sell their own children for alcohol or drugs. It's not a pretty sight.' She drew Lily aside, leaving Prissy to settle Charlotte. 'There's going to be a terrible scene when Matt discovers Molly has eloped, and I tremble to think what he'll say if he finds Ma here.'

'We'll think of something,' Lily said with more hope than conviction. 'How long is it since Molly and Armand went missing?'

'Three hours at the most.' Nell shivered. 'Let's go downstairs and sit by the fire. You can have your tea and then you must be on your way. The girl can stay and look after Ma but you must be here first thing in the morning to take her home.'

Gabriel rose from his chair as they entered the parlour. 'Is there anything more I can do, Nell?'

'Only if you can perform miracles and bring Molly back before Matt finds out what the silly girl has done.'

'Have you any idea where they were headed?' Lily asked hopefully. They won't be able to get married until morning, and even then they will have to make arrangements. We might be able to find them if only we knew where they'd gone.'

'We might?' Gabriel raised his eyebrows. 'Are you including me in this scheme, Lily?'

She met his gaze steadily. 'I don't think I could do it alone.'

'And you won't have to. Of course I'll go with you, Lily.'

The warmth in his voice was balm to Lily's troubled soul. The smile in his eyes was for her alone and she felt strangely light-headed and unaccountably happy. 'But as we don't know where they've gone it's impossible.' She could not bring herself to look away and break the spell that seemed to bind them.

'They were heading for Dover.'

Nell's voice shattered the moment, bringing Lily tumbling back to earth. 'They were going to France to get married?'

'That's what Molly told me. I tried to stop her but I might as well have attempted to prevent the tide from coming in. She laughed in my face as she walked out of the door.'

'Then we must go after them,' Lily said firmly. 'They won't have reached Dover yet. They will have to change horses and maybe they've put up overnight at an inn.'

Nell clasped her hands in despair. 'Her reputation will be ruined. It won't make any difference whether or not you catch up with them. It's a disaster whichever way you look at it.'

'Not yet it isn't.' Gabriel retrieved his hat and coat. 'If we can get to them in time reputations will be saved, and you could have Molly restored to you by midday tomorrow or soon after.'

Lily's hopes were raised, only to be dashed by a seemingly insuperable problem. 'But we've no means of transport and no money to pay for its hire.'

Nell shot a suspicious glance in Gabriel's direction. 'I thought you were a man of means.'

'I have a modest income left to me by my mother,' Gabriel acknowledged. 'But I've had unexpected expenses recently.

Lily knew that he was referring to Christian Smith and her heart sank. She had almost forgotten the reporter and the sum of money Gabriel had paid him. 'So it's hopeless,' she murmured, bowing her head. 'There's nothing we can do.'

Shrugging on his coat, Gabriel set his top hat on his head at a jaunty angle. 'Leave it to me. Give me an hour and be ready for a long journey, Lily. I'll be as quick as I can.'

The fire had gone out and Lily awakened with a start, gazing sleepily around the parlour lit by the glow of a single guttering candle. She stretched her cramped limbs, reaching her hands out to the fire but it had died away to a pile of silver ash. Dozing in the chair opposite her, she could just make out Prissy's shape. Gradually the events of the past few hours came back to her. Nell had gone to bed soon after Gabriel's departure, and Prissy had kept her company while she awaited his return. The sound of the front door opening and footsteps echoing off the flagstone floor made Lily rise unsteadily to her feet. She held her breath wondering if it was Gabriel or her brothers returning from their night watch. She breathed a sigh of relief when Gabriel strode into the room.

'I've got a carriage and pair waiting at the end of the alley. Are you ready?' He picked up her cloak, shaking it and holding it out with a flourish. 'Shall we go?'

'What's going on?' Prissy sat bolt upright.

Lily placed her finger on her lips. 'Hush, Prissy. We're going to find Molly. I want you to stay and look after Ma for me. We'll be back as soon as possible.'

'Don't worry, Prissy,' Gabriel said cheerfully. 'I'll bring Lily home safe and sound together with the errant sister. Take care of yourself and Charlotte, and don't let the Larkins bully you.'

'They won't get the better of me,' Prissy said stoutly.

'You don't grow up one of ten nippers without learning how to stand up for yourself.'

Lily leaned back against the padded velvet squabs of the five-glass landau, revelling in the luxury of travelling in style. She had noticed a coat of arms emblazoned on the door, and even though she knew nothing of heraldry, she realised that this elegant equipage must belong to a person of high rank. She stole a sideways glance at Gabriel, feeling suddenly shy in the shared intimacy of the confined space. He turned his head to smile at her. 'We'll catch up with them, Lily. Don't worry.'

His hand sought hers and she felt a tingle run down her spine at his touch. 'I'm not at all worried now, but I'd like to know how you managed all this when I know you gave all your money to that hateful Christian Smith.'

'I have an influential contact who loaned me his carriage and pair.'

'It must be someone with a title who is extremely wealthy. Who is this person, Gabriel?

'Let's just say he's an art lover.'

'That's only half an answer.'

'He's a titled gentleman who was a great admirer of my father's works. He bought several and he's been showing an interest in my efforts. There was a painting of mine that he wanted for his private collection, although I'd been reluctant to part with it.'

His eyes were deep in shadow but Lily sensed the deep emotion underlying his words. She covered his hand with hers. 'It was *Lily in the Flames*, wasn't it?'

413

He nodded wordlessly, raising her hand to his lips.

'But you were going to enter it for the Summer Exhibition.'

'He paid me a fair price, and the loan of the carriage was a bonus. There are more important things to think of now, and Molly is just one of them.'

Lily's breath hitched in her throat. 'And the others?'

'Our future, Lily. Yours and mine. We can't live on fresh air.'

She withdrew her hand, shivering as a chill ran through her blood. 'I've told you before that you aren't responsible for me or Ma. We aren't related in any way.'

He drew her into his arms, pressing his lips gently against her forehead. 'But I want to be related to you, Lily. I want to hold you in my arms forever and tell you that I love you, and that I've loved you since that first moment when you almost tripped over me on Bell Wharf.' He drew away just far enough to gaze deeply into her eyes. 'I adore you, Lily. It's as simple as that.'

His lips claimed hers, robbing her of speech. Shock and astonishment melted away as Lily gave herself up to sheer delight. Her lips parted beneath his and as if moving of their own accord her arms slid around his neck. Everything seemed to fit. Her body moulded into his as if they had been made for each other. Her heart was beating to the same rhythm as Gabriel's and her senses soared towards heaven. Even without knowing it, this was the moment for which she had been yearning and only now did she understand the reason

414

why. She loved him with every fibre of her being. She was his, heart and soul, body and mind. They were as one in the swaying darkness of the carriage as it sped through the narrow city streets.

When he released her in order to draw breath, she blinked dazedly into his smiling eyes. She knew every contour of his face: the tiny laughter line at the corners of his blue eyes, the quirk of his lips when he smiled and the way his dark hair tumbled over his forehead, all were indelibly etched on her heart. If they were parted now never to meet again, she knew she would not forget a single detail. Now she had his kiss imprinted on her lips. She would remember the taste of him and the masculine scent of him, which would linger on even if he was far away from her. Only now could she empathise with the love that her mother must have felt for Everard, and the passion that had led her to desert her family. Only now could she understand the terrible feelings of loss that her mother had experienced after her lover's untimely death.

Lily raised her hand to caress Gabriel's cheek, needing to feel the warm touch of his flesh to convince herself that this was real and not a dream. 'I love you too,' she whispered. 'I love you, Gabriel.'

He silenced her with a kiss that she wished would never end.

She slept in his arms, waking only when the motion of the carriage changed as it slowed down and the horses' hooves clattered in the cobbled yard of a coaching inn.

Opening her eyes, she raised her head. 'Gabriel?'

'We have to change horses,' he said, easing her into a sitting position. He kissed her on the forehead, and brushed her lips with a feather-like salute. 'You are beautiful, my Lily.'

She smiled. 'I am yours, Gabriel. I can't believe it's happened, but in spite of everything I couldn't be happier.'

The carriage door opened and the groom let down the carpeted steps, proffering his arm to help Lily alight.

The air was cold and crisp. A white frost iced the cobblestones and the roof of the inn glittered in the moonlight. An ostler hurried from the stables to see to the horses and the coachman climbed stiffly down from the box. Light spilled out onto the yard as a door opened and the innkeeper staggered sleepily towards them. 'May I offer you a room for the night, sir? Or some refreshment for the lady and yourself while you wait for a change of horses?'

'What time is it, landlord?'

'Two o'clock, sir.'

'Have you taken in many travellers last evening, landlord?'

'Just passing trade, sir. Will you be wanting a room?'

Gabriel glanced at Lily. 'I think we should rest, don't you?'

She nodded her head. Her heart was thumping against her ribs and her whole body seemed to flame with unaccustomed sensations that brought a blush to her cheeks.

'Two rooms, please, landlord. One for myself and the other for my sister.'

It was not what she desired, but she realised that Gabriel was acting as his conscience dictated. Ashamed of her own thoughts, Lily knew that she would have gladly shared his bed and that made her little better than the mother whom the family had looked upon with such scorn and derision. She bowed her head, humbled and yet unrepentant.

Next morning, after a surprisingly good night's sleep, Lily was awakened by a maidservant bringing her a jug of hot water and a cup of hot chocolate. She filled the washbowl, set the cup down on a table within reach of Lily's bed and proceeded to clean out the grate, chattering nonstop as if eager to pass on a tasty morsel of gossip.

'We had another young lady pass through here yesterday with a foreign gent. They said they was brother and sister too, but he weren't English and she was, so that was obviously a piece of nonsense. We see it all here and we can tell them as are pretending to be married and are really doing something they oughtn't.'

Reaching automatically for the cup of hot chocolate, Lily's pulse raced. 'Do you remember what the young lady looked like?'

'Course I do, 'cos she looked a bit like you.' The maid sat back on her haunches, glancing over her shoulder at Lily. 'Same colour hair and eyes but she was more of a flighty piece. She'll lead the foreign cove a pretty dance I says to Cook. She had him wrapped round her little finger. Brother and sister, all my eye and Betty Martin.'

Lily gulped the hot chocolate, burning her mouth in her haste to swallow. 'What name did they give?'

'I dunno, but I heard the froggy-fellah call her Mary – no, perhaps it was Molly. I never paid much attention to it at the time.' She scooped the ashes into the empty coal scuttle and clambered ungracefully to her feet. 'I could light the fire for you, but I expect you want to be on your way. The gent is in the dining parlour and he's ordered breakfast, so I don't suppose you'll want to keep him waiting.'

Lily put the drink aside, swinging her legs over the side of the bed. 'Will you tell him I'll be down directly? We must be on our way as soon as possible.'

'Related to you, was she?' Calmly, as if it were an everyday occurrence to harbour runaways, the maid left the room without waiting for an answer.

Ten minutes later Lily entered the dining parlour to find Gabriel seated at the table drinking coffee. He rose to his feet and his welcoming smile made her dizzy with delight. She had been wondering if their passionate embraces in the carriage had been a figment of her imagination, a delightful dream that would vanish in the morning light, but she knew in that instant that it was real. She was in love and loved in return.

As if their emotions were now joined by an invisible silken cord, Gabriel seemed to sense her agitation and his smile faded into an expression of deep concern. 'My love, what's wrong?'

Lily crossed the floor to fling her arms around his neck. 'They were here last evening. The maid told me.'

He held her close. 'That's good news. At least we

are on the right track and with luck we'll catch up with them before they reach Dover.' He kissed her briefly on the lips. 'We'll leave as soon as you've had something to eat. No arguments, Lily darling. I'm taking care of you now.'

She sat down at the table but she was too overwrought to manage more than a few mouthfuls of freshly baked bread and butter. She managed to swallow some coffee, but her throat constricted with emotion every time she looked at Gabriel, and her appetite deserted her. She could hardly believe that a man of his background and brilliance would fall in love with a girl raised on the docks, but every word he uttered and each loving look went some way to convince her that a miracle had happened.

They left as soon as Gabriel had paid for their accommodation and he instructed the coachman to stop at every coaching inn on the road to Dover. At the second stop Gabriel returned to the carriage with the news that the eloping couple had spent the night at the inn, claiming as before to be brother and sister. He grinned, taking Lily's hand in his. 'They believed the fiction as little as the landlord of the inn where we spent the night. I never want to be mistaken for your brother, Lily. As soon as we get back to London I'm going to speak to Matt and tell him that I intend to marry you as soon as possible.'

Lily struggled with her emotions; she wanted to laugh and cry at the same time. 'Oh, Gabriel.'

He wrapped his arms around her. 'Is that all you can say? Am I not to know whether the answer will be yes or no?'

This was not the moment to cry all over the man she adored. 'You haven't asked me yet,' she murmured, blinking away tears of happiness.

'I want to do this properly,' Gabriel insisted. 'You must have time to think and I need to know that our marriage won't tear your family apart. The Faulkners have done enough damage to the Larkins, and I want our life to be free from feuds and bad feeling.'

'I want that too. More than anything, but . . .'

He silenced her lips with a tender kiss. 'Our future happiness will stand the test of time, it's Molly we must think about now. The landlord at the last inn said they left only an hour or so before we got there. Armand must be confident that they are not being followed. He's in for a shock.'

Lily nestled against him, resting her head against his shoulder. She did not want the journey to end, although she knew they must face the inevitable scene when Molly realised that she was to be taken home unmarried and with her reputation in tatters. Perhaps Armand would play the gentleman and do the honourable thing, but Lily was not so sure. If he was anything like his father he might already have taken advantage of her sister and yet think himself free to walk away. She hoped against hope that this was not so, although she had reluctantly to agree with Grandpa that it was unlikely that a man of his wealth and position would want a girl like Molly for his wife.

They arrived in Dover a little after midday. A pale primrose sun shone from an azure sky and wispy white clouds cast shadows on the turquoise calmness of the English Channel. Lily stepped out of the carriage and breathed in the fresh salty air. The waters of the Thames must have mingled with the sea somewhere along the way. Her imagination had taken her to the coast often but this was the first time she had seen the sea, and the furthest she had ever travelled from London. Gabriel slipped his arm around her shoulders. 'It's beautiful on a day like this, but the weather can change in a moment.'

'I wish I could paint it,' Lily whispered. 'I can see so many different colours in the waves, and that dark line on the horizon is almost purple.'

He gave her a hug. 'You are a true artist, my darling, but we're here on a mission.'

'And what would that be, mate?'

Lily froze at the sound of that all-too-familiar voice. She did not need to turn her head to know that trouble had followed them to the coast.

Chapter Twenty-two

'What in hell's name are you doing here, Smith?' Gabriel demanded, turning to glare angrily at the man in a loud check suit with a bowler hat set jauntily over one eye.

'It's nice to see you too, guv.' Christian tipped his hat to Lily. 'And you too, miss. Down here to take the sea air, are you?'

Lily slipped her hand into the crook of Gabriel's arm and felt his muscles tense. 'What do you want, Mr Smith?' she asked warily. 'Did you follow us?'

He struck a casual pose as if enjoying their discomfiture. 'I think that's my business, miss. I go where my nose for news leads me.' He paused and grinned. 'That's a good 'un – a nose for news. I must tell my editor and maybe he'll up my wages.'

'Come to the point, man,' Gabriel said angrily. 'Why are you here? I thought we'd settled our business.'

A sly smile spread across Christian's untidy features and Lily noticed for the first time that his nose deviated slightly to one side, as if it had received a hefty punch at some stage in his life, and one eyelid drooped slightly as if he were permanently winking. He licked his full lips as if enjoying himself hugely. 'That particular transaction was done, but now I'm off on a new tack.'

'Come away, Gabriel.' Lily tugged at his sleeve. 'He's just trying to annoy you and we have more important things to do than argue with him.'

'You won't be interested in what I have to say then.' Christian leaned against the sea wall with a nonchalant shrug of his shoulders.

'We're here on private business,' Gabriel said coldly. 'Go about yours and leave us alone.'

Christian tapped the side of his crooked nose. 'If I was you I'd be trying to book a passage on the next boat crossing the Channel. The birds have flown, guv. They'll be well on their way to Calais with a fair wind behind them.'

Freeing himself from Lily's restraining hand Gabriel lunged at Christian, grabbing him by the lapels of his tweed jacket. 'What are you saying? Out with it or I'll take great pleasure in flooring you.'

'Go ahead, mate. It'll look good on the front page of my paper, that together with the scandal of the wealthy Frenchman's son seducing a poor girl from Shadwell.' Christian raised his hands to break Gabriel's hold. 'And there's the matter of Sir Cloudesley Forrest's latest acquisition. I ain't seen it yet but my source tells me that *Lily in the Flames* is nothing short of a masterpiece. Seems to me you owe me a debt of gratitude for the name at least, and add your imminent rise to fame with the suicide of your father and we've got another front page story.'

Lily was about to speak but a look from Gabriel silenced her. She had never seen him so furious. She would not have blamed him if he had punched

Christian, but he seemed to have his temper under control. 'What exactly do you know, Smith? You could be making the whole thing up as far as I'm concerned.'

'Nice try, guv, but my source is employed at Boodle's. We have an arrangement whereby he passes on juicy snippets that might be of interest to my readers, and he just happened to overhear a conversation between Sir Cloudesley and a gent who answered a description similar to your own. My source, a very reliable person indeed, saw the said painting and immediately recognised the lady as being the very same young person who made the front page of my paper.'

Lily shook her head. 'That wretched article caused me no end of trouble, but even if what you say is true, it doesn't explain how you came to follow us here.'

Christian puffed out his chest. 'That's where brainwork comes into its own. When Sir Cloudesley gave orders for his carriage to be brought to the front entrance and it was the gent who brought the painting that went off in it, my mate knew there was a story there. He sent a message to me and I thinks to meself, now where would young Mr Faulkner be dashing off to at this time of night?' He tapped the side of his nose. 'There's always a lady in it somewhere, and I guessed it was you, miss.'

'But you couldn't possibly have known where to find me.' Intrigued and curious, Lily forgot to be angry.

'I've been keeping an eye on both of you. I went first to Cock and Hoop Yard, and I came across a simpleton by the name of Sally. She told me that you'd gone to a place where they kept big birds on the stairs.

I'd been watching the Larkin family so it weren't difficult to work out that sweet Sal meant Pelican Stairs. You led me a merry dance but I caught up with you in the end, and when you took off again I knew I was on to a big one.'

Gabriel clenched his fists, but Lily was too caught up in Christian's story to allow him to put an end to the explanation. 'Go on, then,' she said eagerly. 'How did you know we were following my sister?'

'Greasing a palm or two at the inns was enough to work out what had happened.' He held his hand out to Gabriel with a suggestive smirk. 'It always works, as you know full well, guv.'

'I may not have the funds to bribe you or to sue you for libel, but Sir Cloudesley almost certainly will put an end to your tittle-tattling, gossip-mongering ways.'

'Who said anything about bribery?' Christian demanded. 'I'll make more out of this story than you could lay your hands on, mate.'

'If I were you I'd be wary of offending people in high places,' Gabriel said coldly. He turned to Lily with an attempt at a smile. 'Come, my love. We'll leave this vermin to mix with the other sewer rats.'

Christian's laughter followed them along the quay as they walked away. 'I take it you'll be going to France then. Maybe I'll follow you, after I've sent my story to London, that is. I'm off to the telegraph office now.'

'He won't, will he?' Lily asked anxiously. 'Things are bad enough without Matt reading it in the newspapers.'

'He may be bluffing.'

425

'But you don't know that for certain.'

'No, sweetheart, I don't. But I'll send a telegram to Sir Cloudesley and hope to God that he uses his influence with Smith's editor to put a stop to the whole sorry story.'

'But what about Molly and Armand?'

'I'll book a passage on the next packet boat to Calais.' Gabriel hesitated, turning to her with a thoughtful frown. 'But first I'll take you back to the inn where we stopped to change horses. I'll send the carriage back to London and you can wait there for me.'

'Can't I do something useful, Gabriel? I'm not a helpless little female who has to be cosseted like a child.'

He touched her lips with the tip of his finger and a smile lit his eyes. 'Very well, I'll telegraph Sir Cloudesley and you can book our passage on the steam packet to France. That way we might even be able to give Smith the slip.'

Leaning over the rails of the paddle steamer, Lily watched the white cliffs of Dover until they disappeared from view. Gabriel's arm around her shoulders gave her a feeling of warmth and security. Nothing else seemed to matter as the ship sped towards France quite literally under its own steam. As the salt wind whipped her hair from beneath her bonnet and a fine mist of sea spray moistened her lips, she could only marvel at modern machines that defied the wind and tide. Grandpa had always said that one day steam would take over from sail, but she had not believed him until now. She could feel the engine throbbing like a beating heart through the deck timbers, accompanied by the plashing of the paddlewheel as it sliced through the waves. If they had not been on such an urgent quest she would have been happier now than at any given moment in her life. She was in the arms of the man she loved, and now that they had lost sight of land they were free from the cares and worries of the people on shore. She smiled up into Gabriel's face and she knew for certain that he shared and understood her feelings.

'Well, so here you are.'

Christian's coarse voice shattered the moment into a million tiny shards.

'I thought we'd left you behind in Dover,' Gabriel said calmly.

Lily felt his fingers tighten on her shoulder and she saw his jawline harden.

'Not a chance, guv. I told you I was following the story.' Christian doffed his hat to Lily. 'I'll leave you two lovebirds to enjoy the trip, but I'll be there when we land in Calais. My editor can't wait to have the rest of the story. Will it be pistols at dawn? If you need a second, I'll be only too willing to oblige.' He strolled away, adopting a rolling gait to compensate for the movement of the deck beneath his feet.

'You won't fight Armand, will you?' Lily could barely frame the words. Until Christian mentioned such an outcome, the possibility of a duel had never crossed her mind.

'Not I, darling. I'm not a coward but neither am I foolhardy.' He twisted a stray lock of her hair round his finger and his smile faded. 'You do realise that your own reputation will be compromised by the very fact that you've accompanied me?'

'I don't care what anyone says or thinks. I never want to be parted from you, Gabriel.'

'That's just as well then, since we'll be spending the rest of our lives together.' Drawing her into his arms, Gabriel's mouth sought hers in a salty kiss.

It was dark when the paddle steamer moored alongside the quay wall in Calais.

'Where are we going first?'

Gabriel turned on Christian with a snarl. 'Go away, Smith. We don't want anything to do with you.'

'Come now, that's not the attitude. I've got contacts over here as well as in England and I can help you to find the runaways. On your own you'll struggle with the language and waste precious time. Unless of course you think you know better.' Christian struck a pose, angling his head with a cocky grin.

Lily tugged at Gabriel's sleeve. 'He's right, even though I hate to admit it. We could go all the way to Paris and still not find them.'

Gabriel hesitated, eyeing Christian thoughtfully. 'Very well, as time is of the essence, what do you suggest?'

'I know an inn on the outskirts of the town where we can get a decent meal and a clean bed for the night. There's no point trying to follow them until daylight, and in the meantime I'll make a few enquiries.'

'You speak French?' Lily asked.

'My mother was born in Calais. She was lady's maid working in a mansion up West, and my pa was a footman. I've got scores of relations in this town, all of 'em nosy buggers like me, so it shouldn't be hard to find someone who's seen Labrosse and your sister. She's not the sort you could pass by without a second glance.'

'We can manage on our own, thanks,' Gabriel said stiffly.

Lily squeezed his hand. 'No, Gabriel. That's just your pride talking. I think we should accept Christian's help if it means we get to Molly sooner.' She thought for a moment that he was going to be stubborn, but a reluctant smile lit his face and he raised her hand to his lips.

'You're right, Lily. Go ahead, Smith. Lead on.'

The inn was packed with customers and the air was thick with strange-smelling tobacco smoke and the mixed odours of garlic, wine and brandy. Christian spoke the language fluently enough to order a meal and book rooms for the night. Translating the innkeeper's response, Christian announced with a deep-throated chuckle that Lily and Gabriel would have to share a bed. Lily's heart leapt but a quick glance in Gabriel's direction put paid to all thoughts of a night spent in his arms. In the end it was Christian and Gabriel who shared a room and Lily went to bed alone.

Next morning, after a breakfast of croissants washed down with several cups of coffee, they set off in the direction of Paris, following a report from one of

Christian's many cousins that a young woman answering to Molly's description had been seen getting into a private carriage accompanied by a man with a decided limp. This was enough to convince Lily that they were on the right track, and Christian went off to hire a vehicle that would take them on to Paris.

The carriage when it arrived turned out to be a rickety contraption that smelt strongly of the farmyard, with straw on the floor and worn leather squabs, but as it was the only transport available they had no choice other than pay for its hire. The driver, who turned out to be Christian's second cousin once removed, wore a tricorne hat and a caped greatcoat with a greenish tinge to the material which suggested it might have once belonged to the man's grandfather or even his great-grandfather. Taciturn and patently disapproving of foreigners, he refused to hurry his ageing nag. Christian elected to ride on the box beside his relative, leaving Lily and Gabriel to endure the discomfort of travelling inside the vehicle as it rattled over ruts and potholes on the uneven road surface.

'How far is it to Paris?' Lily asked after enduring two hours of the bone-shaking journey.

'Over a hundred miles,' Gabriel said grimly. 'And at this rate it will take us several days to get there.'

'We'll be too late,' Lily murmured, resting her head against his shoulder. 'If he doesn't marry her she'll be ruined, just as Nell predicted.'

'He'll do the right thing, I promise you that.' Gabriel tightened his arm around her waist.

Lily closed her eyes. She was emotionally exhausted

430

and physically tired after a sleepless night spent in the stuffy bedroom at the inn, with the noise from the bar continuing into the small hours followed by the clarion call of an amorous cockerel that began before dawn. The rocking and swaying of the vehicle lulled her into a deep sleep from which she was rudely awakened by a sudden jolt as the carriage came to a halt.

'What's happened?' she demanded, blinking as the sunlight streamed through the open door. But Gabriel had already alighted and she could hear raised voices. Struggling to her feet, she clambered to the ground, shielding her eyes as she took in the scene of chaos ahead of them. Christian's cousin was attempting to quieten a pair of horses that had broken loose from the shafts of an upturned carriage. The driver lay in a motionless heap at the roadside and Lily approached him warily, praying silently that he was not dead. She looked to Gabriel for assistance, but he had scaled the body of the carriage and was tugging at the door in an attempt to free the occupants. Christian climbed up beside him and they worked together. There was nothing Lily could do to help them and she went down on her knees beside the coachman. She loosened his cravat and was relieved to find that he was breathing.

'Monsieur,' she said, giving him a gentle shake. 'Are you all right?'

He opened one eye, staring at her dazedly. 'Don't parley French.'

'Neither do I.' Lily breathed a sigh of relief. 'I thought you were dead, mister.'

He raised himself on one elbow, holding his hand to his head. 'Not a chance, ducks, but I got a lump the size of an egg on me head. Fetch us a drop of brandy, will you? I keep a flask in the bottom of the box seat for emergencies.'

Lily rose to her feet. 'I don't think it's there now,' she said, eyeing the splintered remains of the coach.

He dragged himself to a standing position. 'What a bloody mess. I'll get the sack for this, but it weren't my fault.'

Lily was torn between paying attention to the coachman's tale of woe and watching Gabriel perched precariously on top of the coach. 'Be careful,' she cried anxiously. 'Do take care, Gabriel.'

'Is that you, Lily?' A small voice from the interior of the carriage made Lily's heart miss a beat.

'Molly?' She picked up her skirts and raced towards the vehicle despite Gabriel's warning to stay clear. 'Molly, it's all right. We're here to help you.'

'Move away,' Gabriel shouted. 'This thing could topple over at any moment. Stand back, Lily. We'll get them out.' With a mighty heave of his shoulders he wrenched the door open.

Christian leaned inside. 'Grab my hand, miss.'

'Madame,' Molly said loudly. 'It's madame, you oaf.'

Tears of laughter and relief trickled down Lily's cheeks. Only Molly would put her new title before her own safety. 'Do as he says, Moll.'

Moments later, Christian heaved Molly out of the carriage. She was dusty, dishevelled and visibly angry as Gabriel lifted her to the ground. She pushed him away.

'Leave me be, you idiot. This gown cost a fortune and your hands are filthy.'

'A word of thanks wouldn't go amiss, Molly Larkin.'

She tossed her head and her hair spilled over her shoulders, turning to flame in the pale sunlight. 'It's Madame Labrosse now, Mr Faulkner. I'm a respectable married woman.'

'So he did the right thing,' Gabriel said wryly. 'That's something, I suppose.'

'It's wonderful news. I'm so happy for you.' Lily wrapped her arms around Molly, giving her an affectionate hug. 'But is Armand all right?'

Molly's face crumpled. 'Oh, dear. I don't know. It was dark in there and everything was upside down.'

Christian lowered himself into the shell of the carriage. There was a moment's silence as everyone held their breath. A cold breeze rustled through the trees on either side of the road, and in the distance Lily could hear the rumble of steel-rimmed wheels and the drumming of horses' hooves. 'There's something coming,' she said anxiously. 'We must stop them or there'll be another accident.'

Gabriel leaned into the carriage. 'Is he all right, Smith? We must get him out quickly.'

'Can't tell,' Christian called faintly. 'Get down here and give us a hand.'

The body of the carriage rocked dangerously as Gabriel lowered himself into the interior.

'How did this happen?' Lily demanded.

'I don't know.' Molly covered her eyes with her

hand. 'I was asleep and there was a fearful din and a crash . . .'

Lily turned to the coachman. 'Please do something.'

He hesitated, staring at her dazedly, but the approaching vehicle was getting closer every second and the sound seemed to register in his confused brain. Acknowledging Lily's plea with a vague salute, he staggered off along the lane waving his arms in an attempt to flag down the carriage. Lily could hardly bear to look as the driver of the equipage heaved on the reins and the horses slithered to a halt, whinnying with fright and rolling their eyes. The carriage door was flung open and Philippe Labrosse alighted from the vehicle.

'Oh dear,' Molly murmured. 'My father-in-law doesn't look too pleased. Armand invited him to our wedding, but this is the first time I've seen him since he was last in London.'

'What happened, Walton?' Philippe addressed himself directly to the coachman. 'Where is my son?'

Walton pointed a shaky finger at the upturned coach. 'It was an accident, guv. A wild boar ran out at us terrifying the horses. They bolted and we hit a rut in the road. The wheel came off and the shafts broke. I don't remember the rest.'

Labrosse slapped him across the face with his glove. 'Idiot. This wouldn't have happened if a Frenchman had been driving.' He turned his angry gaze on Molly, who was attempting to hide behind Lily. 'You caused this. Am I too late to stop this charade?'

'My sister is lucky to be alive, sir,' Lily protested. 'Please don't speak to her like that.'

'This has nothing to do with you.' Labrosse walked away from them to stand beside the wreck of the carriage. 'Where is Armand? Where is my son?'

Gabriel stuck his head out of the coach. 'We're trying to get him out, Labrosse. Climb up and give us a hand or else keep quiet.'

Philippe beckoned to the coachman. 'Get up there and help them, Walton.'

'Me head, guv. It's splitting.'

'Do as I say or you'll be sorry.'

Reluctantly, Walton tried to heave himself onto the coachwork but slid to the ground, clutching his head. Lily ran forward as he attempted to rise to his feet. 'Stay where you are. You'll topple the whole thing over.' She lifted her skirts, tucking them into her drawers as she made her ascent taking care not to upset the delicate balance, which would bring the whole thing crashing down to the ground. She peered into the dark space below. 'Can I do anything to help?'

'He's cut his head, and I think his arm is broken,' Gabriel called back. 'We need something to tie the arm in place before we try to lift him.'

Balancing precariously, Lily slipped off her petticoat and proceeded to tear it into strips. She dropped them into the carriage. 'Lucky I put on fresh linen yesterday,' she said, smiling. 'Ma always said we should wear clean underwear in case we got knocked down by a horse and cart and taken to hospital. It seems she was right.'

'That's fine,' Gabriel called. 'I'll buy you a new petticoat as soon as we get back to London.'

'We're going to Paris,' Molly protested. 'You can get a new petticoat in Paris. I'm sure my husband will be pleased to buy you two or three if you like.'

'Husband?' Philippe roared. 'So I'm too late to stop the young fool from making the worst mistake of his life?'

'Yes, pa-in-law,' Molly retorted with a pert smile. 'I'm afraid you are. We was married last night by a man in a top hat and Armand's got the papers to prove it. I'm your daughter-in-law now so you'd better get used to it.'

Philippe threw up his hands. '*Merde*. I could not believe it when I read the telegram Armand sent to me. I hoped I was in time, but no, it was not to be. This is a disaster.'

Lily tugged at his sleeve. 'Never mind that, monsieur. Look, they're pulling Armand from the wreckage. Don't you think there are more important things to worry about at the moment than your hurt pride?'

'I will have this marriage annulled,' Philippe muttered. 'My son deserves better.'

Clawing her fingers, Molly lunged at him, but Lily caught her round the waist and dragged her a safe distance from Labrosse. 'No, that's not the answer, Moll. Armand needs you now.'

Philippe turned away in disgust, but even as he made a move towards his son Molly pushed past him and ran to Armand, throwing her arms around his neck. 'Armand, my darling. Are you all right?'

Pale-faced and with his left arm strapped to his chest, Armand managed a weak smile. 'A few bruises, *ma chérie*. Nothing to worry about.'

'I think his arm is broken,' Gabriel said. 'He needs to see a doctor.'

'We must make haste to Paris where my personal physician will treat Armand.' Philippe glared angrily at Molly. 'You will return to England with your sister.'

Molly's smile froze and her bottom lip trembled. 'But I am Armand's wife. My place is with my husband.'

'My lawyers will sort this matter out. I have nothing further to say to you.' Philippe eyed the wreckage of the carriage and the horses now tethered safely to a tree, and his gaze travelled to the shabby vehicle owned by Christian's second cousin. The Frenchman had remained on the driver's seat with his hat pulled down over his eyes and was apparently sound asleep.

'Papa, no.' Armand slipped his uninjured arm around Molly's waist. 'We are legally married and there is nothing you can do about it.'

'Go with her and I disown you.'

'You can't do that to him,' Molly cried passionately. 'What sort of man are you?'

'I love her, Papa,' Armand said faintly. 'Don't make me choose between you.'

'The marriage cannot have been consummated,' Philippe snarled. 'It can be annulled and you will be a free man.'

Molly flung herself between father and son. 'That's where you're wrong, mister. We did plenty of consummating last night at the inn. I'm his missis good and proper.' She turned to Armand. 'Tell him, Armand. Tell him.'

Lily groaned inwardly. She could see Christian taking

437

in every word that was being said and no doubt filing it away in his head to be written up for a newspaper story as soon as they returned to England. It was not difficult to imagine how the news would be received at home. Matt would be furious and Nell heartbroken on seeing their family's name dragged though the mire. Grandpa and Aggie would back each other up as never before in their disapprobation, and easy-going Mark might lose his chance with Cobbold's pretty daughter Flossie. Then there was Ma. Add this to her mourning for Everard and it might tip her over the edge completely. Lily sent a desperate silent plea to Gabriel and as they exchanged glances she knew that he had understood.

He cleared his throat, addressing Philippe. 'May I suggest that we get Armand to the nearest doctor, Monsieur Labrosse? A long journey with a possible broken bone would do him no good at all.'

'Yes, Papa,' Armand murmured. 'That is a sensible suggestion. I fear I might . . .' He slid to the ground in a dead faint.

'Well, you're a fine lot I must say.' Christian picked up his bowler and rammed it hard on his head. 'That poor bastard is in agony and all you can do is stand round arguing. If that's how the toffs behave then give me the common man any time.'

'He's right,' Lily cried passionately. 'Armand must be seen by a doctor and Calais is only a couple of hours away, less if you take him in your carriage, Monsieur Labrosse. You fast horses will get him there in no time.'

Labrosse frowned, as if considering all the possibilities. With a resigned shrug of his shoulders he beckoned to his coachman and groom, issuing instructions in rapid French. They leapt to do his bidding, picking up Armand and carrying him to the waiting carriage. Molly followed him, shooting a defiant glance at her father-in-law. 'Don't you dare try to stop me, mister. I'm going with my husband and that's that.'

Lily laid her hand on Labrosse's arm. 'She really does love him.'

He brushed her off as if she were an irritating insect. 'Would she love him if he had no money? Can you answer that, Mademoiselle Lily?'

'I think she would,' Lily said slowly. 'Yes, monsieur. I think that for once in her life my sister really cares more for another than she does for herself.' She turned to Gabriel, who was standing close behind her. 'It's back to Calais then.'

He took her hand in a warm grasp. 'Are you all right, my love?'

'Of course. Nothing can harm me when I'm with you.'

'Ahem.' Walton cleared his throat noisily. 'What happens to me, guv? I can't walk all that way and I ain't no bareback rider.' He jerked his head in the direction of the horses, tethered to a branch of a tree.

'You must come with us,' Gabriel said firmly. 'That's if you don't mind sitting beside a newsman who will plaster your life story all over the front pages if you aren't careful.'

Christian grinned. 'I think I've got enough material

to fill my column for a week. D'you play poker, mate? I've a feeling we might be stuck in Calais for a day or two.' With a cheery wink he strolled off to awaken his cousin by knocking the tricorne hat off his head.

Christian's prophesy proved surprisingly accurate as the weather took a turn for the worse and raging storms and wild seas stopped all sailings to and from Calais. Labrosse had booked into a hotel on the seafront, refusing to pay for Molly's accommodation and ignoring all the pleas from his son, as Molly related tearfully when Lily and Gabriel arrived a couple of hours later. Walton had told them where Labrosse usually stayed, but they had booked into the inn where they had spent the previous night. Armand, Molly explained through angry tears, had been given a strong sedative by the physician and was in no position to argue with his autocratic father. 'He won't let me stay with Armand. He means to separate us forever.'

'I'm sure that won't happen,' Lily said, casting an anxious glance at Gabriel. 'If he truly loves you Armand won't allow anything to keep you apart, least of all his hateful pa.'

'You don't know Labrosse. Armand's told me some dreadful stories about his father. What he did to you was nothing compared to how he's treated other people, Lily.' Molly sniffed and blew her nose on a hanky provided by Christian, who hovered in the background.

'Look, this ain't my business,' he said gruffly. 'I'm

going back to the inn. Walton and me have got a game laid on for tonight. You're welcome to join us, Gabriel old boy.'

'Thanks, Christian, but I'm no gambler, and I'm a bit short of reddies at the moment.'

'Then you was diddled, mate. I reckon old Forrest saw you coming. That painting would have fetched a small fortune if you'd put it up for auction.'

Gabriel pulled a face. 'Maybe, but I've more important things to think about now.' He kissed Lily's hand. 'Lily's agreed to marry me and that means more than fame or fortune. All I've got to do now is to convince her family that I can support a wife.'

'Good luck, mate.' Christian tipped his hat and strolled off in the direction of the inn.

'That's all very fine for you,' Molly said, sniffing. 'But I am married and I'm not allowed to be with my husband.'

Lily slipped her arm around her sister's heaving shoulders. 'Come back to the inn with us, love. Maybe Monsieur Labrosse will see things differently in the morning.'

Molly shook her head. 'I'm going to have one last try. I'll appeal to Monsieur Labrosse's better nature, if he has one. I can't bear to leave Armand to his father's tender mercies.' Ignoring Lily's protests, she left them in the hotel foyer while she went upstairs to find her father-in-law.

She returned half an hour later in floods of tears and it took Lily some time to calm her down.

'It will be dark soon,' Gabriel said, glancing out of

the window at the lowering sky. 'We'd best go now, Lily. We don't want to get caught in the storm.'

Lily slipped her arm around Molly's shoulders. 'Come with us, love. We'll sort it all out in the morning. You can't stay here, that's for certain.'

With Lily clutching one arm and Molly the other, Gabriel battled his way through the strengthening gale. The rain started before they had gone more than a hundred yards and lightning rent the dark sky, followed by a huge crash of thunder. With their heads down, they fought against the wind and rain, but a different danger threatened as they turned into the narrow side street which led to the inn. Seemingly from nowhere, three men leapt out at them brandishing weapons.

'Which of you is Madame Labrosse?' The voice was unmistakeably English but a second flash of lightning revealed that the man wore a neckerchief tied around the lower part of his face.

'What do you want?' Gabriel demanded. 'We have no money.'

'I am Madame Labrosse,' Molly said, pulling free from Gabriel's grasp. 'I am married to Armand Labrosse.'

'No,' Lily cried, as the man drew a pistol from his belt. She made a grab for Molly just as Gabriel leapt in between her and her assailant.

Chapter Twenty-three

A loud crump of thunder accompanied the crack of a gunshot and Lily uttered a terrified scream as Gabriel fell to the ground. Almost immediately appearing from the depths of darkness, three men fell upon their assailants brandishing cudgels. Molly stood motionless, as if turned to stone, ignoring Lily's pleas for help as she attempted to staunch the blood from Gabriel's wounded shoulder. The fight raging over their heads barely registered with Lily as she concentrated her efforts on saving the life of the man she loved. Gabriel attempted to sit up but his eyes rolled upward and he collapsed onto her lap.

'For God's sake don't just stand there, Molly,' Lily cried in desperation. 'Fetch help. Gabriel's been shot.'

Molly stared at her as if she had spoken in a foreign tongue. Her lips moved soundlessly and she buried her face in her hands, shaking her head.

'Help,' Lily cried. 'Someone help me.'

A body flew past her, falling with a dull thud onto the cobblestones. Another of their attackers hurtled through the air and landed close by with a man still pummelling him.

'The bastards shot him. We were too late.' Christian knelt beside Lily, taking a close look at Gabriel's wound.

'I think the bullet went straight through his shoulder,' he said cautiously. 'But he needs a surgeon. Gaston.' He turned to his cousin who was struggling to his feet, having rendered his opponent unconscious. In a stream of rapid French accompanied by meaningful gestures, Christian sent him staggering on his way. 'He's gone for the doctor, who just happens to be another distant relation of mine.'

'Why did they attack us?' Lily whispered dazedly. 'We've done nothing to them.'

A flash of lightning revealed that it was Walton who had been grappling with the third assailant and he forced the man to his knees. 'These men work for Labrosse. I recognise this 'un. Ain't that right, matey?'

The man grimaced, raising his hand to his bleeding and swollen lips.

'He don't speak English,' Walton said with apparent satisfaction. 'I can call the stupid bugger anything I like and he don't know the difference.'

'We should call the police,' Lily murmured faintly as she continued her efforts to staunch the flow of blood from Gabriel's shoulder. 'They tried to murder us.'

Christian picked up his bowler hat and dusted it off on his sleeve. 'Looks to me like they was after her.' He jerked his head in Molly's direction. 'My guess is that Monsieur Labrosse decided to get rid of his daughter-in-law by any means, fair or foul.'

Molly sank to her knees, uttering a stifled moan. 'It could have been me lying there on the ground, dying.'

'Gabriel isn't dying,' Lily said angrily. 'He saved your life.'

The man on the ground moaned as he started to regain consciousness but Walton pushed him down with the toe of his boot. 'Make a move and I'll give you another pasting, cully.'

Christian eyed Gabriel with a worried frown. 'We'd best get him to the inn, I told Gaston to take the sawbones there. We'll leave these fellows to the gendarmes.' He turned to Walton, who was still grappling with his captive. 'Let him go. I need you to help me carry this chap.'

With a none too gentle shove, Walton allowed the man to lumber off into the darkness. 'I've got you marked, mate,' he shouted. 'You won't get far.'

Lily dropped a kiss on Gabriel's forehead as Christian and Walton lifted him gently from her lap. She shuddered at the sight of the blood pooling on her skirt, and as she rose to her feet she was shaking uncontrollably.

'What shall I do?' Molly moaned. 'Where shall I go? I want to be with Armand.'

Lily gave her a pitying look. 'Don't you ever think of anyone but yourself?'

'No,' Molly said truthfully. 'Why should I? Who will look after me if I don't stand up for myself? You were always the baby of the family, Nell was more like a mother than a sister and so perfect that it made me want to scream. I was the middle one and no one noticed me unless I put up a show, but Armand loves me for what I am and I want to be with him.'

Touched by her sister's obvious sincerity, Lily held out her hand. 'Come with us to the inn. We'll send word to Armand at the hotel, and let him know that you're safe. The rest is up to him.'

Molly managed a smile. 'Thank you, Lil.'

They arrived to find the doctor waiting at the inn. A room had been made ready and Gabriel, now fully conscious, was able to walk upstairs with Christian's help. Lily followed them, but the doctor refused to allow her into the room, addressing her volubly in French.

'He won't let me in, Christian.' She had to raise her voice to make herself heard above the doctor's vociferous argument.

Christian poked his head round the door. 'Best do as the sawbones says, Lily. I'll call you when he's done.'

Reluctantly, she made her way downstairs to the private parlour that the landlord had provided, where she found Molly huddled up by the fire sipping something from a glass that smelt suspiciously like alcohol. 'It's brandy,' she said defensively. 'I need it for my nerves. Why don't you have some?'

'I might,' Lily said, forcing a smile. 'But not until I've made certain that Gabriel is all right. The wretched doctor won't let me into the room.'

'I want to go home, Lily. I don't like it here, and I hope they throw old Labrosse into jail. He's a murderer, or he would have been if Christian hadn't come along when he did.'

'We'll go home,' Lily said firmly. 'As soon as Armand and Gabriel are well enough to travel, we'll go back to London where we belong.'

'I won't be living in Paris.' Molly's bottom lip trembled. 'And I suppose I can say goodbye to fashionable gowns and a big house with my own carriage and pair.'

'I suppose you should. But you still have Armand.'

Molly sighed. 'Yes, and I do love him, even without his fortune. I hope he'll still want to marry me after all this.'

Lily stared at her aghast. 'But you said . . .'

Molly had the grace to blush. 'I know what I said, but it wasn't true. We didn't have time to get married. I just told old Labrosse that so that he'd have no choice but to let me stay with Armand.'

Three days later the party arrived back in England. No arrests had been made in Calais, as it seemed that Labrosse had influence with everyone from the mayor to the chief of police. Walton had elected to stay in France, having set eyes on a pretty chambermaid at the inn who happened to be the landlord's daughter. Gaston had offered him a job looking after his horses, and it looked as though his future was settled and that he might soon become part of Christian's extensive family.

They had travelled on the London, Chatham and Dover line and Christian parted from them at Victoria Station. Lily threw her arms around him and kissed him on the cheek. 'I used to hate you,' she said, smiling. 'But that's all changed now, Christian. You saved our lives and I can't thank you enough.'

He flushed brick-red, looking sheepish and quite

unlike his usual self. 'It was nothing. I'd have done the same for anyone.'

'No, I won't have that,' Lily insisted. 'I don't know why you appeared out of the blue on that stormy night, but it seemed like a miracle.'

He shook his head. 'Can't claim holy intervention, Lily love, it was one of my many cousins who knew Labrosse's men by sight. We were just having a drink in the bar when Jean Paul told us that there was trouble brewing. It ain't often a chap gets to use his fists without being arrested for being drunk and disorderly, so I couldn't resist the challenge. Anyway, I'll write it up for my paper with me as hero for once.' He returned her embrace. 'This ain't goodbye, girl.' Releasing her, he produced a newspaper from his pocket which he handed to Lily. 'I bought this off a newsvendor just now. It seems you're famous and so is your bloke.' He tipped his hat and sauntered off into the crowd.

'What is it, Lily?' Molly demanded eagerly. 'What does it say?'

Lily unrolled the paper and gasped as she saw her portrait reproduced on the front page. The title *Lily in the Flames* leapt out at her in bold type. She held it up for Gabriel to see. 'Look, it's the painting of me that you sold to Sir Cloudesley.'

Gabriel steadied the fluttering sheets of paper with his good hand. 'Well I'm damned.'

'Is that all you can say?' Molly snatched the newspaper from him and waved it in front of Armand. 'Look, it says that it's being exhibited on loan to the National

448

Gallery. Lily and Gabriel are famous. We'll be invited to all sorts of important events and charity balls.'

'You'll be rich as well as famous, old boy,' Armand said, slapping Gabriel on the back and immediately apologising for causing him pain. 'I'm sorry, I forgot your injury. It was fortunate they didn't wing your right arm because I think you'll be inundated with work if this is anything to go by.'

'I'll need it to support my wife,' Gabriel said, smiling at Lily. 'But first I have to make my peace with the men in her family.'

'I too will have some explaining to do.' Armand slipped his arm around Molly's waist. 'I don't know if they'll allow Molly to marry a penniless foreigner. But for my papa's untimely intervention we would already be a respectable married couple.'

There was a hint of spring in the air as they reached the old inn on Pelican Wharf. The sky was the colour of a robin's egg and the sun sparkled on the river, turning the tea-coloured waters of the Thames to viridian green. There was a faint flush of new growth on the trees surrounding the Prospect of Whitby, and even the city stench seemed less noxious as they waited for someone to let them into the house.

Lily had expected Aggie or Grandpa to be the first to greet them but it was Prissy who opened the door. Her face broke into a huge grin and she flung her arms around Lily with a cry of joy. 'You're home. I was beginning to think you was all lost at sea.'

'We sent you a telegram,' Molly said, sweeping past

449

them. She paused in the hallway, sniffing the air. 'I can smell lavender and beeswax. Someone must have been polishing. Everything is shiny.'

'That's me,' Prissy said proudly. 'I been working night and day to put this old house right, and you'll find another difference too. Come inside, all of you.' She ushered everyone in before closing the door with the air of a proud hostess. 'Go on through to the kitchen and you'll see what I mean.'

'Where's Ma?' Lily asked anxiously as a feeling of guilt assailed her. She had put her mother almost completely out of her mind during their frantic days abroad, but now she had to face the fact that Ma might be in bedlam for all she knew.

'You're just in time for dinner,' Prissy said, grinning. 'I'm sure there's plenty to go round.'

Taking off her mantle and tossing it on a chair together with her bonnet, Lily entered the parlour and was struck by the difference that had been made in less than a fortnight. Everything gleamed, from the brass candlesticks on the mantelshelf to the highly polished floorboards and furniture. A fire burned in the hearth and there were daffodils in a pewter mug on the dining table. The windows, which before had been caked with grime inside and out, were now sparkling clean. The reflected rays of the sun on the water made diamond-shaped patterns on the ceiling. 'You have been busy, Prissy,' Lily said appreciatively. 'I know Aggie couldn't have done all this.'

'And why not, you cheeky young madam?' Aggie waddled in from the kitchen, holding out her arms to

Lily. 'So you've come back.' She gave her a fond hug and then held Lily at arm's length. 'Where's the wedding band then? Has he made an honest woman of you?' She shot a darkling look in Gabriel's direction. 'Good Lord what happened to you?' She glanced over his shoulder at Armand. 'And you too, both of you with arms in slings? What's been going on in them foreign parts?'

Molly rushed forward to hug Aggie. 'I'm going to be married very soon, so don't get in a state. I'll soon be Madame Labrosse, although poor Armand nearly died when our carriage overturned, and Gabriel was shot by Armand's Pa. What d'you think of that?'

'I think I'd best sit down,' Aggie wheezed, collapsing onto the nearest chair. 'Best go and fetch the missis, Prissy. She needs to hear all this.'

Prissy nodded and disappeared into the kitchen, reappearing seconds later with Charlotte, who was enveloped in a white apron, her cheeks flushed and her eyes sparkling. 'My dearest girls, you've come home.' She held out her arms. 'Come to Mama, darlings.'

Moving automatically, as if they had suddenly reverted to their childhood, Lily and Molly walked into their mother's embrace.

'You look so much better, Ma,' Lily murmured.

'See my ring, Ma,' Molly said, waving it beneath her mother's nose. 'It's a real diamond, none of your French paste for me.'

Charlotte smiled. 'You haven't changed at all, my little firethorn.'

'I prefer to think of her as a briar rose,' Armand said,

smiling. 'I hope we have your blessing for our forth-coming nuptials, Madame Larkin.'

'I prefer to be called Mrs Faulkner,' Charlotte said with dignity. 'As you see I am in mourning for my dear departed Everard.'

'We haven't forgotten him, Ma.' Lily beckoned to Gabriel. 'We have something to tell you also.'

'Not now, darling,' Charlotte said, making an obvious effort to control her emotions. 'I have a meat pie in the oven and I don't want the pastry to burn. My boys will be home soon and hungry as hunters.' She hurried into the kitchen, mopping her eyes on her voluminous apron.

Lily turned to Prissy, eyebrows raised. 'She's cooking dinner?'

'That's right,' Prissy said proudly. 'It's a talent she'd forgotten she had in all those years of being waited on and pampered.'

'And it's given me a rest from all that peeling of taters and chopping onions until me eyes were red raw,' Aggie added with a pleased grin. 'I got time to play backgammon with your grandpa, and she does the marketing too. It's been a godsend.'

Lily and Molly exchanged looks of astonishment. 'We've been gone such a short time,' Lily said faintly. 'It seems everything has changed.'

'It's all due to her,' Aggie said, pointing at Prissy. 'She's worked wonders in the house; she's got the old man eating out of her hand and he's not the only one.'

Prissy's face was suffused with a sudden blush. She shrugged her thin shoulders. 'That's enough of that talk, Aggie. I only done me bit.' She cocked her head on one side as if listening to a sound unheard by anyone else, and she turned to look out of the window.

Following her glance, Lily realised that it was the sight of Matt, Mark and Luke striding along the quay wall that had made Prissy's eyes light up and her lips tremble with emotion. 'Which one of them has made your heart beat faster?' Lily whispered.

Prissy gave a guilty start. 'I dunno what you're talking about. I'm going to help the missis serve dinner.' She hurried into the kitchen, closing the door behind her.

'It's Matt she fancies,' Aggie said, as if reading Lily's thoughts. 'She's got him wrapped round her little finger. You'll see.'

Lily ran to open the front door. Matt was first over the threshold and he stopped short, staring at her with surprise written all over his strong features. 'Lily, you're here.'

'We're home, safe and sound. Well, Molly and I are fine, but Gabriel and Armand have been injured.' She reached up to kiss him on the cheek, inhaling the familiar smell of smoke and charred wood that clung to her brothers after attending a fire.

Bestowing a perfunctory kiss on her cheek, Matt strode into the living room with Lily hurrying after him. Glancing round, he shot a darkling glance in Armand's direction. 'I'll deal with you later, Labrosse.'

Mark stood in the doorway, grinning. 'You're safe and sound, Lil. That's all that matters. That goes for you too, Molly. We thought we'd never see either of you again. It's good to have you home.'

'I second that.' Luke caught Lily up in his arms and kissed her on the tip of her nose. 'You're famous, little sister. Have you seen the newspapers?'

'I have,' Lily breathed. 'It's wonderful, isn't it? But Gabriel deserves all the praise; I just sat for him doing nothing.'

Matt's stern gaze rested on Gabriel. 'I want to speak to you – in private.'

His tone was anything but encouraging and Lily's heart sank. 'Why, Matt? What are you going to say that can't be heard by all of us?'

'That's between the two of us.'

'No, it isn't. It concerns me too. Gabriel has asked me to marry him and I've said yes.'

'We'll see about that,' Matt said grimly.

'Hold on, old chap.' Mark clapped him on the shoulder. 'Give the poor sod a chance to explain.'

Matt shook him off impatiently. 'Give an account of yourself, Faulkner.'

'Stop it,' Lily said urgently. 'Don't talk to him like that.'

'This is men's business, Lily. Keep out of it.'

'Don't speak to her in that tone of voice.' Gabriel spoke for the first time, his face pale and his eyes flashing angrily. 'I love Lily and I intend to marry her as soon as the banns are read.'

'Over my dead body,' Matt said coldly. 'One Faulkner is bad luck, but two spell disaster. Our family has suffered once thanks to your father and now you want to drag my sister into a life of debt and depravity.'

'Matt, no,' Lily cried passionately. 'It's not like that.

454

Artists are respectable people; they just live differently to us.'

'You were brought up to be honest and decent, Lily. I'm not having you mix with the likes of them. You saw what it did to Ma. She's just getting over it now, but you'll go the same way if you marry him.' He turned on Gabriel with a savage snarl. 'Get out of my house. Come near my sister again and you'll be sorry.'

Gabriel opened his mouth as if to argue, but Mark moved to Matt's side, fisting his hands. 'I'm sorry, mate, but you heard him. You ain't ruining our little Lily.'

'Luke.' Lily turned to him, holding out her hands. 'You know better than this. Help him.'

He shook his head. 'Those friends of Ma and Everard let me down too, Lily. I took my poems to the publisher and he threw them out. Laughed in my face, he did. They're not interested in people like us unless it's to poke fun at our clothes and our way of speaking. You'll be just another oddity to exhibit, not a real person to them.'

'That's not true,' Gabriel protested angrily. 'I love Lily and I'll protect her for the rest of my life. I won't let anyone hurt her.'

'Get out,' Matt said angrily. 'Go and don't come back. If you try to see her again you'll have us to contend with.'

Gabriel hesitated, his emotions clearly written on his face as he gazed at Lily. 'All right, I'm going now, but I'll come back for Lily as soon as the banns are read.'

'I'm coming with you.'

Lily attempted to follow him but Mark barred the way. 'Let him go, Lil,' he said softly. 'He ain't worth it. Like father, like son. You're one of us again. Don't spoil it.'

'But he's injured,' Lily sobbed. 'He needs someone to look after him.' She broke free from Mark's restraining hands, facing her brothers with tears running down her cheeks. 'He saved Molly's life, you idiots. And I love him.' She made for the door but Matt slammed it shut, leaning against it with his arms folded across his chest.

'No, Lily. It won't do. I'm not having my sister running off to live with an artist. You'll stay here even if I have to tie you to a chair.'

She turned to Nell who had emerged from the parlour, her face pale with anxiety. 'Tell him he can't do this to me, Nell.'

'Matt's right,' Nell said slowly. 'And Eugene would say the same thing.'

'Damn Eugene,' Lily cried passionately. 'And damn you all for treating me like this.' She pushed past Nell, making her way into the kitchen where she flung herself into her mother's arms. 'Ma, tell them they can't do this to me. I love Gabriel and he loves me.'

Charlotte stroked Lily's tumbled hair back from her forehead. 'My darling, I know how you feel, I really do, but I think Matt's right in this. You should stay here with us and give Gabriel time to sort out his finances and find a home for you . . .'

'But we have a home. There's the house in Cock and Hoop Yard. We were happy there, Ma.'

Prissy laid her hand on Lily's shoulder. 'We don't have it now. I went to collect our clothes and someone else was living there. So I went round to see Mad Maggie and she told me that Gabriel had only paid a week's rent in advance. When we left all of a sudden they didn't know what had happened and they let the house to a juggler, his missis and seven nippers who are all part of their stage act.'

'You must understand that I'm only looking after your interests, Lily.' Matt had come into the kitchen unnoticed by her. She could not bring herself to look at him. She had to hold back the bitter words that filled her mouth like bile.

'And a fine way you chose to do it,' Prissy said, shaking her head. 'You men are all the same, you think with your fists. Can't you see that the poor girl's in love? Ain't you got no heart, Matt Larkin?'

Lily held her breath. If anyone else had taken that tone with Matt they would have been cut down to size, but he eyed Prissy warily, looking distinctly uncomfortable.

'I did it for the best,' he murmured.

'You fly off the handle and then regret it.' Prissy wagged her finger at him. 'I think you should apologise to Lily, and to Gabriel when you see him next. He intends to do the right thing by her; it's not history repeating itself and you've got to put the past behind you. This is now and then was then.'

Charlotte released Lily with a gentle pat on the cheek. 'Prissy's right, Matt. Give him time to put his house in order.'

457

Matt shuffled his feet, looking for all the world like a small boy caught stealing jam tarts from the pantry. 'There's already been talk. Lily's name has been bandied round the docks. She's left us open to the local gossips.'

'Let them talk all they like,' Prissy declared stoutly. 'Words can't hurt us if we stick together. Now go and wash that dirt off your face, Matt Larkin. I ain't sitting down to eat with a sweep.' She shooed him out through the scullery into the yard.

Lily stared after them in disbelief. 'Am I imagining things or did Prissy just take Matt in hand?'

'Love is a wonderful thing, darling,' Charlotte said, opening the oven door and lifting out a pie with a tempting golden crust. 'Call the others in for their dinner, Lily. We'll eat like a civilised family for once.' She paused as she placed the steaming dish on the table. 'And don't look so tragic. Gabriel won't let you down, he's too much like his dear father, and Matt will come round given time. Just wait and see.'

'I haven't much choice, it seems.' Lily wiped her eyes on her sleeve and went into the parlour, where she found the rest of her family waiting in silence. Grandpa Larkin scuttled towards her, holding out his hands and beaming.

'My little Lily. I just got in from the pub and they told me you'd come home. Don't take no notice of Matt, we're all on your side.' He shot a warning glance at Mark. 'And don't you say nothing to upset the girl. Just stop and think how you'd feel if old Cobbold said you couldn't see young Flossie ever again.'

Mark met Lily's gaze with an apologetic smile. 'Sorry,

Lil. It's just that we don't want to see you hurt. After Ma getting all tangled up with them arty folks it's no wonder Matt behaved as he did.'

Nell rose to her feet, holding her hand out to Lily. 'We all love you, Lily. We just want you to be happy.'

'Like me and Armand,' Molly said, smiling up at Armand and tucking her hand through the crook of his arm. 'We're going to be married as soon as possible.'

'So how will you support a wife now that you've been sacked by that libertine of a father?' Grandpa demanded.

'I have contacts in London,' Armand replied calmly. 'I had already been offered a position as manager in a rival shipping company here in London before I proposed to Molly. I didn't say anything at the time because I had a feeling my papa would react badly. I hoped and still hope that Papa will come round in time, but I will accept the job now. Molly and I will be comfortable enough.'

'Shall I have a carriage and pair then, Armand?' Molly's eyes shone. 'And new gowns and a hat with feathers and flowers on it?'

'In time, *ma chérie*, but for now we will have to live in the small house I bought some time ago in Cinnamon Street.'

'Do you hear that, Lily? I'm to have my very own house. You shall come and visit me and take tea with me in my parlour.' Molly did a little dance, twirling round on her toes and clapping her hands.

'But what about this house?' Lily asked anxiously. 'Your father owns it and he won't hesitate to throw my family out on the street.'

459

Armand shook his head. 'No, Lily. I bought the freehold of this old place myself some years ago. I leased it to my father's business, but that expired some time ago. It is mine and I give it to Molly's family with all my heart.'

Prissy stuck her head round the door. 'Grub's up. The missis says come and get it while it's hot and no nonsense at the table.'

Although it was the last thing she wanted, Lily had no option other than to live at home, helping her mother and Aggie with the household chores, and listening to Molly chattering about her forthcoming wedding. Armand had posted the banns at St Peter's Church and he had taken up his new appointment with a company that plied its trade between London and the Caribbean islands. He had returned to his house in Cinnamon Street, and when Molly was not attending the dressmaker for fittings for her wedding gown she was busy choosing curtains and furnishings for her new home. Lily accompanied her on these trips to warehouses and markets, and although a three-bedroom house in Cinnamon Street was not the same as a mansion in a fashionable part of Paris, Molly did not seem to mind.

Lily was happy for her sister, but as the days went by with no sign of Gabriel, her heart ached and she was secretly afraid that there would be no place for her in his new life. Using Silly Sally as an unlikely go-between, Gabriel sent loving notes keeping Lily informed of his movements. He was lodging with Magnus the Magnificent and Mad Maggie, but rarely at home as invitations to meet prominent people in the art world flooded in. The newspapers were filled with praise for his work and Sir Cloudesley, who had previously been better known in the gaming clubs than in the world of art and culture, had earned a reputation as the man who had discovered the fresh new talent that was taking the art world by storm. There were words of praise from members of the Pre-Raphaelite Brotherhood which Lily was eager to show her mother. Charlotte pored over the articles which mentioned the friends she and Everard had welcomed to their home in Keppel Street. If she was envious she did not allow it to show, and she seemed content to remain quietly at home, getting to know the children she had once abandoned. Lily felt for her mother, and she took solace from the time they spent together sketching and painting. Charlotte had been earning a little money by drawing portraits of local children, for which she charged a few pennies.

'You are wasting your talents, Ma,' Lily said one afternoon as she examined a charcoal sketch of Silly Sally who had called with yet another note from Gabriel. Aggie had taken the girl under her wing, insisting that the poor creature needed feeding up. Sally needed no second bidding and was a willing sitter. Her wild curls and gamine features made her an appealing subject, and it was one of these drawings that particularly caught Lily's eye. She was holding it up to the light in the window when she saw a familiar figure approaching the house. She ran to open the door.

Chapter Twenty-four

'Christian, what brings you here?'

He doffed his bowler hat with a flourish. 'I came to see how my Lily in the Flames is doing.' He put his hand in his breast pocket and took out a battered envelope. 'Gabriel sent this for you, my duck. It's an invitation to the private viewing of the exhibition.'

Lily took it with trembling fingers. 'Why didn't he bring it himself? I want to see him.'

'He didn't want to cause any further upset with your family, but he said to tell you that the first of the banns has been called, and that he loves you more than life itself.' Christian pulled a face. 'There, I've said it. I'm an unlikely Cupid, but it was sincerely meant. He's making plans for your future together, Lily. He's determined to win your brothers over, so he begs you to be patient, and I'm to take you to the exhibition tomorrow, if you'll come with me.'

'He will be there, though?'

'Of course he will, ducks. He's doing all this for you.'

Lily knew that what Christian said was true but a niggling doubt refused to go away. If Gabriel loved her so desperately, would he not have tried harder to see her? She tucked the invitation into her pocket, holding the door open wide. 'Come inside and meet Ma. I'm sure she'd love to see you.'

Tucking his hat beneath his arm, Christian walked past her and went into the parlour where he stopped, staring at Charlotte. He bowed from the waist. 'You must be Lily's older sister, ma'am.'

Charlotte looked up and her face was wreathed in smiles. 'You flatter me, sir. I'm Charlotte Faulkner; my late husband was Gabriel's father.'

'Christian Smith, reporter for the *Daily Globe*. No flattery intended,' Christian said with apparent sincerity. 'If you'll pardon my saying so, ma'am, I can see where Lily gets both her looks and her talent. Gabriel has told me that she's an accomplished artist in her own right, as I see you are, ma'am.'

'Oh, he's a one,' Sally giggled. 'What about me, mister?'

He struck a pose. 'You are a princess amongst women, miss. A veritable Helen of Troy whose face launched a thousand ships.'

Sally shot an anxious glance at Lily. 'Does he mean me face is all smashed up? I mean, if it's been bashed against the side of ships ...'

Lily placed her arm around Sally's thin shoulders. 'He means you're very pretty, Sally. Helen of Troy was a great beauty.'

'Oh,' she murmured, mollified. 'That's the ticket then.'

'May I ask why you're here, Mr Smith?' Charlotte asked, dimpling. 'We get so few visitors these days.'

'He brought me an invitation to attend the viewing of Gabriel's work, Ma,' Lily said hastily, before Christian could turn anyone else's head with his sweet talk. 'Christian is the one who started the whole thing with his article about Lily in the Flames.'

Charlotte rose to her feet, scattering charcoal all over the floor. She held out both hands. 'Then I have you to thank for reuniting me with my dear daughter, and subsequently with my whole family. You don't know how much it's meant to me, Mr Smith.'

He took her right hand and raised it to his lips. 'Glad to have been of some small service to a beautiful lady. And I hope you will accept my condolences for your tragic loss. I covered the story of Mr Faulkner's death for my paper.'

Charlotte's eyes filled with tears which, Lily noted with a wry smile, made them appear larger and more luminous, unlike ordinary mortals whose eyes might redden or their noses start to run when they cried. No one, she thought, would think that her mother was in her forties, or that she had borne six children. Her figure was voluptuous but shapely and her face amazingly unlined, but perhaps that was because Ma never let anything worry her. She was flirting openly with Christian, and although Lily did not doubt her mother's genuine love for Everard, she could see that Ma's broken heart was mending nicely. She left them to entertain each other while she went outside to sit on the wharf and reread the gilt-edged invitation and Gabriel's note.

Dangling her legs over the wall with the Thames lapping gently a few feet below, and the sounds of the river all around her, she immersed herself in the words written from Gabriel's heart.

'Lily, for goodness' sake get up.'

She looked up, startled by Nell's crisp voice. 'I'm not doing any harm, Nell.'

Nell was leaning on Eugene's arm, shaking her head. 'You're too old to behave like that. Come inside before Matt comes home and sees you showing your petticoats for all the common sailors to see.'

Eugene patted her hand. 'She's having a quiet moment, my dear. I can understand that in a household the size of yours such time is precious.'

'I suppose you're right, Eugene.' Nell's face lit with a smile as she looked up into his eyes. 'Will you come in for a cup of tea?'

'I most certainly will. I have something very particular to ask Matt and your grandfather.'

Lily looked up into his face, startled by the tender tone in his voice, and she could see that Nell's ivory pallor had deepened to blush rose. 'Why you sly old thing, Nell,' she cried, leaping to her feet. 'You never said a word.'

'It's not official – I mean, he hasn't exactly asked me yet.' Nell broke off in a state of confusion.

'Quite so,' Eugene said seriously. 'Did you mention a cup of tea, dearest?'

As they passed her and went into the house, he turned his head and Lily could have sworn that he winked at her. So Nell was going to marry Eugene. She had no doubt that her sister would accept the schoolmaster, who was proving to be everything that Nell wanted in a man, and it seemed that he had a sense of humour too. Both her sisters were happy in love, and in less than a week Molly would be walking up the aisle with Armand. Lily stared at the note clutched in her hand and raised it to her lips. Tomorrow she would see Gabriel and be introduced into his world. If only Matt would relent, she thought sadly. She was determined to marry the man she loved, but the thought of causing another rift in the family made the decision to flout her brothers agonising.

'Of course I'm coming with you,' Charlotte said, tying the ribbons of her bonnet at a fetching angle beneath her left ear. 'Do you really think I'd miss an opportunity to meet my old friends? Besides which, my presence will lend respectability to your clandestine meeting with Gabriel. I am, after all, his stepmother.'

'No you're not, Ma,' Lily said patiently. 'But I'd be glad of your company all the same.'

'Is Christian coming to call for you?' Charlotte asked casually, primping in front of the mirror above the mantelshelf.

'Yes, Ma. You know he is.'

'I know no such thing, but it's important to be escorted to these functions by a gentleman, and a gentleman of the press ensures that we get privileges other people cannot aspire to.'

'Yes, Ma.' Lily peered out of the window. 'He's here. Let's go before Aggie and Grandpa get wind of what we're doing.'

'I'd like to see them try to stop us.' Charlotte slipped a shawl around her shoulders with a flourish. 'I'm ready.'

The journey took much longer than Lily had anticipated and she sat in her corner of the hackney carriage staring out of the window while Ma and Christian chatted as if they had known each other for years. Lily was too nervous and excited to listen to them, but she was vaguely aware that Ma was in fine form, and Christian was hanging on her every word. The city streets flashed past the windows and heat rose from the cobblestones together with the stench of horse dung and blocked drains. Lily clutched her reticule containing the invitation to the viewing and she was thankful that Christian was paying the cab fare. Her hands were damp with perspiration and her heart beating erratically as the cab drew to a halt in Trafalgar Square.

Christian leapt out first, handing her down before helping Charlotte to alight. He led the way into the gallery with Charlotte on his arm and Lily following close behind. Her hand flew to her mouth to stifle a gasp of pleasure as she saw her portrait hanging in pride of place, lit by the sun beaming through a skylight. She could almost smell the smoke and burning timbers and hear the crackle of the flames as they devoured the warehouse. The girl standing in the well of the cart stared heroically ahead, her flaming hair seeming to be part of the conflagration itself.

'Lily, my darling.'

She turned at the sound of Gabriel's voice, and the look in his eyes made her tremble with delight. It was all she could do not to throw herself into his arms. She hesitated, taking in his smart black suit and immaculate white shirt. He looked distinguished and so handsome that it took her breath away. 'You aren't wearing a sling,' she murmured, suddenly shy in the midst of the exalted company.

'No,' he agreed, taking her hand and raising it to his lips. 'My wound is healing nicely.' His eyes shone as they met hers. 'I've missed you every moment of every day, my love.'

'Me too,' Lily murmured, casting an anxious glance to see if anyone was watching them, but Ma and Christian were chatting to some important-looking men with goatee beards and shiny shoes. 'Can we go somewhere more private, Gabriel?'

He squeezed her fingers, holding on to her hand as if he would never let her go. 'Not yet, sweetheart, but we'll slip away as soon as I've done my duty here.' He slid his arm around her waist. 'There is someone I want you to meet first.' He led her through the crowd of well-dressed art lovers to the end of the gallery where a tall, thin man was standing in front of a set of watercolours. Gabriel tapped him on the shoulder. 'Harry, old boy, I want you to meet the artist.'

As the man moved aside Lily was amazed to see that the paintings which had been the object of his intense scrutiny were her own work. 'I don't understand.'

Gabriel smiled. 'May I introduce Harry Lockwood, darling? He's the most influential art critic in London. Harry, this is Miss Lily Larkin, the artist.'

Harry Lockwood eyed Lily as critically as if she had been one of the exhibits and then a slow smile spread across his gaunt features. 'Miss Larkin, I must congratulate you on your efforts. Your work shows freshness and a naivety that are quite charming. I hope to see more of your paintings.'

At a loss for words, Lily bobbed a curtsey.

'Charming,' Harry repeated, patting Gabriel on the shoulder. 'Quite charming. Miss Larkin will go far, given the right mentor and the opportunity to exhibit her paintings.'

'I knew you'd say that,' Gabriel said, beaming. 'Not only is she an inspiration as a model but she is talented as well, and I adore her. We're to be married very soon.'

'Congratulations, old man.' Harry took Lily's hand and kissed it. 'I wish you all the happiness in the world, and every success in your career, Miss Larkin.' He strolled off to study another work on the far side of the gallery.

'Me, a real artist,' Lily breathed. 'Why didn't you tell me you'd put my paintings into the exhibition?'

'I wanted to surprise you,' Gabriel said, brushing her cheek with his lips. 'And I must confess I didn't know they had been accepted until last night. Anyway, that will all change soon. In no time at all we'll be man and wife, and I'll never leave you again, Lily.'

'You know that I want that more than anything in the world,' she said in a low voice, 'but where will we live? How will we manage for money? And what will Matt say? I can't go against him and cause the family more pain.'

'But you want to be with me, don't you?' Gabriel's eyes darkened as they held hers in a gaze that pierced her soul.

'You know I do.'

'I have several commissions which will bring in a steady income. We'll manage somehow, darling. My rooms in Cock and Hoop Yard aren't palatial but they'll do for the time being, and as soon as I receive the money for my paintings we'll move to somewhere more suitable. Do you think you could stand living in two attic rooms with a struggling artist?'

Lily clasped his hands in hers. 'I'd live in a garret and eat nothing but bread and water as long as we were together.'

'It won't be quite that bad,' he said, chuckling. 'But tomorrow, first thing, I'm going to Cock Hill to have it out with your brothers. I'm not going to make the same mistakes as my father, God rest his soul. We're going to be married with the blessing of your family; I promise you that, Lily.' He glanced over her shoulder, frowning. 'I'm going to have to leave you for a few moments, darling. Lockwood is beckoning to me and he's too important to ignore at this stage in my career.'

Lily made her way through the crowd to rejoin her mother and Christian. She felt happier than she had for a very long time. Gabriel had promised that he would sort things out tomorrow. She could barely wait.

Next morning, as she stood outside the house on Pelican Wharf, Lily was joined by Prissy who had just come back from market with a basket overflowing with her purchases. 'What are you doing standing out here without your bonnet?' Prissy demanded. 'You'll get freckles all over your nose and that ain't pretty.'

Anxious as she was, Lily could not help smiling at

470

Prissy's motherly concern. 'I'm waiting for Gabriel. He said he was going to sort things out with Matt and the boys.'

'It's about time someone did,' Prissy said, nodding sagely. 'Your brother needs a firm hand.'

Lily was quick to notice the faint flush that coloured Prissy's cheeks and the sparkle in her eyes whenever Matt's name was mentioned. 'You're fond of Matt, aren't you?' she said softly.

'He's all right.' Prissy shrugged her shoulders.

'Come on, Prissy, you can't fool me,' Lily said gently. 'I've seen the way you look at him, and what's more I've seen the way he looks at you when he thinks no one else is watching.'

'I dunno what you mean.' Prissy made for the side door, but Lily caught her by the arm.

'Admit it; you've got a soft spot for my eldest brother and he for you.'

'I like him a lot, but a man like him ain't going to pay no heed to an ignorant country girl like me.'

Lily wrapped her arm around Prissy's thin form. 'You're not ignorant. In fact you've got a wiser head on your young shoulders than all the rest of us put together.'

Prissy sniffed and wiped her nose on her sleeve. 'That's not true. I'm just good at keeping house and looking after people. I've had enough practice, heaven knows.'

'And that's a talent that Nell, Molly and me have got to learn,' Lily said softly. 'You do it naturally, Prissy. You've turned that old barn of a place into a real home, and you've got the boys eating out of your hand, including Matt. He took it worst of all when Ma left and he didn't seem to be interested in girls, at least not in the way that Mark and Luke were. But he's different with you. He listens to you, Prissy, and I think he loves you.'

Prissy looked up, her blue eyes swimming with tears. 'Do you really?'

'I wouldn't say it if I didn't think so.'

'No, you must be wrong.' Prissy shook her head vehemently. 'He wouldn't want someone like me.'

'You're not afraid to put him in his place. He needs someone who will stand up to him, and he'd never put up with a silly girl who demanded his attention all the time and talked about nothing but folderols and fripperies. Matt's not like that.'

'He's wonderful,' Prissy breathed, closing her eyes. 'If I had one big wish I know what it would be.'

Lily glanced over her shoulder at the sound of approaching footsteps and for a moment she thought she was seeing things. She blinked hard. 'I think your wish and mine might have been answered, Prissy,' she murmured as she saw two familiar figures striding towards her. They appeared to be deep in conversation and her breath hitched in her throat. She hardly dared to hope as Matt and Gabriel drew nearer, with Mark and Luke close behind them. Anxiously she scanned Matt's face for signs of outrage, but she could see that he was smiling. He threw back his head and laughed, slapping Gabriel on the back.

'It's all settled, Lily,' Matt said, encompassing her and Prissy in a warm smile. 'Gabriel's worn me down and I'll not stand in your way any longer.'

Prissy uttered a shriek of joy and threw her arms around Matt's neck. 'You're a toff, Matt Larkin. A real toff.'

He lifted her off her feet, planting a kiss on her lips. 'I've wanted to do that for a long time, Prissy. You've done something to me, girl. I dunno what it is but I like it.'

'Well I'm blowed, you dark horse.' Mark slapped him on the back. 'I thought you hated women.'

'I hadn't met the right one,' Matt said, grinning. 'I've been plucking up the courage to make the first move, but she did it for me.' He kissed her again, receiving a round of applause from his brothers.

Gabriel slipped his arm around Lily's waist. 'It seems like a happy outcome after all, my darling.'

Still clutching Prissy as if he was afraid she might suddenly fly away, Matt nodded his head in agreement. 'You can marry your bloke, Lily, and I wish you well.' He picked up the heavy basket of meat and vegetables that Prissy had put down, proffering his arm to her. 'Let's go inside. I want to put everyone straight as to how to treat you now, Prissy. You've been treated like a servant and it's got to stop.'

'Yes, Matt,' Prissy said meekly. 'Anything you say.' She tucked her hand in the crook of his arm, but paused as they reached the door, turning to Lily with a broad grin. 'I done it, Lily. I done it.'

'I wish you well too, Lily,' Mark said, giving her a

smacking kiss on the cheek. 'And you'd better treat her right or you'll have me to answer to, Gabriel.'

'I'll treasure her for the rest of my life,' Gabriel said softly.

Luke nudged his brother out of the way. 'I'll write a poem for your wedding day, Lil, and I'm going to speak to Christian about getting a job on his newspaper. It may not be poet laureate stuff, but I think I've got a talent for putting things into words.' He gave her a hug, turning to Gabriel with a wide grin. 'It looks like she's all yours, old chap.' He hurried into the house, leaving them alone on the quay wall.

Gabriel took hold of Lily's hand, looking deeply into her eyes and smiling. 'I'm no poet when it comes to writing down how much I love and adore you, but I think you know how I feel.'

She nodded her head. 'I do.'

'And I've managed to convince your brothers that I'll spend the rest of my life trying to make you happy. You know that too, don't you?'

She smiled. 'I do, Gabriel.'

'According to Lockwood the exhibition was a huge success and I've already sold two of my works, so now I can ask you humbly and from the bottom of my heart if you'll consent to be my wife, my dearest Lily.'

'You already know the answer to that, my love.' She slid her hands around his neck, drawing his head down until their lips touched in a kiss that sealed her pledge to love him until the day she died.